SHADOW POINT

SEMPER CONSIDERED THINGS for a moment, then gave his waiting officers their orders.

'Mister Nyder – put out extra fighter screen patrols and have all your attack craft squadrons put on standby, ready for emergency launch. Tell your pilots to see off any more incursions into our defence zone from any of the alien craft. Let's see how they react when we hang the "no entry" sign up on the door. Comms – signal the *Graf Orlok* and tell them to proceed at speed to the last known position of the *Mosca*. If we can't raise them, maybe *Graf Orlok* can. And signal *Drachenfels* to do likewise with the *Volpone*. Tell that old rogue Ramas that–'

He was abruptly cut off by the urgent voice of a communications officer.

'Sir, flash-comm signal coming through from the *Drachenfels*. They're in combat with hostiles. They're reporting they're under attack by at least one eldar vessel!'

More Warhammer 40,000 from the Black Library

• OTHER WARHAMMER 40,000 TITLES •

EXECUTION HOUR by Gordon Rennie
ANGELS OF DARKNESS by Gav Thorpe
SOULDRINKER by Ben Counter
FARSEER by William King
STORM OF IRON by Graham McNeill
NIGHTBRINGER by Graham McNeill
PAWNS OF CHAOS by Brian Craig
EYE OF TERROR by Barrington J. Bayley

• GAUNT'S GHOSTS •

FIRST & ONLY by Dan Abnett
GHOSTMAKER by Dan Abnett
NECROPOLIS by Dan Abnett
HONOUR GUARD by Dan Abnett
THE GUNS OF TANITH by Dan Abnett
STRAIGHT SILVER by Dan Abnett

• THE EISENHORN TRILOGY •

XENOS by Dan Abnett
MALLEUS by Dan Abnett
HERETICUS by Dan Abnett

• LAST CHANCERS •

13TH LEGION by Gav Thorpe
KILL TEAM by Gav Thorpe

• SPACE WOLF •

SPACE WOLF by William King
RAGNAR'S CLAW by William King
GREY HUNTER by William King

More Gordon Rennie from the Black Library
Zavant – A Warhammer novel

A WARHAMMER 40,000 NOVEL

SHADOW POINT

Gordon Rennie

A BLACK LIBRARY PUBLICATION

First published in Great Britain in 2003 by
BL Publishing
Willow Road, Lenton,
Nottingham, NG7 2WS, UK

10 9 8 7 6 5 4 3 2 1

Cover illustration by Paul Dainton

A CIP record for this book
is available from the British Library

ISBN 1 84154 263 6

Set in ITC Giovanni

Printed and bound in Great Britain by
Cox & Wyman Ltd, Cardiff Rd, Reading, Berkshire RG1 8EX, UK

See the Black Library on the Internet at
www.blacklibrary.com

Find out more about Games Workshop
and the world of Warhammer 40.000 at
www.games-workshop.com

IT IS THE 41st millennium. For more than a hundred centuries the Emperor has sat immobile on the Golden Throne of Earth. He is the master of mankind by the will of the gods, and master of a million worlds by the might of his inexhaustible armies. He is a rotting carcass writhing invisibly with power from the Dark Age of Technology. He is the Carrion Lord of the Imperium for whom a thousand souls are sacrificed every day, so that he may never truly die.

YET EVEN IN his deathless state, the Emperor continues his eternal vigilance. Mighty battlefleets cross the daemon-infested miasma of the warp, the only route between distant stars, their way lit by the Astronomican, the psychic manifestation of the Emperor's will. Vast armies give battle in his name on uncounted worlds. Greatest amongst his soldiers are the Adeptus Astartes, the Space Marines, bio-engineered super-warriors. Their comrades in arms are legion: the Imperial Guard and countless planetary defence forces, the ever-vigilant Inquisition and the tech-priests of the Adeptus Mechanicus to name only a few. But for all their multitudes, they are barely enough to hold off the ever-present threat from aliens, heretics, mutants – and worse.

TO BE A man in such times is to be one amongst untold billions. It is to live in the cruellest and most bloody regime imaginable. These are the tales of those times. Forget the power of technology and science, for so much has been forgotten, never to be re-learned. Forget the promise of progress and understanding, for in the grim dark future there is only war. There is no peace amongst the stars, only an eternity of carnage and slaughter, and the laughter of thirsting gods.

PROLOGUE

THE BURNING GOD sat immobile upon his smouldering throne, feeling the pulse and flow of the life energy of the place ebb through him. He had sat there for an eternity as mere mortal beings reckon such things, dreaming dreams of battles past and battles still to come, and thinking thoughts which not even the longest-lived of his race's savants could ever truly fathom.

There were others of his kind out there in the universe beyond, other fractured splinters of the same original being, dreaming their own dreams and feeling the life-flow of their own home-worlds pulse through them. So few of them left, the burning god lamented. Once there had been worlds upon worlds of them, and in his dreams he could still see them as they once were. He saw a race at the height of its glory, revelling in its own power and majesty, capable of reforming entire worlds to suit its own purpose, able to reach out to probe the deepest mysteries of time and space. All gone now, it lamented. Now there were only these few poor remnants left, seeds drifting in the gulfs of space, a scattered diaspora struggling to hold back the tide of darkness which would one day still rise to engulf all that had once been.

But not yet, the warrior god knew. Not yet. Not while it and those like it still existed to protect all that remained of their race and hold back the darkness for just a little longer.

Slowly, though, in a period reckoned over decades, the warrior god had been stirring in its sleep. There was war being waged amongst the stars, it knew. There was always war – the lesser, younger races seemed to be have born both for and from war – but it knew that, somehow, this war was different. It heard the distant wraithbone voices singing of war between the mon-keigh corpse-worshippers and the human servants of the Great Abomination, and the songs interrupted its dreams in a way in which they never had before.

The burning god looked into its dreams of the future for answers, and saw that, for the first time in millennia, it would soon be called upon again. Its dreams were troubled. It saw a convergence of many intersecting fate-lines ahead of it, and, after that, its dream-images of the future were too vague and indistinct to be properly discerned. Something lay just over the horizon of its perception, a shadow point where many possible futures lay in wait, which not even its near omniscient dream-vision could bring properly into focus.

For the first time in long, long millennia, the burning god knew something approximating fear, and its fear communicated itself through ancient wraithbone pathways to the living mind of its drifting homeworld. The wraithbone amplified the dreaming god's concerns and communicated them to the other drifting islands out in the darkness, the faint but growing alarm call spreading through the far-flung diaspora like ripples across the surface of a pond.

Slowly but surely, the first stirrings of a call to arms began amongst the closest neighbouring islands, and the burning god's dreams of bloody and fiery carnage to come began to seep into the minds of its warrior acolytes.

Within the god itself, the ancient furnace of its heart began to beat with greater strength as it pumped torrid streams of living fire though the god's immobile limbs, shaking off the languor of too many millennia of inactivity. The burning god was beginning to stir to life, and, when fully awakened, its wrath would be terrible to behold.

PART ONE
CONSPIRACIES

ONE

THEY HAD BEEN torturing the warp spawn creature for six days now. Endless torture without relief or remission, using methods known only to the Inquisition's finest interrogator-adepts. For six days now, they had been working in shifts to visit miseries and abominations on living flesh that could not easily be imagined by most ordinary subjects of the Imperium; and, no matter what they did, no matter what manner of gruesome cruelties they inflicted, they had so far been neither able to kill it nor to induce it to give up whatever warp-born secrets it had to tell.

It was contained within a null-field in an adamantium-walled chamber buried three hundred metres below the surface. There was no way that the sound of its screams and babbling, blasphemous shrieks could even be heard outside the examination cell, and yet, somehow, some aspect of its agonies seemed to transmit themselves up through the layers of armourplas and adamantium shielding which entombed this deepest and most secret sub-level of the Inquisition fortress. Its screams echoed silently in the minds of everyone within the place, penetrating through whatever psychic wards and screens existed to protect the citadel and its occupants from daemonic intrusion. Only a precious, oath-sworn few even knew of the thing's existence, and, yet, somehow all sensed its presence. There had been a wave of suicides and murderous fights amongst the prisoners held in the ordinary detention levels above, Horst knew, no doubt prompted by the invisible currents of psychic horror emanating up from the thing imprisoned down here. Even the hand-picked and veteran members of the senior inquisitor's retinue seemed shaken and unnerved by such close proximity to the entity.

Remarkably, however, the creature's presence amongst them had had a most unexpected effect on the soul of at least one unwilling guest of the Inquisition. Two days ago, guards had come running in answer to the cacophony of screams and babbling pleas coming from the cell of Gorgio Nepheris, the so-called 'bodygatherer fiend of Bergamo', and captive of the Ordo Hereticus.

For two months now, the renegade surgeon had held his silence, revelling in his own planet-wide infamy and answering with a mocking smile his interrogators' demands to recant his sins and reveal the whereabouts of the remains of his many missing victims.

Now, however, the terror of the back-alleys of Bergamo, the third largest city here on the Gothic sector world of Lethe, had brushed minds with the thing held in the crypts below and had understood something of what true evil really was. He was currently to be found in a confession chamber, begging forgiveness from a stern-faced Ecclesiarchy confessor as he kept a small team of scribes busy with a non-stop, babbling litany of the details of his multitude of crimes.

The size of this list, and the enormous and previously unsuspected numbers of his victims over the course of his century-long murder spree amongst the poor and destitute of Bergamo had stunned even his interrogators.

Horst had little doubt that this catalogue of atrocity, when finally completed and codified, would be enough to allow the local Arbites force to clear out several record rooms of files on hitherto unsolved cases, and hopefully bring some kind of comfort into the minds of the families of Gorgio's many victims, a figure which had so far stood at some twelve thousand dead, though the number was reckoned to possibly double by the time the repenting heretic had completed his confession.

It was a pitifully small solace, Horst knew. The confession and, eventually, the execution of one lone heresy-ridden maniac. Significant only in local or perhaps even planetary terms, but completely infinitesimal in scale compared to the tumultuous events happening throughout the Gothic sector. This was why he was here on this world when so many possibly greater and more urgent matters called for his attention elsewhere within this war-torn sector of Imperial space. This was part of the mission he had embarked upon when the High Masters of the Inquisition had first despatched him to the Gothic sector eleven years ago, when they had first suspected the stirring to life of forces within the Eye of Terror, when they had dimly perceived the first awful warp-whispers of the Despoiler's intent to unleash a new and deadly Black Crusade upon the worlds of the Imperium of Mankind.

As he exited the elevator and walked down the corridor towards the single adamantium-reinforced and rune-inscribed door at the end of the passage, Horst recalled other passages from that mission, and other stages on the journey which had led to this moment.

PURGATORY, NINE YEARS ago. Smoke, ugly and black, filled the skies above the world, casting a gloomy shroud over the devastation below. Horst had seen such scenes before, on a score of worlds across the Gothic sector, but with a growing feeling of dread, he already knew that this one was different from and far more ominous than the other Chaos raids that had plagued the sector in recent years.

With a feeling of apprehensive dread that grew stronger with every step he took, he climbed up the jagged and fused sides of the still-smoking giant impact crater where the other members of the Inquisition survey team were already gathered. There was a small fleet of Imperial battle and rescue craft in orbit above the world, all from various arms of Imperial service, but the inspection of this devastated area of the planet's surface had been claimed by the Inquisition alone, and Horst had imposed a five hundred kilometre exclusion zone around the site. What lay here – or at least the evidence of what perhaps had lain here, Horst reminded himself, feeling that sense of dread grow ever tighter within him – was for the eyes of the Emperor's most trusted servants only.

Standing with the others, he stared into the deep, still-smouldering wound which had been gouged into the earth. A glance at the map display on his data-slate confirmed the almost unbelievable. According to the information, this twelve kilometre-wide gaping abyss of burning gases and smouldering, still semi-molten rock had, until just a few short days ago, been the location of a heavily-defended Imperium planetary base, home to thousands of Imperial Guard troopers, Adeptus Mechanicus adepts and servants of the myriad of other branches of Imperial government.

All across the planet's surface, other settlements and Imperial outposts had been struck and obliterated during the lightning-fast raid, but this, Horst knew, was the main object and target of the attack. Here the fell touch of Abaddon the Despoiler could truly be seen on the surface of Purgatory, scarring the face of the planet forever.

Horst looked down, and, through the haze of burning, sulphurous gases, saw the marks on the sheer sides of the crater, where, from high above in space, an orbiting warship had directed a coruscating beam of lance energy down onto the planet's surface, blasting away the topsoil and all of the fortress built upon that topsoil, and probing deep into the underlying bedrock of the planet.

How many lance-armed warships would it take to accomplish such a task, the inquisitor asked himself? He both marvelled and feared the thought of the massive outpouring of firepower that must have been required to carve such a wound through the planet's dense, rocky crust. And then a second, more troubling, thought suddenly struck him. What if it wasn't a fleet of warships? What if all this were the work of something else, some terrible new addition to the Despoiler's armoury which they had yet to encounter?

He shook his head, trying to dispel his gloomy mood. The potential ramifications of all that had happened here were bad enough, without adding to them with increasingly troublesome thoughts about some fictitious, planet-blasting super-weapon now possibly in the hands of the Imperium of Mankind's most hated and implacable enemy.

He looked again into the depths of the crater, rechecking the stream of info-runes now scrolling across the face of his data-slate. Despite the enormous energy stream that had been unleashed on the surface here, it was plain to see that it had somehow been expertly contained and targeted to an almost uncanny degree of precision. The overlaying surface material had been simply blasted away, yes, but, after that, the energy stream had been tightly focussed as it drilled down into the planet's crust, obliterating dense rock and mineral deposits in micro-seconds as it pushed deeper down into the planet's core, almost as if it were probing in search of something.

But probing in search of what, Horst wondered, already sickly suspecting the answer to his own unspoken question.

'Drones and servo-skull scouts have been despatched into the fissure. We estimate it to be at least eighteen thousand metres deep,' reported Monomachus, taking up his customary position alongside his inquisitor master, 'so it may take them some time to make a full survey. Residual energy from the massive weapon discharge which created the fissure, along with local interference from some of the mineral and ore deposits in the surrounding bedrock, may also affect surveyor readings and delay a fully accurate understanding of what is, or may once have been, down there.'

'But?' queried Horst, silently fulminating against the habit apparently ingrained in all of the Machine God's servants of taking seemingly forever to get to the point.

Monomachus tapped rune-keys on the brass façade of his antique data-slate, pausing also to silently commune with the interconnected machine-minds of his brother tech-priests and their mechanical server-devices, not only here on the planet's surface but also those aboard the Inquisition lightship in orbit overhead.

'But already we are detecting strong traces of psychometric radiation of a probable xeno-origin emanating upwards from the fissure bottom. The traces are strong, but are already starting to decay.'

'Hypothesis,' demanded Horst, knowing that the tech-priests were slaves to statistics, facts, figures, and long-established analytical models, and hated any kind of open, unsupported conjecture. It was Monomachus's ability to break free of such dogmatic behaviour and make intuitive leaps of informed opinion which made him such a valued member of the inquisitor's entourage.

'As I said, it may be some time before a fully accurate survey can be made, lord inquisitor, but it is my considered opinion that the spot we are now standing upon was indeed, until very recently, the hidden resting place of the xeno-artefact known as the Hand of Darkness.'

HORST'S BOOTED FEET noisily crunched over the brittle, ossified material that carpeted the ground for hundreds of kilometres in all directions, the noise sounding like the sharp crack of las-fire in the still, silent air of Ornsworld. Reluctantly, he looked down at the bone-chaff beneath his feet, picking out the details of tiny human-like bones over which he walked. They might easily have been mistaken for the remains of children, but Horst knew otherwise.

He lifted his gaze and looked around him, seeing the endless bone-litter, the piles of skull cairns dotted all across the horizon and the smoke plumes from the cremation pits which still rose up into the skies now over a week since the last of Abaddon's extermination legions had left this world.

He heard the crunch of more booted feet behind him, and turned to see the figure of Monomachus behind him, the tech-priest distastefully gathering up his gold-silicate robes in an effort to keep the long hems clear of the corpse-material littering the ground.

'How many?' asked Horst.

There was a characteristic pause of several seconds before Monomachus answered. In that time, the inquisitor heard the faint whirring of the cogitator machinery within his Adeptus Mechanicus advisor's rebuilt metal cranium. Other than that, the only sound to be heard in this tainted place was the whistling insect drone of servo-skulls as they drifted lazily over the scene, recording all evidence of the atrocity for the Inquisition's closed library archives, although some of the footage, suitably edited for mass consumption, would no doubt turn up in Imperial propaganda vidpict-casts.

'Three or four million, at this site alone,' intoned Monomachus, his typically blank-toned delivery giving scant homage to the enormity of the scale of the atrocity contained in that number. 'Preliminary orbital-drone scans show another twelve sites across the planet's surface of at least a similar magnitude, as well as possibly up to sixty other lesser massacre sites.'

Horst's only reply was a weary grunt. He personally had little fondness for the stunted abhuman breed known as ratlings, but they were part of the Imperium of Mankind and part of the Emperor's divine plan, and he regretted the deaths of so many of them, as he would that of any of the Emperor's loyal servants.

Ornsworld was the main home of the ratling sub-race and the recovery from this attack on the world would be long and painful, if indeed the planet and its population ever fully recovered at all from the decimation which had been visited upon them. For the next few generations at least, Horst coldly calculated, the Imperial Guard would have to make alternative arrangements for the recruitment of its quartermasters and sniper specialists.

He was standing in what had once been the central square of the ratling settlement known as Samstown, but the anonymous, burnt-out ruins around him showed little discernable evidence of what had once been the settlement's main focal point. Horst had never been on Ornsworld before, but he was familiar with its numberless similar counterparts scattered across the length and breadth of the Imperium, and, without too much effort, he could well imagine the look and feel of the place.

Over there would have been the local Administratum building, the centre of the Imperial bureaucracy on Ornsworld, and facing it almost in rivalry from the other side of the square would have been an Ecclesiarchy temple dedicated to whatever form of the Divine Emperor the ratlings had been given to worship. No doubt around the fringes of the square would also have been clustered the headquarter buildings of many local provincial trade guilds and merchant houses, since ratlings were nothing if not enterprising and industrious in the acquisition of wealth and material comforts.

All of it was gone now, swept away in mere hours as the gaze of the Despoiler fell upon this tranquil and unremarkably ordinary backwater Imperial world, located well away from the front-line planetary systems and main attack routes leading out from the Eye of Terror.

When his vox crackled into life, Horst easily recognised the brief series of staccato identity code blips hidden within the seemingly random-sounding burst of radio static.

'Horst here. Where are you, and what have you found, old friend?' he answered.

The voice which answered him was typically gruff and irreverent. Half a century of dispensing the Emperor's harsh and often brutal justice to the subjects of the Imperium had done little to improve the Senior Arbitrator Haller Stavka's notoriously blunt manner.

'In the hills, inquisitor, about sixty kilometres north-west of your position. It took a bit of doing, but we finally got one of these little bastard runts to act as guide and lead us to the site. No wonder the Hereticus could never find the place. The woodlands are so dense up here, and there's so many deep ravines and dead-end canyons that you could spend a lifetime crawling through these bloody hills and never find anything. It wasn't so hard to find the way as we got closer, though. After a while, we just followed all the damn buzzards in the sky above us, and they led us straight to it.'

'And?' Horst fought to quash the tight, underlying tone of apprehension in his question.

'I'll say that for these little half-pint bastards, they must have put up a hell of a fight defending the place, not that it did them any good in the end, of course. We found them all over the place, but the ones who were still alive at the end made their last stand in the inner temple part of the cave system.'

'The xeno-artefact?' Again, Horst struggled to control the anxiety in his voice. There was a pause before Stavka replied, although Horst already knew what the answer would be.

'Gone, inquisitor. Just like on Purgatory.'

THE DOOR AT the far end of the corridor opened, and Horst saw the stolid figure of Stavka emerge from the interrogation cell beyond. Even though he was out of uniform and wore only leather breeches with a simple, rough-spun tunic and a belt with holstered bolt pistol sidearm, there was little mistaking him for anything other than the capable and veteran servant of the Emperor's law which he had been for all but the last two decades of his life.

From the Imperial eagle emblem branded into his shoulder to the grim, impassive fix of his jaw to the rippling muscles beneath the surface of his scar-crossed arms, this was clearly a man well used to the often violent imposition of the Emperor's justice, a loyal and capable servant of the Imperium who would not flinch in the face of whatever task was required of him.

Even so, Horst could see the anxiety written across the arbitrator's uncharacteristically pale features. Stavka had been supervising the interrogation of the warp-spawn thing for over thirty-six hours now, and the strain on the man's face was clearly evident. Once again, Horst silently asked himself for perhaps the thousandth time if he was truly justified in taking such an extreme course of action. The creature's very presence here was an abomination, he knew. It was an unnatural, tainted thing, and the corruption it carried could potentially spread further – much further indeed – than this time and place.

Stavka nodded in salute to Horst as he met the inquisitor at the entrance to the interrogation chamber.

'It's been asking for you, inquisitor,' he said simply. 'By name.'

'HORSSSSSST,' HISSED THE daemon-thing in undisguised pleasure, one of the torture-inflicted wounds in its throat splitting open wider and warping to form a crude mouth. 'Why haven't you come down to see me earlier? I've been bored waiting for you. You should be more careful with your choice of minions. These ones here make for such dull company.'

A queer, bubbling laugh emerged from the ruin of its face, and it writhed in pleasure, straining against the bindings which held it down onto the pitted, filth-stained surface of the interrogation slab. Its skin was criss-crossed with scars and open wounds, some of the wounds horribly opening and closing in synch with the creature's mouth as it talked. Something that wasn't blood bubbled hotly out of the torture-openings in its body. Its skin was blackened and charred in those portions where the mystic binding wards and glyphs had been carved or tattooed into its flesh. Beneath the tight, stretched drum of its skin, the musculature of its unnatural body seethed and broiled in urgent agitation.

Other than the sick laughter of the warp spawn, the only other sound in the chamber was the droning chanting of the chorus of three Inquisition-approved Ecclesiarchy confessors as they endlessly recited prayers of protection and the sacred words of the litanies of binding. One of them swung an incense burner filled with potent and blessed unguents in a vain attempt to dispel the vile, hot reek of the thing which filled the air in the close confines of the underground chamber, and Horst silently gave quick thanks for the rebreather implants inside his throat and nostrils as he leant forward to confront the daemon-creature.

'You know me, warp-spawn?'

It laughed again, a hideous, high-pitched, almost childlike giggle. 'Perhaps, perhaps not, noble Inquisitor Horst. Perhaps we met during your famous scouring of Cato, or perhaps it was earlier than that? During that incident in the tunnels beneath Pazzazu?'

Horst visibly flinched at the mention of the so-called 'hive of damnation'. Not even his brethren in the innermost circles of the Inquisition knew the full facts of what he had seen and endured in that hellish network of underhive passages and crypts, and he doubted that anyone born in the last century or so even knew the name of that once most infamous of hive cities, so rigorous had been his ruthless subjugation of the full facts of his investigation there, and the forces it had stirred up. The daemon-thing cackled in delight, and Horst angrily cursed at himself, realising that, in falling for a trick that even a novice interrogator apprentice might have avoided, he had allowed the creature to open up a possible weakness in his mental defences.

'Warp spawn, is that all you have to offer me?' he said, deliberately putting a heavy sneering tone into his voice. 'Half-truths and lies? Vague hints of ancient events of no interest to anyone in these last hundred years? You disappoint me. I thought even a minor warp-born such as you could have done better than that.'

Again, the creature cackled, clearly relishing the encounter. 'Ah, but Gideon, isn't that why you had me summoned? To hear the whispers carried on the currents of the warp? To know the shape of the future? To learn what plans the Despoiler has been weaving all this time?'

Horst's expression was stony and impenetrable, betraying no hint of the thoughts which lay behind it, but, whatever the daemon was searching for as it carefully studied his reaction, somehow it found it. It laughed in satisfaction, forming new mouths to further express its hellish delight.

'Ah yes, the Despoiler, who stood with Horus as the walls of your precious corpse-emperor's palace came tumbling down before them. Abaddon of old, who still desires above all else the prize which was denied to him and his master those ten thousand years ago. He's come again, Gideon, out of the Eye of Terror, out of a place which you cannot and should not dare try to imagine, and all I see for you and the other servants of the corpse-emperor is a darkness of fear and futile sacrifice. Enjoy what time you have left, Gideon,' it laughed, 'for the Despoiler's plots are nearly done, and soon these worlds you cling to so tenaciously will all be gone!'

Horst was turning angrily away even before the last echoes of the creature's mocking, multi-voiced laughter had died away. 'Have the chamber sealed and leave this thing here to rot,' he instructed Stavka. 'Let us see if it's still laughing in a thousand years' time, cut off from the warp, bound inside this body and encased within a hundred tonnes of reinforced rockcrete.'

He took four steps – perhaps two more than he had expected – when the daemon-creature's voice shrilly rang out from behind him.

'The sleepers will be awakened! The Talismans of Vaul, that is what the Despoiler truly seeks here. And, oh yes, Gideon, just wait and see the light that will shine forth from those pretty baubles! Your day will come! The six will become one, and then all shall fall together!'

It screamed to itself in mad laughter and then started to babble in a confused chorus of voices. The printer mechanism of the cogitator device set up in a corner of the room clattered noisily as its auto-transcription abilities strove to keep up with the wild stream of gibberish and prophecies fed to it from the audio receptors of the servo-skull monitors hovering above the interrogation slab.

Later on, Horst and Monomachus would spend long hours going over these transcripts and the accompanying vidpict records of the creature's interrogation, but Horst knew that such second-hand evidence was no substitute for actually being here and facing the thing, listening to the fear and hate in its chorus of voices.

He leant closer, wary of some warp-born trick from the thing imprisoned on the slab, but keen to pick up more of the pattern he was beginning to discern amongst the torrent of nonsense words the daemon was now screaming in various different-toned voices. A second's concentration, a clearing away of all the extraneous gibberish using a mental trick which Monomachus had taught him, and, suddenly he heard the strain of prophecy amongst the stream of daemonic gibberish.

'Fularis, Anvil and Fier,' trilled the daemon in a grotesque and child-like song-song voice, repeating the couplets over and over to itself. 'Rebo, Schindelgeist and Brigia. The day will come. Six become one! All shall come together!'

Stavka too had heard the daemon's words and instantly grasped something of their meaning. 'Fularis, Anvil and the others,' he started, 'they're all Imperium worlds where–'

A sharp look from Horst cut him off. At the inquisitor's silent, urgent gesture, he quickly joined Horst in the passageway outside.

'Let it babble on until it's finished, but I think we've already heard the best of what it had to tell us.'

The one-time Arbites officer nodded grimly in agreement. 'And after that?' he asked, looking questioningly at Horst.

'As we agreed beforehand,' said Horst, looking his subordinate straight in the eye. 'Maximum containment. Nothing said or done in that room leaves this place.'

Stavka nodded in understanding, his hand unconsciously shifting towards his holstered bolt pistol. He saluted briefly and turned and re-entered the room.

Horst's thoughts were deep and troubled as he made the journey back to the elevator platform which would take him back up to the main levels of the citadel and forever away from this tainted place. The summoning of the daemon would surely damn him in the eyes of many of his fellow inquisitors, the so-called 'puritan' faction who zealously followed the ancient maxims of Imperial dogma to the very letter. It was, he admitted, a dangerous and desperate thing to do, an act which was, at best, an admission of his failure to divine the plans and purposes of the enemy by any other means. What he was about to do next would, he judged, leave him equally damned in the eyes of others within the Inquisition.

'Talismans of Vaul', he murmured to himself, repeating one of the things the daemon had said. He did not fully understand the true import of everything the daemon had spoken of, but already his worst suspicions were deepening, and he recognised at least part of that phrase.

Vaul.

When the High Lords of Terra had despatched him here to the Gothic sector to investigate what had only then been a series of bewildering if seemingly random attacks by Chaos raiders across the fringes of the sector, he had little imagined the strange and terrible places the course of that investigation would lead him to. Now, as the forces of the Despoiler broke out of the Eye of Terror and plunged all of the Gothic sector into ferocious, full-scale war of a level not seen since the time of the Great Heresy, his investigation into the enemy's true purpose was nearing an end, and this last stage of that journey would take him in a new direction and possibly towards the strangest and most dangerous encounter of all.

Vaul. An eldar word. One of their damned alien heathen deities, he knew. Well, when this is all over then, if the fanatics of the Ordo Malleus don't get me, he thought to himself, their brethren in the Ordo Xenos most assuredly will.

The moment of humour was short-lived. As he entered the elevator and activated the command rune for the surface levels, he could already hear the first bolt pistol shots ringing out from the place he had just left.

DAYS LATER, HORST and his entourage pushed their way through the bronze doors, entering the Lord Admiral's strategium chamber beyond in a clash of heavily booted feet and weapons on armour. Navy armsmen guards raised the blunt-nosed barrels of their deadly shotcannon weapons in sudden alarm, but were quickly quelled into submission by the sight of the Inquisition emblem upon Horst's carapace-armoured chest-plate, as well as by a warning growl from Stavka and the rest of Horst's bodyguard retinue: veteran warriors gathered from half a dozen different branches of the Imperium armed services.

Horst took the scene in with a glance. A group of Imperial Navy officers, the proof of their various exalted ranks indicated by the colourful plumage of gold braiding and glittering medals decorating their dark blue uniforms, stood around the spinning strategium globe at the centre of the room. Around them were waiting phalanxes of adjutant officers, scribe adepts, Munitorium officials, tech-priests and even, standing to one side in the wide chamber, the distinctive crimson and gold robes of a cardinal-prince of the Ecclesiarchy, attended by his own smaller courtly entourage of followers.

All eyes were upon Horst and his group, many navy officers openly gawping in surprise at this unforgivable breach of protocol. Only one figure amongst the cluster of senior navy personnel gathered around the hologram display failed to react or show any sign of alarm at this unwarranted invasion of the very centre of Battlefleet Gothic Command. The man, a tall and elegantly thin naval officer wearing the resplendent uniform of an admiral of the Segmentum Obscuras fleet continued to lean forward in inspection of the strategium display, staring in close concentration at the complex ballet of planet and battle-squadron runes projected across the three-dimensional map of the Gothic sector. He seemed to be caught up in deep contemplation of some remote and complex long-range strategy equation, the workings of which only he could truly fathom. The flickering light from the display played across his face, reflecting off the trademark cyber-device implanted in place of his missing right eye and throwing his distinctive hawk-like features into stark relief. It was a face now familiar to the inhabitants of every civilised Imperial world within the Gothic sector from the endless propaganda vidpict-casts which had become a feature of daily life since the start of the war.

Not even the lowliest rating or indentured slave-worker aboard any of the hundreds of Imperial Navy warships under his command would be in any doubt about the figure's identity, even without the magnificent diamond-inlaid and gold-woven rank sash he wore across his tunic breast.

'My dear Horst,' said Lord Admiral Cornelius Ravensburg, in the tell-tale clipped accent of the hereditary navy aristocrat class of Cypra Mundi, 'always a pleasure to welcome a member of the Imperial Inquisition aboard my flagship, even if the visit is both unannounced and unexpected. I take it then that you are not here to check anything as mundane as mere naval strategy?'

The voice of the commander of Battlefleet Gothic concealed a dry, slightly mocking tone. It had been five centuries since the Inquisition had conducted a merciless purge of suspected and widespread seditious elements amongst the senior officer cadre of Segmentum Obscuras, but such events lingered long in the memories of the institutions of the Imperium of Mankind, and there had traditionally been a great deal of hostile resentment to the agents of the Inquisition amongst the upper echelons of Battlefleet Obscuras.

Horst sensed Stavka bristling in anger at the Lord Admiral's tone, but Horst himself knew that this was not the time to dwell on any of the petty resentments and rivalries that existed between so many branches of Imperium authority. He bowed slightly in a modest deference to Ravensburg's rank, and, when he spoke, his tone was polite and conciliatory.

'Forgive the intrusion, Lord Ravensburg, but I must speak to you most urgently. What I have to tell you is too precious to be trusted to any courier vessel or astropath communication, and involves vital information concerning the enemy's underlying motives in launching their assault upon the Gothic sector.'

'Motives? We already know all about their motives, lord inquisitor,' said one of the other navy officers, looking disdainfully at Horst and his entourage. It was Ravensburg's chief adjutant, Commodore Admiral Kirponos. Horst had heard that the commodore had been a brave and fearless ship's captain, and now he had the proof, for even here at the very heart of Gothic Sector Naval Command, it took a brave if perhaps rash man to stand up against the authority of a Lord Inquisitor emissary of the High Council of Terra. The navy commander stared Horst in the face as he continued.

'We face another Black Crusade, this much we know. Both the Inquisition and the High Lords of Terra have confirmed this, and the crusade's motives are no different from the previous ones which have assaulted the Imperium for the last ten thousand years: wanton destruction of Imperial worlds, the defeat of the Emperor's armed forces, the overthrow of Imperial order and the subjugation of the Emperor's subjects. These are the only motives which count in the minds of our enemies. Twelve times before, the Imperium has faced and withstood such assaults. This time, with the Emperor's grace and with the forces under the command of the Lord Admiral, shall be no different, no matter how many "Planet Killer" weapons the enemy may possess. The Despoiler and his heretic lackeys will be defeated and sent back into their Eye of Terror bolt-hole to lick their wounds for another thousand years.'

Yes, a brave man; the Imperium needs more like this one, thought Horst, realizing that this was neither the time nor the place to impose the full crushing weight of his authority upon Kirponos, and the other loyal servants of the Emperor assembled here. He would need the co-operation and trust of men such as this in the days to come, he knew, and he needed to make allies of them, not enemies.

'So I pray, lord commodore,' said Horst, bowing in the man's direction, 'and, like you, I too assumed that we were facing a Black Crusade, and not a mere series of raids as we first assumed. However,' he continued, directing his gaze towards Ravensburg and deliberately bringing a more authoritative tone into his voice, 'I now have good reason to believe that what we are witnessing is something else, part of a larger and hidden stratagem which could herald something far greater and more terrible than any Black Crusade.'

He paused to allow his words to take effect, hearing the muted gasps and quickly-stilled utterances from amongst the throng of navy officers. When he continued, his next words were aimed solely at Ravensburg.

'The Despoiler moves in shadows and lies, my lord, hiding his secrets within other secrets, and his plans are already far further advanced than we could almost fear possible. We must act soon to counter him, or else we risk losing far more in this war than the entire Gothic sector.'

Horst locked eyes with Ravensburg, holding the Lord Admiral's gaze for a moment in a long look which communicated much about the inquisitor's mood of deadly earnestness. Ravensburg paused for a moment, holding the other man's gaze, and then spoke.

'Tell me what you require, lord inquisitor, and I will do everything in my power to make it so,'

'What I have to tell you is for your ears only, lord admiral.'

Ravensburg nodded, and made a curt gesture of dismissal to his staff. 'Gentlemen, leave us, if you please.'

Both men waited as their entourages and attendants, together totalling over two hundred in number, left the strategium chamber. Stavka was the last to exit, and would stand guard at the doors, permitting no one to enter until he had received the correct vox code signal from Horst. Ravensburg waited until the doors had been swung shut before turning to look expectantly at Horst.

Horst began to talk. When he had finished, some three hours later, the nature of the things he had told Ravensburg and the conclusions the two men had come to would change not only the course of the Gothic Sector War, but also even possibly alter the fate of the Imperium itself.

TWO

WITH A RUMBLE like the voices of angry gods, the two metre-thick blast doors ground open before Siaphas, permitting him entry into the Warmaster's throne room.

The squat, hulking shapes of the two daemon-possessed dreadnoughts on either side of the entranceway turned towards him, emitting low electronic snarls of warning. Blood-slicked servo-motors hummed and deadly heavy bolter weapon arms were aimed in readiness at him. Flickering pencils of red light played over Siaphas as the dreadnoughts' targeter senses zeroed in on him, and the Chaos sorcerer felt cold, inquiring tendrils of daemon-thought probing at the surface of his consciousness.

His fanged lips formed and spoke a word of power, and, with an angry mechanical growl of what sounded almost like disappointment, the daemon guardians of the entrance to the Warmaster's throne chamber retreated back to their guard-posts on either side of the doorway.

'Enter, Siaphas of Eidolon,' intoned the cold, mocking voice of Abaddon the Despoiler, 'and be welcome amongst us.'

Siaphas shuffled forward, the thick, flesh-fused mass of his left leg dragging heavily behind him. He was a champion of Tzeentch, and he was here at the Warmaster's summons as a one-time commander of one of his master's legion armies, but, somehow, he sensed that something was strangely amiss on this occasion. Fear flickered through his mind and the dark, twisting thing within him, that part of him which he had long ago offered up to the Lord of Change, lapped eagerly at such thoughts, relishing the taste of his terror.

He moved towards the Warmaster's throne dais, aware of the many eyes upon him. This was the first time for more than four years that he had been permitted into the Warmaster's presence, and he was keenly aware of the suspicious glances and whispered sniggering from amongst the groups of courtiers flanking the procession-way leading towards the Despoiler's throne. There were many old enemies of his here, Siaphas knew, long-time rivals and also more than a few former allies whom he had been happy to use and then ruthlessly discard during what had been a swift and deeply satisfying ascent up through the ranks of the Despoiler's warlord cadre.

And then, four years ago now, had come the invasion of Helia IV. It had been Siaphas who had first suggested the strategy of unleashing terror fleets on the Imperial worlds within the Gothic sector. It had been Siaphas who had cast the warp-runes and declared the omens favourable for the attack on the world of Helia IV, and it had been Siaphas who became the object of the Despoiler's wrath when the invasion fleet and three entire Chaos Legions of troops had been all but annihilated by the Imperium fleet which had unexpectedly arrived to defend the world from the Warmaster's attack. It had all been the fault of that fool Varro, of course. It had been he who had led his fleet straight into the jaws of the Imperial trap, but Varro was gone, vaporised along with his flagship the *Lord Seth* during the battle, and the fury of Abaddon's displeasure had fallen solely on Siaphas alone.

The sorcerer knew that he had been fortunate to survive the experience. The Warmaster did not tolerate failure, and the normal penalty for those who disappointed him was to be consigned to an eternity of suffering as flesh-fodder, doomed to serve as the physical vessel for a warp daemon. There were many such daemon-possessed creatures serving throughout the ranks of the Despoiler's forces: as commanders of his Chaos hordes; as navigators aboard his warships, using their mystic daemon-sight to guide his fleets through the warp; as familiars for his sorcerers and as advisors within his own throne room, offering the Warmaster whispered counsels that came direct from the great Powers of the Warp themselves.

There was one such creature present here now, hunched at the foot of the steps of the Warmaster's dais, drooling black slime from between its bloody lips as it strained against the heavy rune-marked iron chain around its neck, growling in discontent at its imprisonment, chained as it was to the stone slabs of the dais steps and trapped inside a too-weak physical shell and cut off from the limitless freedoms of the warp. In a sudden flash of unwelcome prescience, through his own warp-given mystic powers, Siaphas for a moment saw his own face reflected in the creature's shifting features, reminding him that there was still an agonised vestige of the body's original human occupant trapped in there with the daemon-thing spirit, and reminding him again of just how fortunate he had been to escape a similar fate.

As he approached the Warmaster's dais, he looked around, quickly spotting the figure of his benefactor standing in the shadows behind the throne. Zaraphiston was Abaddon's chief lieutenant and personal Chaos sorcerer; he had also been Siaphas's mentor. It had only been through Zaraphiston's personal intervention that Siaphas had been allowed to escape the awful fate that would otherwise have been his due punishment for failing the Warmaster.

Siaphas searched the face of his one-time mentor and patron for any flicker of acknowledgement or clue as to why he had been summoned back to Abaddon's court after four years in exile amongst some of the most obscure and far-flung reaches of the Warmaster's domain, but all that met him in reply was the carefully-guarded blank gaze of the elder sorcerer's hooded eyes. After millennia in the service of the Despoiler, the Chaos sorcerer was a master in keeping any sign of his true feelings or motivations well buried.

Siaphas secretly knew that Zaraphiston bore little love for the Despoiler, and suspected that his former master's ambitions went far higher than merely being content to serve as Abaddon's pet sorcerer.

Zaraphiston was not alone in this regard: many before him had plotted in secret against the Warmaster and the husks of their daemon-devoured remains were there for all to see, hanging around the walls of the vast chamber alongside all the other captured war banners and heraldries of thousands of Imperial Guard regiments and more than a hundred Space Marine Chapters, mute evidence of the Warmaster's victories over his enemies.

No, Siaphas knew, as he painfully threw himself to his knees and bowed in supplication before the figure seated on the throne, Abaddon the Despoiler, Warmaster of Chaos, Commander of the Black Crusades and Heir to the Glories of Horus, was not an opponent to be underestimated. That was why this shameful display of abeyance was necessary; it was the only way to find the path back into Abaddon's favour and into the ranks of his warlord commanders. There were many others here who harboured the same secret ambitions as Siaphas and his master Zaraphiston, who were not content to accept the rank positions within the Legions of Chaos which Abaddon had already deemed was the highest position that any of them would ever attain within the service of the Powers of Chaos. There were many here who were not content to merely serve, but wished to rule instead, and Siaphas was one of them.

He would not waste this opportunity, he promised himself. He would carry out whatever trifling and unworthy task the Despoiler required of him, and then he would be free to reclaim his place amongst his peers. Free to plot and scheme amongst those with similar ambitions to his own. There were many within the Legions of Chaos who considered this assault on the Gothic sector to be a foolhardy and dangerous venture. They whispered that the Warmaster had been led astray by false prophecy voices within the warp; that, after ten thousand years, the heir of Horus was finally losing his grip on power; that this war should have been won by now and that, with another and more able Chaos Legion commander seated on the throne of the Warmaster, it still might not be too late to salvage the damage done by Abaddon's endless schemes within schemes and private vendettas.

Sometimes, such whispers reached the ears of the Warmaster himself, and he was able to trace them back to their source. The remains of such unfortunates were still here for all to see on the walls around the throne room, so Siaphas was careful to mask his thoughts from Abaddon's all-seeing gaze, and show the Warmaster only the same fawning, unquestioningly obedient façade as that presented by all the rest of the Despoiler's witless and craven lackeys.

So, mindful of what was expected of him, Siaphas prostrated himself before the Warmaster's throne. 'It is my pleasure only to serve you and the Powers of the Warp, Warmaster,' he dutifully intoned, not daring to raise his head until Abaddon had spoken.

'Indeed,' came the reply, in a disdainful voice containing less warmth than the chill depths between the furthest stars. 'Rise, loyal Siaphas, and hear why we have at last sent for you again.'

Siaphas rose to his feet, and looked up at the figure on the throne. The eyes of Abaddon the Despoiler, as dark and fathomless as the outer gulfs, stared back at him, catching him in their cold gaze and seeming to strip him bare of all defences. For a moment, Siaphas wanted to confess his many disloyalties and those of others to the Warmaster, but then his mystic training took hold once more and he managed to break the spell, looking quickly away under the clumsy pretence of bowing his head in supplication. The possessed thing crouching at the foot of the throne dais snickered in cruel humour at the sorcerer's discomfort, and its mocking laugh found subtle echoes amongst the watching crowd of courtiers.

Siaphas's mind seethed with hatred and humiliation, but he choked the feeling back down within himself. 'My life and soul for Chaos, Warmaster,' he managed to stammer out. 'Tell me what you require me to do, and I will move the stars to fulfil your command.'

'The war goes well,' intoned Abaddon in his cold, dead voice, 'but our enemies grow ever more desperate as the tide of battle continues to turn against them. In their desperation, they reach out in search of allies. They must not be allowed to succeed. This is the task we require of you, sorcerer.'

Hope and relief surged through Siaphas. This was more than he had ever dreamed of, and already that aspect within him which belonged to the Changer of the Ways was spinning the first plots and schemes using visions of the forces and resources which would no doubt be put at his disposal. 'You honour me, Warmaster,' he said, careful to keep out of his voice any hint of what was going on in his mind. 'What forces will I be given to command in your name? What size of warfleet? How many legions of troops?'

'Warfleets? Legions?' answered the Despoiler, with a mocking edge to his voice. 'You misunderstand, little sorcerer. The enemies of the false emperor seek allies, but we have found allies of our own. Contact has already been made, and now you and one other will join them as my ambassadors to ensure that their part of the bargain is carried out as I have commanded. Do this thing, and the favour of the Great Powers will be upon you. Fail, and we will not be so merciful as we have in the past.'

Siaphas's thoughts were a turmoil of confused emotions. To be the Warmaster's personal envoy was an honour granted to few, but why had he, who had been out of favour for such a dangerously long time, been chosen for this task? Who were these mysterious allies, and what prize could have tempted them to strike a bargain with one as notorious as Abaddon the Despoiler?

Siaphas risked a quick glance at the figure of his patron standing to the side of the throne. Zaraphiston stood silent and immobile, his face hidden within the shadows of his hood, but Siaphas had to suppress a smile as he saw his former master's hand brush casually and haphazardly on the rune-inscribed hem of his robes. To anyone watching, it might have looked like an unconscious gesture, but to a student of the master Chaos sorcerer, it was a clear signal, communicating much in the placement of the fingers and the gold-threaded rune signs which they briefly touched upon.

The thought flashed through Siaphas's mind. A warning! There is a trap lying in wait here, but also a great reward for the one who can safely bypass it and prove their worth to the Warmaster. Siaphas casually inclined his head, letting Zaraphiston know that his warning had been received and understood, before replying to the Despoiler.

'Who is to be the other envoy on this mission, Warmaster?'

Abaddon smiled thinly and gestured towards the crowd of courtiers. At his command, the crowd instantly parted, and a tall, muscular figure in brass and steel armour strode forward, blood and other fluids dripping from the jangling, hooked chains embedded into its flesh. It grinned a lipless grin, for much of the original flesh of its face was missing, replaced by a patchwork of dead skin taken from its battle victims, and growled in savage pleasure, raising its inactivated chainaxe in salute to the figure on the throne.

'Hannibar of Barca,' the Warmaster said. 'He will accompany you on this mission. It is my unalterable command that you both fulfil the separate roles I have intended for you.'

'Warmaster,' said Siaphas, bowing again as he pondered this new and most unwelcome twist to events. That there was a double meaning in what the Despoiler had said was obvious, but why, of all candidates, would Abaddon have selected the Beast of Barca for this mission? Hannibar was notorious, a mindless animal in human form, and one of the followers of that arch-maniac, Kharn the Betrayer.

Like Siaphas, the Khornate berserker champion had seriously fallen from the Warmaster's favour. He and his legions had been ordered to attack and seize the Imperium mining world of Achilia, with the aim of enslaving its population and turning the outpost into a supply and refit point for the Despoiler's warfleets. Instead, the berserker fool had allowed his troops to not only butcher the entire population but was further unable or unwilling to control them when, their bloodlust unfulfilled, they then fell upon and massacred those contingents of other Chaos troops which had supported them in the initial invasion.

The Warmaster was not slow to show his displeasure. The mines and workshops of Achilia were still manned with an army of slave workers, but it had been Hannibar's own troops who had taken the place of the exterminated civilian population, while Hannibar himself had been banished to the remote fringes of the war where he might learn to tame the worst excesses of his Khornate bloodlust.

So, thought Siaphas, two pariahs, both now summoned back to the heart of the Warmaster's power. It was surely no coincidence or show of unlikely clemency on the part of Abaddon that both of them had been selected for this mission, and Siaphas remembered Zaraphiston's warning of a hidden trap. He warily eyed the glowering figure of Hannibar, who, if his mind wasn't empty of all but the usual tedious Khornate blood-frenzy, was no doubt making similar calculations of his own. Which one of them was the trap for? One, or both? What was the Warmaster's hidden purpose in putting the two of them together like this? Siaphas decided that more information was urgently needed.

'These allies you speak of, Warmaster, who are they, and how will we make ourselves known to them?'

Again, the figure on the throne smiled in secret amusement and gestured towards his Chaos sorcerer. 'You must be weary after such a long journey from whatever remote part of our domain you have travelled from. Rest and recover some of your strength. Afterwards, when you are ready, I have no doubt that our good and loyal Zaraphiston will tell you everything you need to know.'

IT WAS SOME three weeks after the departure of the two envoys from the Warmaster's court that a scout raider craft dropped out of the warp on the edge of a desolate and forgotten star system on the edge of the Cyclops Cluster. It made its way quickly in-system to take orbit around the system's third innermost planet, a barren rock so insignificant that only the most dedicated of the Imperium's cartographer-adepts could have located its details in the vast and still incomplete index of mapped star systems which lay within the Imperium's sprawling and ever-changing borders.

A shuttle, black and sinister, dropped from the orbiting ship towards the planet's surface, landing at the point of the precise co-ordinates given to them days ago and depositing three elite squads of Black Legion Chaos Marines on the dead and dusty plain. Two of the squads instantly fanned out to secure the perimeter of the landing zone while the other began a careful search of the area. It took less than a minute before a voxed shout alerted the squad commander that they had found what they came for.

It sat in the middle of a dust-filled crater. A squat, featureless obsidian canister roughly half a metre high and with no visible seams or means of opening. The planet was barren and airless. No wind or breeze existed to stir the dead dust of the place, and so it was with a feeling of unsettling disquiet that the squad commander noted that the desert surface of the sand remained undisturbed for hundreds of metres all around the canister. Whatever had placed the object there had left no evidence of its passing.

With an angry curse, he commanded a Marine to run forward and snatch up the canister before he and his squad retreated back toward their waiting shuttle, nervously training their weapons on a landscape which had not seen the tread of another living thing in millennia. Less than three minutes after touching down, the shuttle was in the air again, abandoning the world to whatever forgotten ghosts walked upon its dead surface.

SIX DAYS LATER, the canister lay on a black marble plinth within the private chambers of Abaddon. The Despoiler stood in contemplation of it, secretly marvelling at the chilling alien blankness of the thing. The scabbarded daemon blade hanging by his side stirred in disquiet, giving forth a faint psychic rustle of distrust, and Abaddon turned to see Zaraphiston entering the chamber.

'You sent for me, Warmaster?' he purred with his usual unctuous, too-quick-to-please tone. 'I assume we have received an answer from our potential new allies?'

Abaddon gestured at the canister. 'Open it.'

The Chaos sorcerer bowed at the command and stood over the plinth, contemplating the object upon it for a few seconds. Then, with his scaled hands, he made passes over the canister, running his fingers above its featureless surface while whispering words of power. In the dim light of the room, a faint glowing nimbus of energy became apparent around the object. A few seconds later, a sequence of strange and elaborate rune-marks became fleetingly visible there too. Zaraphiston's long, nimble fingers moved quickly, following the runes and lightly touching them in a complex sequence only he could follow.

With a quiet, rasping hiss, the top of the canister dilated open like the iris of an eye, although there was no visible mechanism involved in the process. An acrid vapour spilled out, tainting the air with a bitter-sweet chemical taste, and, beneath that, the faint smell of something rotting and organic.

'Well? What answer have they sent us?' asked Abaddon, as Zaraphiston reached into the canister and removed its contents.

The severed and perfectly preserved head of Hannibar of Barca dangled there, the circumstances of his death written there in the frozen expression of agony etched into his cryogenically preserved features. However the Khorne berserker had died, it had neither been quick nor easy, that much was plain to see.

Abaddon smiled at the sight of the gruesome missive-object. 'Excellent. Then their answer is "yes".'

THREE

LILEATHON WATCHED IMPASSIVELY as the last doomed human vessel continued valiantly, if futilely, to fight on. It had been stripped of its shields, its main drive had been crippled by a torpedo hit and it could neither move nor manoeuvre. Its hull was punctured in more than a dozen places and its internal atmosphere was bleeding out into space, and yet the human barbarians within refused to yield to the inevitable.

The slender dart shapes of her life-mate Kornous's Eagle formation glided in for another and surely final bombing strike on the vessel, and, even as Lileathon watched the images projected on the delicate wraithbone membrane of the pict-skin, she saw the remaining working turret defences on the enemy vessel's hull open fire at the oncoming bomber craft. She smiled in appreciation as she watched the Eagles dance through the hail of fire, leaving the confounded human gunners pointlessly chasing the ghostly after-images thrown out by their targets' holofield generator defences.

'Your orders, craftmistress?' echoed Kornous's mind-voice over the wraithbone device-amplified communication link. 'Do you require any of the mon-keigh animals as captives?'

Even over the wraithbone-comm link, which often missed
subtle inflections of meaning and cadence, the knowing
humour in his mind-voice tone was clear.

'Mael dannan,' replied Lileathon, using the shared warrior-
cant dialect of their now-vanquished craftworld. *Dannan*, the
word for death, but used only in terms of the culling of animals and other lesser creatures.

Mael dannan. Total and merciless extermination.

The Eagle bombers bore mercilessly on, skipping effortlessly past a storm of las-beam fire, spinning a dizzying path
through a wall of crude mon-keigh explosive projectile
munitions. They bore relentlessly down on the target. In
times past, Lileathon had taken on the aspect warrior path of
Amon Harakht, of Eagle pilot. That part of her which would
always be of that aspect could well remember the surge of
exultant pleasure which must now be filling the minds of the
bomber pilots as they heard the over-excited, screaming
crescendo of their craft's infinity circuits and saw the bulky
shape of their doomed target looming ever larger through
the crystal-glass canopies of their cockpits. She watched the
last few moments on the pict-skin screen, marvelling at the
skill and artistry of the bomber pilots. She had seen this final
killing stroke performed a thousand times, had performed it
herself a thousand times more, but still the pleasure never
left her.

The Eagles bore on, until the pitted and battle-scarred hull
of their target must have filled their entire universe, and then,
at the last possible moment and with only scant metres to
spare, they broke formation and peeled away, their navigator-
companions simultaneously giving the mind-thought order
to their crafts' infinity circuit systems. A brood of missile-
slivers launched away from each craft, piercing the target vessel's hull in a space of time immeasurable by the crude
animal-minds of the vessel's occupants. Another infinitesimal moment later, and the missiles' sonic charge warheads
detonated deep within the target, unleashing a carefully
orchestrated symphony of destruction. The human vessel did
not so much explode as *shatter*, transformed in an instant
into a rapidly expanding sphere of twisted metal and fragmented ruin.

The eldar vessel's pack of killers raced ahead of the wreckage wave, the squadron's infinity circuit comm-channels filled with a hot, excited mish-mash of victory shout-thoughts and bravado chatter.

'Swift victory, sure death,' thought-talked Lileathon in the proper rite of celebration, using her Eclipse class cruiser's superior infinity circuits to reach into the minds of the over-excited aspect warrior pilots and install a necessary sense of calm and authority. 'Return home to receive your craft-world's blessings.'

One by one, the pilots swiftly responded to the order, but she maintained her vigil at the pict-skin screen until she was certain that all the bomber craft were returning to their launch-bays. As a one-time aspect warrior pilot, she well knew the dangerous ferment which often seized the minds of those who chose the aspect warrior path.

We are slaves to our emotions, she thought. This weakness – this inability to control our animal-selves – almost destroyed us once. We must not succumb to this mon-keigh aspect within ourselves again. We must keep in check our baser nature if we are ever to survive.

A flickering glance across the other pict-skins confirmed that, elsewhere, the battle was likewise going in their favour. Four mon-keigh transports lay crippled and helpless, offering themselves up as easy victims to any of the other Eagle formations still at loose across the battle zone. Three more transports and one escort craft had been reduced to burned-out hulks, while what remained of the human convoy was making a desperate, limping run for the warp jump point on the fringes of the system, still impossibly far-distant, given their present speed and predicament.

Fast-attack eldar vessels, Hemlock and Nightshade destroyers, harried them all the way, and Lileathon saw the last surviving human escorts turn, outmanoeuvred and out-gunned, to face their pursuers in a desperate and doubtlessly ill-fated attempt to buy time for the rest of the convoy to reach the safety of the warp jump point. The eldar ships accelerated at speed towards the enemy warships, their commanders no doubt revelling in the promise of such easy kills.

'They fight bravely, the humans,' offered Ailill, second-in-command of the *Vual'en Sho*, watching the denouement of the battle as it was projected real-time upon the augur chamber's pict-skin screens. 'We must give them that much, if nothing else.'

'We give them nothing,' replied Lileathon, making no attempt to disguise the contempt in her voice, shading the meaning of her words with the inflection reserved for an enemy considered beneath contempt.

'They are enemies. It is dangerous not to accord your enemies at least some measure of respect,' ventured Ailill.

'They are animals. They have no souls, and so they are incapable of possessing the virtues of bravery or nobility of spirit,' she replied.

'And yet they continue to fight when there is no hope of victory, as they do now. Even the lowliest animal knows when to flee or, if cornered, when to offer its throat in surrender to its conqueror.'

Lileathon was not to be distracted by her second-in-command's philosophical musings. 'They fight, because they know no other way, because their animal natures compel them to do so. If they have any courage, then it is merely the courage of a savage beast, that manner of mindless savagery which may drive an animal to gnaw at its own trap-imprisoned limbs.'

We have more important matters to attend to, she added in mind-speech. *Let the issue be at an end.*

'Wisdom commands,' genuflected Ailill, the unmistakeable body language of his stance and carefully subservient gesture making clear his unspoken opposition to his craftmistress's opinion.

He disagrees, but our ways permit him to do so, thought Lileathon. That is why our ways are superior to the ways of the mon-keigh and their mindless subjugation to the will of their corpse-god. Lann Caihe. *Water bringer*. That is what his role means in our language. He is older and more cautious than I. His task is to bring water to quench the fires of my fury when they threaten to become too uncontrollable. He brings balance to my command, just as our race's task is to bring balance to the universe. That is why all that we are and all that we have been cannot be allowed to be extinguished without a struggle.

Light flared on one of the pict-skin screens as another ship exploded, calling her attention back to the here and now. She saw one of the human vessels – so ugly, she thought to herself, so bulky and graceless, so unlike the graceful, slender-lined shapes of our ships – slowly breaking up as it was rent apart by a series of internal explosions, one entire side of its hull stripped away by the deadly, nimble touch of a pulsar lance. The eldar on the command bridge of the *Vual'en Sho* paused for a few seconds in their tasks to watch the last few moments of the human ship's death-throes.

'One of their troop transports,' judged Ailill. 'A bad loss for them, several thousand warriors less to battle the servants of the Abomination.'

'Or several thousand warriors less to attack and extermi-nate us,' countered Lileathon. 'Count yourself fortunate, Ailill. You still have a craftworld home, while I saw mine destroyed by the mon-keigh savages, and heard the mind-screams of our world's Dreaming Ones as their spirit stones were ripped out of the living wraithbone.'

Ailill said nothing. All across the command deck, the eyes of many other eldar were upon her, and even the gentle, calming mind-speak whisper of the wraithbone all around them seemed to falter and quiet. To those of her race, a craft-world was a sacred, living thing, the sanctuary which nurtured and protected them in the cold gulfs between the stars, and to speak of the death of one of these ancient and impossibly precious refuges was to bring fear and horror in the minds of every eldar listening.

'The mon-keigh and their corpse-god oppose the Great Abomination, as do we,' she continued, studying the pat-terns of the field of battle on the tactical pict-skin screen, 'but they are also the Abomination's greatest source of power. They are weak and stupid, and their god is old and failing. Their empire is doomed, but in its death-throes, it lashes out blindly at all around them, including us. They understand so little, and all which they do not understand, they condemn and seek to destroy. That is why we cannot depend on them to hold the line against the Abomination, and that is why we must prevent them from building their strength to strike at us.'

Ailill said nothing, but made the sixth variation of the ninth gesture of contrition. Sorrow expressed at the touching upon of another's grief. Lileathon made the corresponding gesture of forgiveness. Her story was well known amongst the eldar of Ailill's craftworld. Her own craftworld destroyed, she and the other survivors of the unwarranted attack on Bel-Shammon fled into the labyrinth of the webway, taking refuge amongst the craftworlds of their brethren eldar. A refugee even amongst a race of refugees, the fires of vengeance burned hot and fierce within the proud young warship captain, as the ships of this human transport convoy had just found out to their cost.

The humans' war had spread out all across the Gothic sector, even into those regions which they had normally left well alone in centuries past. Regions marked as uncharted or uninhabited wilderness space on their crude star charts, but which every vessel's captain knew all too well to be inhabited by races other than theirs. The humans had lost many ships over the millennia in attempts to probe into these regions and for many years now there had existed an unspoken concordat within the humans' naval forces that such areas would be left well alone, and the races within them allowed to remain unchallenged.

Now, though, the urgent requirements of war brought the humans into these dark regions. They came in search of convoy routes which would allow them to evade the enemy's prowling wolf pack fleets, or seeking new resource planets to provide the raw materials for the manufacture of their crude but often highly effective armaments. This system was part of one such region. In itself, it was insignificant and unremarkable, a dying dwarf star circled by four dead planets, but drifting far distant through the outer fringes of the system was the craftworld of An-Iolsus, birthplace of Ailill and the other eldar aboard the *Vual'en Sho*, and the adopted home of Lileathon herself. The system and the barren reaches of interstellar space around it were sacrosanct while the craftworld was even remotely nearby, and it would be over a century and a half yet before An-Iolsus's slow, millennia-long course would carry it beyond the furthest borders of the system, and so the eldar of An-Iolsus had reacted with brutal and immediate force to the humans' incursions into the region.

This was the third such convoy which Lileathon's reaver fleet had ravaged, and that aspect of her which she had surrendered to the warrior calling exulted in the carnage she and the vessels under her command had wreaked amongst the human trespassers. She had stood on this deck and watched in satisfaction as star-bright beams of pulsar lance energy effortlessly laid open the thickly-armoured hulls of the human vessels; as flights of eldar torpedoes, mind-fast and almost impossible to detect, ruthlessly and effectively hunted down and destroyed the slow and ponderous enemy ships; as squadrons of Darkstar fighters and Eagle bombers danced their deadly ballet around their targets, filling the darkness of space with the light of exploding enemy craft. She had seen all this, and yet it was not enough. Still, the humans came.

They do not yet understand that this region of space is forbidden to them, she thought, feeling the old, familiar fury of the warrior aspect well up within her, *and so the more vessels they attempt to send into these reaches, the more we will enforce that understanding upon them.*

With difficulty, she tamed such wild thoughts, knowing that the command deck of a flagship cruiser was no place to allow full vent to the most extreme emotions of her aspect warrior mind. She looked again at the scenes on the tactical pict-skins, speaking aloud orders to the crew members around her.

'Mainsail thirty degrees to sunward. Increase speed by two *urs* and set in a pursuit course following the main body of enemy vessels. Escort vessels *Medhbh's Shield* and *Lament of Elshor* will accompany us. The remaining vessels will seek out and destroy the enemy stragglers which have already been abandoned in the enemy's escape towards their precious jump point.'

Delicate eldar fingers flickered in complex patterns over crystal and wraithbone control settings. There came the quiet whispering of Thought Talker communications officers as her orders were disseminated to the rest of the reaver force. There was a palpable surge of energy within the wraithbone structure of the *Vual'en Sho*, and all within the vessel felt something of the surge in their own minds: a rising tide of bloody-edged excitement at the prospect of the slaughter to come.

Lileathon felt it, and welcomed it, but at the same time her superior aspect warrior senses detected a note of faint discord within the mood of the moment. She mind-reached out in search of the puzzle, and found it. A vague forbidding dissonance emanating from far away, but growing nearer and stronger even as she observed it. The ship's wraithbone spirit sensed it too, and picked up on it, broadcasting it to the mind of every eldar aboard the cruiser. The ship's spirit-song changed as systems powered down, apparently of their own volition, and, scant seconds later, the other ships in the reaver fleet did likewise as their own vessel-minds responded to the silent call of the command ship.

Eldar eyes looked at Lileathon in question, everyone on the command deck radiating the same range of confused emotions: puzzlement and surprise, mixed with a vague and angry accusation as they suddenly found themselves denied the prize that had been promised to them.

She looked at the ritual place where the Thought Talkers stood, angrily gesturing at them in curt command. *Explain. Now.*

'A summons from An-Iolsus, craftmistress,' said Nemhain, the oldest and most experienced of the quartet. 'We are to break off and return immediately to the craftworld.'

'Now?' asked Lileathon, looking towards the pict-skin showing the image of the remaining escaping mon-keigh vessels.

'An-Iolsus has spoken,' bowed the Thought Talker. 'Its summons carries the word and name of Lord Farseer Kariadryl himself.'

Lileathon and Ailill exchanged glances and mind-thoughts, the same reaction passing between them. Kariadryl, a farseer so old and venerable that he had seen many farseer brethren pass along the journey from birth to spirit stone while he still walked the witch path. What could have happened to have roused him from his reveries inside the dome of crystal seers?

'Wisdom commands,' said Lileathon, giving the required obedient reply and indicating to her crew that they were to comply immediately with the summons-order from the craftworld. A few seconds later and the *Vual'en Sho* was swinging about to sunward, abandoning the chase and setting its prow towards the system's hidden webway portal, located at a point in space between the orbits of the third and fourth planets.

'*Ceiba-ny-shak,*' she cursed to herself in the coarsest possible dialect of Bel-Shammon battle-cant, taking a last look at the rearward-view pict-skins and the image projected there of the human vessels as they escaped to undeserved safety. The mon-keigh aboard them had eluded her, she knew, but the next of their species to cross her path would not. In the name of the murdered kin of Bel-Shammon, the next time she would kill five, ten, a hundred times the number of humans who had escaped her wrath today.

As ALWAYS, KARIADRYL's dreaming mind took pleasure in the smallest of things. At the moment, his universe centred on the tiny jewel-carapaced insect-drones which drifted lazily through the humid, misty air of the dome chamber, looking like small drifting starpoints of light in the dim ambience of the place.

The tiny mechanoid creatures were a marvel of technological achievement, nano-devices the secrets of which had taken the eldar thousands of years to attain, and far in advance of anything the galaxy's younger and less refined races could yet manufacture. Their purpose was to tend and clean the crystalline wraithbone material of the spirit trees which filled the dome all around the resting farseer. Kariadryl could – and, on at least one occasion actually had – spend days studying the patterns of the creatures as they drifted through the chamber in their never-ending work, seeing in their behaviour an endless and silently joyful symphony of movement and purpose.

How many of them are there, he wondered. Tens of thousands? Hundreds of thousands, even? And, yet, each year

there seemed to be a few less, a fact which he doubted anyone else even noticed or cared about.

We are a dying race, he reminded himself, *without even the
ability to repair or replace these precious little things. Study the
patterns and facts of the smallest of things, for that is where the
greatest truths are to be found.*

He sighed, and began to stir himself, seeing the patterns of
several possible near-futures shift and coalesce into one clear
moment-soon-to-come. Someone was coming, and soon his
rest would be necessarily disturbed. He had lived a long life,
even by the standards of his long-lived kind. A long and
arduous life. Limbs and joints once supple and strong ached
in the humid heat of the dome chamber. Eyes which were
once a deep golden hue had faded to a milky amber, while
hair that was once raven black was now shocked with bright
silver. The intricately-worked wraithbone staff was now
more than just an affectation of rank, and he leaned on it
heavily as he began to climb awkwardly to his feet.

He remembered days more than one and a half millennia
ago, when, as a fleet-limbed young warrior amongst the
ranks of his craftworld's guardian militia, he had fought and
triumphed in the great *dithyandli* competitions of martial
strength, besting the champion guardians of three other
craftworlds, the mighty Ulthwé amongst them. He had considered then setting his life's course along the path of the
warrior, but the fatelines had led him to his true calling
along the witch path.

He sighed again, casting his gaze across the thousands of
wraithbone trees which filled the wide expanse of this place,
the crystal dome of seers. One day, not too distant now, his
spirit would take its place here amongst his brethren, and his
journey along that long and often shadow-shrouded path
would finally be at an end. It was not a thought which
daunted or alarmed him, and he had already left instructions as to where he wished his spirit stone to be planted in
the rich psycho-plastic loam, so that it might take root and
form the seed of another crystal tree, releasing his spirit to
join those of the others in the craftworld's infinity circuit
mind. He looked at the spot he had long ago picked out,
between the spirit trees of Agilthya, his first soul-mate, killed

twelve hundred years ago defending an Exodite world from an ork attack, and that of his old mentor Dodona, who had travelled this same path nearly a thousand years previously. He often communed with their soul-spirits here inside the dome, and those of other friends, rivals and lovers, but it would be good to finally be at one with them all.

But not yet, he reminded himself. Not while there was still one last vital task to perform.

He heard the silent psychic murmur pass through the spirit-mind of the crystalline forest, and turned to see the three figures which his farseer prescient-sense had told him minutes ago would soon be here.

They stood silent and reverent in a clearing amongst the trees, awaiting his attention. Darodayos, Craftworld An-Iolsus's master warrior and keeper of the shrine of Kaela Mensha Khaine, and two of his aspect warrior lieutenants, Chiron of the Dark Reaper aspect, and Freyra of the Striking Scorpion aspect. Freyra shared kinship with Kariadryl, being the grand-daughter of a brother dead these last eight hundred years, and so there was an extra gesture of familial respect in the bow she offered to the farseer.

Kariadryl returned the warriors' greetings, noting how oddly ill-at-ease Darodayos seemed here in the craftworld's most precious and sacred place, then realising that it was because the aspect lord was without his warrior's mask and weaponry, removing them as a mark of necessary respect before entering the dome, the one place in the craftworld where weapons of any kind were forbidden. Without his fierce aspect warrior's mask to hide them from view, Darodayos's features were sharp and keenly intelligent, although his discomfort at his surroundings was betrayed by eyes which constantly searched for threats which could not exist in this of all places, and by hands which protectively sought out the empty places on his belt-harness where sword and shuriken pistol would normally have hung.

He is far upon the warrior path, Kariadryl thought. *Perhaps too far to turn back now. Soon, in only a few decades, perhaps, he will turn his back on all else which he could have been and take on the title of exarch.* It had been many centuries since An-Iolsus had witnessed the nomination of one of its own to the rank of exarch, an eldar who had become trapped in one aspect role, dedicating their existence solely to the pursuit of war, although Kariadryl could remember when there had always been at least one such terrifying and awe-inspiring figure aboard the craftworld.

We are a dying race, he told himself again. *We only have to open our eyes to see the evidence all around us.*

'The summons has been received and acknowledged?' the farseer asked, already knowing what the answer must be.

'She is coming,' replied the aspect lord. 'The *Vual'en Sho* and the other craft under her command are returning to An-Iolsus.'

'You do not approve of the choice of Lileathon for this task?' The inflection Kariadryl used made his words less of a question and more of the statement. The aspect lord considered the matter for a brief moment before giving his answer.

'Her soul is not in harmony. She is too full of anger and a thirst for vengeance to be trusted with the task you have commanded.'

'Anger? A thirst for vengeance? Strange to hear one of the warrior path condemn such traits in another. Are these not aspects of one's own soul-self which all who walk the path you have chosen must find and embrace within themselves?'

'We use them as tools,' replied Darodayos. 'Emotions to be mastered and used to give us greater strength of purpose. The *eshairr* Lileathon does not use them in such a way. She allows them to use her as their tool instead. She has allowed her hatred of the humans and her grief at the destruction of her craftworld to blind her to all else around her.'

Eshairr, noted Kariadryl. The fourth of the five words for outcast, only one meaning above the level of true outcast, the murderous eldar pirate raiders who roamed space killing at will, and who were without both honour and craftworld. Had Darodayos used that term in Lileathon's presence, the life-blood of one or the other of them would surely have been spilled.

'There is truth in much of what you say,' conceded Kariadryl.

'And still you insist on using her in this matter, despite all I and others have said.' The aspect lord shifted stance, assuming the correct posture to signify his official opposition to the farseer's command.

'So noted,' nodded Kariadryl, making the gesture of conciliation. 'Nevertheless, Lileathon will accompany me on my mission, as will you, Darodayos. An-Iolsus commands it,' he added, gesturing around them at the crystal forest of the craftworld's collective spirit-minds, 'and I shall need your strength and counsel close by my side.'

The aspect lord's voice and expression were sharp with displeasured surprise. 'Accompany you? It was our understanding that we were to lead this expedition. There is much danger in what lies ahead, Lord Kariadryl, we do not need the witch-gift of farsight to know that much, and An-Iolsus has much need yet of your wisdom and seer-vision. You should not take such a risk.'

'I can, and I must,' answered the farseer. 'There are matters of prescience which are yet far from assured.' He broke off for a moment, looking at Darodayos and whispering to him in mind-speech.

'Chiron and Freyra, how far can they to be depended on?'

The answer came back almost instantaneously. *'I trust them with my life, lord farseer. And with yours.'*

Kariadryl nodded in acknowledgement. 'Then I must tell you that in this matter, there are shadows across the path of the future. Even to one with the gift of farsight, the outcome of events we are about to set in motion, and those which have already been set in motion, is unknown. Too many fatelines intersect together at some point in the *kilithikadya*, in the near-future-to-come, obscuring the way ahead.'

'You speak of a *fhaisorr'ko*, a shadow point,' said Darodayos, noting the farseer's surprised reaction to his use of the term. 'A convergence of many possible futures which not even the farsight of our race's greatest seers can discern. Yes, the ways of the witch path are not unknown to even an aspect initiate such as this one,' Darodayos added with the hint of a knowing smile. 'If that is the case, Lord Kariadryl, then my concerns about your involvement in this expedition are multiplied many times over. If you cannot see the future ahead, then the danger to you becomes more than can be safely imagined.'

'An-Iolsus shares your concerns, friend Darodayos,' said the aged farseer, indicating the crystalline forest around them with a sweep of his withered hand, 'but, if we do face a shadow point, then my presence becomes even more vital. It is only by being there, standing at the centre of the moment of convergence, that I will be able to see and choose the one truth path ahead amongst the many other false futures.'

The aspect lord paused in thought for a moment, considering the farseer's words, and then, with an air of reluctant obligation, bowed respectfully to Kariadryl.

'Wisdom commands, lord farseer. I go now to make the necessary arrangements for the expedition, ahead of the arrival of the *eshairr* outcast Lileathon and her vessels.'

He bowed again and departed, accompanied by his two lieutenants.

Kariadryl watched them go, wondering if they had detected any hint of the half-truths he had told them. Yes, his farsight had detected the mystic shadow point ahead, but his gift of prescient-vision was far in advance of that possessed by many of his brother farseers, and it had shown him tantalising hints of the form of things to come. These were not mere *ferishimm* visions, fragment pieces of false futures or possible futures still waiting to be born into realtime, for his farsight was powerful enough to tell the difference between such phantom visions. No, they were images from the *t'hao-ny*, the true future-yet-to-be, and they showed mind-pictures of things that would and must come to pass if the course of the true future were to be safely found amidst the entrapping maze of the shadow point ahead.

He closed his eyes and focussed his farsight again, seeing the same images which he had already committed to memory a thousand times before.

A laughing mon-keigh giant, his brutal, scarred face splashed with blood, his bare, thickly-muscled arms covered in the crude, tribal tattoo-markings typical of his barbaric race. He had weapons in his hands, crude and noisy mon-keigh weapons, and he laughed as they spat forth metal death into the bodies of his unseen enemies. Was this terrifying vision that of friend or foe,

Kariadryl wondered, knowing that only the events which awaited him within the darkness of the shadow point would reveal the truth.

He concentrated further, and the torrent of mind-images continued.

The eshairr outcast Lileathon upon the command deck of her vessel. The features of her face were twisted in violent anger. She was shouting orders, and the void around her ship was filled with a flurry of destructive energy. Gunfire. A space battle. There was another vessel there too, alongside Lileathon's ship. The other vessel's hull-lines were vulgar and ugly in comparison to the sleek, almost organic shape of the eldar craft. A human warship. A monkeigh craft, the fury of its firepower unleashed in the same direction as that of the eldar ship beside it.

Now do you see, Darodayos, Kariadryl asked himself? Now do you see why the *eshairr* outcast must go with us? She is there already at the shadow point, waiting for us in a future which, for better or worse, I know will come to pass. Already the shape of the hidden future commands that she be there with us.

He looked further. More visions swam up into focus.

The webway. Its shifting psycho-structure was as familiar to Kariadryl as the walls of his own living chambers, although it had been over a century since he had left the craftworld to walk the webway's strange and near-limitless paths. There was something there in the webway, something vast and terrible, travelling even now towards the shadow point and carrying with it portents of futures the shapes of which even the veteran farseer hesitated to look at. He saw the presence's name written in the burning trail it left in the wake of its journey through the webway, and his mind recoiled in fear at the promise of the bloody-handed slaughter the burning lord carried with it.

He saw the shadow point itself. A giant, glittering black gem blocking the route ahead to the future. It was slowly spinning, presenting first one facet to his gaze, then a different one. Even as he watched, images flickered and cascaded across its clouded surface, tantalising hints of futures yet to be, some of them perhaps also never to be.

Himself, lying dead on the barren surface of some bleak and sterile world.

A human, stern and hawk-faced, dressed in the strange uniform of one of the corpse-god's bewildering number of warrior tribes. He is aboard a starship, shouting orders in vain as his vessel turns to fire around him.

A great battle among the stars, greater than any Kariadryl had ever seen before, greater perhaps than any he had heard tell of except in the dimmest and oldest of legends. Mon-keigh and eldar ships together, fighting not against one another but combining against a mutual enemy.

A star exploding, its ancient nuclear heart as old as the galaxy itself and now ripped asunder by a force more destructive and deadly than a thousand of the mon-keighs' proudest battlefleets. The other stars witnessed the death of one of their own, and the galaxy mourned its passing and feared the awakening of weapons the secrets of which it had long hoped had been lost forever.

The faces of Darodayos, Lileathon and other elder known to him. They were imprisoned somewhere terrible, a no-place at once both strangely familiar and grotesquely alien. They were screaming, all of them, their broken bodies pinioned down upon machines constructed of gleaming bone and metal, while twisted, barb-fleshed things stood over them and opened them up with fingers transformed into thin, cruel scalpel edges.

All this he was able to see, but nothing else. The shadow point spun faster, throwing a shroud of darkness around itself, the darkness reaching out towards the bright goal of the farseer's mind. With a wrench, he tore himself free of its grasp, returning his mind and soul to the here and now.

He stood still for a moment, taking comfort in the psychic refuge of the dome, dwelling on what he had just seen. Only some of these visions would come to pass, but which ones? And there was something else too, something still hidden within the obscuring deadness of the shadow point. Something abominable, and yet also perversely familiar. A thought, or something less than a thought, a vague and nameless dread which he dare not even give proper form to, worked itself loose from the place where he kept his deepest and most secret fears.

'Shea nudh Asuryanish ereintha Asuryanat,' he intoned to himself. *May the blessings of Asuryan protect the children of Asuryan from abomination.*

His invocation of the most potent and dire of all the prayers to the greatest and oldest of the eldar gods sent a rustling shiver of psychic alarm through the spirit-minds of the dome. Kariadryl laid a hand on the crystalline bark of one of the nearby trees, recognising as his flesh touched it the psychic resonance of the bonesinger Cathrhal, who had once been a rival of Kariadryl's for the love of his eventual first soulmate Agilthya, and who had saved his life a century later, fending off a human chainsword blow which would have otherwise decapitated the injured Kariadryl.

'Rest easy, brother,' he whispered. 'Forgive me. I did not mean to disturb your dreams with my thoughtless words.'

A motionless current stirred through the dreaming minds of the spirits of the dome. Kariadryl felt it, and felt the craft-world's concern, concern for him and for the future of them all. He mind-spoke thoughts of reassuring calm, and felt the mood of the infinity circuit ease in return. He made his way to the exit, turned and bowed respectfully one last time to the forest of glittering, diamantine trees.

'Farewell, old friends. An-Iolsus commands, but I look forward to resting here a while with you again when I return.'

As he left, he heard the disquiet in the spirit-minds' voiceless murmurings, and the faint, sad whispers of final farewell from those who in life had been closest to him. He sighed to himself. Perhaps a century or two ago, he could still have easily guarded his thoughts from the spirits within the craft-world's infinity circuit, but this gift seemed now to have deserted him. They had seen what he had seen, and they saw and understood the lie in the words he had just spoken.

FOUR

HALF THE GALAXY away, another craftworld drifted serenely in the dark, uncharted places between the stars. Its name was unknown to the librarian-scribes of the Inquisition's Ordo Xenos, whose task it was to compile secret lists of such things. Its history was untouched by contact with the Imperium, for it lay far beyond the Imperium's borders, and its inhabitants neither knew nor cared about the squabbling affairs of such a vulgar, upstart race. It lay almost at the very limits of the webway, and there were few of those ancient routes which still connected to it.

And so, by choice or circumstance – none within the craftworld could remember, so long ago was it – they existed in almost complete isolation. Detached and unruffled, there they existed at the hour of the sunset passing of their race in a state more akin to that of the long and blissful days enjoyed by their ancestors in the time before the great, self-inflicted cataclysm

Aloof. Idyllic. Untroubled.

So it was that the young aspect initiate drew disapproving glances and reproachful mind-thought queries from his elders as he hurried along the tranquil, pearl-floored passages of the craftworld's outermost western spiral. The turbulent emotion which filled his as yet untutored mind communicated itself into the minds of those around him, and, after a moment's thought, many of them would have identified it as something similar to panic, or the closest equivalent to it that an eldar mind could produce.

This note of discordant and unfamiliar emotion transmitted itself through the craftworld, jumping from one eldar mind to another, and so, by the time the young initiate reached his destination, the one he had been searching for had anticipated his arrival.

She stood waiting for him in a gallery lined with wraithbone sculptures. The delicate psi-material of the figurine shapes was sensitive to the mood of nearby minds, and they writhed and contorted into unfamiliar and anxiety-ridden shapes as the initiate approached. A display of crystalbone chimes shook in sympathetic distress at the sculptures' plight, but were hushed into calmed silence by a mind-command from the gallery's sole occupant.

In his panic, the initiate forgot the normal courtesies due to his craftworld's most high-born.

'My lady, there has been an incident at the Shrine of Kaela Mensha Khaine. The shrine has been opened!'

'The Shrine of the Bloody-Handed God?' It took the eldar noblewoman a moment to remember where the shrine was located within the vast labyrinth of the craftworld. She had never visited the place herself. Few of the tens of thousands aboard the craftworld ever had. They maintained a full force of guardians raised from amongst the population, and every eldar here was fully prepared to sacrifice their lives in defence of their craftworld, but the ways of war were not their ways, and there were few amongst her people who chose to dedicate themselves to the worship of the eldar's dark and enigmatic god of war.

'How can this be? Who would dare intrude on that place without risking the anger of the god?'

When the initiate answered, it was in a voice barely more than a terror-struck whisper. 'My lady, you do not understand. There has been no intrusion. The shrine has been opened from the inside, and the chamber beyond is empty. *The avatar is gone.'*

The gallery chamber was filled with the sound of the crystalbone sculptures, all of them chiming urgently and without harmony. They would chime for many days, untamed by the sternest of thought-commands, sending out an unheard warning to the cosmos.

Let the enemies of the children of Asuryan beware. The Bloody-Handed God is on his way.

FIVE

'SPOOK? HESH? OBSCURA? Morpho? Kalma? Spur? Whatever you're looking for, we've got it. Big battle coming. If we're all gonna die, might as well get high!'

Maxim Borusa had to admit that his new front-man was good. Good at handling the customers, good at handling the merchandise, good at spotting troublemakers. And not too greedy either. He'd only once caught the little creep stealing more of the takings that he should have, and a few minutes with Galba and Corba and a couple of broken fingers – nothing too severe, Maxim didn't want to damage a potentially very valuable new employee – had been enough to sort out that little misunderstanding.

Yeah, Maxim thought, as he sat at the back of the abandoned, lower-deck gallery that he and his crew had claimed for their own, the guy was good. In fact, life was good generally. He sat back on a crate throne from where he could keep a careful eye on the proceedings. His tunic, emblazoned with the gold-fringed red rank sash of a senior chief petty officer, lay nearby, as did his chainsword belt and scabbard and twin bolt pistol holster, all of them within easy reach should he have any urgent need for them. A ship-whore, her eyes filled with the tell-tale glaze of tajii root intoxication, sat on his lap, giggling and squirming playfully in response to the idle movements of one of his big, paw-like hands beneath her sequined blouse.

Girls like this one weren't allowed aboard naval ships, Maxim knew, but, of course, neither were many other things that people needed and wanted, like all those little illicit lux-uries which helped make life aboard one of His Divine Majesty's warships slightly less hellish, and so there were always openings for a smart operator to do well for himself.

Yeah, life was good, Maxim thought. When he first came aboard the *Macharius* he had been just another prison world conscript, kept in chains and with a life expectancy that could probably have been measured in months. Now, six years later, he was one of the most senior non-commissioned offi-cers amongst a crew of almost thirteen thousand, a familiar face on the command deck, a figure of fear and respect throughout the vessel, and, here below decks, the biggest fixer and criminal operator aboard the ship. He had a crew of almost fifty answering directly to him, all of them hand-picked by him. Hard, brutal sons of bitches, every one of them, and, if need be, he could probably call up a full force of three or four times that number. His own private army, loyal only to him.

Not that he usually had need of such a show of strength, of course. There were plenty on the bridge who knew what he got up to here below-decks, but as long as you played it cool, didn't get too greedy and didn't leave too many bodies lying around the place as a result of one too many disagree-ments with your business rivals, then they were generally happy to turn a blind eye to what was going on.

Yeah, old Captain Semper wasn't a bad sort, Maxim thought. A bit of a cold fish, maybe, your typical Cypra Mundian officer nob really, but he knew what the score was. He knew that, to keep order aboard ship, even the harsh, unforgiving type of Imperial Navy order, you had to leave a few outlets for the ordinary crew to blow off some steam.

Steam control, that's what Maxim liked to think he pro-vided. He remembered the steam tunnels below the hives of

Stranivar, filled with the excess bleed from the torrents of thermal energy that was pumped up from the bubbling, magma-heated, sunless seas deep below the planet's surface, energy which provided much-needed heat and power to the giant, ancient hive structures. Good places to hide from the Arbites bastards, those tunnels, and good places to take shelter during the tri-annual Big Chill season, when the hiveworld's eccentric orbit took it away from its sun and out towards the heatless depths of the planetary system.

That was when the deadly cold of the planet's atmosphere cut through the hive's ancient, battle-scarred adamantium walls in a way which no lance beam ever could, penetrating down into the deepest levels of the hive. You had to fight for the safest places in the steam tunnels, fight over displaced gangers and the ghulaki scavenger things which made their permanent homes in the tunnels. If you were unlucky, you and your entire gang might be suddenly scalded to death in an explosive rushing of super-heated steam which often blasted at random through some of the tunnels, but it was still better than freezing your bolters off in the dismal under-hive regions above.

There were other things down there in the steam tunnels, servitor mechanoids which went about their endless tasks completely oblivious to the gangers around them, even to the extent of carrying out their work in the middle of pitched inter-gang gunfights. The gangers knew well enough to leave these things alone, for they maintained the ancient steam pressure systems throughout the tunnel network, and any attempt to interfere or damage these systems or their custodians could lead to catastrophe.

Steam control, that's how Maxim saw his role aboard the *Macharius*. Just like those servitors, operating the systems that keep the steam pressure within safe limits. And if he made a little on the side for himself? Well, that was only fair, wasn't it, considering the risks and effort involved in what he did?

Everyone understood that. Everyone except that silver skull bastard, Kyogen. The *Macharius's* senior fleet commissar was gunning for him, Maxim knew. He had his people all throughout the ship, on every deck and in every crew team:

spies and informers, reporting everything they heard back to
the big, scar-faced commissar. Maxim had already found
three of them within the ranks of his own organisation, and
had taken appropriate action. Even when not in battle, there
were at least a dozen deaths a week on the *Macharius*, an
unremarkable statistic which passed as the normal hazards
of duty aboard a navy vessel. Crewmen crushed by heavy
machinery in the torpedo room or flight bays, crewmen
vaporised by energy surges while working amongst the
innards of the ship's power systems, or even, for those
wretches unfortunate enough to be consigned to the lowest
decks where the ship's atmosphere processing systems were
at their least dependable, suffocated, poisoned, frozen or
killed by sudden air pressure changes.

Lots of ways to die, smiled Maxim, and lots of ways to con-
veniently and blamelessly dispose of Kyogen's little spies.

Like this one, he thought, running another scarred hand
over the soft flesh beneath the girl's top. Yes, it had been
remarkably convenient how she had turned up at just the
right time, arriving, so she claimed, as smuggled cargo
aboard a lighter craft during their last re-crewing stopover at
Luxor III. She was a looker, he had to admit. Just his type –
also convenient, he noted – and athletic too, but she liked to
ask questions, and she liked to be with him whenever he
wasn't on duty on the command deck. She especially liked
to be with him at times like this, when he had business to
conduct.

A honey-trap, he thought to himself. Why, Commissar
Kyogen, you sly old goat. And I thought you were too much
of an Emperor-loving puritan to stoop to such tricks!

Still, he knew he would have to do something about this
one. He sighed to himself. It really was a pity, since he actually quite liked having her around. No doubt the coming
battle would provide a few convenient opportunities to settle the problem.

As if on cue, a series of deep, sonorous chimes rang out,
broadcast through the ship by the inter-deck vox-callers.
Three chimes. Battle imminent.

Speaking for himself, Maxim liked battles. Not just personally, but professionally, too. Good for business, a great

big battle. Half the crew aboard any warship liked to get hopped up on narc-stimms just before a battle. Narc-stimms took the edge off the fear of knowing that, at almost any second, you and the other thousands of poor bastards around you stood every chance of being obliterated from existence without a moment's warning. Others wanted something that would help them tune into the madness of battle, figuring their best chances of survival lay in adding to the insanity rather than trying to isolate themselves from it. Maxim didn't care.

Whatever his customers' preferences, he had the product to match their needs. Kalma and obscura for the ones who needed to pretend it was all happening to someone else; heavy-duty hallucinogenics like morph, zziz and halo for the ones who needed to pretend it was happening in a completely different universe to the personal universe-for-one they were inhabiting. 'Slaught, spur and havoc for the ones, mostly armsmen and the members of boarding assault parties, who wanted a little something extra in their bloodstreams and nervous systems to give them that added boost for when they met the enemy face to face.

The warning caused a stir amongst the line of customers, and they pushed forward, eager to get what they had come for and return to their stations before the next warning sounded.

Not being at your battle stations by the time the two-chime warning sounded was a capital offence, one ruthlessly enforced by Commissar Kyogen with his usual efficient, favourless zeal.

'Back! Get back.' warned Galba, waving a snub-nosed autopistol at the line. 'Plenty for everyone, and plenty of time to get it. Kolba, his twin/cousin/lover/ganger-brother – Maxim was never sure of the exact nature of the relationship between the two of them, and didn't much care – stood nearby, backing up Galba's actions with a meaningful sweep of the long barrel of his shotcannon. The crowd backed off respectfully, knowing from experience of too many close-combat boarding actions exactly the kind of slaughter the weapon could achieve in a confined, target-filled space like the one they were in now.

'Next!' called the front-man, beckoning forward the man
at the head of the line. 'What you looking for, friend?'

"Slaught, as much as you got. The red vial mix only, none
of that kalma-cut stuff you tried to sell me last time.'

The front-man looked at the customer, coolly appraising
him. 'Man knows his 'slaught. Red Dragon mix it is. I know
how much you boys in the enginarium like to ride the
dragon.'

Maxim looked over, the exchange catching his interest.
The customer was squat and heavy-set, his dark-coloured
skin oddly taut and withered in the manner typical of those
who worked in the ship's engineering sections, where the
heat and radiation from the ship's fiery plasma reactor hearts
could penetrate the thickest plasarmoured work suits to
braise and burn flesh.

The enginarium sections weren't part of Maxim's turf.
They belonged to a senior Engineering rating called Sejarra,
a limping, squint-eyed little runt who was Maxim's main
rival in the steam control business. Maxim had given Sejarra
that limp. Next time, the big hive worlder promised himself,
his aim would be better.

Kolba shot a querying glance at his boss. Maxim nodded
the okay. Sejarra controlled the narc-stimm supply business
in the enginarium, but if this guy wanted to buy from
Maxim, or, as the quantities he was buying here seemed to
suggest, set himself up freelance in the same business, then
that was his lookout. Independent operators trying to set up
on their own in Sejarra's turf had a nasty habit of falling into
plasma furnaces.

The front-man caught the exchange between the crew-boss
and his pet killer. 'Okay, friend,' he said to the customer. 'So
what you got to offer us in exchange? No navy scrip, and
none of that stuff they call currency on half the mudballs in
this arse end of a sub-sector. Like for like, that's what we like
to see.'

The engineer moved forward, laying a cloth-wrapped
bundle on the makeshift table-crate before the front-man.
Maxim's man unwrapped it, revealing an oddly-wrought
bolt pistol. He held it up, showing it to Maxim. With its
brass markings and ornamentation, gargoyle-mouthed

muzzle end and strange hand-grip that didn't seem quite made to fit a normal human hand, it was clearly a Chaos weapon. Maxim knew there was a high demand for these things, and that he could probably trade it for a small fortune at the next port world they visited. There were always plenty of mincing, rear echelon Munitorium adepts or reservist Imperial Guard officers keen to acquire such trophies, no doubt so they could display them to swooning, weak-kneed aristocratic ladies and tell them heroic tales of how they took it from the dead hand of some Chaos warlord they had just slain in single combat.

'Not bad,' judged Maxim grudgingly, careful not to give away too much of his interest in the offer. 'Got any shells for it? They're worth more if you have a full mag of shells.'

'Funny you should mention that...' grinned the customer, reaching casually into his heavy, kevlar-quilted engineer's jacket.

As he did so, there was the beginnings of a minor commotion at the back of the queue. Kolba, distracted by the customer, missed it. Galba caught it, but a split-second too late. Maxim, who had survived dozens of ambushes in the tunnels and caverns of his brutal hiveworld home, and who had planned dozens more, saw it coming a split-second before it happened.

He roared in anger, hurling the girl off his lap directly into the line of fire. Shots rang out, and a volley of bullets and las-blasts intended for him struck her instead, tearing her apart. The front-man still sat there, his numbed mind racing to catch up with what was happening. It was a race he would never win. He keeled over, dead before he hit the ground, as the engineer customer levelled the autopistol secreted inside his jacket and fired two closely grouped bursts of shots into his face and chest.

Maxim was moving now, reaching for his own holstered weapons while keeping one eye on the progress of the mayhem around him. There was more gunfire from the back of the disintegrating queue, more quilt-jacketed engineers emerging out of hiding to join the fray.

Sejarra's crew, Maxim knew. Looks like the sneaky little runt was trying to expand his business ventures beyond the limits of the enginarium sections, using the cover of the imminent battle as an opportunity to make his move.

He saw Kolba spin and fall, shots punching into the carapace-armoured vest he wore on such occasions. He saw Galba shout in fury and return fire on his twin/cousin/lover/ganger-brother's attackers, stray shots from his stuttering autopistol slamming into the bodies of the panicked customers.

Maxim saw one of the shots lift off the top of the skull of a junior tech-priest, and uttered a typically harsh Stranivar curse to himself. The tech-priest was a valued and regular customer, and a useful source of all kinds of valuable little tech-devices which he used to pay for his secret obscura habit. That was one source of supply which would be closed to Maxim now.

The fall-guy for the ambush was coming at him now, kicking aside the body of the front-man and charging straight at Maxim, keeping up a continuous stream of fire with his autopistol. Maxim rolled, reaching out for and missing the holster belt hanging nearby, as autopistol shells chewed apart the crates around him.

Instead, his scrabbling fingers found the hilt of his chainsword. He drew the weapon in one smooth motion, searching for and activating the power switch. The weapon roared into hungry life. The assassin was almost on top of him now, and Maxim felt an autopistol shot take away some of the meat from the top of his left shoulder. From the ground, Maxim swung the chainsword in a low horizontal arc.

A second later, the assassin fell to the ground, landing beside him, the stupefied expression on his face showing that he was still trying to wonder what had happened to his legs from the knees down. Maxim didn't give him a chance to work out the answer, and shot him in the forehead with his autopistol.

He stood up, emptying the remainder of the clip into the chest and stomach of the next stupid bastard to fancy their chances against Maxim Borusa, then did a quick head-count as he discarded the spent weapon and successfully retrieved his bolt pistol.

Bodies littered the floor, most of them customers caught in the crossfire. Maxim recognised the forms of three of his own men amongst them, and, even as he watched, he saw that useless Balaamite yokel Gorgakor hit the far wall of the chamber, his body dancing idiotically under the impact of the bullets pummelling into it. No big loss to his organisation, Maxim judged. The lazy agri-worlder had been a dead weight for a while, and there would be any number of potential replacements for him coming aboard the next time the re-supply shuttles arrived with their press-ganged cargo at their next port of call. Still, his death meant one gun less against Sejarra's crew, so Maxim figured that he needed to do something to even up the odds.

He tracked targets, his aim hesitating as the running forms of non-combatants passed through his field of fire. Not that he cared much about causing a few friendly fire casualties amongst non-combatants, but it was bad business to gun down your customers without good cause. Finally, his aim settled on a clear target. A group of Sejarra's gunmen, clustered together and metres from the nearest cover.

Amateurs, he thought. They wouldn't have lasted five minutes on Stranivar, never mind the hiveworld's notorious Lubiyanka prison moon. Really, he was doing the Emperor a favour, he told himself as he pulled the triggers on his bolt pistols. Halfwit fools like them didn't deserve a place in His Divine Majesty's glorious Imperial Navy.

The gunmen blew apart in a scattering of shattered limbs and viscera under the impact of the bolter shells. Maxim checked his remaining shell-count and scanned for further targets.

Kolba was back on his feet now, blood flowing through at least one of the bullet holes punched through his chest-plate as he scattered shotcannon rounds into the ranks of Sejarra's men, showing far less discretion in his choice of targets than Maxim had. Galba was with him, partially supporting him as his twin/cousin/lover/ganger-brother's legs threatened to give out from under him, and their combined fire was enough to drive the enginarium gangers back into cover.

Maxim was moving forward now, firing his twin bolt pistols, keeping up a steady litany of shots, adding his firepower to that of Kolba and Galba, boxing in their targets with streams of fire from two simultaneous directions at once, keeping them confused and off-balance. Maxim grinned. Sejarra's crew had lost the initiative now. With every moment that passed, he could feel the direction of the battle swinging in his favour.

A shape rose up from behind an equipment stack. Maxim swivelled towards it, raising one bolt pistol in readiness, but before he could fire, the figure tumbled to the ground, a knife hilt buried in its throat. Maxim looked round, and saw a man – no, more of a boy, really, barely old enough to know the feel of a shaving blade on his face – crouching nearby. Maxim nodded his unspoken thanks at the lad – a powder-monkey from one of the starboard-side gun bays, he hazily recalled, who liked his kalma cut with a little cloudy obscura resin – and made a mental note of the boy's quickness and ability for future consideration. Maxim had no doubt that he would have dealt with the threat in time, if the boy's knife hadn't got there first, but that kind of resourcefulness and skill with a knife could surely be put to use somewhere within his little business operation.

Besides, he thought, stepping over the dying, groaning body of another of his men, there seemed to be a few unexpected openings in the organisation at the moment.

Sejarra's boys had had enough. The gunfight should have been over by now, and the lookout pickets Maxim had posted to guard the approaches to the gallery would be pulling back now, threatening to cut off their escape, while others would be summoning reinforcements from nearby.

They tried to make a break for it, the less experienced of them going first. The first three were cut down in the crossfire from Kolba, Galba and the others, unintentionally creating a distraction which allowed the rest of them to run for the exit passage. Maxim had been waiting for them. Two went down hard, bolter shells exploding into their retreating backs.

Maxim smiled as he drew a bead on the next one, a short figure with a familiar limp. He fired, his pistol clicking on empty. He brought his other pistol up to bear, but it was too late, and his target had already disappeared round the corner. Maxim wasn't stupid enough to follow, not when the

chances were that Sejarra would have left a man there waiting to plug a few rounds into the first warm body to come
round that corner. That would be what Maxim would have
done under the same circumstances, and he rarely made a
mistake of crediting an enemy as having any less intelligence
than himself.

So that was twice he'd had Sejarra in his sights, and the little runt was still alive. Maxim swore. His enemy wouldn't get
that lucky a third time, that much he was sure of.

From the passageway beyond came the sound of the vox-
callers.

Two chimes. All crew to battle stations. Galba shot a nervous glance at his gang leader.

'Battle time, boss. What we going to do about all this?' he
asked, gesturing at the carnage around them.

'Relax, if I know old Semper, then he'll be taking the Mach
right into the thick of things.' He grinned. 'So, if we're all still
alive at the end of this, no one's gonna notice a dozen or so
extra bodies in amongst all the others the clean-up crews
sling through the airlocks.'

He did a quick headcount, coming up with himself,
Galba, Kolba and four others, plus the knife kid, who still
hadn't run off along with the other non-combatants. 'Okay,
round up about ten others. I want Horke and Vannan especially, if you can find them. Any officers try to give you a hard
time, tell 'em they're seconded to inspection tour duties with
Chief Petty Officer Borusa, by order of Lieutenant Ulanti.
That'll shut 'em up quick. And tell everyone to bring
weapons.'

'Inspection tour?' There was confused doubt in Galba's
voice.

'As chief petty officer, I've got rights of access to just about
every area of the ship. I take my responsibilities seriously,
Rating Second Class Galba. I need to know that everyone's
carrying out their Emperor-ordained duties faithfully and
efficiently, especially when we're in battle.'

Galba smiled. So did Kolba, despite the pain of his
wound. Their smiles were like the hungry snarls of a predator. Eager understanding shone in their eyes. 'Rights of
access, boss... you mean like the enginarium?'

'That's exactly what I mean,' grinned Maxim. 'So come on, let's go find our old pal Sejarra and spring a little surprise inspection duty on him.'

They moved out, leaving their dead behind him, Kolba first making sure that the scattered merchandise was safely gathered up and returned to a secure hiding place. Maxim turned round just before they left the gallery, seeing the knife kid still standing there, looking expectantly at him. Maxim hesitated a moment, and then nodded. The kid happily ran to join them, scooping a gun out of the hand of a dead man.

They moved swiftly and purposefully along the gangway beyond, as the ship trembled under the impact of the first incoming enemy fire glancing off its void shields. Seconds later, the final warning chime sounded over the vox-callers.

One chime. Battle commencing.

Maxim grinned again. He loved a good battle. So useful for covering up so many different things, with no one the wiser afterwards about what you'd really been up to.

SIX

'FULL AHEAD, BATTLE speed. Helm – engage port-side manoeuvring thrusters and bring us around one point to starboard, on my mark. Maintain formation position and keep us within three unit distances of our wing vessels. Stand by, all stations. Mister Nyder, be ready to fire torpedoes at my command.'

Leoten Semper stood in his customary position on the bridge, mindful of the newly-gleaming commodore rank bars on the epaulettes of his tunic; mindful too that, in the unspoken opinion of some under his command, including, most probably, some here on his own command deck, he had yet to prove his right to wear the new rank insignia. His promotion to the brevet rank of commodore-captain had been a battlefield necessity, made during the third Battle of the Moons of Pergamum several weeks earlier, when a lucky lance strike had struck the bridge of the battlecruiser *Lord Huascar*, killing its captain. Commodore Haruna had been the commander of the battle-squadron, and Semper, named in the mortally-injured man's dying words, had assumed command of the Imperial forces and driven the opportunistic Chaos raid back out towards the system's outer fringes. Battlefleet Command had allowed the temporary promotion to stand, but Semper was all too aware that his sudden elevation had been at the expense of several other ship's captains within the battle-squadron, all of whom had greater seniority than him in terms of years of service.

If any of this troubled him, he never allowed it to show externally. He stood there, the calm and steady centre of the vortex of activity which filled the command deck of His Divine Majesty's Ship, the *Lord Solar Macharius*. Brightly-robed tech-priests communed together, whispering secret Machine God words to the machine-mind spirit within the ship's mighty logic engines, assuring it of its survival in the battle just about to begin. Choirs of servitors droned in chaotic unison, relaying the streams of information flooding in from all sections of the ship, and from the other vessels in the battle group. Gunnery officers bustled amongst themselves, checking and rechecking likely target patterns and firing solutions. Ensigns and junior officers received reports from duty stations on every deck of the ship, and relayed them to senior officers who, in turn, reported in to Lieutenant Hito Ulanti.

The ship's second-in-command digested the information and communicated its summary to his captain with a single nod, and a few brief words.

'All stations standing by and ready to commence battle.'

Semper nodded in acknowledgement, and looked out through the command deck's front viewing bay. Through the metre-thick armoured glasteel, and still thousands of kilometres distant, but magnified by the viewing bay's in-built augur systems, he saw the wide scattering of targets ahead.

At a casual glance, it looked like a field of large asteroids, but a closer inspection of the magnified augur screen images and the telemetry data being gathered by the ship's surveyor showed that several of the asteroids were firing huge and crude thruster rockets in an attempt to manoeuvre into position, while the upwards-fluctuating energy signals surrounding many others showed them preparing to do likewise.

Ork roks. Asteroids taken over and colonised by the green-skin creatures and turned into crude but highly effective mobile fortresses. Twenty-eight of them counted so far in this cluster, with Emperor knows how many others scattered throughout this, the Mather system, creating a deadly obstacle to any Imperial convoys attempting to traverse this area of space. Two years ago, the last time a small Imperial force had been despatched to Mather to scour the system of any greenskin presence, just four of the asteroid fortresses had been detected and destroyed. Now, as was so typical of the creatures, they had seemingly emerged from nowhere to multiply and fester in even greater numbers than before.

'Weeds,' he murmured to himself, not realising at first that he was speaking aloud.

Ulanti, standing nearby, caught the word but not its meaning. 'Captain?'

'Weeds,' Semper repeated, gesturing at the constellation of asteroid-vessels before them. 'My grandfather was an admiral in Battlefleet Tamahl, and I remember a childhood visit to his estate on Cypra Mundi after he had been granted permission to retire. If the crew think this particular Captain Semper is a stern taskmaster, Mister Ulanti, then he didn't know my grandfather. He was a holy terror amongst both the Emperor's enemies and his own men, and my cousins and I were terrified of the old devil.' A hint of a smile crossed Semper's face as his mind recalled the events of the past. 'I remember one time, though, when he seemed almost human to me. He took me out to the fields of his estate – after a lifetime of warfare amongst the stars, he relished the quiet tranquillity of the countryside – to help him supervise the planting of next season's crops.'

Ulanti feigned polite interest, wondering where all this was going, especially with battle imminent. Also, as a hive-worlder, even a highborn aristocratic one, he had lived most of his life in a world where the open elements promised nothing but danger and toxic death, and so Semper's talk of idyllic pastoral scenes meant almost nothing to him.

Semper sensed his second-in-command's slightly baffled impatience, and allowed himself another brief smile. 'That season, my grandfather had been having some trouble with

weeds amongst his beloved rakki-fruit crops. They'd had to
replant the crop three times already, and I can remember
seeing him getting down on his hands and knees amongst
the servitor-workers and pulling the weeds out of the earth
with his own hands. "Damned greenskins!" he called them,
hurling them away as far as he could. "Always watch out for
them, Leoten," he told me. "Just when you think you've dug
them all up, there's always more of them popping up as
soon as your back's turned."

Semper glanced at Ulanti, still seeing puzzlement in the
younger man's face. 'My grandfather knew all about orks,
Hito. He won his admiral's spurs against the greenskins during the Caudium Campaign, and he took part in the
scouring of the Achilia Reaches. I didn't know what he
meant then, but I've fought those savages since, and now I
know exactly what he was talking about all those years ago.'

He pointed at the asteroid cluster dead ahead of them, the
details and numbers of the ork rok-fortresses there becoming more apparent the closer they drew to them. 'Weeds,
Mister Ulanti. No sooner do we wipe them out, than they
grow back again.'

Flashes of light from the pattern of roks signalled the commencement of hostilities. Ork munitions – massive,
unwieldy and potentially devastating – flew through the
void to detonate harmlessly in space well ahead of the
advancing Imperial battle-line.

'Typical greenskins, no real command ability to speak of,'
grunted Werner Maeler, the *Macharius's* efficient Gunnery
Master. 'We're well out of range, and they still can't wait to
open fire. Still, at least the energy release from their weapons
fire gives our gunnery surveyors an easier target to lock onto.'

Semper signalled to a communications officer. A comm-
net channel opened up, linking him to the bridge of every
other ship in the Imperial Navy formation.

'Semper to battle-group. To arms, gentlemen. Let us tend
to the Emperor's garden,' he ordered, knowing that he was
about to prove once and for all his right to wear those new
rank epaulettes on his shoulders.

* * *

THE *MACHARIUS* POWERED forward, its gargantuan plasma engines spilling out a fire cloud trail in its wake. To its starboard lay the Gothic class cruiser *Drachenfels*, an old and dependable comrade vessel, and the Dauntless class light cruiser *Triton*. *Triton's* sister ship *Mannan* and the Lunar class cruiser *Graf Orlok*, an old but less dependable comrade vessel, were arrayed to the *Macharius's* port side, while the Dominator class cruiser *Fearsome* flew within the arrow-head formation formed by the other cruisers. It was the clenched fist inside the armoured gauntlet, its deadly prow-mounted nova cannon weapon aimed at the heart of the ork forces. Accompanying it were the escort carriers *Vengeance of Belatis* and *Memory of Briniga*, merchantmen transports converted to military use and named after just two of those many Imperial worlds which had been destroyed during the war.

Swarms of close-range attack craft, wide-winged Marauders and vicious little snub-nosed Thunderbolt fighters, surged forth from makeshift launch bays in the carriers' hulls, forming up into attack formations of their own. Dual squadrons of Cobra destroyers swept out wide along the battle-group's front, guarding its flanks and extending its firepower all across the enemy's front.

A significant force, by any measure, but one which Semper wished with all his heart he did not now have to lead into battle here. Battlefleet Gothic's resources were stretched to breaking point to meet the threat posed by the forces of Abaddon the Despoiler, and each one of these ships gathered here today to deal with the orks meant a ship less elsewhere within the Imperial line of battle, where it was needed most. Semper and his fellow captains would rather be fighting the Despoiler's warfleets than these greenskin savages, and again he damned the orks to the Eye of Terror and back, and vowed to make the creatures pay for the deadly but very much secondary threat they posed to the Emperor's forces within the Gothic sector, forcing Lord Ravensburg to deploy much-needed warships away from the war's main battle fronts.

'All ships forward. Mister Nyder – range to closest target?'

'Torpedo range is good, captain, but they've put up a fighter screen in front of them. I wouldn't trade ten of those

greenskin death-trap contraptions they call fighters for one
of our Furies, especially with one of my pilots in the cockpit,
but they've got a hell of a lot of the damnable things. Estimate they'd manage to intercept at least half our fish before
they reached their targets, and that's even before the greenskins bring their defence turrets into play.'

Semper nodded. 'Very well. Bring our own fighter wave
forward. We'll dangle some bait in front of their noses, and
see what they do then.'

'STORM LEADER TO squadron. Full thrust forward on my lead.
Let's show these animals what proper flying looks like.'

Amic Kaether opened up the power-feed on his Fury's
engine drives, sending the interceptor fighter hurtling
towards the ork line. Around him, the other craft of Storm
squadron did likewise, forming up around their commander in a perfect and deceptively simple-looking formation.
Around and behind Storm, cruising in matching formation patterns, came the craft of Hornet and Hurricane
squadrons, while Arrow, the fourth of *Macharius's* Fury
squadrons, remained on a tight anti-ordnance defensive
orbit around the advancing cruisers, ready to intercept any
enemy torpedo or bomber craft attacks on the capital
ships.

Kaether grinned. Aube Terraco, his counterpart in Arrow,
was neither a patient nor an understanding man, and would
doubtlessly be chafing in angry frustration at the role
assigned to his squadron for this coming battle.

Kaether had more than a hundred enemy kills to his
credit, the highest kill count of any of the *Macharius's* fighter
squadron commanders, but, in a drunken boast one night in
the pilots' mess, Terraco, with just over eighty kills to his
tally, had promised to surpass Kaether's score before the ship
put into port for its next scheduled refit. Today, Terraco
seemed likely to find little other than some rusty and easily-
destroyed greenskin torpedo passing through his Fury's
weapon sights, while Kaether was flying straight into the
teeth of the enemy force, and, if he survived, would
doubtlessly return to the *Macharius* with his kill tally further
strengthened and his title unchallenged.

Yes, he reminded himself, looking towards the wing formation on his starboard side. Highest-scoring squadron commander, but not the highest-scoring ace aboard the *Macharius*. No, that honour definitely belonged to another. Almost two hundred confirmed enemy fighter or bomber kills, and Emperor knew how many other lesser targets such as assault craft, torpedoes, mine-bombs, landing pods, orbital lighters or even life rafts.

A glance confirmed that the *Macharius's* top fighter ace was there in position on the far starboard side of the formation. It may have been Kaether's imagination, but it seemed to him that the last Fury in line was slightly further away from his nearest wingman than was customary. If so, it was typical of the attitude of the occupant of the fighter's cockpit. He never mixed with his fellow pilots. He never visited the pilots' mess. He never took part in the tight-knit and often raucous camaraderie common amongst the other Fury interceptor pilots, whose life expectancy in front line action during the Gothic War could often be measured in months, and so were granted a grudging amnesty from the generally harsh discipline requirements aboard an Imperial warship. He didn't even share quarters with the other pilots, his veteran ace status and the unspoken disquiet he caused amongst his squadron comrades allowing him private quarters of his own, away from the others.

Kaether looked again, seeing that his formation's far starboard linchpin was proceeding as ordered, flying fast and true, predictably taking no part in the nervous and excited pre-battle banter between pilots, which filled the squadron comm-net channel.

Reth Zane. 'Zealot' Zane, as they called him. Now, four years after the horrific injuries the pilot has suffered in the aftermath of the events surrounding the evacuation and subsequent destruction of the Imperial world of Belatis, he seemed even more remote and less human than ever.

'Form up,' Kaether commanded over the comm-net. 'Be ready to wheel when you hear the word.' Acknowledgment runes flashed across the instrument screen in front of him, one for each of the thirteen pilots under his command.

'Zane?' he added, trying to keep the note of distaste out of his voice. 'You're on the far starboard point, so we're depending on you to get this right.'

'Ready when you give the word, commander,' came the electronically-modulated voice over the comm-net. Little evidence of humanity remained in Zane's voice after the tech-priests and ship's surgeons had done what they could with the charred and ruin-fleshed horror that had been brought to them more dead than alive those four years ago.

The end of Zane's comm-net reply was obliterated in a heavy spray of static, overlaid with bursts of barking grunts and thick, incomprehensibly guttural voices making words and sounds which no human throat could ever produce.

Ork-talk. The voices of the enemy, broadcast on crude but powerful ship-carried transmitters and now cutting randomly into the Imperial forces' own separate comm-net channels. In the cockpit space behind him, Kaether knew his tech-adept navigator Manetho would now be altering the squadron's comm-net frequencies, setting up blocker walls to filter out the enemy interference.

That meant they were close now, Kaether realised. Close enough to have entered the enemy's own comm-net bubble. Close enough to be beginning to take incoming gunfire as the nearest rok-fortresses' defence turrets opened up at them with the first bursts of wild-aimed speculative fire.

Kaether's eyes flickered between the view through his cockpit, as the distant shapes of the ork vessels loomed ever larger before him, and the information scrolling across his instrumentation panel's surveyor screens as the closing distance to the enemy counted down in kilometres and seconds. They were even closer now, close enough to start picking out details on the thick, rocky hides of the asteroid fortresses, close enough to begin to see the bewildering array of thruster engines, weapon emplacements, airlock entrances, attack craft launch bays, observation blisters, torpedo silos and defence turrets which studded their surfaces at seemingly random points. Close enough to see the swarms of fighter-bomber craft which buzzed excitedly in the orbits of the closest roks. As he watched, he saw more and more of them peel away from the main body of ork vessels, unable to resist the challenge of the oncoming Fury squadrons.

Typical greenskins, thought Kaether, confident now that the strategy was indeed going to work. Offer them the chance of a good scrap, and they'll trample each other into the dust to take you up on your offer.

Kaether counted the passing of several more long and drawn-out seconds, leaving the final moment until as late as he dared, balancing how many more greenskin fighters he could draw off against the likely effective range of the increasing numbers of defence turrets now being aimed in his direction.

'Storm Leader to squadron. Wheel!' ordered Kaether finally, almost shouting into his helmet comm-link. 'Zane, show us the road out of here.'

As one, with Zane out on the far starboard wing leading the way, the entire fighter formation pivoted in a wide-arcing 90 degree turn to port, taking them right across the front of the enemy line. They were met by a hail of fire from the nearest rok-fortresses. Explosions filled the void around them, radioactive and more conventional fallout debris buffeting violently against the Furies' armour. Kaether's craft rocked violently, caught in the electronic squall from a nearby ork dirty-bomb explosion, and he saw amber warning runes light up across his instrumentation panel. In the rear of the cockpit, Manetho re-calibrated power-feed systems and whispered prayer-words to the fighter's guiding machine-spirit. A second later, the flashing runes on Kaether's panel returned to a solid and reassuring green. More runes lit up as the other craft in the formation reported in. Thirteen runes. All of Storm squadron had survived the potentially disastrous manoeuvre intact.

'How's the view behind us, Manetho?' he asked over the cockpit's internal comm-channel.

'Busy, commander,' came the simple, understated reply.

A glance at the rearward surveyor screen confirmed the tech-priest's succinct choice of words. Enemy fighter icons crowded across the screen, massing in chaotic and haphazard pursuit of the apparently retreating Imperial fighter wave. Kaether smiled; Manetho had successfully managed to block out the ork comm-net interference, but he could almost imagine the ork warlord commander's screams of frustrated rage as his protective fighter screen disintegrated before his very eyes, his pilots falling for Captain Semper's ploy and chasing off in disordered pursuit of the Imperial feint attack.

He activated his comm-link to the carrier vessel's command deck. 'Storm Leader to *Macharius*. The bait has been taken. The field is yours.'

ON THE BRIDGE of the *Macharius*, communications officers confirmed the incoming signals from their sister ships.

'*Drachenfels* ready.'

'*Graf Orlok* ready.'

'Vanguard squadron ready.'

'Praetorian squadron ready.'

'*Macharius* ready.'

The last confirmation came from Remus Nyder, the *Macharius's* master of ordnance. Semper gestured in acknowledgement and raised his voice, knowing his words would be carried over the comm-net to his brother captains on the bridges of their own vessels.

'Very good, gentlemen. Fire on my mark... *Fire!*'

Seconds later, a deep shudder ran through the hull of the *Macharius*, signalling the launch of multiple torpedo missiles and the commencement of the battle in earnest.

'Torpedoes running true,' announced an ordnance officer. 'Four gone, two still in the tubes.'

'Understood. Commence ordnance reloading on tubes one to four,' ordered Semper.

The torpedoes rocketed away from the ship, the four fiery contrails of plasma gas from their full-burn engines matched on either side by an equal number of torpedo launches from the two other cruisers in the formation. Twelve torpedoes, with the Cobra destroyer squadrons on the flanks also launching six torpedoes apiece.

A total of twenty-four torpedoes, all converging on the same two targets at the centre front of the rok-cluster.

Ork fighters from what was left of the orks' defensive fighter screen scrambled to intercept the deadly missile wave.

What the orks lacked in co-ordination and intelligence, they more than compensated for in terms of firepower and sheer bestial determination. Semper watched the bridge surveyor screen calmly as three of the torpedo icons winked out of existence one after the other, blown apart by the formidable weaponry of the ork craft. Moments later the surviving twenty-one torpedoes were through the fighter screen, running the gauntlet of defensive fire from the target roks' anti-ordnance batteries.

The ork gunners, no doubt urged on by the angry roars of their brutal overseers, threw up a curtain of fire in the torpedo wave's path, destroying not only torpedoes but also more than a dozen of their own fighters which were still pursuing the missiles.

Semper watched as two more active torpedo icons disappeared from the screen, and then two more. There was a sharp intake of breath from one of the other officers on the deck as yet another icon disappeared off the screen.

Sixteen torpedoes left. Would that be enough to accomplish the desired task?

One of the torpedo icons suddenly flashed red. Then another. And still another. In seconds, the screen filled with red-coloured icons. Red for impact detonation. Fourteen red icons; fourteen hits on target. Two of the icons remained unlit. Two of the torpedoes, malfunctioning or possibly with their machine-mind guidance systems damaged by enemy fire, failed to find their slow-moving, lumbering targets and continued their journey, heading into the heart of the rok cluster where it was entirely possible they still might acquire and damage other enemy targets.

The torpedo wave's target had been the two largest rok-fortresses in the enemy front line. The roks were massive, one of them easily over eight kilometres from tip to tip, and possibly as many as four kilometres across. Eight torpedoes struck it, the remaining six finding the other one. Normally, it might have taken several dozen torpedo strikes to destroy targets this large. Not today, however. Today, the Imperium warships were using new ordnance: so-called 'rock-buster torpedoes', specially designed for the task in hand.

The torpedoes struck the pitted and cratered surface of the roks, their armoured nose-cones spinning like giant drill-bits and boring into the porous rock. The missiles burrowed deep into the bodies of the asteroids, drilling through hundreds of metres of rock in seconds. When the high-speed drill motor burned itself out at the end of its short lifespan, it triggered the warhead payload. The torpedoes exploded. Their payload was not the conventional plasma-fusion warheads used in normal ship-to-ship actions, designed to melt and destroy ship's hulls and set their internal compartments ablaze. Instead, the rock-busters' warheads were packed with high explosive seismic charges, designed to shatter and pulverise rock, setting off a chain reaction of aftershocks within the structure of their asteroid targets far in excess of the payload's explosive yield.

To those watching on the command decks of the Imperial ships, it seemed as if the two massive rok-fortresses simply burst apart from within.

The smaller one went first, the majority of it vaporised in a huge secondary explosion as something inside it – some deep-buried power source or magazine cavern full of unstable high explosive ordnance – detonated under the effects of the torpedo strike. The larger one shook and rumbled, and then, slowly, jagged fiery lines appeared all across its surface. The lines split apart, growing ever wider and revealing huge fires consuming the interior of the thing. Chunks of it broke away and were sent spinning off into space, a prelude to what was about to happen. A second later, the entire rok came apart, disintegrating in a ravenous and fiery explosion. Fragments of it, huge and deadly, hurled out with explosive force, raining meteor destruction amongst the roks nearest to it. From the safety of the bridge, Semper saw one jagged shard larger than a frigate strike another rok, piercing it like a dagger and sending it tumbling askew out of the ork formation.

'Two, or maybe even three, down, at least twenty-six more to go,' noted the laconic voice of one of the *Macharius's* senior gunnery officers.

Semper grunted in grim humour at the comment. It would indeed be a remarkable achievement if his force managed to destroy all the roks, even assuming they had enough rock-buster torpedoes to accomplish such a task. Which, as everyone on the command deck knew, was certainly not the case. The new experimental ordnance devices were rare and expensive and so far in short supply. Semper had little doubt that, assuming they actually survived the engagement, he and his fellow captains would be recommending that the rock-busters become part of the standard specialist range of torpedoes available to the forces of Battlefleet Gothic, after their first and highly successful testing here today under battlefield conditions.

'Ordnance report, Mister Nyder?' he asked. 'How many seismic torpedoes do we have left?'

'The rock-busters? Four, captain. Those shiftless Munitorium heretics were probably too busy chasing young adepts or polishing all that gold braid they give themselves to organise the supply of more than eight per ship to those of us who actually do the fighting in this man's war.'

'No sense letting them go to waste, then, I imagine. We have a new target laid in?'

Nyder gestured towards the magnified image of one of the roks on the auspex screen before him. 'The big one here, the one with what looks like the profile of old Lord Admiral Dardania, Emperor rest his devilish old soul, staring out at us from amongst those rock formations on its starboard flank. We're doubling up our fire with *Drachenfels*. They're reloaded and waiting for the word.'

Semper looked at the auspex-magnified image. Curiously, the jagged rock formation in question truly did resemble the unmistakable and craggy countenance of the former Lord Admiral, one of Battlefleet Gothic's greatest and most legendary commanders.

'I wonder, Mister Nyder, would it be a court martial offence to aim our torpedoes at the face of the good lord admiral?' asked Semper, with a half-smile.

Nyder returned the joke. 'If I recall correctly, sir, from what I can remember of the history classes at the academies on Cypra Mundi, the lord admiral was supposed to be a fearsome old ork-hater. I think he'd probably thank us for taking his face off the side of that thing.'

'I concur,' smiled Semper. 'Fire when ready, Mister Nyder. We'll dedicate this kill to the lord admiral's memory.'

FLAME WREATHED THE prows of the Imperial ships once more as they launched another torpedo wave at the target roks. They were close now, close enough to be within range of the ork batteries, and energy bursts erupted around the *Macharius* and its sister ships as the first ork fire impacted against their void shields. The ork fire was still sporadic and uncoordinated, but would soon grow in strength.

The Imperial strategy had been to hit the orks hard and fast, stunning them into a state of helpless panic with a sudden and ferocious assault. The swift destruction of the two large rok-fortresses and the chaos and confusion it had caused amongst the greenskin line had done much to achieve this end, but now the human battle force had to ensure that they maintained the pressure of the attack and that the initiative remained on their side of the engagement.

The second and final wave of rock-busters struck home. Two more roks, considerably smaller than the first two targets, explosively fragmented apart. A third remained mostly intact, but the weapons fire from its batteries slowed to an ineffectual trickle, and it began to drift out of position, its engines and steering systems apparently knocked out of action. Minutes later, its erratic and rudderless course would bring it blundering helplessly into the field of fire of several other roks. A combined salvo of mass-reactive howitzer fire – each shell the size of a Fury interceptor fighter – and traktor beam-launched plasma meteors smashed apart the crippled rok, finishing the task begun by the Imperium torpedoes.

Three more down, twenty-three more to go.

Semper felt a strong impact shudder run through his ship as enemy fire landed its first direct hit on the *Macharius*, stripping the cruiser of one of its void shields. The deck beneath his feet lurched under the shock, and he fought the urge to lean onto his lectern for support, knowing that many eyes would be casting nervous glances at him right now. In many ways, he was a captain of the old school, and firmly believed the old naval collegium maxim: a vessel's strength lies not in its armour or its weapons, but in its captain, and the will of its captain must be stronger than the densest adamantium armour.

'A minor hit on our forward starboard side,' reported Ulanti, consulting the information scrolling across his screen. 'Void shield generators are fully operational, and shield integrity is already regenerating itself.'

'I hope the greenskins can do better than that,' noted Semper. 'We came a long way for this fight, so they'd better not let us down now.'

There was the expected ripple of polite laughter from his officers, but Semper felt the atmosphere on the bridge around him relax a little, his crew reassured by their captain's modest attempt at humour. He looked out at the scene ahead of them, as the cluster of roks loomed ever closer, the tactician in him noting their clumsy attempts at formation change and the likely weaknesses in their incoming gunnery fire patterns, while the warrior in him secretly exulted at the thought of the battle to come.

Their battle plan had worked so far, he reminded himself, and the orks had obligingly taken the bait offered to them earlier on. Would they now fall for the same trick again? The bait was here right in front of them, the *Macharius* and its sister cruisers, so would it be enough to draw out the true prize the Imperial battle-force had come here to engage and destroy?

SEVEN

LIKE THE ORKS themselves, the battle which followed was savage and relentless, chaotic and unpredictable.

Two more roks, smaller than any of the previous targets, fell victim to massed salvoes of torpedoes. After that, the Imperium vessels were in amongst the enemy, able to bring their side-mounted weapons batteries to bear , and using torpedoes for target of opportunity fire on any ork rok foolish enough to drift across their bows.

The orks, in their own way, fought back furiously and without respite.

An ork torpedo struck the *Mannan* midship. The light cruiser staggered under the impact, but limped on, trailing debris and burning gases in its wake, making it that much easier a target for the ork gunners.

The *Macharius* took a heavy cannon battery hit in its thickly-armoured prow, temporarily knocking out two of its torpedo tubes. The impact of the hit set off alarm klaxons throughout the ship. On the command deck, tech-priests redoubled their prayers in praise and reassurance of the ship's troubled machine-mind spirit.

Launching from multiple roks, the orks finally managed to form something resembling an organised attack craft wave. The huge, sprawling wave of ork fighter-bombers targeted the *Macharius* and were immediately intercepted by the carrier cruiser's own protective fighter screen. Too late, Semper remembered that orks, for all their mindless barbarity, were not without intelligence, and were easily capable of a surprising level of natural cunning. The attempted attack on the *Macharius* had been a feint, albeit a highly costly one from the orks' point of view, drawing off the greater part of the Imperial formation's fighter cover and leaving unprotected the two escort carriers at the formation's centre.

A large splinter group of the main ork attack wave peeled away from the main dogfight and fell upon these two targets with gleeful abandon. Swarms of the small but heavily-armed ork fighter-bomber craft made daredevil attack runs on the two carrier vessels, neither of which had any of the armour, shield protection or anti-ordnance defences of a larger and true carrier vessel like the *Macharius*. In minutes, the *Memory of Briniga* was crippled and aflame, while the *Vengeance of Belatis* was desperately launching what was left of its own attack craft squadrons in a race against its own likely and imminent destruction.

Amongst the Imperial cruisers, the *Graf Orlok* was drawn into an unequal duel against the combined batteries of three different roks. Its captain, the notorious Titus von Blucher, owed his position mostly to a shared distant kinship with Lord Admiral Ravensburg, but Semper was surprised and pleased to note that von Blucher seemed to have developed something actually resembling a backbone over the last few years. The *Graf Orlok* mounted an effective fighting retreat, its own batteries of laser cannons and fusion beamers silencing the guns of one of its enemies. Still, the Lunar class cruiser was in mounting trouble, its void shields stripped away and the explosive bloom of successful enemy hits erupting along the length of its hull.

Vanguard squadron came to its rescue, the group of three Cobra destroyers mounting a fast attack torpedo run on one of the roks. The rok shook under the impact of two successful torpedo detonations, but was able to attack in return. A powerful tractor beam was brought into use as a huge and primitive catapult weapon, seizing and ripping away parts of the rok's own asteroid body and hurling them into space at the Imperium ships. The weapon was typically orkish, barbaric and makeshift, and typically highly effective. One of the Cobras, turning too late out of its torpedo run, was smashed in half by the impact of an asteroid missile fully two hundred metres across. *Graf Orlok* and the remaining two surviving Cobras beat a hasty retreat, rejoining the comparative safety of the main Imperial line of battle.

The Imperium line wavered but did not break under the mounting toll of damage. Its vessels kept up their own withering rain of fire upon the enemy roks, and slowly, the pattern of the battle began to show in their favour.

Squadrons of Marauder bombers targeted one of the roks, seeking vengeance for the damage done to their escort carrier motherships. The Marauders – smaller, less well-armed and less well-suited for deep space combat – still excelled under the conditions of this battle, their atmosphere-capable configuration allowing them to manoeuvre at ease amongst the asteroid field, skimming and gliding across the surface of the roks. They laid waste to one of the roks, making low-level bombing runs across its cratered skin, targeting and expertly picking off gun emplacements, torpedo silos, shield generators and engine thrusters with crippling precision strikes from their plasma bomb and armour-piercing missile payloads, and leaving the rok drifting helpless and defenceless, ready for the heavy batteries of an Imperial cruiser to later deliver the final coup de grace.

From its position in amongst the main cruiser formation, the *Fearsome* fulfilled its supporting role to devastating effect. Its massive, jutting, prow-mounted nova cannon wreaked havoc amongst the ork roks, firing explosive projectiles into their midst at near light speed. The *Fearsome's* captain and gunnery officers were veterans in the effective use of the powerful but unpredictable weapon. The slow-moving and clumsy roks made for easy targets, and Fury fighters adapted to specialist reconnaissance duties were in close amongst the enemy target cluster, feeding back accurate and instantaneous telemetry data to the *Fearsome's* gunners. So far, four shots had reduced two roks to just so much drifting and shattered asteroid debris, the last shot striking its target dead-centre and breaking it apart like a giant sledgehammer blow.

The orks retaliated, mounting another feint attack on the *Macharius*, one part of the assault wave splitting off towards its real intended target of the *Fearsome*. As they had already illustrated earlier in the battle, the orks were neither wholly without intelligence or a certain cunning, but ultimately their mindless animal nature triumphed in their assumption that the same trick would work twice in the same battle against the same opponent. Easily able to anticipate the repeat tactic, several squadrons of Furies and Thunderbolts intercepted the attack aimed at the *Fearsome*, and the ork attack wing was annihilated en masse.

A multitude of attack craft dogfights erupted around the *Macharius* as what was left of the desperate forces in the feint assault pressed forward their attack on the carrier for real this time. The cruiser was surrounded by a halo of tiny, flickering lights, the flashes of fighter-mounted laser cannons and the detonations of exploded fighter craft, as the attack craft battle raged around it. A determined thrust by the orks opened up a breach in the fighter screen, two Furies from Hornet squadron falling victim to a combined hail of ork rockets and cannon fire. From his commanding position on the bridge of the *Macharius*, Semper had a clear view of the incident as a flight of four ork fighter-bombers broke through and sped directly towards him, blazing a trail right up the dorsal spine of the ship's main hull and bearing down fast on the ship's command tower. The ork craft were ugly, threatening-looking things, garishly coloured and decorated with outlandish and primitive ork rune-markings, bristling with combined fighter and bomber armaments and powered by crude and outrageously large chemical-reaction engines mounted on their wings and tail.

One of them was clipped by a strafing line of las-fire from a pursuing Fury, and was instantly transformed into an exploding fireball. The other three opened up with their afterburners, and threw off their pursuer, flying with almost suicidal recklessness amongst the thrusting peaks and spires of the ship's upper superstructure.

Semper studied their progress with detached calm, despite the fact that the command deck where he was now standing was almost certainly their intended target. Crude but no doubt all too effective bomb-missiles hung beneath their wings, their warhead nose-cones painted with savage and grinning orkoid faces. Anti-ordnance fire reached up from the defence turrets studded along the *Macharius's* dorsal spine, but the angle of fire was poor, and the ork craft hugged the sheltering cover of the superstructure.

They were in the last stages of their attack run now, forced to finally leave the cover of the hull and arc upwards towards the command tower. Their trajectory brought them within reach of the anti-ordnance defences mounted on the command tower, and up into the arc of fire of the hull defences. They were suitably punished for their reckless final manoeuvre. Lascannon fire and exploding flechette-missile detonations hammered into them from two different directions. The starboard side attacker blew apart, followed seconds later by his portside wingman. The centre fighter, one engine ablaze and one shredded wing trailing fire, continued on towards it target.

Semper stared down the attacker, locking eyes with the grinning, bestial image painted across the fighter's blunted nose: the face, no doubt, of some typically savage and unknowable ork war god. The ork fighter was two hundred metres away, a second later and it was one hundred and fifty metres away. The time to lower the thickly-armoured blast shields over the command deck's vulnerable viewing bay windows was minutes gone.

The fighter opened fire, heavy cannon shells striking the reinforced glasteel of the window and forming cracks in it centimetres deep. Semper wondered why the pilot had not yet launched his primary missile armaments, and could only guess that the damage his craft had sustained had somehow disabled his payload launch mechanisms.

A suicide run then, he thought, wondering if a bomb-laden ork attack craft crashing through the viewing bay and exploding into the interior of his command deck would indeed be enough to cripple his entire ship.

Less than a hundred metres now. Semper could see the pilot inside the cockpit. The atmosphere inside it was on fire, the ork pilot wreathed in flame. He was shouting, his tusk-filled mouth forming sounds which Semper could only guess at. Some bestial ork battle-chant or prayer-words of dedication to yet another ork war god. The expression on his face matched the one of savage, animal joy painted on the nose of his craft.

Fifty metres. Semper resisted the urge to turn or look away. His grandfather may have survived to earn a peaceful and easy death on the family estates, but Semper's father and two of his uncles had all died in the Emperor's service, on the command deck of an Imperial warship. Semper had always imagined that their fate would one day be his too, and he was determined to meet that fate with the same stoicism which they too had faced it.

Thirty metres. A final, desperate burst of fire from one of the command tower's defence turrets blew away the tail of the fighter. The ork craft corkscrewed down out of sight, crashing seconds later several decks down into the armoured front of the tower. Semper felt the impact of the crash as a tremor through the deck beneath his feet.

He turned, catching the look of mutual relief on the face of Ulanti, not realising until this moment that his second-in-command had been standing by him the entire time, facing the prospect of instant obliteration with the same stoic resoluteness.

'Make a note, Mister Ulanti,' remarked Semper, with as much arch reserve as he could still muster. 'Extra target drill needed for the defence turret gunnery crews. And find out who the crew were on that last burst of fire, and send them a case of the finest and strongest grog we have in the ship's stores, with the captain's compliments.'

ELSEWHERE, THE BATTLE continued to rage. The *Drachenfels's* lance batteries gored into the sides of another rok, blasting away or vaporising hundreds of tonnes of soft, porous rock. The asteroid material of the rok's body was streaked through

with deposits of a glittering metallic ore substance. Whatever
the substance was, it was apparently highly fissionable. It
ignited instantly when the star-hot power of the lance beams
touched it, setting off an instantaneous chain reaction
through the interior of the rock. The entire rok disappeared
in a nuclear flash, lighting up the void like a second, short-
lived miniature sun.

The sudden and massive energy burst overwhelmed the
Drachenfels's shields and temporarily blinded its scanner systems. Amongst the surrounding roks, the effects were much
worse. One of them, the closest, was reduced to a burnt-out
cinder by the flash, while two others were caught on the
periphery of the blast and took varying degrees of damage.
Two suffered more damage still, accidentally colliding into
each other as their crews, panicked by the evidence of what
they assumed to be some new and super-powerful human
weapon, fired up crude and unpredictable emergency
manoeuvring rockets.

In his armoured strategium shell deep with his ship, Erwin
Ramas, captain of the *Drachenfels* and a Battlefleet Gothic
legend in his own right, allowed a rasping chuckle to escape
from his lipless mouth.

Who else, he laughed to himself, but the greenskins would
build a fortress base upon an asteroid streaked through with
deposits of enriched plutonium?

RETH ZANE REGISTERED the nuclear detonation as a flash of
buzzing interference cutting through the flow of information
being fed into him through the mind-impulse link with his
Fury's onboard systems. The servitor navigator seated in the
rear cockpit space behind him emitted a brief question in
the form of a transmitted query-equation. Zane ignored the
query, and the event which had prompted it. Whatever that
distant explosion had been, it had no bearing on his divine
work.

They were in amongst the main cluster of roks now, weaving in and out of the asteroids; a vast and chaotic dogfight
mêlée, with Imperium Furies and Thunderbolts and a bewildering array of ork fighter-bombers finding and then losing
each other amongst the deadly maze of drifting space debris.

He was flying lone wolf, without any supporting wingmen, without even a living human navigator, and that suited his purposes perfectly. Back aboard the ship, his fellow pilots shunned his company, and that suited his purposes too. He held no malice nor ill-will towards them. They were, as far as he could tell, good and conscientious servants of the Emperor, but they did not understand his divine purpose.

He was an Avenging Fury. He killed the Emperor's enemies, and he did so under the Emperor's direct guidance and protection.

He had been busy with his divinely-ordained business this day. Six more kills, six more enemies of the Emperor destroyed, six more blessings to be added to the holy shrine he maintained in his personal quarters.

His comrades feared him, he knew, and mocked him. 'Zealot Zane' they used to call him behind his back. 'Machine Zane' they more often called him now. More servitor than man, they whispered snidely amongst themselves. Zane forgave them. They did not understand the transformation which had happened to him in the events during the evacuation of Belatis. He had faced and vanquished an enemy of the Emperor, a daemon of the warp, no less. Protected by the holy aura of the Golden Throne he had survived the encounter, even if much of his body had been destroyed. The recovery had been long and painful, the mastering of a new body which was more machine than flesh even more so, but, throughout it all, Zane knew he would prevail. After all, the Emperor himself was with him.

His comrades saw the injuries he had suffered as a disability, a source of pity and secret horror. To Zane, though, they were a liberation. Only the flesh, the most superficial element of his humanity, had been burnt away in the all-cleansing fire. The most important part, his Emperor-given soul, remained, and his new machine-body freed him from the weaknesses of the flesh, allowing him to better carry out his holy work.

He brought the nose of his Fury up, sensing rather than seeing yet another new kill opportunity. Machine eyes allowed him to see and feel all his fighter craft saw. The distant shapes of two ork craft drifted into view. The ork fighters were difficult for his wing-mounted missile weaponry to lock onto, he knew. The orks' primitive power systems and crude fossil fuel engines threw out unpredictable energy signals, confounding the Imperium's more sophisticated scanning devices.

His machine-augmented brain judged the distance from him to the targets. Machine hands powered up his engines' thruster power, pushing him forward towards the targets at an accelerated speed but which would not yet alert the targets to his presence. Machine patience, freed from the emotions of flesh, calmly counted out the seconds until the moment of interception.

A human soul, free and untainted, exalted in the expectation of the imminent deaths of the Emperor's enemies.

The first target drifted into his cockpit screen's targeting display. Flesh was weak. Flesh would have fired already. Machine patience still held sway, counselling caution, knowing that the target lock-on was never certain in the first few crucial moments.

Machine-mind gave the command. Machine hands moved calmly across the firing controls. The quad-cannons mounted in his Fury's nose fired as one, spitting out a stream of laser energy. The brief storm of las-bolts found and pursued its quarry. The target broke apart in a sudden, fiery burst.

Machine mind calmly replayed the incident, satisfied at its choice of the correct course of action. Human soul offered up a silent prayer of rejoice.

The last remaining target peeled away, hitting its afterburners and tracing a long burning arc across the starfield. Machine mind and machine hands matched the target's movements. Machine eyes kept the target fixed in sight, working with machine mind to calculate angles of fire and likely speeds and trajectories.

The target looped round and reversed its course, coming straight at them. The servitor navigator clicked and whirred in faint alarm. Machine mind did not panic. Machine hands did not waver. Human mind recognised the signs of an experienced and skilled enemy pilot. Human soul thrilled at the prospect of the death of such an enemy.

Human mind took over, doing what no mere machine could not. Flying straight towards the oncoming target. Skilfully jinking the fighter craft through the hail of autocannon fire now filling the void around it. A stray shell careered off the hull just in front of the cockpit. A stream of shells shredded part of his tailfin. Another stray blast blew away the cowling on his starboard engine.

Warning runes flashed across instrumentation panels. Machine mind made urgent calculations and counselled withdrawal. Machine hands longed to seize the control stick and steer them out of the path of imminent destruction.

Human soul ignored them. Human soul and human mind bided their time, Human soul and mind had been here many times before in previous battles.

The Fury jinked aside at the last moment, unleashing two wing missiles at the target. The ork craft disappeared in an explosive rush. Zane's Fury flew through the midst of the still-expanding debris cloud. Pieces of wreckage smashed off its armoured hull, adding to the chorus of warning runes going off within the cockpit.

Zane ignored them all. Machine was strong and efficient, but human was always better. Human was that part of us which belonged to the Holy Emperor, and so was in itself partly divine.

He brought the fighter up tight and fast, skimming low-level across the rocky canyons and plains of a nearby rok. His eyes and the Fury's augur senses scanned the rok's surface, seeking suitable targets. Machine eyes saw the tell-tale heat trails from exhaust vents hidden amongst a cluster of needle-like stalactite rock formations. An extremely tempting and vulnerable target for a bomber run, but not with any of the lesser ordnance his fighter was carrying.

Light flashed out at him from the rim of a crater half a kilometre over. Zane directed his attention in that direction, and saw a cavern mouth set into the wall of the crater, protected by at least two small defence turrets, turrets which were now firing at him. Without the lines of tracer fire coming from them, he might not have noticed the hidden crater at all.

He gave praise to the Emperor for the stupidity and over-eagerness of some anonymous ork gunner as he hit his forward braking jets and guided the fighter down into the crater for a closer look at the potential target within it.

Defence turret fire zigzagged past him, ploughing the surface of the crater and throwing up chunks of rocky debris. He saw light flooding out from the cave mouth, and, within the light, the shapes of ork fighter-bombers sitting there in the wide cavern beyond. Squat, orkoid figures in some form of crude, gas-belching, armoured vacuum suits moved amongst them, and Zane saw fuel cables and power couplings snaking amongst the parked craft, and stocks of munitions piled up nearby. No matter how disorganised and ramshackle the scene, Zane still recognised an attack craft launch deck when he saw one.

One of the orks saw him, and, aggressively if futilely, raised a handgun to fire several shots at his cruising Fury. Zane hits the lift thrusters and pulled up, intending to turn round again and make a proper attack run on the launch bay cavern. A few missiles into the munitions stacks and fuel dumps at the back of the cave would quickly wipe the place clean of all trace of greenskin life.

Tracer fire from the defence turrets chased after him. He easily outran it, arcing up out of the crater. The view through his cockpit window rolled and yawed. Cratered and pitted rock fell away, to be replaced by a glittering starfield. He pulled on the altitude controls, rolling the fighter over as he prepared to dive back down on the target.

A shadow, huge and dark, fell over his fighter, blotting out the starfield above.

The servitor navigator gave an electronic squawk of alarm. Zane looked up, seeing the huge, gaping, brightly painted jaws of a giant creature looming above him in space. Metallic, jagged teeth gaped open, revealing a battery of rudimentary, ugly and deadly weapon barrels clustering within its mouth. A giant red eye, painted onto the side of a hull crudely patchworked together from great, thick slabs of ill-matched metals, glared balefully down at him.

The gargantuan ork cruiser rumbled past overhead, hiding within the cluttered surveyor shadow of the surrounding asteroids. Another ork cruiser vessel, different in outline and configuration, but identical in the same deadly, lumbering purpose followed along behind it, accompanied by a school of smaller and eager-looking escort craft.

Human mind and soul faltered, temporarily overwhelmed by the sheer savage scale and ferocity of the ork vessels. Machine mind took over. Machine hands opened up a comm-channel. Other than the whisper of prayer-words to himself, it had been several days since Zane had spoken aloud, and the sound of his own voice, harsh and machine-formed, almost came as a shock to him.

'Storm Four to *Macharius*. Have sighted two ork cruiser vessels and escorts. They're powering up engines and heading towards you. Be warned, *Macharius*: the bait has definitely been taken, and the prey is coming out into the open.'

EIGHT

'WE'RE SURE THAT it's really them?'

Semper stared at the hazy augur screen images being transmitted back by their forward reconnaissance scout craft. The squadron of ork vessels was just beginning to clear the final fringes of the asteroid field. The smashed and gutted remains of several roks drifted nearby, dead and derelict. The ork vessels moved past them, unheeding and uncaring. They had changed course since their first sighting, taking a vector which would take them away from the Imperial force and out towards the warp jump point on the system's distant outer edge. The consensus amongst the captains of the Imperial battle-force was that the ork commander was cutting and running, abandoning the roks and their crews to their fate at the hands of the Imperial warships' gun batteries.

'As much as we can be,' answered Ulanti, in response to his captain's question. 'The energy signals from ork vessels are notoriously unpredictable, and the greenskins have an irritating habit of tearing down and altering their ships' superstructure at any apparent random whim. Still, as far as we can tell, based on the information from survivors of the ork pirate raids in this sub-sector, those floating junk-piles we're looking at now are indeed the *Wolverine* and the *Sabretooth.'*

Semper looked again at the ship images, seeing the clear evidence of the trademark primitive and brutish ork manufacturing process, seeing the rough patchwork of their thickly armoured skins, seeing the gun batteries bristling across their surfaces, seeing the outlandish greenskin markings and glyphs burned or cut hundreds of metres high into the vessels' flanks.

He had no idea what those markings might mean. Perhaps such primitive pagan symbols actually spelled out the vessels' true names, he supposed. There were Imperium adepts who could read and translate orkish writing, he knew; oddly-minded scribes within the Ordo Xenos or various obscure branches of the Administratum who dedicated their lives to the study of alien races. No captain of the Imperial Navy, however, would ever sully themselves with the knowledge of such things, and so the tacticians of Battlefleet Gothic had merely followed the traditional custom in such matters and assigned their own codenames to the ork vessels in question.

Wolverine and *Sabretooth*, two suitably feral and savage names for the two ork pirate vessels which, together with their attendant flotilla of escort vessels, had been preying upon unprotected Imperial convoys throughout this subsector for months now, each time evading retribution by retreating back into their rok-protected lair here in the Mather system. The cleansing and securing of this system was important, yes, but more important still was the destruction of the two ork cruisers. If they were allowed to escape, then no doubt in a few months' time Lord Admiral Ravensburg would be forced to reallocate more precious resources to clear out the next empty star system to be occupied and quickly infested by these same ork pirates.

Open comm-channels hissed in empty expectation, as Semper's fellow captains waited on him to decide the deployment of his forces for this next final and vital stage of the battle.

'*Graf Orlok* and *Fearsome*, with me. We'll also need *Triton* and Vanguard squadron with us, to take care of their escorts and provide supporting firepower. *Drachenfels*, I need you here to keep these damn roks occupied. *Mannan* and Paladin squadron will assist you, and be seconded to your command. You'll also have attack craft support from my Furies and the fighter and bomber squadrons from *Belatis* and *Briniga*. No heroics, *Drachenfels*,' he added, dryly, 'just make them keep their distance. There'll be plenty of time to deal with them properly after we've run *Wolverine* and its pack-mates to ground.'

The reply over the crackling comm-channel was typical Ramas: a dry, barking laugh, a scathing, impatient edge to his machine-modulated voice, hiding, for those who didn't know the illustrious and irascible captain of the *Drachenfels*, a deep-held respect for those rare few he considered worthy of his friendship.

'Hah! I see you're thinking like a real commodore already, Leoten. The youngbloods get to chase glory and promotion, while the old warhorses like me can only be entrusted to keep taking potshots at a few floating rocks. Good to see some things haven't changed yet in glorious Battlefleet Gothic!' He laughed, the sound turning into a weird electronic whinnying sound as the Adeptus Mechanicus constructed voice-box in his rebuilt throat struggled to interpret the sounds of human laughter.

'Good hunting, *Macharius*,' the master of the *Drachenfels* added in a more serious tone, the traditional good luck message between brother captains of Battlefleet Gothic being too much of a sacred custom for even Erwin Ramas to ignore or make sport of.

'And to you, *Drachenfels*,' replied Semper, signalling for his helm crew to bring them around to their new battle course.

IN NORMAL TERMS, an hour does not seem such a long time. In terms of space combat, a lot can happen in a short hour. In a naval battle, an hour can seem an eternity.

Fearsome drifted somewhere in the mid-distance off the *Macharius's* starboard bow. The Dominator class cruiser's command tower was gone, sheared right off by an ork ram ship attack, and a salvo of giant macro-cannon shells had stitched lines of catastrophic ruin across the cruiser's flanks. Its main hull section was shattered and broken, with an area fully three-quarters of a kilometre long gouged away and missing, as if a giant pair of jaws had simply ripped away a portion of the vessel.

The crews of the other vessels would not have believed it possible had they not seen it with their own eyes. The battle-squadron's comm-channels had been filled with a babble of pleading, desperate voices from aboard the *Fearsome*: the voices of crew still trapped aboard her in airtight compartments, and begging for rescue before they suffocated to death, or before the wrecked and burning vessel exploded or began to break up. Semper had ordered that all comm-links to the *Fearsome* be cut, knowing the damaging effect such pitiful transmissions could have on the minds of a ship's crew during time of battle. The survivors trapped aboard the *Fearsome* would have to wait until the battle was over until rescue craft could be sent to sift amongst the wreckage of the vanquished cruiser. In the meantime, only the Emperor would hear their pleas for help.

One of the *Fearsome's* killers drifted not too far away. *Wolverine* was a fragmenting hulk, with little left to suggest the armoured and heavily armed leviathan it had been less than an hour before. The *Macharius's* Starhawk bomber squadrons, held back from battle with the roks for just this moment, had relentlessly harried and pursued the ork monstrosity, targeting its drive systems and leaving it crippled and limping, unable to outrun the gunsights of the Imperial cruisers' weapons batteries. The *Fearsome's* nova cannon, combined with the prow lances of the *Triton* and the torpedoes and weapons batteries of *Macharius* and *Graf Orlok*, had reduced it to just so much scattered space debris.

The retaliation from the *Sabretooth* and its escorts had been swift and brutal. *Triton* lay somewhere far to the *Macharius's* stern, the light cruiser's engine drives pounded into slag by the *Sabretooth's* macro-cannon batteries. *Graf Orlok* was closer, still nominally in the battle but with the metal-jawed prow of an ork escort vessel buried snout-deep into its forward portside. Ork warriors, huge and savage, wild and merciless, had poured into the interior of the Lunar class cruiser in their hundreds, and the last comm-channel transmission from Captain von Blucher had indicated heavy fighting in his ship's forward sections, with his gun batteries left unmanned as he was forced to withdraw their crews to join the shipboard combat.

Graf Orlok, for the moment at least, was out of the battle, leaving the *Macharius* to face the terrifying power of the *Sabretooth* on its own.

'Vandire's oath! I don't believe it. The bloody thing's powering up and coming round again!'

Alerted by the incredulous voice of one of his gunnery officers, Semper looked at the image on the augur screen, sharing the man's disbelief.

The *Sabretooth* was a wreck, its hull riddled with blast craters and torpedo wounds. Somehow, though, it continued to fight. Semper could only secretly marvel at the very orkoid inability to admit defeat as, in complete defiance of all the odds, the vessel's commander managed to fire up manoeuvring thrusters and to crew to man the gun batteries.

The vessel swung round in space, its side batteries sending out a wave of fire to crash explosively against the *Macharius's* shields and hull. As it did, Semper could see the horrific damage so far inflicted on it. Through the gaping holes in its armoured skin, fires could clearly be seen burning inside its decks and compartments. As it continued to swing round, Semper could see the starfield behind it, visible through the holes blasted clean through its body.

'Vandire's oath,' breathed Ulanti, standing beside his captain. 'What's keeping them going?'

'Sheer bloody-mindedness, Mister Ulanti,' replied Semper. 'You can't convince a greenskin that it's truly dead until you hold up its severed head and show it its own bullet-riddled body.'

The *Macharius's* own gun batteries replied, blowing away more fragments of the unshielded target's hull, but still the monster kept on moving. The dark maw of its prow mouth gaped open in threat, and Semper had a sudden and terrifying vision of the fate of the *Fearsome*.

'Engage portside thrusters. Hard to starboard! Get us out of reach of that damned tractor beam!'

There was that familiar, sickening lurch in the pit of the stomach as the ship swung round and the artificial gravity generators lagged a second or two behind in readjusting to the vessel's new orientation. A further, this time reassuring, shudder ran through the ship as its engines fired up, taking it out of harm's way. The sense of relief amongst the command deck crew was almost palpable.

The elation did not last long. Semper was thrown to the ground as the deck beneath his feet vanished from under him. There was a crash from high above, and the jagged spear of a great, splintered stalactite of machinery crashed into the flag-stoned floor several metres away, crushing and killing a tech-priest and a junior ordnance officer.

There was the scream of tortured metal from all around them, and the whole ship shook under a continuous series of violent, pounding impacts.

Klaxons and warning alarms reverberated from dozens of points throughout the ship. Leoten Semper climbed to his feet, wiping away the blood from his face from a flying metal sliver thrown out by the falling machinery. There was a dry, foul taste in his mouth, and a sensation of sick dread in his heart. His ship, he knew, was now in the deadliest of perils.

The internal comm-channels were filled with panicked damage reports from the intolerable strain now being put on the ship's innermost structural integrity.

'Hull breach… gun-deck three. Requesting permission to evacuate.'

'Fires on decks eighteen, nineteen and twenty-one.'

'Got a hull breach here on forward compartment, deck sixteen. Sealing blast doors now.'

'Enginarium… serious coolant failure on Reactor Tertius… engaging emergency coolant systems.'

'Open the blast doors… We're trapped in here! Emperor's mercy, we can't get out!'

Semper gathered his wits. His ship was in pain, and could be destroyed any minute. 'Mister Ulanti, what's our situation?' he barked.

Ulanti's face was grim. 'Definitely still some life in *Sabretooth*, sir. It's sunk its teeth in, and now it's trying to take a bite of us. A large bite, it would seem.'

Semper cursed. A tractor beam, one of the few high technologies which the orks had managed to master for their own use. And, being orks, that use was as a weapon, of course.

The *Macharius* was caught in the invisible grip of a huge and powerful ork tractor beam weapon mounted in the *Sabretooth's* mouth-like prow. The tractor beam wasn't powerful enough to bodily drag or hurl the *Macharius* through space, as the orks had done with the asteroid missiles which had been directed at the *Graf Orlok* and which had smashed apart one of Vanguard squadron's Cobra destroyers, but it was still easily capable of destroying the ship. The powerful gravitic forces of a tractor beam, recklessly manipulated in the right way, could be used to crush or tear apart a target, or at least a portion of a larger target.

This was what was happening to the *Macharius* now. The tractor beam had seized a large hull section, and was attempting to tear it free from the rest of the ship. Less than half an hour ago, Semper and the crew of the *Macharius* had seen the *Fearsome* ripped apart by *Sabretooth's* savage tractor beam jaws. Now the same thing was happening to them.

Semper could sense his ship starting to tear apart. Metal buckled. Armoured hull plates ruptured. Power conduits exploded or failed. The *Macharius* screamed in torment at the intolerable strain being put upon its metal body.

MAXIM BORUSA HEARD the deep, echoing boom from somewhere deep within the ship's interior, and felt the decking lurch beneath his feet. He uttered a coarse Stranivar curse as the unexpected and violent movement threw off his aim. A bolt shell which should have taken off the head of the figure at the other end of the catwalk instead ruptured a steam pipe several metres wide of its target.

The man, one of Sejarra's thugs, turned and began to bring his own weapon – a battered old stub pistol, Sejarra had a tendency to skimp on arming his boys with the proper heavy stuff, Maxim knew – up to bear, aiming it at Maxim.

'Dumb bastard,' sneered Maxim, putting a bolt shell through his chest, 'should have run when you had the chance.'

Another violent impact shook the ship. Maxim had to grab onto the handrail to prevent himself keeling over the side of the walkway and into the guts of the lower enginarium levels, several decks below. Someone a few decks above wasn't so fortunate, and a screaming body plunged down the metal chasm, which ran almost the full height of the ship, through twenty-two decks of machinery-crammed engineering sections. There was an explosion from somewhere down below, followed by the fiery rush of released plasma and the screams of several men caught in the blast.

Maxim grinned. The ship was clearly taking a pounding from something, but he wasn't worried. Whatever kind of scrap they'd got into, old Captain Semper would see them through it, of that Maxim had little doubt.

And, besides he thought, still grinning, all this internal damage meant casualties, and casualties meant plenty of opportunity to cover up the evidence of his own private little battle right here.

There were shouts – he recognised the voice of Galba amongst them – and the sound of more gunfire from through the maze of machinery ahead of him. Maxim checked the load on his bolt pistol and moved off towards the location, homing in on the familiar and welcome sounds of conflict.

THE SOUNDS OF his ship's distress continued, coming to him both over the command deck's comm-channels and reverberating through the very substance of the ship. Semper knew the *Macharius* was only moments away from suffering irreparable damage.

'Helm – all ahead full. Channel all available power to engines and get us out of this thing's grasp.'

'No!'

It was the voice of Magos Castaboras, the most senior servant of the Machine God aboard the *Macharius*, who had just arrived on the command deck, surrounded by his customary train of tech-priest acolytes. Even with destruction looming, the officers and crewmen present stared in complete disbelief at this unforgivable challenge to a captain's authority here on his own command deck.

Semper stared at the impassive gold-masked face of the senior tech-priest. He had little fondness for the cold and aloof Castaboras. Few aboard the *Macharius* did, but he had no doubt of the man's abilities, or his unsurpassed knowledge of the workings and capabilities of the vessel to which he had so far dedicated more than eighty years of his Machine God-extended life.

'Explain!' snapped Semper, as the sound of the ship's torment grew louder all around them.

The tech-priest spoke quickly but calmly, his voice offering little in the way of accent or human emotion. 'If we engage the engines, we will only hasten our own destruction, struggling in one direction against the force pulling at us from the other, and tearing the ship apart in the process. However, there is another way...'

The tech-priest's last words were almost drowned out by the tortured shriek of metal on metal. Semper didn't hesitate, knowing they likely only had seconds.

'The Magos has command,' he told his officers, doing what many captains would consider the unthinkable, even under such dire circumstances.

Castaboras set to work immediately. 'Engage port and starboard thrusters – anchor us in space. Channel all available power to the defence shields and set the shield frequency to four points above the norm.' He broke off, favouring the officers of the *Macharius* with a rare explanation of his methods. 'Studies have shown that changes in shield frequency can interfere with the gravitic fields of tractor beam weapons. I have never seen it done myself, but the great Magos Technicus Sulpicius the Precise proved in his studies in M.39 that–'

Remus Nyder exploded in anger. 'Look at the shield output readouts, man. You're overloading the generators! And now you talk of "studies", and tell us that we've put the safety of the ship in the hands of the theories of some long-dead damn Machine God prayer babbler who none of us have even heard of!'

Castaboras looked at Semper, directing his reply to him and ignoring Nyder. 'The shields will hold, captain. I know this vessel. I tend to its workings. I commune with its machine-mind. I offer prayers to its sacred spirit. I have faith in its strength, and so too should you and your men.'

The violent shaking took on a different timbre now. A tone of slightly anxious relief crept into the tech-priest's voice.

'It's working. The shields are interfering with the tractor beam. They're boosting the tractor beam's strength, trying to keep their grip on us.' He stepped back, taking firm hold of a nearby instrumentation panel. 'I recommend you and your men hold onto the nearest fixed surface, captain. The venerable magos's studies suggest that the final moment of uncoupling may be hazardous to a vessel's human crew components.'

There was a final scream of metal, matched by the shriek of energy generators overloaded to near destruction. Then, suddenly, the ship was moving, tumbling through space, rolling almost thirty degrees on its portside, its artificial gravity field crucially lagging several seconds behind in adjusting to the ship's radical change of orientation as the *Macharius* was brutally expelled free of the tractor beam's deadly grasp.

Castaboras's warning was well-founded. For a second, Semper found himself in freefall, falling laterally across the command deck, before the firm grasp of Remus Nyder found him and pulled him to safety. Semper nodded his thanks, and hauled himself to his feet. The command deck was still filled with the sound of warning alarms and comm-net distress calls. If anything, the flood of damage reports and distress calls had increased, as the ship took stock of the cost of that last near-disastrous manoeuvre. Still, Semper knew that at least now his ship was safe from imminent destruction.

His ork opponents, however, had different ideas.

The augur screen was cracked, the image on it temporarily flickering and indistinct, but Semper could still make out the flame-wreathed shape of the ork cruiser as it laboriously swung round in space in pursuit of them, presenting its lethal tractor beam maw towards them once more.

'It's still after us!' shouted a young surveyor adept in near panic. 'It's powering up its tractor beam for another attack!'

'No, it's not,' said Semper in determination, looking towards Remus Nyder. 'Mister Nyder, what do we have in the way of torpedoes?'

Nyder checked the information on the data-slate handed to him by one of his junior officers. It made for grim reading. 'Only two in the pipe, captain. It's a hell of a mess down there, I'm told. That last jolt really shook up our torpedo room. I've got two tubes out of action, half my loading crews dead or injured and Emperor only knows how long before we can get the other two tubes loaded and ready to fire.'

Semper looked at the auspex screen, checking the telemetry data scrolling down the sides of the screen and making his own personal calculations about the angle of fire, the closing distance between the two vessels, the current battle status of each of them and the likely outcome of any head-on battle between them. The answer he came up with was not much to his liking, but he was a captain in His Divine Emperor's Navy, and so it was not in his nature to show any sign of fear or weakness on his own command deck and before the eyes of his expectant crew.

'Two torpedoes will be more than enough,' he said, in a voice filled with more confidence than he felt. 'Helm – bring us around. Ordnance – prepare to fire as soon as you have a good angle of shot.'

The ship's manoeuvring thrusters fired again, bringing it round to face the oncoming *Sabretooth*. To the watching crew on the command deck, it seemed to take the prow an eternity to swing through the sixty degree angle which would bring the ship round towards the enemy ship.

All the time, the *Sabretooth* came on. In the minds of some of the more nervous crewmen aboard the command deck of the *Macharius*, the ork cruiser's open maw with the tractor beam weapon hidden inside seemed to gape open to swallow up the entire ship.

Light flared within that maw. 'Power levels are building,' reported a surveyor adept. 'They'll be activating that thing any second now.'

'In position. Target in range. Angle is good,' reported an ordnance officer a second later.

'Fire torpedoes!'

The words were barely out of Semper's mouth before he held the dull roar of the torpedoes' release from their prow silos. The missiles streaked through space towards their target. Light flared stronger between the *Sabretooth's* jaws. Aboard the *Macharius*, they felt the first shifting lurch as the tractor beam's gravity field once again took hold of the ship.

The torpedoes shot between the metal jaws. For a moment, it almost appeared as if the *Sabretooth* had actually swallowed them, and even the most resolute of veteran navy officers watching felt a moment of sickening fear, as it seemed that almost nothing could destroy the vessel.

Sabretooth's head exploded. It keeled over, tumbling away through space, a series of secondary explosions gutting what was left of its shattered innards.

'Double impact. Target destroyed,' recorded the surveyor adept.

'Scan the area,' ordered Semper. 'Surveyors and augurs to maximum. Search for any remaining enemy vessels.' He waited impatiently while his orders were carried out, servitors and tech-priests attuning themselves to the massive flood of information gathered by the ship's electronic senses and sifting through it in search of any further threats. Finally, the answer came back from Hito Ulanti, the second-in-command confirming the scan findings relayed onto the screen of his control lectern.

'No enemy vessels found within surveyor range. The garden is clear, captain.'

For the first time in hours, Semper allowed himself to relax. The battle for the Mather system was over.

NINE

THE *MACHARIUS* LAY inert in space, tending to its wounds. Vacuum-suited work crews crawled across the outside of its hull, inspecting the most recently-inflicted battle damage, and making what immediate repairs they could. Hull breaches were resealed, using whatever materials were available, including the salvaged remains of other vessels destroyed in the battle. Molten metal salves were applied to the wounds in the ship's armoured flanks, adding further to the ancient patchwork of scars which criss-crossed its centuries-old hull.

Inside the ship too, the necessary post-battle rituals of damage assessment and repair were well underway, as was the grim task of recovering and counting the dead and wounded. Ships' surgeons and their orderlies were at work throughout the vessel, operating a strict and merciless triage system on the wounded men brought to them. The walking wounded would have to wait until after the battle for any kind of attention, and the crew decks and dormitories were filled with the moans and screams of the injured. The only relief from the pain at present would be whatever quantities of illicit narc-stimms they had hidden away or could beg from their comrades.

The more seriously wounded lay piled up in corridors and compartments which now served as makeshift field surgeries. Surgeons and orderlies moved amongst them, dispensing crude and swift battlefield surgery with las-cutters, stimm-packs, clamps and flesh-cauterisers. More than one surgeon also carried a chainsword, their blades already clotted with the gory evidence of the number of emergency battlefield surgeries they had already carried out.

The dying, the ones who were beyond help or for whom the surgeons could not spare the additional time needed to tend to their more grievous injuries, were handed silently over to armsmen wearing blood-soaked overalls, who carried them away out of sight of those other wounded still waiting to learn their own fate under the strictures of the surgeons' system. A quick and mercifully-intended piece of knifework by the armsmen, and possibly a few mumbled words of prayer from their killers, and then the bodies were deposited amongst the growing pile of dead, where teams of sweating, gore-covered ratings carried them in relays to the nearest airlock chamber.

'Get a move on. We haven't got all day!' cursed Petty Officer Vorshun, wondering why he always seemed to get detailed with this duty after a battle. His words, and the angry blow he casually directed at the nearest of them with the wooden haft of his billy club, spurred on the ratings under his supervision, and they heaved the last few bodies in through the open airlock door. Vorshun looked at the mound of corpses filling the airlock chamber, and decided that enough was enough.

'Right, that'll do for this one. Stand back while I seal her up,' he warned, casually kicking a corpse's dangling arm back over the other side of the rim of the airlock hatch. He reached for the manual release lever which would seal the heavy blast door, and, seconds later, release the outer door and expel the gory contents of the airlock chamber out into space.

'Hold on, Vorshun, you lazy whoreson! Time and room for a few more yet!'

Vorshun turned in anger towards the latecomers, ready to take out the worst of his temper on whoever dared to speak to him like that. The intended volley of curses died stillborn on his lips when he caught sight of the uniform and rank sash of a chief petty officer. The fury in him turned to fear when he saw the familiar and powerfully-muscled figure which filled out that uniform.

Maxim Borusa came up the corridor with a group of his picked cut-throats, all of them carrying bodies over their shoulders. 'Chief Borusa!' said Vorshun, the surprise in his voice hopefully disguising the fear in there too. 'I didn't know you and your men were working this section.'

'You know me, Vorshun,' grinned Maxim. 'Always willing to lend a hand anywhere I'm needed, and always willing to help our dear departed shipmates on their final journey to the Emperor.'

Maxim turned to his men, indicating the open airlock. 'Right, lads, in they go, and be gentle about it and mind that you treat these fallen heroes with all the respect they deserve.'

His men laughed, and threw their burdens into the airlock to join the other bodies piled there. Maxim went last, lobbing the corpse he was carrying halfway across the airlock with a single shrug of his shoulders, and Vorshun tried hard to ignore the fact that the corpse made a distinct moaning, sobbing sound when it landed.

Maxim turned towards him, a dangerous glint of unspoken threat in his eyes. 'Right, Petty Officer Vorshun, off you go now. Me and my boys will take care of this. I expect you've still got work to do on the next deck down.'

'Right, chief,' mumbled Vorshun, all too glad of the chance to get away from whatever it was the big hiveworld ganger was up to.

Maxim waited until the men were out of sight before he turned and looked into the airlock. The terrified eyes of Ship's Engineer Second Grade Tyrrus Sejarra stared back at him, wide with fear and silent, desperate pleading. It had been a fine piece of work to capture his old rival alive, Maxim thought. Sejarra was gagged and had his hands and feet bound with wire, while the neat little paralysing cocktail of narc-subs which Maxim had mixed up for him had kept him quiet and subdued while they hauled him and the rest of his dead crew all the way from the enginarium to here, taking the longer sub-deck levels to avoid the prowling likes of Kyogen and his spies.

Sejarra's jaws worked feebly, and Maxim realised he was trying to say something beneath the strip of plasti-seal fixed over his mouth and bonded to the flesh of his face. Maxim congratulated himself at his skill in mixing together the ingredients of the cocktail. He had wanted Sejarra subdued – it would have been awkward if the 'corpse' had started struggling or making noises during the journey here – but he didn't want the sneaky bastard so doped up that he wouldn't be able to appreciate what Maxim had planned for him, especially when Maxim had gone to so much effort to get everything organised. So now the drug was wearing off, which, as far as Maxim was concerned, was pretty much perfect timing.

He looked in silence at Sejarra for a few moments, allowing the knowledge of where he was and what was about to happen to him sink into the engineer's drug-dulled consciousness. Sejarra looked around him and started to thrash about in terror, squirming bound and helpless on top of the bloody heap of corpses. Maxim grinned, and looked him straight in the eye.

'Winner takes all, Sejarra. But no hard feelings, right? After all, it's just business. Nothing personal.'

Maxim pulled the lever his hand had been resting on. The airlock hatch slid shut with an echoing metallic clang. Inside the airlock, Sejarra tried to scream, but the sound, already muffled by the gag across his mouth, was swept away in the louder scream of the sudden rushing of air as the outer hatch swung open.

'AND THE ROKS?'

'We're estimating sixteen destroyed or crippled, captain,' answered Ulanti. 'The remainder have retreated deeper into the safety of the asteroid field, where accurate surveyor scans are problematic, to say the least. We can send attack craft reconnaissance patrols in there to find them, but it's the greenies' territory, and they'll be waiting for us. It'll be a damn easy way for us to lose some good pilots.'

Semper sighed, and sat back behind his desk, thoughtfully drumming his fingers on the large ork's skull he kept there as a ceremonial trophy of his first ever boarding action and taste of close-quarters combat. As ever, victory was no assurance of the end to one's problems. The battle was won, but the full cleansing of the Mather system would take many months yet. As much as over a year, perhaps, if his officers' informed judgement that there might be as many as twenty other roks lurking undetected elsewhere in the system was accurate. They would all have to be found and destroyed, every one of them, if Battlefleet Gothic was ever to declare the Mather system finally purged of ork infestation.

Ulanti politely cleared his throat, and Semper realised that he had been pondering too long. The senior cadre of his ship's officers stood assembled in his captain's study, and they were waiting for their captain to give them their next orders. Ulanti, Nyder, Maeler and Khoir Sabattier, the ship's master of arms stood to attention before him. Beside them stood Senior Adept Volterman, one of Castaboras's techpriest lieutenants. Castaboras himself was inspecting the damage to some of the *Macharius's* more esoteric but vital control systems, and, in acknowledgement of the magos's recent actions in saving the ship from tractor beam destruction, Semper had diplomatically granted his request to send an emissary in his stead to the meeting called in the captain's study.

The tall, regal figure of Ship's Navigator Solon Cassander and the dark-robed figure of Ship's Chief Astropath, Adept Rapavna, stood towards the rear of the dark, low-ceilinged room, voluntarily removing themselves from the others in discreet understanding of the discomfort many navy officers felt in the presence of psykers. The tall, imposing figure of Commissar Koba Kyogen lounged against a wall decorated with crystal-framed images of ancient starcharts and tattered scrolls of battle honours won centuries ago by previous incumbents of the captain's chair which Semper was now sitting in.

Kyogen's position and casual stance was deliberate and meaningful. He did not stand to attention like the other navy officers, because a captain's otherwise unchallengeable authority did not apply in the case of a ship's commissar. He stood apart from the others because he was here voluntarily, and not at Semper's orders. So far, he had said nothing. His task was to observe, to watch and remember everything said and done by the *Macharius's* most senior command cadre. His holstered bolt pistol lay across the front of his immaculate, black serge uniformed coat. It was the only sidearm permitted into a captain's chambers, and it was a clear, unspoken reminder of the power of life and death which a ship's commissar held over everyone in the room.

Each officer present had made his after-battle report. Now they awaited their captain's orders on what they and his vessel would do next.

'We leave the hulks where they are,' Semper told them. 'They don't have warp drive capability, so they aren't going anywhere from here. We've accomplished what we came here to do with the destruction of *Sabretooth* and *Wolverine* and their escorts, and we've driven the remaining ork presence in the Mather system back into retreat. This system will be cleansed of any remaining greenskin presence, but it will be the task of others to finish what we have begun here. Lord Admiral Ravensburg and Battlefleet Command, in their glorious wisdom, have decided that there are other duties elsewhere which demand our immediate attention.'

The sense of barely-retrained relief from his officers was almost palpable. While none of them balked at the prospect of battle with the Emperor's enemies, neither did they much relish the idea of the long and tedious work involved in rooting out the remnants of the ork infestation of Mather, especially as it would keep them away from the crux of the real war in the Gothic sector.

Typically, it was Ulanti who was first to ask what everyone else was thinking. 'Then you've been in touch with Port Maw, sir?'

'I have,' answered Semper, indicating towards the figure of the astropath. 'Adept Rapavna has conveyed my battle report to Battlefleet Command, and we have received word back from them in return. A battle-squadron comprising of the *Ark Imperial*, two more squadrons of Cobras and a force of troop transports and warp-towed defence monitors is already in transit to the Mather system. They will arrive in several days and set up in orbit around the system's third innermost planet, which will become the home base for a rigorous scouring of any remaining greenskin presence in the system.'

Ulanti nodded. It was a good plan. The *Ark Imperial* was one of the old super-carriers of the now defunct Majestic class of battleship. Its worn-out warp engines were almost past the point of final repair, and the journey through the warp to the Mather system might be its last, but it would make a fine centre of operations for the purposes of this mission. The ork roks had proven highly vulnerable to attack craft assault, and the *Ark Imperial's* specialist reconnaissance craft and massed wings of bombers would be ideal for seeking out and destroying the things.

'Then what are our orders, captain?' ventured Castaboras's stand-in. 'The ship's sacred machine spirit is in pain. Urgent repairs are needed and sacred rites of re-consecration, and all these things can only be done in an orbital dry-dock.'

Semper held up his open hand, cutting off the tech-priest. 'Our orders, effective immediately, are to make way at once to the Ramilies star fort *Stygian*, in the Elysium system. *Drachenfels* and *Graf Orlok* are to accompany us. We'll apparently have several days there to make good any battle damage and re-crew and re-equip before the commencement of our next mission.'

Semper saw the look of dismay on the tech-priest's face. 'Have faith in the spirit of the *Macharius*, brother adept. She's been injured before, and no doubt she'll be injured again, but she's a strong, stout-hearted old maid, and I haven't seen anything in these damage reports to suggest she won't be able to make it through whatever's ahead of us.'

'Then Battlefleet Command haven't told you what that mission is, captain?'

The enquiry came from Ulanti. Semper hesitated a moment before answering. 'All I've been told is that we are to wait at *Stygian* until the arrival of the *Bernardo Gui*. It will apparently dock with *Stygian*, and a group of passengers will disembark from her and transfer over to us. What our mission and next destination will be, and exactly who these passengers are, Battlefleet Command have not yet seen fit to tell us.'

There was a pause while the others in the room digested this information. Nyder, shifting uncomfortably, was the first to break the silence.

'The *Bernardo Gui*, you say, sir? That's the vessel we are to rendezvous with?'

Semper gave a tight smile, knowing what his Master of Ordnance was really asking. 'Yes, Mister Nyder, you heard me correctly, and you know just as well as I do which branch of the Imperial service that particular vessel belongs to.'

His smile grew tighter, as he looked his officers in the eye. 'We'd better tidy the place up and have the *Macharius* looking its best for the arrival of our distinguished passengers, since it would appear, gentlemen, that we'll soon be playing host to the representatives of His Divine Majesty's most sacred and noble Inquisition.'

MINUTES LATER, AND Semper had dismissed the other men and sent them to oversee the necessary preparations for the ship's departure from the Mather system. All of them except Solon Cassander, whom Semper had requested to stay behind, ostensibly to consult with him on the safest and quickest course through the immaterium to their new destination. The *Macharius* captain had been afraid that Kyogen would stay to observe, and had been secretly relieved when the stern and silent ship's commissar had left with the others. Kyogen, a native Stranivarite, was investigating reports of some minor but troubling incident of typical below-decks mayhem and was keen to begin. Semper had not paid much attention to the details – something about a gunfight in the enginarium section, and possibly another one elsewhere too, and the disappearance of several engineering crew – and had been only too glad to see the back of the man.

Semper sat at his desk again, with Cassander seated on the other side, facing him. Semper did not consider himself to be superstitious – in many respects, he was the epitome of the hardnosed and practical-minded Schola Progenium-trained naval man – and would not wish his crew to know that, from time to time, when he felt it necessary, it was his secret custom to consult the psychic visions of the *Macharius's* Navigator. The mutant warp-sight of many Navigators could see into the future as well as into the immaterium. Solon Cassander was one so gifted, and, now, as Semper watched, the Navigator reached up to remove the gold-woven headband which he wore across his forehead. Semper tried not to stare at the unnatural eye now revealed there, larger than any normal human eye and set into the centre of the man's forehead.

The eye, the trademark of the Imperium-sanctioned and almost priceless mutation of the Navigator strain of genetically-modified humanity which allowed the mighty ships of the Imperium of Mankind to traverse the galaxy, stared back at him, eerie and unblinking. Semper knew that its mystic gaze was fixed not on him but on those images which it saw reflected across the flickering surface of the sub-empyrean, a realm which to Navigators was real and all around them, but the reality and shape of which eluded the understanding and sight of mere normal human consciousness and vision.

'Tell me what lies ahead of us, Master Cassander. Tell me what you see out there in the immaterium.'

Cassander closed his two normal eyed, frowned in concentration, and cast his gaze out into the void at his captain's command. The frown grew deeper as he focussed his concentration. Semper fancied that he saw something – brief, indistinct images of *something* – flicker across the milky surface of the Navigator's third eye, although it may only have been a trick of the low light in the room.

Finally, Cassander heaved a sigh, and opened his two normal eyes again, his third eye closing indistinctively at the same time. He secured the bindings back into place on his forehead, and leaned forward to take the glass of wine which Semper proffered to him, flavoured with silver flecks of the psycho-active substance commonly known as spook. All Navigators, even those seconded to lifetime service within the armed forces of the Imperium, belonged to the Navis Nobilite, the great aristocratic houses and merchant guilds which so dominated the Senatorum Imperialis and even commanded a place amongst the High Council of Terra itself, and Semper had not met one of their kind yet who did not enjoy a few expensive and aristocratic creature comforts. Semper waited patiently while his Navigator drank fully half the glass and composed his thoughts.

'What do you see, Master Cassander?' asked Semper, when he was sure the man was ready to speak.

The Navigator's voice was low and atonal, carrying no trace of an accent or homeworld origin. He was a typical member of his class, reared in seclusion from the rest of inferior humanity, and owing his loyalty solely to Emperor and his Navigator clan rather than any one world or region. 'As you know, captain, the gift of future-sight is never precise or fully controllable. Sometimes the warp shuns its face to those with the sight, and the vision-path to the future is blocked. Then we see nothing, and have no more knowledge of what lies ahead than any other human.'

Semper felt a surge of disappointment. 'Then you saw nothing?'

'Yes, and no, if that can be possible,' answered the Navigator. 'The path was open, but I still do not understand what it was I saw. I saw the future, Leoten, but I did not recognise its shape. It was...' He broke off, nervously draining the rest of the wine, setting the empty glass down and looking across at Semper, his normal expression of calm expectancy replaced with one of troubled nervousness. When he spoke again, it was in a voice barely more than a troubled whisper.

'Shadows, Leoten. I looked into the future, and all I found there were shadows.'

THE HARLEQUIN TROUPE had been on the move for days now, travelling by some of the webway's most secret and hidden routes, the full extent of which were known only to the oldest and most venerable of their kind. They stopped only when truly necessary, eating on the move, and even sleeping too, taking it in turns to use the *lia'dhethi* discipline of mastery of mind and body, the mind resting while the body continued its crude automaton functions. They left the webway only when necessary too, entering the real universe at several different points over the last few days, transferring between one hidden portal and another when there was no other choice, moving swiftly and silently across the surface of worlds which were many light years apart in real universe terms but only a day or two's webway travel from each other.

They did not speak unless necessary, and when they did, they never used another's name aloud. The walls of the webway were thin, and there were things swimming hungrily in the psychic ether beyond those walls, things which prowled eagerly for any clue of power or knowledge over the living, mortal inhabitants of the real universe. Even silence could be used as a weapon against the things which waited for them in the realm of the Immaterium.

The troupe was cautious and alert on every step of their journey. Many of their race thought the webway safe from the dangers which threatened them in the real universe, but those who followed the path of the Laughing God knew better. They knew that the darkest and most secret routes of the webway often hid terrible things, and that, even if many of their race could never admit it, there were those other than the scattered eldar of the craftworlds and the Exodite worlds who knew how to find and access the secret routes into the main webway.

The *athair* leader of the troupe suddenly froze in alert, as the silent mind-speech warning from the *margorach* scout ahead of them echoed through his consciousness. The rest of the troupe reacted instantly to the mutually-shared warning, dancing into position, nimble hands unhesitatingly finding and drawing forth scabbarded wraithbone swords and holstered shuriken pistols. The shifting, mystic stuff of the walls of the webway tunnel flickered and pulsed with the reflected rainbow dazzle of activated *dathedi* holo-suits.

The troupe tensed, ready for whatever threat the Death Jester scout had sensed ahead of them. The *athair* flashed an urgent mind-speech query to the black-armoured scout, demanding more information. There was a worrying pause, before he received back a confused melange of the scout's surface thoughts. He sensed doubt and fear in the Death Jester's mind, and a growing feeling of awe and disbelief.

A matching ripple of fear passed through the thoughts of the rest of the troupe. What, they wondered, could bring fear into the mind of one such as a *margorach* Harlequin, who bodily assumed the role of Death itself in the troupe's mime-pantheon?

In a flash of mind-speech, the troupe saw all that the scout saw, and instantly they knew and understood the reasons for his fear. As one, before even the *athair* could issue the mind-speech command, they dropped to the ground, sheathing their weapons, bowing their heads and kneeling in respectful abeyance to the entity now coming along the webway passage towards them.

They felt the heat of its passing, heard the heavy tread of its feet, recoiled in mental shock as they brushed minds with it and met the furnace fire of its thoughts.

They remained thus as the entity moved unseen amongst them, only daring to raise their heads once it had safely passed them by. It did not acknowledge their salute. It did not even acknowledge that it had ever been aware of their existence as it moved amongst them, its burning gaze fixed only on some remote and unknown destination.

The *athair* was the first to raise his head, not daring to look behind him but still seeing the evidence of the entity's passing. A trail of fiery footmarks, too large to belong to any mortal creature, burned into the supposedly immutable stuff of the webway tunnel's floor.

The troupe exchanged nervous, frightened glances, none daring to share their thoughts with any others, but all of them dwelling on the same terrible, awe-filled knowledge.

The burning god walked abroad, unbidden and uncontrolled. The deadly fury which was the avatar of the Bloody-Handed God was awake, and death and catastrophe surely followed in its wake

PART TWO
CONVERGENCE

TEN

THE PLANET LAY somewhere out in the barren reaches beyond the Quinrox Sound, orbiting a dwindling pair of binary dwarfs. Both stars were dying, one already all but extinguished, slowly collapsing into a pulsar and beaming out its distress as a long and silent electronic death-scream to an uncaring universe. Its twin faced its own imminent death with a little more dignity, diminishing quietly but steadily over the long millennia, the stellar heat of its nuclear fires fading and dying, the very substance of its aeons-old body dissipating and fading away in faint, fiery ribbons into the surrounding void.

The world had two remote and distant siblings. Once it had had more, but the fierce gravitic forces exerted by the binary twins had long since taken their toll, and all that now remained of these worlds were thin garlands of broken rock, strung out in long, elliptical orbits round their murderously uncaring parent stars. One of the remaining siblings swung about in an eccentric orbit of both stars, captured in the orbit of first one then the other, alternately freezing and burning as the parent stars fought a jealous gravity tide tug

of war over their errant child, each seeking to draw it as close
to itself as it could. It was completely uninhabitable, rent
constantly by earthquakes, volcanic eruptions and gravity
storms which stripped away whole segments of its ravaged
planetary surface. The process of its inevitable destruction
was already far advanced, and, in time, it too would end its
days as a scattered belt of asteroid fields, forever orbiting in
mute testimony to its two parents' murderous rivalry.

The other planetary sibling was an adopted orphan: a lone
cosmic wanderer, really more a giant meteorite or rogue
moon, which had long ago been captured in the twins' eager
grasp and had since assumed an eccentric and wild orbit on
the remote fringes of the system, resisting its adoptive parents' insistent but gradually weakening pull and remaining
far beyond both the knowledge of its two siblings and that
invisible but fixed point past which no life could ever flourish upon its dismal and barren surface.

No, the planet drifted alone, safely secured in a narrow
marginal orbit between its two warring parents, heedless of
the fate which had befallen its less fortunate siblings.

It had had several names in its time. Names given to it by
the ancient races that had trodden the stars long before the
birth of humanity, and which had built their monuments
and cities upon its surface. Those races were long gone now.
They had become less than the drifting dust which was now
mostly all that remained of those same supposedly inde-
structible cities and monuments. After these ancient ones
had come the eldar, following in the footsteps of these older
races and seeking to recapture their lost glories for themselves. For a while, the eldar had flourished, achieving many
of their highest and most secret aims, and then, in one brief
but terrible instant, they had fallen, betrayed by their own
hubris and secret, dreadful weakness. After the cataclysm,
the ones who were left had mostly abandoned worlds such
as this, retreating into their scattered and drifting craftworlds
and often closing and sealing behind them the webway por-
tals which led to these now dead and empty worlds.

The planet's surface had known the tread of eldar feet
since then, but these new ones had come like thieves in the
night, moving swiftly and in fear where once their ancestors

had walked proud and confident. They had entered the halls and homes of their ancestors, exploring them in a manner more akin to nervous and over-awed tomb raiders than as presumptive heirs to their ancestors' fallen glories.

After the eldar had come the humans, briefly and almost insignificantly. They had come several thousand years ago, just another explorator team investigating the surface of another dead and empty world. They had made their studies, measured the monuments and scratched around amongst the time-worn ruins, tabulated their findings, then had left again with barely a backwards glance. Just another dead and empty world, they surmised, just another one of thousands of such worlds within their Imperium, an Imperium which, unknown to them, had been built in wilful ignorance upon the ruins of so many other, greater and more ancient civilisations which had ruled the galaxy long before the age of man.

Before leaving, though, they had given the world a name: a name which had only recently been remembered for the first time in centuries. Orders from the office of no less a personage than Lord Admiral Ravensburg himself had sent anxious teams of scribes scurrying into the deepest labyrinth reaches of the Administratum archives on Port Maw in search of the urgently required information. The dusty and long-forgotten transcripts of that ancient explorator mission had been successfully found and recovered, and, once again, the planet's human-given name, a name most probably assigned to it at random by some bored and now long-dead explorator scribe, had been spoken aloud for perhaps the first time ever.

Stabia, they called it. A forgotten and utterly insignificant world on the remotest fringes of the Quinrox Sound, and upon which was focussed the gaze of a select handful of the most powerful men in the Gothic sector. And, beyond them, the secret gaze of others, non-human as well as those who, no matter what they had once been, were now something less than human, was also turned towards Stabia.

The world continued serene and undisturbed in its long slumber, but perhaps even it itself was aware of the forces now descending on it. They came through the warp and through the myriad, twisting paths of the webway, racing towards the prize.

Towards Stabia. Towards the moment of convergence. Towards the shadow point.

Once, long ago, the world now known as Stabia had known the touch of greatness, as the ancient eldar races and those who had sought to follow in their footsteps had walked its surface and left their hidden marks upon it. Now, and soon, Stabia would know something of greatness once more, for it would be upon its lifeless surface that the fate of the Gothic sector, of hundreds of inhabited worlds, and, perhaps the entire Imperium of Mankind itself, would be decided.

In their cells and reliquaries all over the Gothic sector, blind astropath seers consulted the ever-mutable faces of the sacred cards of the Imperial tarot, and paused in fear and wonder at what they found.

In the dome of the crystal seers on far-distant craftworld An-Iolsus, where the dreaming souls of dead eldar gazed forever up through the transparent diamond skin of the dome high above them at the panoply of stars, a faint current of unease breezed through the crystalline forest, disturbing the dreamers' reveries.

In his secure and heavily-guarded sanctum buried deep within the decks of his venerable battle barge flagship *Harbinger of Doom*, Abaddon the Despoiler listened to the prophecy-whispers of his most favoured pet daemon-things and looked out into the face of the warp with his Chaos-given mystic sight. His plans were well advanced now. His allies were not to be trusted, and would certainly betray or abandon him when it best suited their own purposes, he knew, but the factor had long ago been taken into consideration, and the necessary precautions taken. After all, he reminded himself, smiling briefly at the thought, why else would he have entrusted such a task to a treacherous viper such as Siaphas?

Still, there were uncharacteristic doubts in the mind of the Chaos Warmaster. The daemon-prophecies were confused and contradictory, while his own mystic sight could make little sense of the blurred and shadowy future-images which moved fleetingly across the face of the warp. Deep down, the Chaos Warmaster was troubled. His daemon sword Drach'nyen, hanging on the wall in its jewel-encrusted scabbard of tan-hide Space Marine skin, sensed its master's disquiet and made a long, keening sound of displeasure. Beyond the void-shielded entrance to Abaddon's quarters, his phalanx of Black Legion Terminator bodyguards heard the sound and looked at each other in apprehension, understanding what it meant. The command would not come from the Despoiler for perhaps another minute or two, but already one of the Terminators had activated his vox-link to the slave decks below to order living flesh to be brought up to feed the sword's blood-thirst and help assuage the Warmaster's mood.

ELSEWHERE, IN A place remote from but connected to all other places, other minds and eyes looked at the hidden face of events still to come. They saw the same shadows, the same blurred confusion, but these watchers were unlike those others. They and their kind were masters of the shadows, long at home amongst the dark and hidden places of the universe, and they understood the shadow images as all others did not. They saw the shape of the future and they rejoiced at the death and slaughter to come, for it was all that they had anticipated.

Or, at least, so they thought.

By warp and webway, the players in the coming drama drew closer towards the meeting place. Stabia awaited them. The *fhaisorr'ko*, the shadow point, awaited them too. As they approached, their fatelines become even more complex and entangled. The many distorted, mocking faces presented by the mystic shadow point to any who tried to divine its secrets now blurred and changed again, the patterns of intersecting fatelines changing by the moment. Perhaps the very oldest of the ones in the dome of crystal seers, the ones whose life memories reached beyond the dreadful time of the Fall, could have understood what was happening, but they were mostly gone now, their spirits completely subsumed within the soul stream of the infinity circuit, and their voices had not been heard since before even wise old Kariadryl was born. The knowledge was gone now, just another marker on the path of a dying race's slow slide into extinction, and so no eldar alive in the last few thousand years could have known the secret understood by their forebears.

The *fhaisorr'ko* itself is a trap. It does not hide the future from view, for there is no pre-determined future to conceal. Try to penetrate its mysteries and it will show you the future which most favours you, but the shape of that future is no more real than the phantom images which conceal it.

Perhaps Kariadryl understood something of the true dangerous nature of the shadow point, but these darker ones, who had fallen far further and far more terribly than their one-time craftworld brethren ever had, did not, and, in their cruel arrogance and conceit, they had already become entrapped by the beguiling falsehood of the *fhaisorr'ko*. They did not know what the ancient pre-Fall eldar had known: the future within the *fhaisorr'ko* is not set. Anyone within the shadow point can, by their own actions, change their future and that of all others. Nothing is known. Nothing is pre-determined. All is there to be won by any of the participants in the coming shadow play.

IN THE ENCLOSED shell of his armoured strategium, the crippled human husk that was Erwin Ramas floated in an all-enveloping and protecting environment of synthetic amniotic fluid, surrounded by the myriad of wires, tubes, nourishment feeds and tendril-like mechadendrites which kept him alive and connected to the living mind of his vessel. He was asleep, or at least the nearest thing to sleep he would ever know, but, while he slept, that part of him which was so intimately involved with the innermost workings of his ship was awake and active. It communed with the *Drachenfels's* machine-mind, browsing through the never-ending stream of information flowing through the ship's mighty logic engines. It assessed surveyor and auspex readings, and kept half an eye on the ongoing status of the ship's weapons and defence systems. It monitored too the steady input of information from the ship's non-mechanical components: duty logs and crew assessments from his officers, damage repair updates from the vast teams of ratings still slaving round the clock to make good the last of the damage suffered in the battle against the greenskins.

Meanwhile, as that mind impulse-linked part of him continued to function, the human part of him slept, reliving the trauma of old battles and old wounds.

'Enemy contact four hundred kilometres to our rear, and starboard! Sigmuth's balls, look how fast it's coming in. Where the hell were our close-range defence augurs? How did he get in so close to us?'

For perhaps the thousandth time in the last one hundred and fifty years, Erwin Ramas heard the panicked voice of his second-in-command as it rang out across the bridge of the ship. Vhoten Kamares, that had been his name. A good enough number two, Ramas had always thought, but too prone to fright, and almost certainly never destined to rise any higher in Imperial Navy service than the rank he already held.

For perhaps the thousandth time, Ramas turned to look at the image on the bank of augur screens. The image captured upon them was simultaneously beguiling and terrifying. The eldar ship raced towards them with its solar sails fully extended, and, for a moment, the pragmatic Ramas was uncharacteristically reminded of the old spaceman's myths of the vacuum valkyries, vast, angel-like creatures which drifted serenely amongst the scattered wreckage of the aftermath of space battles, gathering up the souls of the dead and dying aboard the burned-out hulks and carrying them off to their earned place by the side of the Emperor. The ominous black maws of the ship's forward-mounted torpedo tubes, however, and the clear and deadly intent with which the vessel bore down on its intended prey, gave immediate lie to this particular piece of fanciful spacer legend.

'Hard to starboard,' Ramas heard himself say, for perhaps the thousandth time. 'Deploy starboard side turrets quintus to octus, and let's give those xenos bastards a good, clean taste of lance fire!'

They were patrolling the trade route circuit between Sicyon and Bladen in the Lysades sub-sector. Nothing too special or demanding. Just another routine patrol mission to fly the aquila eagle standard across one small part of the

Gordon Rennie

Emperor's domain to assure or remind the Emperor's nervous and/or potentially rebellious subjects that the forces of the Imperium were still keeping a careful watch over their worlds.

The eldar attack had come out of nowhere, unprovoked and without warning. They had no way of knowing what the alien ship was even doing here, on the fringes of the sparsely-populated and unimportant Lamont system. Ramas doubted they ever would find out, because, as soon as the attack began, it became his firm intention to reduce the alien vessel to just so much drifting space debris.

Now, as Ramas watched the images projected on his bridge's augur screens, he felt the first stirrings of secret doubt about whether he could make good on that promise. The eldar ship seemed to flicker in and out of existence, its image actually jumping confusedly from one place to another in space. At times, Ramas saw multiple images appearing around it, often merging and blurring into each other. Whatever damnable alien technology the vessel was using to defend itself, it had the same confusing effect on his gunners' targeting systems as it did on the human eye. Lance beams cut through space around the oncoming ship, probing in vain to find it. Ramas saw one energy beam harmlessly pass right through what he would have sworn had been the real target and not one of its phantom after-images.

Ghosts, he thought to himself. It's like trying to fight ghosts.

The catastrophe, when it happened, came without warning. As far as Ramas and his officers were aware, they had never even known the eldar ship had launched any torpedoes, not until the brace of missiles, moving almost impossibly fast and seemingly undetectable to the Imperium vessel's senses, struck the base of the *Drachenfels's* command tower.

An explosion, ferocious, sudden and terrifying, ripped through the floor of the ship's bridge. Ramas saw his second-in-command decapitated by a flying piece of torn deck-plating, and then the blast wave struck him and blew him across the entire deck, smashing him with bone-crushing force against the far wall and impaling him upon the beak point of a gargoyle-faced atmo-breather pipe. Incredibly, Ramas struggled for a few seconds to pull himself off the thing, before realising, just as a second and more powerful blast ripped up through the gaping hole in the floor, that the effort was futile since the first blast had removed his left arm and both of his legs.

For the thousandth time, Ramas saw the eruption of flame from the torpedo-destroyed decks below. For the thousandth time, he saw it burst across the command deck in a living wall of flame, immolating screaming officers, crewmen and adepts as it swept towards him.

For the thousandth time, he opened his mouth to scream too, but all was lost in the hungry roar of flame as the heat consumed most of his lungs and burned away the flesh of his face.

His last conscious memory, before he mercifully passed out, before the rescue crews cut their way into the wreckage of the command deck and found him impossibly hanging there, barely alive, was of seeing the image of their attacker on a cracked but still-functioning augur screen, as the eldar ship executed a graceful, looping turn around its victim and moved off dispassionately towards the system's edge, swiftly disappearing into the blackness of space.

They had had the *Drachenfels* at their mercy, and, in their supreme arrogance, had disdained to deliver the killing blow.

A thousand times he had relived these memories. A thousand times he had relived every moment of the crippling of his ship and the destruction of his body. And, a thousand times, he swore he would one day exact his revenge for what they had done to him and his ship.

Fully awake now, he linked his consciousness into his ship's gunnery systems, for the thousandth time rerunning the unique firing solutions and target pattern equations which he had long ago laid into the ship's logic engines. Trapped as he was in this wreck of a body inside his strategium home, he had had plenty of time and opportunity to prepare for another encounter with the eldar in the last century and a half, should any of their kind ever cross his path again.

Yes, just let the arrogant alien bastards come, he told himself, smiling a lipless smile. Next time, he and his ship would be ready for them.

'PREPARE YOURSELF, MAGE. They are coming.'

Siaphas turned at the sound of the eldar lord's whispering, sibilant voice, the Chaos sorcerer silently angry and alarmed that his mystic senses had not earlier detected the creature's approach.

There is still so much I do not know or understand about these things, he thought once more, again questioning Abaddon's wisdom in forming a pact with such strange and unknowable allies.

The eldar lord stood there in the dim light of the chamber. The surrounding shadows seemed to enfold around him, making him part of themselves. Siaphas's Chaos-altered eyes and mystic warp-sight allowed his gaze to see far beyond mere human limits, but the shadows in which these creatures so often surrounded themselves defied even his abilities to properly see through.

Dark eldar, he thought to himself. An appropriate name, although one he dared not utter in front of them.

The eldar lord's name was Kailasa – Kailasa of the Kabal of the Poison Heart, in the clannish and baroque way these creatures termed themselves. He was entirely encased in armour, coloured dark red and streaked through with shots of some strange black material which glittered and shifted when he moved, breaking up the shape of his body. Whether this was for decoration or, more likely, designed for a defensive purpose in battle, was something the Chaos sorcerer had yet to discover. Cruel, mono-molecular edged blades ran down the seams of the limbs of the eldar's armoured suit, and one hand ended in an ominous, lumpy metal protuberance which could variously be, Siaphas speculated, either an unfamiliar type of hand-held weapon, a mechanical limb attachment, part of the eldar's armour or even a combination of all three.

The dark eldar lord wore a full closed helm, styled in the same design as his suit. Like many of his kind, Kailasa seemed to prefer to go about his business masked, even here, aboard the relative safety of his own cruiser vessel. Even so, Siaphas could imagine the set of the kabal commander's features beneath the burnished and featureless face of the helm: his skin pale and taut across his slender eldar skull, his eyes dark and glittering, full of cruel malice, his lips fixed in a constant and secret arrogant sneer.

Siaphas had served several lifetimes in the court of the Despoiler and had travelled extensively throughout the daemon worlds of the Eye of Terror at the bidding of both Abaddon and Zaraphiston. He thought he had encountered evil and malicious cunning in all its forms, in the inexhaustible variety of the monstrous and degenerate shapes thrown up by the whim of the Powers of Chaos and lovingly nurtured along and brought to full, abominable fruition by the daemonic forces within the Eye of Terror, but these dark eldar creatures were of a more terrible nature than anything he could ever have imagined. He had seen something of the place Commorragh, their hidden fastness concealed within the vast, mystic labyrinth they called the webway, and he was both awestruck and repelled by the cruel depravities which these beings, unclaimed and unwarped by the tainting glories of Chaos, could devise using nothing more than their own still-mortal intelligence and imagination.

Pure hate, that was what they were, he had realised from the time he had spent in their company. Their hate was stellar in its pureness and intensity, directed at a pitiless universe which so uncaringly reduced them to such degenerate circumstances; hate directed at those who had once been their race-kin, and who had not been consumed by the same dire fate which had befallen them.

And hatred too, directed most terribly and secretly at themselves. Siaphas did not yet know the secrets these dark eldar creatures hid about themselves and their past, but he knew that they had once been something far greater than the malice-consumed things which they now were. They secretly hated all that they were and even more secretly coveted all that they had once been, and so they took their pent-up fury out on all other races in the universe.

Hate consumed them, and, Siaphas was sure, fear drove them. They were filled with an overriding fear of something,

something that loomed vast and terrible over them, blotting out all other concerns. Siaphas did not know what the root of this fear was, although he intended to find out, and soon, but already he realised that, in combination with that all-consuming hatred, it was the source of everything which made the dark eldar what they now were.

Yes, dangerous allies, Siaphas reminded himself. But, potentially, very useful ones too. These creatures were a weapon; a weapon which in the right hands could advance the one who knew how to wield it correctly to unparalleled heights of power.

Had the Despoiler made a dual mistake in sending him here, the Chaos sorcerer wondered? The first mistake was perhaps trying to make an alliance with such beings, but the second was surely in bringing Siaphas and these creatures together. The Despoiler, in his conceit and arrogance, thought that the dark eldar existed only to serve him and his purposes, but Siaphas already knew that beings such as these did not comply so easily with the plots and plans of others.

Perhaps, the Chaos sorcerer mused pleasurably to himself, it took a schemer of his own intelligence and vision to truly understand the nature of these dark eldar, and to realise that, with the correct measure of cunning and manipulation, it might be possible to engineer an alliance of mutual benefit with such as they.

Siaphas smiled again at the thought. Perhaps, after so many thousands of years of dominance, Abaddon the Despoiler was indeed finally beginning to lose his grip, for how else could he have made the potentially fatal error of delivering so potent a weapon as these dark eldar into the hands of one such as Siaphas?

'My lord Kailasa,' the Chaos sorcerer bowed, displaying all the gestures of false abeyance and respect which had served him so well during centuries of service in the court of Abaddon the Despoiler, while adding an extra and subtle flourish to his body language picked up from his observations of the mannerism of his dark eldar hosts. 'You are certain of this? I have cast my own augur-spells, and have seen nothing, although I readily admit my own humble inferiority in such matters, in comparison to whatever scrying methods your lordship and his servants have call on.'

Behind his burnished mask, Kailasa smiled in amusement. The mon-keigh sought to use him for its own purposes, he knew. It pleased the kabal lord to continue this amusing fiction for the mon-keigh creature's benefit, if only because it made the end all the more pleasurable when, at the close of the game, the would-be manipulator realised the extent to which he himself had been manipulated right from the very start.

'We are certain,' Kailasa said simply, knowing how much his answer would only further set the mon-keigh's mind pondering. 'Your own forces are ready?'

'They are, my lord,' said the mon-keigh, executing another overly-extravagant and crudely-interpreted flourish. 'They await my signal. When do we make our move?'

'We allow our enemies to gather. We allow them to get a sense of each other. We allow their mutual fears and suspicion to grow.'

'And then what, lord Kailasa?'

Another bow, another flourish, more ridiculous mon-keigh apeing of eldar mannerisms. Kailasa allowed the question to hang in the air for a few seconds before he finally deigned to answer.

'And then, mage, we begin the hunt.'

ELEVEN

'MY COMPLIMENTS, SEMPER. You command a fine vessel, and lay on an even finer spread at your captain's table!'

There was a polite ripple of laughter at Pardain's joke as the admiral crammed another forkful of Stranivarite borsch meat into his mouth. Red juice dribbled down the man's chin, and he dabbed at it with a napkin as he soaked up the mirth of his fellow diners.

Despite appearances, the fat, aged and ruddy-faced rear admiral was nobody's fool. Lothar Pardain – Lothar Rodriguez Ravensburg-Pardain, to give him his full name – was uncle to the commander of Battlefleet Gothic. Unlike other members of the vast and disparate Ravensburg clan such as captain of the *Graf Orlok*, Titus von Blucher, however, Pardain owed his position far more to ability and shrewd intelligence than common nepotism. Semper knew his Battlefleet Gothic history, and knew that Pardain, before accepting a senior staff position at Battlefleet Command on Port Maw, had been a highly able and distinguished commander in his own right. His treatises on orbital siege and close in-system fighting were required reading during Semper's days as a young officer.

'I don't know what qualifications you have as a connoisseur, admiral,' said Semper, lifting his glass in acknowledgement to Pardain and raising another polite ripple of laughter from the other diners, 'but, coming from the man who commanded the battlecruiser *Manifest Destiny* during the Vara Campaign and who also carried the day in the Holy Emperor's favour during the Kierkegaard Heresy, I shall humbly accept your first observation as a compliment of the very highest kind. Your health, admiral.'

Semper downed the glass – full to the brim with the peppery red Cypra Mundian liqueur which the rear admiral had gifted to the ship when he first came aboard at Elysium – in one swift motion, choking back the taste which, as a young cadet at naval academy, he had quickly come to loathe.

The others at the table followed suit. Pardain accepted the toast and then downed his measure in the same way, laughing as he slammed the empty glass down on the table before him.

'Ha, no matter how long it's been, you don't forget the taste of *raikhi* in a hurry, do you, Semper? Emperor only knows why we in the Segmentum Obscuras battlefleets are required by tradition to drink the damnably foul stuff all the time. I once met a Master of Ordnance who told me that the Fury pilots aboard his carrier ship mixed it with promethium fuel from their own fighters for new arrivals aboard ship to drink as some kind of initiation rite into their squadron. Unfortunately, the man was unable to tell me whether, as I suspect, the resulting concoction actually improved the taste of the original drink!'

There was more laughter from the other diners, but this time it was more sincere and heartfelt, encouraged all the further by Pardain's own bellowing laughter to the punchline of his own joke. The mood round the table, until now stiff and formal, palpably relaxed and Semper mentally raised another glass to the rear admiral in appreciation of the adroitness at which the wily old command staffer had broken the ice at the meal.

Gordon Rennie

No, Rear Admiral Lothar Pardain-Ravensburg, holder of
the Obscuras Honorifica, the Order of the Gothic Star crimson class and the Golden Seal of Terra, was nobody's fool,
and it was not difficult to understand why Lord Admiral
Ravensburg had sent him along on this mission as his own
personal envoy and observer.

Pardain crammed in another mouthful of food – Semper
had not been keeping count, but believed that the rear admiral was now on his third plateful – and signalled for one of
the nearby attendants to refill his glass, waving away the
proffered bottle of raikhi.

'Away with that devil's brew, boy,' he jovially told the nervous young ensign. 'Find me a carafe or two of amasec or
some of that agreeably potent Stranivarite spirit which old
Admiral Haasen, Emperor rest his soul, once had the good
grace to introduce me to. Search the ship from prow to stern,
if need be. I know your captain must have a secret store of
the good stuff hidden somewhere!'

More laughter. More breaking of the ice. Semper glanced
down the table, taking stock of the situation. Ulanti, seated
several places down, was talking to the grey and gaunt Commodore Neyland, Pardain's aide-de-camp. Despite the
difference in the two men's ages and temperaments, they
seemed to find common cause in both being blueblood aris-
tocrats of suitably fine and venerable stock. Neyland came
from some far-flung line of nobility which had an impressively tenacious grasp on power in several star systems
within the Gethsemane sub-sector, and Semper looked forward to a full briefing from his second-in-command on
anything relevant to their mission by the Port Maw staff officer. Semper assumed that any titbits seemingly dropped by
accident by Neyland in the course of casual conversation
would be deliberately-revealed information coming, in the
end, from Pardain himself.

Further down the table, Broton Styre and Remus Nyder
exchanged a raucous and increasingly lewd series of anec-
dotes between themselves as the meal continued and the
drink continued to flow, while, seated at the far end of the
table, even Commissar Kyogen deigned to exchange a few
words with his closest dinner neighbour. Semper tried hard

not to stare, struck by the strangely random thought that, up until this moment, he doubted that he had ever even seen the relentlessly stern Ship's Commissar do anything as mundane as actually eating a meal in other human company.

Occasionally, Kyogen would look up and glower in disapproval towards Semper's end of the table. Semper, following the commissar's latest frowning gaze, saw the figure of Chief Petty Officer Maxim Borusa standing to attention in full dress uniform behind where Ulanti was sitting. If the big Stranivarite was aware of the unfriendly attention of the *Macharius's* senior Ship's Commissar, he gave no indication. Semper frowned, sensing coming trouble between the two. He knew something of Borusa's below-decks activities, but feigned to turn a deaf ear to any reports on the subject which managed to reach him. Such things had always gone on aboard the vessels of His Divine Majesty's Imperial Navy, and it was a foolish captain who did not realise that these kind of illicit arrangements, if kept within reason, were necessary for the smooth running of any ship and its crew.

Also, he was forced to admit to himself, he had a grudging admiration for the big hiveworld rogue. He had seen the man in action during the events on Belatis, when Borusa had actually saved his life, and Semper had long ago decided that, even if he were an unrepentant cutthroat gangster and killer, Maxim Borusa was still exactly the kind of man he would want by his side in a tight situation.

Still, if Commissar Kyogen was gunning for the *Macharius's* most valuable and notorious chief petty officer then that was Borusa's look-out, and Semper couldn't and wouldn't intervene if the commissar gathered enough evidence to allow him to take typically swift and summary action against Borusa.

Mindful of his duties as host, Semper turned his attention back to the rest of the table. His other guests, seated on the opposite side of the long table from the navy officers, were noticeably less ebullient in their conversation habits. Semper imagined that the servants of the Holy Orders of the Emperor's Inquisition were not usually selected for service in the Imperium's most arcane and secretive organisation with their more garrulous qualities in mind. Nevertheless, Werner

Maeler seemed to have struck up a tentative exchange with
the Inquisition man seated across from him early in the
meal, and now the two men were deep in conversation. Semper recognised the man as Haller Stavka, Inquisitor Horst's
chief lieutenant. When the inquisitor and his retinue came
aboard, and even before Semper had been introduced to the
man, he recognised Stavka for the ex-arbiter he clearly once
had been. The man was in mufti, wearing a plain black and
grey bodyglove and a rough woollen waistcoat, but, even
without seeing and recognising the tell-tale justice eagle
aquila tattoo on his firmly-muscled shoulder, there was no
mistaking him for anything other than the highly capable
and no doubt brutally lethal servant of the Imperium which
he most assuredly was.

Inquisitor Horst, seated beside his chief lieutenant and
directly across from Pardain, was still predictably much of
an enigma to the officers and crew of the *Macharius*. Tall,
thin and greying – he showed all the signs of expensive and
subtle rejuve treatment, and Semper could only make a haphazard guess at his age as being somewhere between sixty or
as much as four or five times that figure – he was the typical
vidpict propaganda drama image of an Imperial inquisitor,
right down to the Inquisition skull emblem seal of office
which he wore upon his black mesh-leather coat, even at the
dinner table.

Semper knew that many Imperial inquisitors possessed
some form of psychic ability. Semper had the typical loyal
Imperial servant's quiet dread of those touched by the mystic properties of the warp and the things which lurked
within it. Despite this, his position as a commander of a
vessel of the Imperial Navy meant that he was frequently
forced to consort with psychically-endowed Imperial servants such as astropaths and Navigators, and he was aware
of the strange and unsettling sense of otherness which surrounded psykers like an invisible cloak. He got no such
sense from Horst on the several occasions he had met him
since the inquisitor and his retinue came aboard the
Macharius. Nevertheless, it was seemingly some kind of pre-
scient sense which caused Horst to glance up at that
moment and catch Semper watching him.

Horst held his gaze. Sensing a conversational opening, Semper made his play.

'I trust the quarters you and your staff have been given are comfortable and adequate for your purposes, inquisitor?'

'They are most satisfactory, commodore. In return, I trust your officers haven't been too discomforted by having to share quarters for the duration of this voyage?'

'Not as far as I know,' answered Semper, all too aware of the endless litany of complaints of the thirty or forty of his junior officers who had been evicted from their quarters to make room for Horst and his servants.

'I'm curious, though, inquisitor,' continued Semper, 'I admit to having encountered few servants of the Inquisition during my own time of service in the navy, but I wasn't aware that inquisitors travelled with such large personal staffs.'

Horst paused, laying down his glass of amasec. 'The Inquisition is a broad church, commander,' he answered, looking Semper in the eye. 'We all serve the same purpose, my brethren and I, although our methods and philosophies may differ. Some philosophies more than others, perhaps,' he added as a musing afterthought, taking another sip of the fiery spirit. 'While some of my brother inquisitors travel almost incognito and surround themselves with only the smallest band of followers seconded to their service, I believe that the purposes of the Inquisition and the Imperium as a whole are best served by an inquisitor's full use of the power and authority invested in him.'

'How many do you have in your personal staff?' asked Pardain, joining the conversation.

'Ordinarily? Never anything less than between fifty and sixty at any one time,' answered the inquisitor. 'But an inquisitor has the entire resources of the Imperium to draw on, so, when necessary, when I decide that the situation demands it, I have often had good call to second many more than that into my temporary service.'

He looked again at Semper and Pardain. 'Many, many more than that,' he repeated again, significantly.

Both navy officers could not fail to pick up his meaning. Pardain cleared his throat noisily then drained the last of the contents of his glass. Even before he set it back down on the table, the ensign attendant was already starting to refill it.

'Three capital vessel ships of the line, not to mention two Sword class frigates and all the attack craft squadrons aboard this very splendid vessel. You do yourself too little credit, inquisitor. I've known entire planets taken with a smaller "temporarily seconded staff" than the one you have under your command here.' Pardain paused, wiping his lips on a napkin, and gestured towards Semper. 'The good commodore here thought he was merely transporting an honoured guest, but now he learns that in fact he was welcoming aboard his new commander in chief when you transferred over to the *Macharius* at Elysium!'

Despite the apparent humour in Pardain's voice, Semper was uncomfortably aware of the rear admiral's barely-concealed anger at the idea that the naval vessels and their crews might be under Horst's direct command if the inquisitor deemed such action necessary. Aware of the long-standing historical enmity between the Inquisition and the most senior levels of Battlefleet Gothic Command, Semper felt that some subtle diplomacy was called for.

'As you say, inquisitor, and like you and your comrades in the Inquisition, we all serve in different ways, but we still all serve the same purpose. My ship, my crew and my own loyalty to the Emperor are all at your disposal, should you so wish them.'

Horst nodded in polite gratitude in reply to Semper's words. Pardain followed up with a more measured reply of his own.

'As is my loyalty. I meant no disrespect, of course, inquisitor, but I'm sure our good Commodore Semper and his officers would be more assured of the role you perhaps intend for them to play if they actually knew more of the purpose of this mission?'

Horst smiled. 'I thought the Lord Admiral's orders were clear on the matter, Admiral Pardain. We will take up rendezvous station in far orbit around the world of Stabia and await further orders.'

Yes, but who is it that we're supposed to be having this rendezvous with, thought Semper to himself? He wondered again about the possibility of Horst possessing some kind of psychic ability as the inquisitor looked over at him and smiled.

'Patience, commodore. I promise you'll be fully briefed when we reach the rendezvous point.'

A junior helm officer entered the dining room and nervously hurried over to Semper, whispering something urgently into his captain's ear. Semper laid down his cutlery, carefully wiped his lips with a napkin, and rose to his feet. The other conversation round the table died away. The senior officers of the *Macharius* looked expectantly towards their captain.

'I look forward to finally learning more about this mission, inquisitor, especially since it appears it will be occurring even earlier than expected.' He looked towards his officers, who rose as one from the table. For the men of the *Macharius*, at least, the meal was now over and duty called once more.

'Gentlemen, our Ship's Navigator has surpassed himself once more. Our voyage is ahead of schedule and we'll shortly be arriving at our destination. Duty positions, gentlemen. We exit the warp in less than one hour.'

IN A SERIES of closely synchronised energy eruptions, the *Macharius* and its sister vessels burst through the barrier of the immaterium and re-entered the real universe on the edge of the Stabia system.

The *Macharius* led the way, flanked on either side by its two companions, *Drachenfels* and *Graf Orlok*. Two Sword class frigates, the *Volpone* and the *Mosca*, followed in the larger vessels' warp wakes, immediately separating away from the three capital ships to form their own squadron formation.

Surveyor and augur scans from all five vessels probed into the unfamiliar reaches of the system, searching for any source of danger to the Imperial vessels. Quickly, and one by one, the captains of each vessel received the collected information from their bridge crews.

'The system is clear, captain,' reported Ulanti. 'No signs of any potential hostiles or any hazards to navigation, other than those already charted.'

Semper nodded, and studied the data-slate summary of the surveyor scan findings. 'So what do you think, Mister Ulanti?'

'I think, captain, that if I were planning to lay an ambush for someone then this would be the perfect spot to do so. You could hide a Ramilies star-fort or two in the electronic backwash from that damned pulsar and any recently-arriving vessel here would be none the wiser from the scrambled surveyor readings it would get back from the thing. Emperor only knows how many ships you could cloak in amongst those asteroid belts.'

Semper smiled. 'Agreed, Mister Ulanti. By the time you get close enough in-system to see what might be hiding in the petticoats of that pulsar star, then whatever's waiting for you in those rock fields would have had plenty of opportunity to jump out and bite you on the arse.'

Now Ulanti smiled. 'So what are your orders, captain?'

'We're Battlefleet Gothic, Mister Ulanti,' came the expected and welcome reply. 'The best damn fleet in the best damn segmentum in the whole damn galaxy, and we don't turn tail at the suggestion of the possibility of trouble.'

'Indeed not, captain,' said Ulanti, taking his role in the traditional and well-loved old navy man's joke. 'After all, that's what the Holy Emperor, in His divine wisdom, created the battlefleets of the Segmentums Solar, Tempestus and Ultima for.'

'Indeed so, Mister Ulanti. Signal the battle-squadron – all vessels to continue in-system on their current course and speed. Defence shields raised and fully charged. Long-range surveyor scans at maximum powers. Any scan anomalies to be reported at once and fully catalogued and investigated.'

Semper caught the querying glance from his second-in-command.

'We're Battlefleet Gothic, Hito, and that means we don't run away from a scrap, but it also means that we don't go running blind straight into the jaws of trouble like a bunch of over-zealous and battle-eager Space Marines.'

'A sound policy, commodore, although perhaps it's best for you that there aren't any brethren of the Adeptus Astartes around here to hear you express such sentiments.'

Semper turned, seeing Horst entering the command deck and coming towards him. He was accompanied by his Arbites right-hand man, Stavka, who was now wearing a flak vest and a holstered bolt pistol harness. With them also was the inquisitor's other main lieutenant. Semper had only briefly glimpsed the man when he had first come aboard the *Macharius* and he had not attended the earlier meal, even though an invitation had been extended to him. Semper tried hard not to stare too much in curiosity at the glowing circuit patterns of electro-glyph markings on the man's face and shaven skull, nor at the unfamiliar nature of the man's cyber-adaptations. Emperor knows, the tech-priest servants of the Adeptus Mechanicus were common enough aboard an Imperial warship, especially on the command deck, but Semper had never before encountered one such as this.

Officer of the Watch Broton Styre and his armsmen guards bristled in righteous indignation at the sight of the sidearm openly worn by the ex-Arbites man. It was bad enough that non-naval personnel had entered the bridge without first seeking the captain's permission, but the fact that at least one of them – and Semper suspected that Horst rarely if ever went about unarmed – was blatantly carrying a firearm, the most severe kind of breach of command deck security imaginable to the navy men. Semper quelled their indignation with a subtle glance. As with so many other things this was yet another example of the fact that the members of the Inquisition seemed to operate under entirely different rules than those which applied to the more lowly servants of the Imperium of Mankind.

'Inquisitor Horst, welcome to the bridge of His Divine Majesty's Ship, the *Lord Solar Macharius*,' noted Semper, dryly.

If the inquisitor detected any irony in Semper's welcome, he gave no indication. Instead, he indicated the figure of his tech-priest advisor. 'Commodore, with your permission, I would like my associate Monomachus to check your surveyor readings and possibly make some adjustments to their frequency range.'

Navy captains had been known to throw civilians not just off their bridge but right off their ship for such apparent impertinence, but Semper knew that, sadly, such an option did not apply in this case. He acquiesced to the inquisitor's request with a simple gesture.

Monomachus went to work at the bridge's surveyor section. Anxious and irritated surveyor officers hovered around him, maintaining a suspicious watch on everything he was doing.

'We've conducted a full surveyor sweep of the system,' Semper told Horst, careful to keep any irritation out of his voice. 'If there's anything out there other than us, we've not found it yet.'

Horst's reply was smooth and diplomatic. 'I don't doubt the skills of your surveyor crewmen or the quality of your ship's technical systems, commodore, but sometimes it helps to know exactly what you're looking for.'

Monomachus was approaching them now, handing a data-slate to Semper. 'Commodore Semper, with your permission, I would suggest a temporary adjustment of your vessel's surveyor systems' frequency range to the following new settings.'

Semper looked down at the technical data scrolling across the slate's viewing plate, and frowned. 'These frequencies are extremely low-level, and the prime fluctuation vector you're suggesting in these equations is extremely unorthodox. The Despoiler's vessels aren't too dissimilar to our own, with a broadly similar power output signature. Anything two or more ratio levels above these figures is enough to detect anything, friend and foe alike, within a radius of at least three AUs.'

'Indulge us, commodore,' smiled Horst.

Semper nodded curtly to his surveyor officers, who immediately set about making the necessary adjustments to their instruments.

'The surveyor devices will take some moments to match the recalibrated settings we have introduced into them,' warned Monomachus. 'In the meantime, it would be best if…'

He broke off, looking meaningfully towards Horst.

'Tell your crew to be prepared, Semper,' said Horst, taking up the warning. 'Tell them that, no matter what appears on their auspex screens, they are to take no offensive action of any kind. You can consider this a command backed by the full authority of the Emperor's Inquisition.'

'And what exactly are you expecting to find out here, inquisitor?' asked Semper, refusing to be intimidated on the bridge of his own vessel by anyone, even a senior inquisitor.

Horst did not immediately answer. A few moments later, one of the junior gunnery officers did it for him.

'Throne of Earth! There, eighteen thousand kilometres to our starboard rear. Vandire's teeth, they're practically staring right up our arse!'

A loud babble of exclamations and oaths from tech-adepts and surveyor officers quickly confirmed the sightings. Semper looked at the data-images suddenly appearing on the augur screens all round the command deck. He kept his composure, but it took all his will not to react in the way which his every command instinct compelled him to.

Eldar vessels. Three of them, all easily within striking distance of the *Macharius* and its sister ships.

The newly recalibrated surveyor readings clearly showed the signatures of three alien ships – one capital class ship and two escorts – keeping perfectly synchronised formation as they shadowed the Imperial ships' course into the Stabia system.

'Remember my command, commodore, and pass it on to your fellow captains. No hostile action is to be taken against the alien ships unless they attack first, or unless I command it. Maintain your present course in-system, and have your communications officers closely monitor these comm-net frequencies. They may have to make some changes to their equipment. If that is the case, then Monomachus will be glad to show them how.'

Semper looked at the comm-channel frequency information on the data-slate handed to him by Horst. As with the surveyor settings, the information displayed was strange and unfamiliar, the frequencies at the far end of the spectrum from those used by the Imperium. He handed the data-slate to a communications officer, and looked speculatively at Horst.

'I assume then that we have just made a successful rendezvous with the parties you were expecting to meet here, inquisitor?'

Horst smiled. 'I understand your concern, commodore, but, if we achieve everything I hope, then what we do today may change the course of the war and save untold numbers of worlds.'

ERWIN RAMAS SIFTED through the streams of new data flooding into him through the mind-link with the *Drachenfels*. He had received the almost incomprehensible orders relayed from the inquisitor aboard the *Macharius*, and, like the other vessels in the Imperial formation, his crew had recalibrated their surveyor systems in the same way as the *Macharius* had. Now the four eldar ships stood revealed to the *Drachenfels's* electronic senses, and Semper studied their detestably alien and unfamiliar shapes with a detached and coldly cruel interest.

It had been more than a hundred and fifty years since he had last encountered the eldar, but here they were again, cruising through space well within range of his vessel's lance turrets like a peace-time flotilla parading before some local planetary dignitary at a ceremonial review of the fleet.

Ramas didn't know what dangerous foolishness the Lord Admiral and that damnable inquisitor on the *Macharius* had had in mind when they had come up with the idea for this mission the *Drachenfels* and its two sister ships had been despatched on, but he knew one important thing.

The eldar were not to be trusted. He'd follow orders and hold his fire, but, at the first sign of treachery from those xenos scum, he'd let fly with everything the *Drachenfels* had.

He reached out through the mind link into the ship's matriculators, retrieving his precious firing solution programs. He activated them, running them in a practice simulation through the *Drachenfels's* logic engines, his mind flickering back and forth between the simulation and the real-time information relayed to him by the ship's surveyor and auspex systems. He compared the two data streams, and then merged them, using the surveyor-gathered information on the nearby eldar ships as the new model for the firing simulation.

Ramas's equations had been good, he knew, and the logic engine-created phantasm images were fine enough for what they were, but it was always better to have a real target and hard data to work with.

The logic engines waged the imaginary battle amongst themselves. Non-existent lance beams cut through an imaginary void to find and strike illusionary targets. Phantom explosions erupted in an intangible battle-zone which existed only in the ship's dreaming machine-mind.

Ramas studied the results, and made the necessary corrections to his firing solutions and targeting equations. He ran the simulation again. This time, he was far more satisfied with the outcome.

He smiled his lipless smile. He would follow orders, but he would watch the enemy ships and be ready for the first sign of treachery. When that happened, he promised himself, they would find him more than ready and prepared to settle old scores.

SOMEWHERE ELSE WITHIN the Stabia system, hidden vessels watched and waited. They hid in shadow, cloaked from the senses of the other vessels, even those of the eldar ships. They monitored the transmission bursts that passed between the two groups of ships. The occupants of these hidden watcher ships could not decode these transmissions, but their meaning was clear enough.

Slowly, the two formations split up, spreading out to take up preset positions throughout the small solar system. The remaining two ships, one eldar, one human, remained in high orbit above the dead world, each of them balefully studying the other as their comrade ships warily stalked each other in wide, elliptical picket guard orbits, their scanner senses trained more on each other than in search of any unknown threat which might be waiting out there for them.

Aboard the hidden watcher ships, power and propulsion systems were slowly nursed into life, and the abominable, twisted things they carried in their prison-holds were roused and brutally herded into their waiting positions aboard barb-prowed boarding torpedoes and assault craft.

Swiftly, silently, the dark eldar ships slid out of their place of concealment, like an assassin's poisoned dagger being stealthily drawn from its hidden sheath.

The hunt had begun.

FOR THE FIRST TIME in millennia, the burning god walked upon the earth of a world. Wherever it walked, destruction followed in its wake.

The world itself was unimportant. Once it may have belonged to the children of Asuryan, but they had abandoned it long ago, retreating back to the comparative safety of their craftworlds.

Now other, lesser, races had chanced upon the world, not caring or knowing anything of its previous inhabitants, and, in their ignorance and conceit, these new would-be conquerors had built their settlements upon the ruins left behind by their vanquished betters.

The burning god was angry. So much of the webway had been lost since it had last walked its secret, mystic byways. Passages were blocked off or too unstable to be safely traversed. Whole sections had disappeared or been destroyed. Several times now, it had been forced to make detours, seeking alternative paths towards its destination via several remote and long-unused nodal points.

This world was one such nodal point, containing several hidden but still-active entrances to the webway. The burning god had exited the webway several hundred kilometres to the south, amongst the ruins of what had once, long-ago, been an Exodite colony. Little remained of the place's delicate wraithbone towers and shimmering crystalline fortifications, though. Instead, the burning god had found the place overrun by the planet's new inhabitants, the universal pestilence known as orks. Foolishly, the greenskin animals had built their own foul settlement upon the ruins of the Exodite colony. Emerging through the hidden webway portal which, unknown to the orks had been active and amongst them all along, the burning god had immediately set about showing them the error of their ways.

When it left the place, nothing but dead ashes remained.

Travelling across the surface of the world, it encountered more of the creatures. Its anger grew with each encounter, anger at the realisation that all the children of Asuryan had once achieved here had been swept away by the seemingly endless tide of greenskins.

Now, reaching its destination, it found that this place too had been colonised by the ork pestilence. The animals seemed to have been warned of its coming and rode out to meet it in battle. They bore down on it in waves of their bizarre and noisome vehicles. They whooped and shouted in excitement, firing their weapons into the air.

The burning god met them with the full force of its rising anger.

Another wave of gunfire struck it as it stepped through the tangled, burned-out remnants of an orkoid vehicle, crushing the wreck beneath its burning tread. The gunfire increased in intensity. Many of the projectiles – crudely-cast metal slugs – vaporised into molten mist even as they struck the white-hot iron exterior of its armoured skin. Other, larger calibre shots impacted against it, although it barely registered the blows.

The burning god growled to itself in irritation, turning its glowering gaze towards the source of the gunfire, and sent out a blast of glowing fire with one sweep of its rune-carved sword blade. The line of greenskin vehicles exploded in sequence, the mystic fire jumping from one to the other, consuming their screaming crews in a halo of black fire and detonating ammunition stocks and primitive fossil fuel tanks. Ork infantry ran in panic from the conflagration, and were reduced to ash by another sweep of the burning blade held in the god's hand. Their shrieks mingled with the sword's scream as it gloried in the psychic aura of their death agonies.

Three more of the orks' crude, smoke-belching vehicles rode towards it, spitting out streams of rapid-fire projectiles from the swivel-mounted weapons built upon them. The burning god blew one apart with a brief flick of its mystic blade. The next was armed with some kind of flamer weapon. Had it been able, the burning god might have laughed at the pathetic futility of the attack as the flamer vehicle's gunner directed the weapon at it and enveloped it

in a heavy blanket of chemically-produced flame. The burning god strode through the wall of fire, and swung its sword,
shearing through bike, driver, weapon and gunner with one
simple slash.

The third vehicle, a rumbling half-track loaded down with
howling orks, bore down straight at it. The burning god
braced itself in readiness. The orks did not realise it, but,
even if they had had one to use, not even a traktor beam
weapon could have moved the avatar from the spot where it
now stood.

The vehicle impacted against the burning god, completely
destroying itself just as if it had run straight into the immobile, immovable foot of one of the humans' great Titan
war-machines. Screaming orks, bursting into flames as they
came into contact with the super-heated air around the
burning god, flew through the air amidst the wreckage of
their vehicle. The burning god lowered its guard and moved
on, walking through the scattered wreckage, the heat of its
passing detonating the vehicle's fuel tank and causing
ammunition-loaded weapons in the hands of dead and
dying orks to explode apart.

More gunfire buzzed through the air around the burning
god, the occasional heavier round splattering in a molten
mess against its skin. It saw its objective before it, the distinctive, conical-shell shape of the ancient temple of Asuryan
still visible amidst the desecrating jumble of barrack huts,
watchtowers and weapon workshops that the ork animals
had constructed around it.

A haphazardly-designed battlement wall ran round the
settlement, its single gate made from a section of scavenged
space vessel hull, and firmly barred against the burning god's
advance. The battlements were lined with orks, and sweating
teams of smaller orkoid creatures laboured to turn a huge
rusty capstan wheel, bringing the wide muzzles of the turret
weapons on top of the gate swinging round towards the
burning god.

The god spoke, uttering a few sounds which only the most
venerable farseers would recognise as being words of power.
As it spoke, it thrust its burning blade into the ground at its
feet. The earth erupted open, and a blazing line of fire ran

towards the gate with preternatural speed. Immediately, the ork shouts of triumph and scorn from the battlement walls turned to howls of fear and panic. A few seconds later, the fire line found its target. The gate and large portions of the battlements on either side of it blew apart in an incandescent fireball.

The burning god walked on, oblivious to the soil, battlement wreckage and orkoid remains showering down all around it from the sky.

It strode through the cratered hole where the gates had stood. A crude, clanking ork machine-thing lumbered forward to meet it. The burning god advanced on it, ignoring the pounding hail of shells from the machine's weapon arm which hammered against its iron skin. Reaching the machine, the burning god severed the thing's clumsy power-claw limb with one blow from its wailing blade. Sparks and black hydraulic fluid sprayed out from the twitching metal stump, and the machine-thing staggered back as if it were in pain. The burning god ran it through with its sword, the weapon wailing with surprised glee as it tasted the flesh of the ork pilot hidden inside the machine.

The burning god continued into the ork settlement, killing everything that attempted to stop it.

A massive ork in primitive power armour charged at it, roaring in ferocious anger as it swung a whirring, double-handed chainsword round its head. The burning god reached out and grabbed the ork by the throat, lifting it clear off the ground. Holding it by one hand, it shook the screaming ork as if it were nothing more than a puppet. The unnatural heat from its hand melted through the stuff of the ork's armour, igniting the creature's flesh. In seconds, the creature was ablaze from head to foot. The burning god shook the blazing puppet-thing, causing pieces of it to fall to the ground in a rain of fiery gobbets. Finally, it dropped the empty, fire-blackened armour to the ground and continued on.

A strange, giggling ork in brightly-coloured robes danced and capered before the god on the steps of the temple building, waving a brass-knobbed staff at the burning god as it chanted out a stream of gibberish. The air between them swam with psychic energy, and flickering ribbons of destructive warp power crackled harmlessly against the god's skin.

The avatar killed the ork psyker with one fiery glance. The ork collapsed onto the steps, rolling in agony. Smoke and weird-coloured flame emerged from its mouth, nose and eyes as the contents of its skull ignited from within.

The burning god entered the temple. It could sense the faint aura of the hidden webway portal buried deep amongst the building's foundations. It would take some time to locate the portal, and more time still to activate and open it.

Unhurried and relentless, the burning god continued on its journey. It sensed the events unfolding at its ultimate destination. This detour and the unnecessary distraction of having to deal with the greenskin animals had cost it much precious time. Now it was no longer sure it would be able to arrive in time to change the course of those events.

TWELVE

'As COMMANDER OF this vessel and the man responsible for your safety, inquisitor, I really must protest in the strongest possible terms to this course of action.'

Yes, and also as the man whose head Lord Admiral Ravensburg will surely serve up on a silver platter to the Inquisition and the High Lords of Terra, should anything happen to their personal envoy to the Gothic sector, thought Semper, no longer caring about the unknown possibilities of Horst's mind-reading abilities.

'Duly noted,' said Horst smoothly, as they rode the elevator together down to the shuttle bay. 'You may, if you wish and with my full approval and Inquisitorial authorization, register your protest with Monomachus, who, in the event of my not returning from the planet below, will convey it to Battlefleet Command when this mission is over.'

Horst caught the look of surprise on Semper's face. 'If, as you suspect, this is indeed some kind of xenos trick, commodore, then my mission is already a failure. The war will go as it has done already, and the interests of Battlefleet Gothic will be poorly served by blaming one of its most able commanders for my mistake. This mission is my idea alone, and I take full responsibility for its outcome, including the possibility of my own death.'

Semper nodded in silent thanks, surprised by Horst's words. While he was still dwelling on the inquisitor's unexpected depths of selfless practicality, the elevator doors rumbled open, and they strode together out into the shuttle bay flight deck. Rows of booted feet crashed together in unison at their arrival. Now it was the inquisitor's turn to be surprised as he looked at the four squads of armsmen lined up on the shuttle deck, all of them in carapace armour and bearing fearsome shotcannon weapons and holstered navy pistols.

'I assume this is something more than an honour guard formed to see me politely aboard my shuttle,' noted Horst dryly, seeing the strings of ammunition bandoliers worn by each armsman, and the bulging pouches of grenades, power cells and rebreather rigs hanging from their equipment harnesses. Hito Ulanti and Maxim Borusa, both also in full naval battle dress, stood nearby. Ulanti was armed with his sabre and a holstered laspistol. Borusa had a brace of holstered navy pattern pistols and a heavy bolter, holding the cumbersome heavy weapon as if it were nothing more than an ordinary bolter.

'Let's just call it an extra precaution, inquisitor,' answered Semper. 'You have your mission, but I also have mine, and that mission it to safeguard your life to the best of my abilities. With your permission, Lieutenant Ulanti and four squads of my ship's best armsmen will accompany you and your group down to the planet's surface, to provide additional security.'

Semper saw the look of wry amusement in Horst's eyes 'We can't have it said that Battlefleet Gothic and the captain and crew of the *Macharius* don't know how to look after their guests,' he added, with the same wry smile.

'A fine idea,' nodded Horst, diplomatically. 'It will be reassuring to know that the forces of Battlefleet Gothic will be watching over us both from up here and closer by on the planet's surface.'

A klaxon sounded, signalling the beginning of the shuttle launch procedure. The deck shook under the impact of dozens of pairs of heavy boots as the armsmen squads and Horst's bodyguard marched up the ramps into their separate shuttles. The shaking increased tenfold as, one by one, the three armoured troop carrier shuttles fired up their engines in preparation for take-off.

Semper retreated back towards the deck's safe zone. He spotted Ulanti climbing the entrance ramp of one of the shuttles, and saw him turn to salute him from the top of the ramp.

Semper returned the salute. 'Good hunting, Hito,' he shouted as an afterthought, aware that his words would certainly be lost amongst the rising howl of the shuttle engines. It was the traditional good luck farewell call of Battlefleet Gothic, exchanged whenever a ship left port for battle or just routine patrol. Its use here seemed somewhat inappropriate, Semper knew – this, after all was supposed to be a parley with what could incredibly turn out to be potential allies – but he was unable to explain why he had suddenly felt the urge to use it now.

A foreboding, he thought briefly, and then did his best to dismiss the thought. He did not trust xenos, but he had his orders, and he knew that, on this mission, battle was to be avoided at all costs.

Ulanti paused at the shuttle hatch, grinning and flashing his captain a friendly salute of acknowledgement. He may not have heard Semper's words, but he had obviously guessed their meaning.

The howling scream of the shuttle engines increased in pitch even further. The very air of the launch bay throbbed with the vibration, and the atmosphere of the place was filled with the heavy chemical reek of expelled promethium. Semper turned to exit the bay, leaving only the servitors and human ground crew in their thickly-armoured protective suits to conduct the final technical checks in the almost unbearable atmosphere of the shuttle bay, just prior to the final launch moment.

As he turned, he almost collided with the black-coated figure of Koba Kyogen. Semper immediately noticed the ammo pouches and rebreather rig Kyogen was wearing, even as the Ship's Commissar offered him a stiff-armed formal salute.

'Permission to join the mission to the planet's surface, commodore. As Ship's Commissar, I believe it is my duty to oversee the actions of the crewmen you have selected for this mission, particularly since they may come into contact with xenos abominations. If this is the case, then I must be on hand to keep a close guard over the morale of our men, and to protect their minds and spirits from any signs of alien contamination. The servants of the Inquisition might be used to bargaining with the enemies of mankind, but the men of the Imperial Navy are thankfully not.'

His voice was thick with undisguised scorn for the idea of this attempted parley with the alien eldar, and there was nothing but pure loathing in the way he had described them as 'xenos abominations'.

'Permission granted, commissar,' Semper said, almost shouting over the sound of the shuttle's engines. Kyogen nodded in thanks, although both men knew that the request had been purely cosmetic, since commissars could and did do exactly what they wanted aboard an Imperial Navy vessel.

Kyogen sprinted across the deck of the launch bay, scrambling up the ramp of one of the shuttles just as it began to retract into the underside of the shuttle's hull. He stumbled at the top of the ramp, fire traces from the shuttle's roaring belly thrusters licking at the tails of his heavy commissar's coat, and a surprised-looking Hito Ulanti, assisted by two armsmen, leaned out to haul him into the safety of the shuttle's interior, just as the airlock hatch began to slide shut.

Semper saw all this through the glasteel viewing plate set into the heavy-duty blast doors which now sealed off the launch bay from the rest of the ship. A few seconds later, and the image was gone, washed away by the torrent of flame which now filled the interior of the shuttle bay as the pilots of all three craft brought their engines up to launch thrust.

A few more seconds, and the fire was extinguished as all remaining oxygen inside the place was siphoned away and the launch bay doors rumbled open, exposing the bay to the vacuum of space. Released from their grav-lock moorings, the three shuttles lifted off and exited the *Macharius*.

* * *

MOMENTS LATER, FLYING in triad formation, the shuttles made rendezvous with the waiting flight of Fury escorts. The Furies, a model adapted for planetary atmospheric flight, took up a protective position around the shuttles and guided them down towards their destination.

Inside the lead shuttle, Koba Kyogen settled into his seat harness, staring in sullen challenge at the figure seated across the narrow, cramped aisle. Maxim Borusa stared disinterestedly back, chewing slowly on a fresh wad of tajii root. The two men's eyes met and locked in undisguised mutual hostility.

'Good to have you with us on this little jaunt, commissar. Me and the rest of the boys feel more reassured, knowing we've got a silver skull like you along for the ride and watching our backs.'

Maxim grinned, launched a thick stream of tarry tajii root juice at the decking in front of Kyogen's gleaming, black polished boots and then settled back into his seat, closing his eyes and seeming to simply will himself to sleep through the remainder of the short but violently bumpy orbital descent down towards the surface of Stabia.

When he opened his eyes again, twenty minutes later as they touched down upon the planet's rocky surface, Kyogen was sitting exactly as he had been the last time Maxim had looked at him, still staring fixedly at Maxim, the way a predator measures up its intended prey.

'WE SHOULD NOT be doing this. They are mon-keigh, they are animals without souls. They cannot be trusted, and they should not be bargained with. Let them die at the hands of the Abomination. What do we care of the fate of them and their corpse-god emperor?'

Lileathon stood upon the bridge of the *Vual'en Sho*. Around her, the pictskin-projected images of the human ships swirled and spun in the incense-hazed air of the command deck.

Kariadryl sensed the bristling outrage of the Aspect Lord, Darodayos, standing beside him. Others of his bodyguard retinue also reacted with quiet yet distinct displays of disapproval at the eshairr outcast's lack of respect to craftworld

An-Iolsus's most venerable farseer. The Dark Reaper called Chiron shifted in unease, the heavy plates of his carapace armour striking noisily together in less than subtle warning. Freyra, Darodayos's other Striking Scorpion lieutenant, hissed in angry indignation at this seeming display of contempt to Kariadryl and quietly assumed the ominous body language stance that signified the assumption of *thyerr shumon*: declaration of support, backed up by force of arms, if necessary, towards an insulted kinsman.

Kariadryl reached out with his mind to cast a subtle aura of calm over the proceedings, and looked towards Lileathon, gesturing to her in respectful supplication. No matter what he and the others may think of her, she was the craftmaster of this vessel, and their lives were all in her hands. Now was not the time to provoke a fight.

'An-Iolsus commands, honoured sister and craftmaster. The agents of the mon-keigh corpse-god have made known to us something of the true plans of the enemy they fight. If what they have revealed to us is true, and that is what we are here to determine, then An-Iolsus and its sister craftworlds can no longer afford to stand by and allow the servants of the Great Abomination to achieve their victory. If a temporary pact with the mon-keigh is the price we must pay for keeping the Talismans of Vaul out of the hands of the Great Abomination, then that is what we must do.'

The old farseer's words sent a ripple of distress out amongst those gathered on the command deck. If he closed his eyes and concentrated, Kariadryl knew what manner of thoughts his keenly-attuned psychic senses would pluck from the minds of those around him.

Doubt, confusion and fear, all of them focusing in shock on the bombshell which Kariadryl had quietly allowed to drop.

The Talismans of Vaul, whispered half a hundred eldar minds on the bridge of the *Vual'en Sho*. Could such a terrible possibility be true, they asked themselves, in intense fear and unease? Could the followers of the Great Abomination truly have found a means to awaken and mobilize such devices and turn them to its own use?

It was a thought few eldar minds wished to entertain, and which cast a pall of apprehensive fear over all present on the command deck. As for Lileathon, Kariadryl was quietly satisfied to see that his words seemed to have had the desired effect on the troubled soul of the young firebrand commander.

'An-Iolsus commands,' she acknowledged, chastened by the knowledge Kariadryl had just revealed. She stepped back, her expression reflecting the troubled nature of her thoughts. Her second-in-command, the older but more cautious Ailill, smoothly took over in her stead.

'Lord farseer, the humans have launched their shuttle craft and are beginning their descent to the planet's surface. We have received the signal indicating that they are ready to meet you there.'

Kariadryl nodded, and looked at the pictskin images swimming in the air above them. He could see the small shapes of the shuttle craft and their escorts falling away from the looming bulk of the human star vessel. He studied the shape of the massive vessel for a moment, his eyes taking in the harsh, unfamiliar lines of the thing, and seeing the rows of launch bays and gun ports which studded its crenellated hull. Others of his race might profess to find the human vessel crude and primitive, a typical product of the barbaric mon-keigh, but to Kariadryl it represented all that he found most secretly terrifying about the humans. Massive and overwhelming, brutal and threatening, it seemed solid and formidably permanent in contrast to the slender, delicate, wraithbone-formed vessels of the eldar. Kariadryl could only imagine how many teeming thousands of humans there were aboard the massive cruiser, but he was all too painfully aware of the far lesser number of eldar – barely more than a thousand – who made up the crew of the *Vual'en Sho*.

And the humans had – how many, he wondered – thousands or tens of thousands of such vessels, spread all through the galaxy? In stark contrast, An-Iolsus could only muster a handful of ships, most of which were held in reserve for the defence of the craftworld itself. In his darkest thoughts, Kariadryl strongly doubted that the entire eldar diaspora, scattered as it was across dozens of craftworlds all through the galaxy, could gather its collected forces together in greater numbers than even the size of the single battlefleet group which the humans used to control this sector of their far-flung empire.

We are a dying race, he mournfully reminded himself: the evidence of our decline is all around us. Each day there are less of us, and more humans. One day perhaps there shall be none of us left at all.

And who will there be then to guard the things which the elder ones have left behind, he asked himself? That was why this mission was so important, he realised, even if these others did not. The humans were savage and primitive in comparison to the eldar, but they were also the new heirs to the galaxy and its secrets, just as the elder themselves had inherited it from those races who had gone before. It must fall to the likes of Kariadryl to educate this new upstart race and teach them something of the deadly inheritance which might one day yet be theirs.

I have so little time left, lamented the ancient farseer, *and still so much left to do.*

Aware that he had allowed his thoughts to drift – how much he envied his brothers and sisters in the dome of the crystal seers who had all the time in the universe to let their minds drift in endless thought-dreams, and how much he looked forward to finally joining them – he turned his attention back to the present matters.

'Are the preparations ready for our own arrival on the planet?'

'They are, lord farseer,' answered Darodayos. 'The temporary webway portal is open and stabilised, and I have sent scouts on ahead. They report that the surface area is secure and that there is no sign of any human deception.'

Kariadryl nodded, and bowed to Lileathon.

'Then it is time we took our leave of you, honoured craftmaster. I thank you for the protection and hospitality you have offered us, and I look forward to seeing you again, sister, when we return aboard at the successful completion of our task.'

'An-Iolsus commands,' replied Lileathon, returning the bow and giving the customary blessing of farewell. 'Asuryan

watch over you and our brothers and sisters, and bring you
safely back to us once more.'

'SQUAD HALLER REPORTING. North Two perimeter secured. No
sign of any hostiles.'

'Squad Hoth. Nothing out here either. Just more bloody
rocks and flying dust.'

One by one, the reports came in from armsmen squads
now patrolling the perimeter of the meeting point. Situated
in the relative shelter of the strange alien ruins at the centre
of the secure zone, Ulanti didn't envy the armsmen their
duty. The planet's atmosphere was breathable, but endless
storms swept its barren surface, and the air was filled with a
flying, swirling hail of choking dust and tiny silicate fragments, making rebreather masks and goggles an absolute
requirement.

The journey from the landing zone – a three-kilometre
hike across open ground, leaving one armsmen squad and
several of Horst's people behind to guard the waiting shuttles – had been a rude and shocking introduction to the
realities of life on Stabia. For the members of Horst's Inquisition retinue, it had been bad enough, but for the crew of
the *Macharius*, who were experiencing the usual problems
associated with suddenly having to readapt to planetary
environment conditions after months or even years aboard a
space vessel, it had been tough going in the extreme.

Razor-edged flakes of wind-hurled silicate dust flayed at
their exposed skin, clogging up the workings of weaponry
and equipment, and finding a way into every crevice and
joint in armour and environment suits. The ground was
alternately composed of areas of jagged, uneven rock and
expanses of deep and treacherously unpredictable dust
bowls. Neither environment was particularly easy for booted
feet more used to the firm, level decking of an Imperial warship, and twice they had had to interrupt their journey to
pull people out of deep dust craters. The prospect of sudden
and horrible death was a familiar companion for anyone
who served aboard a vessel in His Divine Majesty's Imperial
Navy, but drowning in a bottomless dust-hole on some
Emperor-forsaken planet, choking to death as the dust

poured into a mouth screaming wide in terror, was no way for a navy man to die, and Ulanti had ordered his people to take the utmost care in this unfamiliar terrain.

And then they had reached the meeting point co-ordinates indicated in the few brief, terse, coded transmissions they had received from the eldar command vessel, and come across this collection of strange and puzzling ruins.

It was impossible to tell how old the ruins were, although they were clearly xenos in origin, and just as impossible to determine what catastrophe might once have occurred here. Had this place been destroyed by war or natural catastrophe, or had it been merely abandoned long ago by its original creators, allowing the deprivations of the passing millennia and the caustic environment to take their steady toll?

Whatever the truth of the matter, the ruins themselves revealed little. The Imperial men had initially mistaken the buildings for natural rock formations when they had first seen them looming out of the shifting curtain of the dust storm. It was only as they drew closer that they saw there was a guiding intelligence to their lines and unusual symmetry.

Ulanti ran a hand over the stonework beside him, marvelling at the strange, melted wax look of the material. Shot through with rainbow streaks of mixed colour and with an oddly viscous quality, it was more like plastic than stonework. He took his hand away, disturbed by the faint crackling sensation which he felt, even through the material of his glove.

'Static electricity, we think,' commented Horst, appearing suddenly beside him. 'It seems to repel the dust, which must be why this place wasn't buried under the stuff long ago. How it's generated, or how the integrity of the field has been maintained for maybe thousands of years is something none of my people have yet been able to explain.'

Ulanti snapped to attention in the inquisitor's presence. Horst settled himself down on a nearby piece of stonework – it might have been the beginnings of a piece of oddly-formed statuary, a chair or the left-over stump of a pillar – and signalled the young navy officer to relax.

'At ease, lieutenant. Your captain and Admiral Pardain aren't here now, and I'm never one to stand on ceremony once I'm out in the field. I assume your patrols haven't found anything?'

If Ulanti felt any discomfort in the presence of this inquisitor, who had been sent to the Gothic sector as the personal envoy of the High Lords of Terra themselves, he didn't allow it to show.

'Nothing at all,' he replied. 'I'm co-ordinating our patrol efforts with your man Stavka. If anything tries to cross any point along the joint perimeter, we'll know about it soon enough. No word from the *Macharius*?'

The dust storm and the strange composition of the mica fragments it was composed of was making long-range comms transmissions from the planet's surface something of a problem, not to mention the effects of the unpredictable electronic interference from this system's binary star pulsar. They had been able to talk to the *Macharius* since their arrival on the surface of Stabia, but sometimes only intermittently, and all such communications had been an ongoing struggle against the natural forces which ruled the planet Stabia and its solar system.

'I was able to speak briefly to your captain some minutes ago. They're maintaining a careful watch on the eldar command ship, but so far there's no sign of them launching any kind of shuttle craft.'

Ulanti looked at Horst, both men wondering the same thing. 'Which rather begs the question, sir, if they didn't get here before us and they don't seem to be in too much of a hurry to get down here by shuttle, then how exactly do they plan to put in an appearance at this rendezvous?'

Horst nodded. 'Tell me the truth, lieutenant, what do you really think of this mission? Don't be afraid to speak your mind.'

Ulanti paused, considering his reply carefully before offering it to the inquisitor.

'As I said to Captain Semper, sir, if I were seeking to lure an enemy into a trap then this system would be perfect for my purposes. And now here we are on a planet within that system, on unfamiliar terrain, bogged down by unfavourable atmospheric conditions, with unreliable communications and waiting for someone who doesn't seem in too much of a hurry to present himself.' Ulanti broke off, hesitating for a moment, and then looked directly at Horst.

'If you ask me, inquisitor, this entire mission is just one big ambush waiting to happen.'

Horst uttered a sharp, barking laugh, and clapped a hand on Ulanti's shoulder, leaning on him as he hauled himself to his feet again. 'Hah, perhaps you should talk more with Stavka, lieutenant, since he's very much of the same opinion. Well spoken, Hito. The Emperor needs more servants who aren't afraid to tell a senior inquisitor that he's most likely walked straight into an obvious trap. If you ever tire of service in the navy, I could always use a man like you in my own organisation.'

Ulanti opened his mouth to answer, intending to politely decline the inquisitor's tentative but apparently serious offer, but was abruptly cut off by a strange, hissing scream which came from somewhere close amongst the ruins. The very molecules of the air seemed to vibrate with the force of the thing, and, at the same time, the swirling maelstrom of the dust storm was lit up by a eye-searing flash of light.

'An explosion!' shouted Ulanti, drawing his laspistol and placing himself protectively in front of Horst. 'An orbital strike, possibly. We're under attack!'

'More like a teleportation shockwave,' answered Horst, knowing that even this was not strictly true. Teleportation technology was rare enough – amongst the forces of the Imperium, only the Space Marines of the Adeptus Astartes were equipped to withstand its potentially lethal rigours – and he had found no recorded evidence of its use amongst the eldar. Nevertheless, piecing together many fragmented clues and suppositions, there was plenty of evidence to suggest that the eldar race possessed some advanced form of transportation technology unknown to the Imperium, since there were so many reports of eldar raiders appearing suddenly on a planet's surface after somehow having been able to completely bypass and elude any orbital or planetary system defences which might have been in place. Indeed, despite the numerous encounters between eldar and Imperium naval forces, and the confirmed sightings of the same eldar ship at points many light years apart from each other, there was a great body of evidence to suggest that the eldar ships were not even equipped with warp drive technology. If they did not have warp engines, how then were they able to travel the distances between the stars?

There is still so much we do not know or understand about them, Horst thought to himself, drawing his weapon and moving towards the source of the unknown phenomenon. *Perhaps I am a fool, then, to have trusted such creatures and to have put myself and these other loyal servants of the Emperor in such jeopardy?*

They were outside now, in a clearing in the centre of the ruins. The figures of armsmen and Horst's bodyguards appeared from amidst the swirling dust screen, drawing protectively towards Horst and Ulanti. All of them had their weapons drawn.

On the vox-channels, there was a babble of excited, panicked voices sounding over the crackling hiss of the storm. One of Stavka's men struggled with the settings of an auspex device, receiving back from it only a static scream which was a lesser echo of the larger sound which still filled the air all around them.

'Switch that thing off,' ordered Stavka, angrily, striding forward out of the dusty murk, wielding a combat shotgun and issuing commands to those around him. 'Use your infra-red filters. Advance in three-man squads. Keep in touch with the squads around you. Find whatever the hell that blast came from, and be prepared to fire upon hostiles.'

'No! No firing unless you're fired upon first,' bellowed Horst, countermanding his second-in-command's order. 'I repeat – hold your fire. Whatever comes out of this dust, the first man who fires upon it without provocation will be summarily executed. I speak in the name of the Emperor's Inquisition!'

There was a light glowing through the swirling dust ahead of them. From their initial reconnoitre of the ruins, Ulanti estimated it to be coming from an area containing a wide circle of unusual, free-standing monolith structures. The area and the structures had been investigated by Horst's people, but, as with so much else here, little had been determined about them, including for what purpose they might have originally been constructed. Taking a firmer hold of his laspistol, Ulanti had a distinct feeling that they were perhaps about to find out.

He felt a presence beside him, and heard a surprisingly familiar voice whispering the words of an Ecclesiarchy-approved catechism of blessed protection. The voice may have been familiar, but the tone of nervous fear in it was not. Ulanti turned in surprise, seeing Commissar Kyogen at his shoulder. The big Ship's Commissar gripped the handle of his chainsword tightly, staring into the concealing curtain of the dust storm, a look of glassy fear in his eyes.

Ulanti did not like the cold and detached Kyogen – as far as he was aware, no one aboard the *Macharius* had ever warmed to the man – but he did not doubt the commissar's courage or ability. Now, for the first time, he saw fear in the man, and Kyogen's secret weakness was exposed to him.

Aliens, thought Ulanti, knowing the fear and horror which Imperial anti-alien propaganda had successfully installed into so many of the Emperor's subjects. *He's afraid of anything xenos-bred.*

The light was dimming now, fading away along with that hellish sound, and an uneasy stillness fell over the scene. For a few moments, nothing happened, and then they appeared out of the swirling murk of the dust storm.

One second they were not there, and the next they were. From seemingly nowhere they appeared, tall and graceful figures, long and lithe of limb, clad in armour which, in stark contrast to the functional armour worn by the servants of the Imperium, had been constructed with artistry as much in mind as practicality. They carried weapons whose unfamiliar, elegant lines did not disguise their clearly lethal intent.

The advance line of eldar warriors stopped, aggressively sweeping the barrels of their weapons in arcs back and forth along the line of human troops. Nervous fingers hovered over gun triggers and firing studs. Mutual suspicion and animosity crackled in the air between the two groups.

An eldar warrior, taller and more magnificently armoured than the others, stepped forward, taking in the vista of nervous, afraid human faces with one sweeping, arrogant glance. His gaze settled for a moment on Ulanti, and the young navy lieutenant had to restrain the urge to protectively bring his weapon up to bear as he felt the alien's keen and frigid intellect focussing briefly upon him. A cold, mocking smile flickered across the creature's delicate, almost albino features, and then it suddenly stepped back. It neither gestured nor said anything to its companions, but Ulanti was left with the distinct impression that some kind of secret communication had just taken place.

The advance line of eldar opened up in its centre, and another, smaller group of aliens advanced towards the watching humans. Most of them were in armour, clustering protectively around a figure in their centre, and then, at a gestured command from that figure, the rest of the group stopped and grudgingly allowed the figure to advance toward the humans on its own.

This second eldar carried an aura which drew every human eye upon him. He looked more frail and slow than the others, and, even though Ulanti had never seen an eldar before and had no means of judging such things in their terms, there was an unmistakable sense of venerable age about him.

And great wisdom, too, held in those almond eyes. The eldar scanned the ranks of the humans, that unsettling, inscrutable gaze quickly coming to rest on Inquisitor Horst.

The eldar took several more steps forward, until it stood before Horst. The two beings, human and eldar, regarded each other for a moment, the tall, slim eldar towering almost half a metre above Horst, then the alien gracefully inclined its head and executed what might have been a respectful bow.

'Welcome, human-called-Horst,' it said in perfectly-spoken but strangely enunciated High Gothic. 'This one you would term "I" is kin-called Kariadryl, second-born of the union of Ky-Danae and Darandera, and honoured to be the farseeing one of the craftworld An-Iolsus. You called into the void, brother, and I have answered, and now we have much to discuss.'

THIRTEEN

ON THE SURFACE of Stabia, the parley had begun. Out in space, on the fringes of the Stabia system, the battle was also beginning.

The Sword class frigate *Volpone* was patrolling the system's perimeter and maintaining a close watch on the eldar vessel doing likewise. Or at least, thought the vessel's angry and frustrated captain, Vanyan Karasev, that was what they were supposed to be doing.

Karasev was that rarity in Battlefleet Gothic, a ship's captain who did not belong to the traditional and sprawling naval aristocracy class of Cypra Mundian nobility which had produced officers and captains for every battlefleet in the Segmentum Obscuras since time immemorial. Karasev had achieved his rank purely through his own drive and ability, and, secretly amongst the upper cadre of Battlefleet Command, great things were expected of him. The captaincy of a capital class vessel would one day be his, although Karasev himself suspected that, had he been one of the Cypra Mundian elite, he would probably already be standing on the bridge of a Lunar or Gothic class cruiser somewhere,

directing the wrath of the Emperor directly upon the enemies of mankind.

Not that he took his current command or mission less
seriously, but, at that moment, his fiery Stranivarite temper
was up, as, for the fourth time in as many hours, his surveyor
officers had once again allowed the eldar vessel ahead of
them to slip out of the reach of his vessel's scanners.

In truth, he knew it was not his crew's fault. The eldar vessel had been arrogantly showing off, almost taunting them,
as it executed a bewildering series of complex manoeuvres,
shocking them with its sudden turns of speed and confounding the abilities of their surveyor systems by
modulating the density and frequency of its energy signature, alternatively fading away completely from their augur
screens and then appearing elsewhere from its last reported
or estimated position in a sudden flare of energy signal.

And now it was gone again, disappearing from their surveyor screens after executing a rapid turn sunwards and
vanishing without trace.

Like many ambitious men, Karasev was neither patient
nor understanding, and the mood on the command deck of
the *Volpone* was tense as his crew endeavoured to re-establish
surveyor contact with the alien ship as their commander
hovered ominously over them.

'Surveyor contact, two AUs to starboard, and closing!'
declared a surveyor officer almost triumphantly.

'Clarify,' barked Karasev, already troubled by this latest
development. A shared look with his second-in-command
confirmed the same thought. At its last recorded position,
the eldar ship was ahead of them and pulling away from
them at speed. Now it had somehow slipped round their
starboard flank and was closing on them instead, appearing from out of nowhere and at an alarmingly close
distance.

'Definitely closing,' confirmed the ship's chief surveyor
officer, reading the data from his control lectern screen.
'Energy signature is completely changed from the last time
we acquired it. It's–' The officer suddenly broke off, and
looked at his captain in confusion. 'According to these readings, it's an Imperial ship. A Praetor class frigate!'

Karasev and his second-in-command exchanged surprised looks. 'Someone's a long way from home,' noted the second-in-command, dryly. The Praetor class vessel was in service amongst many of the local Imperium battlefleets of the Ultima Segmentum, but, as far as Karasev was aware, it had never been used within the Segmentum Obscuras, and certainly not by Battlefleet Gothic.

'More to the point, why weren't we told there were other Imperium forces in the area?' said Karasev, trying to conceal the uncertainty he was feeling. Everything about this mission had been unorthodox so far, to say the least. Could it be possible that there was indeed another, more secret, Imperium force in the system, sent along to provide additional, security for Semper's battle squadron?

'I want to see this thing on vidpict, and I want more information on it. Open hailing frequencies, and identify its transponder codes or energy signature. I want to know exactly what vessel it is.'

The bridge crew went to work carrying out their captain's orders. The main augur screen crackled into life, displaying the hazy, reconstructed image being picked up by the ship's augur systems. Seeing the image on the screen, Karasev allowed himself to relax a little as he recognised the unmistakable and reassuring hull shape of an Imperium warship. Still, the outline of the ship seemed to oddly waver and flicker. Karasev looked in silent question towards his Chief of Surveyors.

'Probably vidpict interference from the pulsar,' commented the officer. 'This whole system's just one damn big electromagnetic swamp.'

It was a reasonable enough explanation, Karasev knew – Emperor knew they had had enough trouble with the surveyor systems since the moment they had arrived in this blighted excuse of a star system – but something deeply worried him about the situation. Something was wrong here, he knew, but he just could not see what. The reports from his bridge crew did little to dispel his unease.

'Comm channels are garbled. Could be spill from the pulsar, but we're getting nothing on the hailing frequencies, and we can't pick up any transponder coding from the vessel.'

'Vessel drawing closer. Nothing in the registry to identify it.'

Karasev looked at the screen, seeing the ship continue its silent, steady approach. The feeling of unease worsened. He was just about to order a course change away from the ship, and for the *Volpone's* gun batteries to be run out and readied to fire, when the image on the screen suddenly warped for a second.

At first he thought that it was just more vidpict interference, but then he told himself that, no, it had definitely been the image of the ship itself which had changed, while the starfield behind it remained in clear focus. For a moment – just the briefest of moments – the image of the frigate had flickered off, revealing the merest, snatched glimpse of... *something else* behind or beyond the façade of that image.

Another ship, Karasev told himself irrationally, unable to deny what he had just seen with his own eyes. *It's a projection concealing a completely different ship!*

'Battle stations! All power to defence shields!'

The order was only half out of his mouth when he saw the second impossible thing happening on the augur screen before him. Torpedoes fired from a prow which had no torpedo tubes. Suddenly there were torpedoes streaking through space towards his vessel, travelling at a velocity no Imperium-made torpedo could match.

Karasev stared sickly at the data on his command lectern, seeing the torpedoes eat up the distance between them and his vessel, and knowing that he had made the greatest and final mistake of his career. A caustic Stranivarite oath which could never have come from any Cypra Mundian aristocrat escaped from his lips.

'Signal the *Macharius*,' he ordered, determined to at least give some useful purpose to his final moments. 'Tell them we have been betrayed and are under attack from the eldar!'

Moments later, the torpedoes struck home. The *Volpone*, its eight hundred crew and Captain Vanyan Karasev and his highly promising career disappeared together in an abrupt and fiery conclusion.

* * *

THE *VOLPONE'S* KILLER cruised forward, slipping harmlessly past the expanding cloud of wreckage of the destroyed Imperial frigate, effortlessly shrugging off the false ship image projected by its mimic engines. The image of the Praetor class frigate wavered and faded away. In its place was the sinister and predatory shape of a dark eldar cruiser, the strange black material of its smooth, featureless and shell-like hull seeming to draw in the light from the starfield around it.

On board the vessel's bridge, the dark eldar commander savoured the thrill of the kill, while lamenting the necessity of having to completely destroy the human vessel without being allowed to take prisoners. Slaves, whether intended for use as sacrifices, torture fodder, cruel and terrible haemonculi experimentation or merely forced labour, were the currency of her kind, and a ship's captain who returned from a raiding mission with their slave holds full of fresh, valuable new flesh could expect to receive the favour of their kabal lord.

This, however, was no mere raiding mission, and there were greater prizes at stake here than the opportunity to take a few hundred human slaves. The Kabal of the Poison Heart had lost much prestige and status in the recent Wych cult schism which had convulsed Commorragh society, and the kabal's fortunes had waned as those of its enemies had risen. Shorn of many of its traditional allies, most of whom had been all too happy to abandon pacts made more out of fear than respect or loyalty and go over to the side of their enemies, the kabal had been left isolated and facing extinction. In the deadly, ever-shifting pattern of brutal intrigue, assassinations and constant internecine warfare that passed for politics in Commorragh, the Kabal of the Poison Heart would not be the first ancient clan to be wiped out without trace or subsumed completely into the ranks of a more powerful rival, and it would certainly not be the last.

Archon Satikus however, could not have maintained his position as kabal lord of the Poison Heart for these last few thousand years, ruthlessly despatching countless claimants and pretenders to the title, without possessing some measure of cunning and guile. This secret alliance with the creature known as Abaddon the Despoiler would, if it were to become known to the rest of their kind, be enough to ensure the Poison Heart's swift and certain destruction by the combined might of all the kabals in Commorragh, but, as there were great risks in this venture, so too were there potentially great rewards.

To arrive back in Commorragh with holds full of thousands of human slaves; not mere sub-standard civilian chattel gathered in plunder raids on isolated settlements and colonies, but the finest specimens from the crews of the humans' warships. Strong bodies and more resistant flesh, capable of withstanding greater and crueller abominations than their weaker brethren.

But there was better than that.

To arrive back in Commorragh with a prize greater than more mere mon-keigh slaves. To display before the other kabals hundreds or perhaps even thousands of those who were once their kin, but who long ago abandoned the inhabitants of Commorragh to their fate at the hands of the Great Devourer, and who denied them a place of safety amongst their own ranks. Yes, what tortures, what exquisite, long-lasting suffering wouldn't any of her kind wish to see visited upon those most hated of their former brothers, the eldar of the craftworlds?

But, oh yes, there was even better than that.

To arrive back in Commorragh with a prize greater even than so many craftworld eldar. A prize great enough to make Lord Satikus risk all to capture it, even the complete destruction of his kabal. What Archon in what other kabal wouldn't want to acquire such a prize for himself? What price might such a prize attain at exclusive auction amongst the highest kabal lords? How much of its former power and prestige would the Poison Heart recover when Lord Satikus paraded his rare, precious prize before his peers?

Yes, how much power and glory would be theirs, when they offered up the soul of a farseer to the One Who Thirsts?

The cruiser commander smiled at the thought, and turned her attention back to the business of the hunt.

The dark eldar cruiser sped on silently through the void, bearing down swiftly on its next chosen target.

* * *

ELSEWHERE IN THE Stabia system, the *Volpone's* destruction would have registered as a sudden, tell-tale energy burst on the pictskin sensor screens of any nearby eldar craft. As it was, the craftmaster and crew of the nearest eldar vessel, the Aconite class frigate *Medhbh's Shield*, were too occupied with other, more pressing, matters to notice the incident.

Their attacker had appeared from literally empty space, it had seemed to Craftmaster Hora Kyrrl. It was almost as if it had unfolded from the blackness of space itself. Kyrrl was young as his race judged such matters, and, relatively unversed in the deeper, darker secrets of the history of the eldar, and at first he had not recognised the attackers for what they truly were. The ambush had been swift and sudden, and it was only after the enemy cruiser had launched torpedoes, only after the *Medhbh's Shield* had been struck amidships by two of them and suffered a catastrophic energy drain which had left it floating powerless and defenceless in space, only after the enemy ship had come alongside and launched a boarding assault on their victim, that Kyrrl's worst fears had been confirmed.

'The Dark Ones,' breathed one of his thought-talkers at the first, terrible sight of their attackers in the flesh. The thought-talker was old, and perhaps had previous, first-hand experience of such things, things which went unspoken amongst the eldar, but, for the younger eldar such as Kyrrl, it was as if part of their race's darkest, most sinister legends had come to life. At first, he wondered – hoped even, that all this was just some particularly vivid kind of *ashytii*, a nightmare dream from his unconscious mind, born out of the eldar's shared race memory of all their kind had endured and suffered since the terrible time of the Fall, but that notion was quickly dispelled as the thought-talker next to him fell screaming and gurgling to the ground, his torso shredded apart by a hit from one of the enemy's weapons.

The dark eldar swarmed aboard, entering the ship from both sides of its hull and on most of its decks. Kyrrl's thought-talkers were either dead or were unable to penetrate the psychic cloud of darkness which had enveloped the ship, shutting it off from contact with the other eldar vessels in the system. From the moment the first dark eldar warrior stepped through the breach in its hull, the survival of the *Medhbh's Shield* could be measured in mere minutes.

Kyrrl's helmet communicator was filled with the screams of his crew as they died under the Accursed Ones' blades and weapons, and, far worse, his mind was filled with the babbling pleas and cries of those crew unlucky enough to fall alive into the hands of their shadow brethren.

Hails of shuriken pistol fire and the strange but deadly splinters of crystal material produced by the weapons of the enemy filled the passageway, striking the smooth, bone-like material of its walls and tearing long, jagged scars. The infinity circuit mind of the ship screamed in silent, psychic agony at the violations being done to it, at the tainting presence of the abominations now forcing their way aboard it. Kyrrl and the remains of his Guardian squad retreated up the passageway, heading towards the sacred wraithbone core which housed the ship's precious infinity circuit mind. They left their dead and injured where they fell. The dark eldar pursued them relentlessly, firing as they came.

The Guardian in front of Kyrrl suddenly spun and fell, his arm sheared away at the shoulder by a hit from a splinter rifle. Kyrrl turned and fired, decapitating the Guardian's attacker as a volley of razor-sharp shards of metal from Kyrrl's shuriken pistol, propelled at enormous speed by the gravitic forces inside the pistol's firing chamber, tore through the dark eldar warrior's throat and embedded themselves in the chest of a second warrior following close behind.

The dark eldar fell back, and, for just a moment, Kyrrl allowed himself the tempting fantasy that perhaps they were retreating back to their vessel. The illusion was shattered in another hail of splinter weapon fire, striking down two more of the defenders, and pinning the others down as a trio of grotesque figures broke away from the ranks of the dark eldar and charged towards Kyrrl and the others.

'Asuryan preserve us,' gasped Melishya, a female steersman, staring in revulsion at the creatures dancing and capering up the passageway towards them. 'What are those things?'

Kyrrl shared his crewman's reaction of repulsed shock, but did not hesitate as he sent a first and then a second hail of shuriken fire into the body of one of the creatures. It staggered, almost falling as the razor-edged, tiny spinning discs of shining metal ripped bloody holes through its body. Seconds later, though, and as Kyrrl watched in complete disbelief, it was on the move again, dancing and capering up the passageway towards them as it raced to catch up with its companions.

Looking at the things, Kyrrl could only guess what kind of creatures they may once have been. Their bodies had been wracked and distorted out of shape by the most terrible tortures or surgical alterations. They were naked save for leather harnesses which held their torture-ravaged bodies into some semblance of normal form, and their flesh was pierced in dozens of places with barbed hooks and pins, holding open the mouths of unhealed wounds or surgical excavations and revealing gleaming bone and pulsing, blood-slicked organs within.

Repulsed, sickened and filled with an awful dread of the grotesque creatures, Kyrrl and those around him opened fire as one. The creatures screeched in vile, ecstatic pleasure as the shuriken fire tore into them, chopping through limbs and slicing clean through flesh and bone. Kyrrl saw one of the things, a shuriken shot carrying off a good third of its malformed head, continue on towards them, gibbering madly to itself. Another one, flayed by round after round of repeated shuriken hits, only succumbed after all its limbs had been shot away. Its limbless torso, pierced in a dozen places, flopped to the ground, where it wriggled in a spreading pool of its own fluids.

And then the creatures were amongst them, and upon them.

The claws of one creature took away the face of a Guardian who Kyrrl remembered had had the makings of a skilled apprentice bonesinger. A second creature fell upon Melishya, ravaging her with black-stained adamantium teeth and claws. She shrieked in pain and terror, her blood splashing against the armour of Kyrrl's breastplate. Kyrrl dropped his pistol, its disc supply now spent, and reached for his chainsword.

There was a flash of sudden hot pain in his sword arm as he drew the weapon. For a moment, he wondered what had happened, wondered why his sword could still be in its finely-decorated leather sheath when it was also still grasped in his hand, and then he saw the creature with the knife in its hand, and felt the hot streaks of blood pumping out of the stump of his wrist. The creature slashed at him again, opening up his body from midriff to shoulder, and Kyrrl fell to the ground, the strength spilling out of him in a torrent of red.

The creature stooped down towards him, the knife ready to strike again, when a voice, harsh and commanding, sounded from behind it. The creature cringed back in fearful, animal-like abeyance, and another figure stood over the mortally-injured craftmaster. Cruel, pitiless, green-coloured eyes set into a pale face of exquisitely-refined beauty stared down at him. A hand sheathed in a delicately-crafted armoured gauntlet, the fingers tipped with tiny, fine-edged cutting blades, reached down towards him. Kyrrl felt a brief, searing, pain in his forehead, and then the hand came away, holding the blood-smeared spirit stone which had been embedded in the flesh there.

Despair like nothing he had ever felt before filled Kyrrl, and he knew his very soul was forfeit to a force too terrible to be openly contemplated by the eldar mind. The dark eldar warrior smiled, brandishing its shining prize.

'Fear not, "brother", it cooed to him. 'I won't let you die, at least not yet. My surgeons are skilled, and eager for new flesh to work upon. They'll be upset at the loss of one of their pets. I think they'll be glad of the opportunity to fashion themselves a new replacement for the one you helped destroy.'

'ZANE, WHAT ARE you doing here? You're not scheduled to be running any patrol missions for another two duty shifts.'

They were on the cavernous flight deck within the *Macharius* which was home to both Storm and Hornet squadrons. Kaether had been making the final adjustments to his flight suit, ensuring that the plug-in nodes of his helmet were clear and that his suit's emergency oxygen supply was unobstructed, when Zane had appeared, also dressed in full flight suit. He had his helmet off, and Kaether forced himself to look the pilot in the eye, reminding himself that Zane was still the best Fury pilot in his squadron. The fact that the man's face, like much of the rest of his body, was a nightmare of scarred and surgically-rebuilt horror should have had no bearing on the respect due to him as the top-scoring fighter ace aboard ship.

'My apologies, commander,' said Zane, in that disquieting electronic monotone voice which was all the tech-priest surgeons' efforts had left him with. 'I request permission to join your flight patrol. I was praying in my quarters when the thought came upon me that you and the Emperor might have need of me today.'

Some of the other pilots shuffled nervously upon hearing this. It was undisputable that Zane's solo actions in combat against a daemon creature had possibly saved the entire ship during the evacuation of Belatis some years ago, but no one was truly willing to speculate as to the cause of the circumstances which had allowed him alone to know of the creature's presence aboard ship and to have been able to hunt it down and destroy it. Some claimed that it was as Zane said, and that he had been an instrument of divine intervention. Others thought that he was simply mad, and had simply been in the right place at the right time.

Kaether was not sure what to believe. He believed in the power of the Emperor, even if that power was located on remote and far distant Terra, and he believed in the divine righteousness of the need to protect mankind from its many enemies, but he was in essence a practical, pragmatic man and, day to day, mainly put his faith in his own abilities and those of his pilots. The promise of divine protection was all very well, but Kaether preferred the more solid assurance of a Fury interceptor, fully checked-out and fuelled and armed, and a pair of trustworthy wingmen on each side of him.

Zane waited patiently while Kaether considered the request. There was an uneasy mood aboard the ship, Kaether knew: pilots and crewmen whose training and combat experience had taught them that all aliens were the enemies of mankind were now disturbed by the uncomfortably close presence of the eldar vessel nearby, and the idea that Zealot Zane had received some kind of divine premonition would do little to dispel that unease.

Still, thought Kaether, no matter how uncomfortable Zane made him feel, there was something about the man which compelled attention. He turned to the tech-priest in charge of the launch preparations. 'Prep Storm Four for immediate launch.'

Zane nodded in curt thanks. 'What the hell,' Kaether told him, 'six Furies are better than five, I suppose, and the extra show of strength won't go amiss as far as putting on a show for our new eldar friends goes.'

Climbing into the cockpit of his command Fury and allowing the ground crew technicians to strap him into the flight harness, Kaether, still unsure why exactly he had acceded to Zane's request, was struck in answer by a sudden thought, and laughed softly to himself. Manetho, undergoing the same process in his customary navigator's position in the rear cockpit space, picked up the sound over his helmet comm-channel.

'Something funny, commander?'

Kaether laughed again. 'I think we may be in luck on this mission, Manetho. Don't tell anyone yet, but I think I may be coming down with a touch of divine inspiration myself. That'll make two holy madmen in the squadron, so the Emperor can't fail to be watching over us now.'

Manetho's caustic and jesting, and also highly blasphemous, reply was thankfully lost in the shattering scream of a Fury engine powering up as the flight prepared for take-off.

OUT IN SPACE, in the void between the *Macharius* and the *Vual'en Sho*, a flight of Eagle bombers with a small, accompanying escort made long, looping patterns across their designated patrol circuit. They had received stern commands to remain a strict distance from the human ship, but, at several points in the course of the patrol, the bomber flight's commander had allowed his formation to 'accidentally' wander across the invisible border line between the human and eldar ships.

In the command blister of the lead Eagle, Kornous smiled at the thought of the alarm aboard the mon-keigh vessel, the stupid, ape-like human creatures gibbering words of anxiety at each other in the crude, barbaric sounds that passed for mon-keigh language. Perhaps he would be censured for such a breach of orders when he returned to the *Vual'en Sho*, although he doubted it. Craftmaster Lileathon was his life-mate, but, more than that, she was also a fellow survivor of the destruction of their original craftworld Bel-Shammon, and Kornous knew that she hated the mon-keigh with the same bright, terrible passion as he did himself.

No, she might berate him before the eldar of their adopted craftworld of An-Iolsus, but alone, in their quarters, clinging naked to each other and whispering between themselves words spoken only in the dialect of their extinct home, she would say other, far different things to him.

Theirs was a love born of hate and bitterness: two desperate, lonely exiles, cast adrift amidst an entire race of lonely exiles. The hate of each of them fed and fuelled the hate of the other, and soon, though neither knew it, that hate would bear deadly and violent fruit.

Kornous thought-signalled his steersman to bring the Eagle around towards the human ship again. The mon-keigh vessel loomed large before him, its image magnified a hundredfold by the wraithbone-infused crystal material of the cockpit blister. He studied the shape and form of the enemy vessel, his keen eye picking out possible avenues of attack through the overlapping fields of fire of its defence turrets and then seeking and finding vulnerable points of weakness across the surface of its armoured hull.

His hands twitched in frustrated, unfulfilled eagerness to pass across the crystal control nodes on the instrumentation panel in front of him, the pattern of their movements, combined with a simple thought-command from Kornous, enough to launch the Eagle's lethal cargo of missiles.

In his mind's eye, Kornous saw the missiles of his bomber and those around it streak away towards their target. In his mind's eye, he saw the wave of missiles strike the mon-keigh ship. Many of them smashed themselves to pieces against the mon-keigh ship's dense armour, but enough penetrated through to accomplish their task.

In his mind's eye, he saw the missiles detonate in sequence within the body of their target, saw the shape of the human cruiser heave and convulse as its metal innards were pulverised under the hammer blow impacts of the missiles' sonic warheads; saw, moments later, the target begin to break apart, its shattered internal structure no longer able to hold it together.

Saw, a few scant moments later, the enemy vessel consumed in a white flash as primitive mon-keigh plasma reactors catastrophically ruptured apart.

All this he saw in his mind's eye, and all this he desired with all his life-force.

With a mental sigh, Kornous signalled the steersman to change course again, taking them away from the human ship. He watched as the image of the ship slid away out of view. It didn't matter, of course, for he had already committed the details of all its potential vulnerabilities to memory.

'Mael dannan,' he whispered to himself, in mocking farewell salute to the mon-keigh ship.

Mael dannan. Words from the warrior-cant language of his original home craftworld.

Total and merciless extermination.

'THEY'RE LOOPING AWAY again, sir, same as they did the last few times.'

Semper studied the icons on the surveyor screen, confirming for himself the information relayed to him by one of his junior officers. The eldar attack craft formation was indeed moving away from the outer periphery of the *Macharius's* defensive range.

'Typical attack pilot grandstanding, perhaps, A show of bravado. Maybe their bomber and fighter crews aren't that much different from ours after all,' mused Semper, only half-seriously.

'Or perhaps they're testing us,' suggested Nyder, gruffly. 'Practising attack runs and testing the range of our defence turrets and the reaction times of our fighter patrols. Or goad-ing us even, maybe. Trying to find out how far they can push us before we'll react.'

Semper grunted in reply, acknowledging the potential truth of Nyder's comment, even if it was not exactly what he wanted to hear at this moment in time. He looked towards his communications crew.

'No word yet from the *Mosca*?'

'Nothing yet, sir,' saluted an officer. 'Same with the *Volpone*. Damned pulsar interference is still playing merry hell with our comm-channels.'

'Any word on the last transmission we heard from the *Volpone*?' Their last contact with the patrol frigate had been over an hour ago, but it had been garbled and indistinct, almost obliterated by pulsar-created static.

'Nothing yet, sir. We've given it to Magos Castaboras to play with. He's running it through the logic engines to see if he can filter out any of the interference and make some sense of what the *Volpone* was saying. We should have something from him soon.'

Semper grunted again in acknowledgement, a sure sign that he was troubled or irritated. He considered things for a moment, then gave his waiting officers their orders.

'Mister Nyder – put out extra fighter screen patrols and have all your attack craft squadrons put on standby, ready for emergency launch. Tell your pilots to see off any more incur-sions into our defence zone from any of the alien craft. Let's see how they react when we hang the "no entry" sign up on the door. Comms – signal the *Graf Orlok* and tell them to proceed at speed to the last known position of the *Mosca*. If we can't raise them, maybe *Graf Orlok* can. And signal *Drachenfels* to do likewise with the *Volpone*. Tell that old rogue Ramas that–'

He was abruptly cut off by the urgent voice of a commu-nications officer.

'Sir, flash-comm signal coming through from the *Drachen-fels*. They're in combat with hostiles. They're reporting they're under attack by at least one eldar vessel!'

The words were barely out of the man's mouth before a second shout from a surveyor officer. 'Eldar cruiser is coming about. Strong energy surge detected – it's powering up weapons and defence systems!'

A glance at the augur screens confirmed everything the surveyor officer said, and instantly brought to life all Semper's worst fears about this mission and the true, treacherous intentions of the alien eldar.

'Battle stations!' he bellowed. 'We're about to come under enemy attack!'

DOWN ON THE surface of Stabia, the dust storm seemed, if anything, to have worsened in intensity. Ulanti and Kyogen sheltered in what they had laughably termed the Imperial forces' command point, even if it was little more than a half-roofed ruin. The eldar were encamped in the ruins on the other side of what appeared to have once been some kind of central plaza or square. Horst and the eldar's apparent commander – Ulanti was unsure what exactly the alien's status was: some kind of high priest was the nearest he could judge – were sequestered in a temple-like building in the centre of the open area, talking over whatever urgent and covert matter it was that had caused them to arrange this parlay in the first place.

The building the meeting was taking place within appeared to be the only intact structure in the entire area. Stavka and a handpicked guard of the inquisitor's senior armsmen were hunkered in the ruins nearby, staring through the swirling dust in sullen, suspicious hostility at the similar eldar retinue stationed likewise nearby on the aliens' half of the area. The eldar commander's chief henchman or champion warrior, the same one who had been first to appear and who had regarded Ulanti and the others with such detached contempt, stood there fixed and immobile, a figure of awe and fear in his unfamiliar, peacock-hued armour, his alien weapons held at the ready. If the eldar warrior even noticed the dust storm raging around it, then it certainly gave no indication.

'Arrogant alien bastard,' growled Kyogen, studying the figure of the eldar through an infra-red augmented auspex scope, a piece of equipment borrowed from one of Horst's retinue, and just about the only thing they had which could pierce the veil of swirling dust. 'Look at it, standing there like it owns the whole galaxy. How much longer do you think this is going to take? The sooner we're done with this and away from these xenos scum, the better.'

Ulanti didn't much care for the commissar's comments, just as he found increasingly unnerving the way Kyogen kept flipping the activation stud of his chainsword on and off, setting the weapon's monomolecular cutting blade in brief but noisy whirring motion, or the way in which his hand constantly strayed towards the holstered bolt pistol at his side, playing with the holster's brass clasp. The man was clearly rattled by being in such close proximity to the eldar, and Ulanti seriously, if silently, questioned his fitness for a mission such as this.

There were, however, matters which were troubling him even more urgently: their inability to make contact with the shuttles still waiting at the landing zone, for instance. The shuttles, with their powerful onboard comms equipment, were their main link with the orbiting *Macharius*, and Ulanti and the others had heard nothing either from the shuttles or the *Macharius* in the last hour. He had despatched a squad of armsmen, led by Borusa, back to the landing zone to investigate. So far, they had heard nothing. Hedging his bets, and suspecting that there was some undetected aspect of the alien ruins which might be hindering normal communications above and beyond the effects of the dust storm, Ulanti had also sent a second and smaller armsmen squad to accompany a comms officer equipped with a backpack vox set to search for a clearer transmission zone beyond the area of the ruins.

'Ravensburg,' came a shout from the area of the perimeter guard, a panicked-sounding voice giving the codeword which would tell the nervous armsmen sentries to hold their fire. A few moments later, one of the armsmen Ulanti had sent to accompany the comms officer came scrambling into the ruin. Red-faced with exhaustion, he tore off his rebreather mask, gasping for breath in the dust-choked air. Ulanti noticed that the man was stripped of weapons and all other non-essential equipment. A messenger runner, sent back ahead of the rest of his comrades and bearing news which could not wait for the arrival of the comms officer.

'Beg to report, sir,' gasped the man, still managing to present a passable salute to Ulanti and Kyogen. 'We made contact with the Mach, although it didn't last long. They're under attack, sir. They're in battle with the alien ship!'

Ulanti's laspistol and Kyogen's bolt pistol were in their hands instantly, even before the first sounds penetrated through the blanket of the dust storm from the events now unfolding on the edge of the ruins. Gunfire, the familiar, barking roar of navy shotcannons mixed with the hissing crack of alien weaponry. And, following soon afterwards, human-voiced sounds of alarm and the screams of human pain.

'Ulanti to all units,' he shouted into his comm-unit, not knowing how many of his men could hear him amidst the confusion of the storm and the sudden alien assault. 'It's a trap. The eldar have betrayed us! We're under attack!'

FOURTEEN

THE FIRST KAETHER and his squadron knew of the emergency was when an entire series of amber and red warning runes flashed into life across his control console, as his helmet's comm system was filled with screaming static, and his craft was violently buffeted by invisible waves of energy.

His veteran pilot's instincts immediately knew the cause of the power surge interference which was currently threatening to overwhelm his Fury's control systems, but his conscious mind took several vital more seconds to realise what was happening.

'Evasive manoeuvres! The *Macharius* is raising its shields,' confirmed Manetho, from the cockpit space behind him. 'We're too close! We're caught in the flux of the energy back-wash!'

Kaether fought with the controls, powering the Fury out of the grip of the invisible force which was threatening to destroy it. He fed more power to the engines, seeking to put as much distance as possible between himself and the *Macharius*, and the energy force it was now throwing out. As the Fury turned and looped in a safe course away from the massive shadow of its mothership, he caught a brief glimpse of the Dictator class cruiser as it swung across the portside view from his cockpit.

It was moving, engaging the main drive engines, the tell-tale plumes of plasma fire along the sides of its hull showing that it was firing up its manoeuvring thrusters. Slowly, ponderously, the three kilometre-long bulk of the warship was swinging round in space.

'They're making evasive manoeuvres,' Kaether realised, almost shouting into the squadron comm-net. 'They're under attack!'

Even as he looked, he saw the eldar cruiser swing round towards the *Macharius*. In comparison with the Imperium vessel, the movements of the alien craft were lithe and graceful; it seemed almost to turn on its own axis without the visible aid of any manoeuvring thrusters. Despite the seductive grace of the manoeuvre, despite the way in which the strange craft's giant, almost sail-like appendages spread out, their delicate crystalline veins and surfaces scintillating as they caught the sunlight from Stabia's two stars, Kaether recognised the manoeuvre for exactly what it was.

An attack.

Now he knew he and his squadron were in even greater danger. Tiny as the Furies were in comparison to the leviathans of the *Macharius* and the eldar ship, it was highly unlikely that any of his squadron would actually be hit by the incoming weapons fire from the eldar ship, but that was not what worried Kaether.

The *Macharius* had its shields up now, probably at full strength, judging by the amount of feedback wash which was still cutting into the Fury's own onboard systems. The shields would bear the brunt of the enemy's initial attack, protecting the ship from serious harm, but the impact of the enemy weapons fire against the powerful void shield barrier would unleash an energy burst of ferocious strength, more than capable of annihilating any attack craft caught in its reach.

Kaether opened up with the Fury's afterburners, punching the space fighter at speed away from the *Macharius* and out of the danger zone. The rest of the pilots in the patrol flight followed suit, just as the eldar ship opened fire.

Kaether saw a brilliant, stuttering stream of lance fire burst from the alien ship's prow. His cockpit surveyor screen flared brilliant red, overloaded by the readings it was receiving back as the energy beams cut through space around his flight. Despite conventional wisdom, he had to jink his Fury out of harm's way, as one burst of energy bolts passed lethally close to his fighter.

The long, stuttering line of energy fire struck the *Macharius* square on, hammering against the invisible barrier of its void shields. The eldar ship kept up the punishing torrent of fire for far longer than Kaether would have believed possible, certainly for far longer than the recharge capacity of any Imperium-built lance battery could have managed. Exhausted by the relentless battering they were being subjected to, the *Macharius's* void shields collapsed in an implosion of energy. The remainder of the eldar lance fire slashed across the Imperial cruiser's hull, laying open its armoured flanks and blowing apart launch bays and shuttle docks.

Wounded, violated, the *Macharius* still swung ponderously round in space, completing the rest of its manoeuvre.

The blast wave thrown out by the collapsing void shields sped out in pursuit of the escaping Fury flight, crackling bursts of electromagnetic energy and fiery plasma squalls snapping angrily at the fighters' tails. At the head of the scattered formation, Kaether rode out the effects of the shockwave, gripping the flight controls tightly and mumbling the words of half-remembered prayers as he felt his fighter shake violently around him.

Only after the dissipating shockwave had passed, only after the flashing runes on the instrumentation panel in front of him returned to something resembling normalcy, only after the feedback scream had faded away to be replaced by an excited babble of voices from the flight controller officers aboard the *Macharius*, did Kaether allow himself to look at the panel showing the squadron status runes. Four runes were still lit; two were not.

Two Furies gone, destroyed by the energy wave from the collapsing void shields. Lerovo and Selle. Two good pilots. Two men who had been with Kaether and Storm squadron since almost the start of the Gothic War.

Finally, through the babble of comm-net voices and the communications-disrupting after-effects of the shockwave, Kaether was able to make contact with the *Macharius*. The orders he received were exactly what he had expected.

'*Macharius* to Storm Leader. We are under attack. Engage nearest enemy targets at once.'

Kaether smiled. He didn't have to check with Manetho to find out what those nearest targets might be.

KORNOUS'S MIND WAS a storm of cold, fierce fury. They had received word from the *Vual'en Sho*. The mon-keigh had betrayed them yet again. One of the mon-keigh ships had attacked and destroyed the *Lament of Elshor*, and they had lost contact with *Medhbh's Shield* and could only presume that it too had been destroyed. The killers of these two craft were on the loose elsewhere in the system, beyond Kornous's reach, but the human flagship was right here in front of him, already under vengeful attack from the *Vual'en Sho*, and Kornous was determined that it would not escape unpunished.

With a single, powerful thought-command, communicated in a way which offered no opportunity for question, he directed the flight of Eagle bombers towards their target. Forewarned of the mon-keighs' treachery, the *Vual'en Sho* had struck first, but, for all its barbaric crudeness, the mon-keigh vessel was larger and more powerful, and Lileathon's vessel would stand little chance against it in a straight duel. Both vessels were carriers and both would now be scrambling to launch their fighter and bomber squadrons. Whichever vessel got its attack craft into space first would almost certainly win the battle. A successful bombing attack now on the mon-keigh ship's launch bays, with its flight decks crammed with fuel-and-munitions-laden attack craft, would leave it crippled and at the mercy of the *Vual'en Sho's* other bomber wings.

Kornous was determined to land that knock-out blow, and punish the mon-keigh for their endless deceit and upstart arrogance.

A flicker of doubt – a mind-thought warning from Kelmon, commanding the Eagle craft on his far starboard, passed through Kornous's consciousness. Kelmon had detected a wing of human fighter craft speeding towards them on an intercept course. Kornous surveyed the sensor information fed to him through the bomber's infinity circuit matrix, and then dismissed his wingman's warning with a contemptuous mental shrug.

A mere four craft, he almost laughed to himself. What could such things – rudely built, powerfully but crudely armed, piloted by soulless mon-keigh animals – achieve against his own craft and crew?

The answer was not long in coming.

Suddenly, shockingly, the Eagle on Kornous's near portside exploded apart, struck by a hail of lascannon fire at a range and accuracy which the eldar commander did not think possible of mere mon-keigh gunnery skills.

The Eagle squadron split apart at his command, offering their enemies a spread of fluid, fast-moving targets, forcing them to break their own formation in response. The human fighters split into two sets of pairs, closing in on their designated targets.

At Kornous's mind-thought command, one of those targets, Marhwdron's craft on the far starboard, peeled away from the others, abandoning its bombing run but drawing off the two enemy fighters from the main battle, leaving just two of them still in the fight.

The eldar craft opened fire with their forward turrets, infinity circuit-linked scatter lasers filling the space around the human fighters with bright-splashing las-fire. To Kornous's almost incredulous consternation, the two mon-keigh craft weaved a skilful – or perhaps merely just fortunate, he thought to himself – path through the twisting maze of weapons fire.

The two Furies opened fire in return, the accuracy of their fire proving that their survival so far had not been a matter of mere good fortune.

The Eagle on Kornous's portside spun away as missiles blew off one of its wings and shredded its tail. From the craft behind him came a collective mental death-scream as a volley of lascannon fire from the other human fighter blew apart its cockpit section.

The fighters flew in tandem through the midst of the dispersed Eagle formation, their rear gun turrets spitting out fire at the eldar bomber craft. Seething with fury – how could two mere mon-keigh craft wreak such havoc? – Kornous linked into his craft's infinity circuit systems, using his own consciousness to boost the efforts of his craft's defensive turret fire.

Massed fire from linked series of shuriken cannon gored the belly of one of the fighters, flaying through plasteel armour. Fire from another of the Eagles struck the other human fighter, blowing out one of its wing-mounted engines, but the Eagles did not escape the exchange unscathed. Combined autocannon fire from the two Furies riddled the hull of another Eagle, crippling it and causing multiple casualties amongst its crew.

Even through the protective firewall installed in his craft's mind-link communications systems, Kornous could easily sense the pain in the mind-voice of the co-pilot of the damaged Eagle. Her pilot commander was dead, blown apart by human auto-cannon shells, the bomber's hull was punctured in dozens of places and she herself was badly injured, struck by shrapnel from an exploding control console. Despite her wounds and the damage to her craft, the young eldar pilot was requesting permission to carry on towards the target.

Kornous ordered her to return to the *Vual'en Sho*, with a single angry command. Eldar blood was too rare and precious to be wasted in noble but futilely suicidal gestures.

Inwardly, he cursed to himself. Five of his Eagles were gone, leaving just two of them to continue the bombing run. The mon-keigh had been lucky so far, but, as they closed in on the target, the favour of Asuryan would be with them now, Kornous knew.

One of their pursuers, the one with the crippled engine, fell back, reluctantly abandoning the chase. The other one, with the shredded fuselage, wheeled and gave pursuit, its pilot pushing his damaged craft hard to make up the lost ground between him and his targets. Had it been any other kind of being, Kornous would have been grudgingly impressed at the pilot's furious bravery and single-minded dedication to the chase. As it was nothing more than a mon-keigh, Kornous knew all the pilot was really doing was brutishly obeying its basest animal instincts to keep on fighting, even at the cost of its own life. At the speed he was pushing his crippled fighter, the foolish mon-keigh pilot would soon realise the error of his ways when the thing simply tore itself apart around him.

They were close now. The shape of the target loomed up ahead of them. Defence fire flashed out from it, but the two Eagles skipped effortlessly past and through, Kornous almost laughing at the predictable patterns of the humans' gunnery abilities.

Two of the cavernous launch bays buried into the hull of the vessel flared into angry life, and two separate swarms of fighters buzzed out of them. Hurriedly launched, and seeking targets already dangerously close to their mothership, it would take several seconds – several vital, precious seconds – for the fighters to organise and acquire their targets. Kornous denied them that vital leeway, diving into the midst of one of the groups and commanding his craft's gunners to open fire.

Two of the Furies exploded apart, caught in the streams of shuriken and pulse-laser fire. Another few seconds, another relentless and close-range burst of pulse-laser fire, and another human fighter was gone. The rest scattered in panic, inadvertently opening up a path towards the target. By the time they regrouped and gave pursuit, Kornous would already have launched his missiles and be on his way back to the *Vual'en Sho*.

The other Eagle was gone, fallen prey to the other swarm of human fighters. That made Kornous, and the clusters of sonic warhead missiles carried by his Eagle, all the more precious. He would have to pick his target carefully.

As if in answer, light flared within another launch bay, signalling more attack craft firing up for imminent launch. This was the moment when attack craft were at their most vulnerable. A successful hit on that launch bay would probably destroy an entire squadron of craft, the chain reaction explosion blowing back into the flight deck hangars beyond, destroying even more of the human ship's complement of attack craft and crippling its ability to launch any more.

Kornous smiled, seeing the gaping mouth of the target launch bay open in front of him. '*Mael dannan*', he whispered to himself, thought-triggering the missile firing systems.

A split-second later, his Eagle shuddered violently. It was too soon and too violent to be the after-effects of the missile launch, Kornous knew, with a sudden sick realisation. In the remaining split-second which remained of his life, he looked into his sensor systems and saw the impossible.

The damaged Fury, the one which should have torn itself apart long ago, was sitting on his tail and blowing his craft apart with tight, concentrated bursts of lascannon fire. Kornous's scream of rage at his unjust fate was lost in the conflagration as a lascannon shot hit one of his missile warheads, detonating it and utterly vaporising Kornous and his craft.

Of the missiles which he had managed to launch, most spiralled off into space. A few, unguided and unaimed, smashed harmlessly into the densely-armoured sides of the *Macharius*.

ZANE THROTTLED BACK on his Fury's power systems, avoiding the expanding debris cloud which was all that remained of his target. As damaged as it was, his Fury would need little more encouragement to explode apart around him from an impact with even the smallest fragment of spinning debris. Other than the hissing of escaping air from his Fury's oxygen supply, there was no other sound in the cockpit. Certainly nothing from the space behind him, where the junked, bleeding remains of his servitor navigator still sat in place, killed by the strange razor shards of enemy fire which had penetrated the craft in their pass right through the middle of the enemy formation.

Zane permitted himself a small moment of human pleasure, offering up a prayer of thanks to the Emperor who had guided his hand in those last few moments. Machine mind had told him that what he was trying to do was impossible, that it was almost certainly a pointless, futile gesture which would lead to the destruction of him and his craft, but Zane had not listened. Human spirit and human hands, guided by the greater hand of the Divine Emperor, had carried him through.

'Storm Leader to Storm Six. Fine shooting, Zane. Return to the *Macharius* before that crate falls apart around you. I'll follow you in.'

It was the voice of Kaether, trailing far behind in his own crippled Fury and carefully nursing an engine thruster which was threatening to explode apart on him any moment. Together, the two of them had almost single-handedly seen off an attack which would have left the *Macharius* almost defenceless against the enemy's own attack craft. Assuming they survived the battle which was still only just beginning, another piece of *Macharius* legend had just been created.

'Understood, commander. Returning to base,' was Zane's only reaction to his place in this legend.

STANDING AT HER position on the command deck of the *Vual'en Sho*, Craftmaster Lileathon suddenly cried out and reeled back, gripping onto her control lectern for support. Ailill and several nearby crew members rushed to her aid. She raised her head and glared at them in fury, stopping them in their tracks with a single thought-command.

'Back.'

Ailill knew what that look meant, and what had made his craftmaster cry out in the way she had. Standing near her, he had caught something of the psychic echo of it himself. Kornous, her soul-mate and one of the few remaining survivors of craftworld Bel-Shammon, was dead. Even his spirit gem, that part of him which would protect his soul from the abomination of the Great Enemy was gone, vaporised along with the rest of Kornous's craft, or drifting lost and unrecoverable somewhere out there in the void. Kornous, and all he had been, was lost forever to the eldar race, and to his still-living soul-mate.

Up until now, Ailill had still hoped some kind of ceasefire could be arranged with the human force. Details of what had happened to the other eldar ships in the Stabia system were still vague and confused. *Medhbh's Shield* had disappeared without trace, and was presumed lost. It was assumed that it had been attacked and destroyed by one of the human vessels, although Ailill was unsure how the swifter-moving eldar frigate, with its superior communications and detection capabilities, could have been taken by surprise by any lumbering human warship without managing to get a warning out first.

Its sister ship *Lament of Elshor* had definitely been attacked by one of the human ships, and had been able to communicate this fact to the *Vual'en Sho* before its destruction by the human cruiser's fearsome arsenal of lance batteries, but even this dire situation was not as clear as it seemed. According to communications signals intercepted from the human craft, the human ship claimed to have come under attack first, from another as yet unidentified eldar vessel. Unable to track down its elusive attacker, it had instead turned its guns on the *Lament of Elshor*. Other human communications intercepts also suggested that the humans had lost two of their own patrol vessels. A partial signal from the *Lament of Elshor*, sent just before its destruction and as it desperately tried to disengage from battle with the larger and far more powerful human ship, suggested that it too had detected the presence of an unidentified ship in the area.

Too many unknown elements were at work, Ailill thought. Too many anomalies and strange variables. There was something deeply wrong here, he felt. Deep down in his soul, something screamed at him in warning. As second-in-command, as the vessel's *Lann Caihe*, or water bringer, it was his duty to bring such doubts to the attention of his craftmaster. She was the fire which he was required to quench with water, bringing harmony to the command of the *Vual'en Sho*. But Ailill knew that the moment for such action was past, that whatever reason he might have tried to have brought to the mind of his impetuous commander would be nothing compared to the savage, vengeful emotions now sweeping through her mind. One glance at the set of her hate-filled features, one psychic brush with the maelstrom of her grieving, rage-possessed mind confirmed that everything now was lost.

'Attack,' she commanded, in a tone which dared any to try and argue otherwise. 'Send them all to their precious corpse-god. We'll stack them in cairns a hundred high

before that living abomination they call an emperor, and it
still it won't be enough to make up for the loss of Kornous
and the others.'

IN THE DEPTHS of the warp, the shadow point opened wider.
Darkness, vivid and crawling, spilled out of it, threatening to
engulf all.

SOMEWHERE NEAR THE edge of the Stabia system, Titus von
Blucher, captain of the Lunar class cruiser *Graf Orlok*, prepared to end his life in a manner very different from the way
in which he had lived it.

Blucher was not a particularly brave man, but nor was he
a coward. The fact was, he had never been required to exhibit
any of the greater qualities associated with a captain in the
Imperial Navy at any time during his ascent through the
ranks of Battlefleet Gothic. Family connections, blueblood
string-pulling and no small element of good fortune had
conspired to assure his swift and reasonably effortless rise to
the position of cruiser captain, a fact which had greatly ran-
kled many within the battlefleet, most especially those
officers of arguably greater, or at least equal, ability but who
also lacked von Blucher's shared aristocratic family heritage
with Lord Admiral Ravensburg.

The outbreak of the Gothic War, which could easily
have been the breaking of the man, had in fact been
something of the making of him. His command skills had
proven to be competent enough, and, while better captains and more illustrious vessels had fallen prey to the
war's voraciously endless appetite for carnage and
destruction, von Blucher and the *Graf Orlok* had survived,
achieving enough to earn the grudging respect of many
within Battlefleet Gothic.

Some doubters still remained, but, if they could see him as
he was now, seated on the command deck of his ship and
preparing to face his vessel's almost certain destruction, their
doubts would finally have been silenced.

'Twelve thousand kilometres, and closing,' counted off a
surveyor officer, as they watched the enemy target icons on
the augur screen advance relentlessly towards them.

The three Chaos vessels – one Carnage class cruiser, identified by its energy signature as the *Despicable*, a vessel which had erroneously been reported as presumed destroyed during a skirmish in the Lysades sub-sector eight months ago, and two Infidel class escorts – had appeared on the surveyor screens over an hour ago, following a possible warp exit energy burst some time before. Moving to investigate, and still searching for the missing frigate *Mosca*, the *Graf Orlok* had encountered the three Chaos vessels on a course heading in-system towards the *Macharius*.

Damn this pulsar interference, thought von Blucher, staring at the closing enemy target icons. If it wasn't for the random electronic noise being thrown off by the warp-damned thing, they'd have been able long ago to detect the enemy squadron's approach and get a warning signal out to the *Macharius* and the *Drachenfels*.

As it was, they were condemned to fight an almost suicidal holding action, unable to outrun their faster enemies, desperately trying to buy time to make contact with the other ships and warn them of this new threat.

Von Blucher's strategy so far had been simple, but relatively effective. Spreads of multiple torpedo fire had succeeded in scattering the formation of Chaos ships, even managing, at an impressively extended range, to land one successful hit on the cruiser. After that, he had put up a fighting retreat, deliberately leading the Chaos ships on a tangent course away from the other Imperial ships' locations, while turning every so often to fire off broadsides at his pursuers. So far, this tactic had paid off, succeeding in damaging one of the escorts and stripping the shields several times from the cruiser vessel. Now, however, that game was almost played out, and the enemy had closed to lethal range, bringing its deadly prow-mounted lance armaments to bear.

For some minutes, turning to starboard and presenting its broadside flank to the enemy, the *Graf Orlok* was able to trade blows with the Chaos ships. A well-aimed lance strike exploded the prow of one of the escorts, possibly crippling it. Broadsides of massed turbo-laser and macro-cannon fire stripped the Carnage class once more of its shields, landing hits across its sloped topside and opening up several breaches in its hull.

But, outgunned and outnumbered, for every hit the *Graf Orlok* inflicted on its opponents, it received many more in return.

Expert weapons fire from the Carnage picked off the *Graf Orlok*'s two starboard side lance batteries. A torpedo strike from the undamaged Infidel penetrated through to the enginarium section, knocking out two of the Lunar class cruiser's plasma reactors and causing a crippling power loss just when it needed power most. The Chaos ships showed no mercy on their stricken target, relentlessly pummelling it with volleys of broadside fire.

Explosions wracked the *Graf Orlok* from prow to stern. A wave of macro-cannon impacts gutted two entire decks of gun batteries on the starboard side, and detonated one of the secondary magazines. Hundreds died in the initial explosion, thousands more in the resulting conflagration as firestorms swept through decks and galleries, consuming everything in their path. Fires burned out of control throughout the forward section of the ship, isolating more than a thousand desperate crew in the torpedo rooms. Trapped, they faced a choice between asphyxiating to death as the fires consumed the remaining oxygen in that part of the ship, or, perhaps more mercifully, dying in a sudden explosive holocaust when the advancing fires ignited either the torpedo warheads or the missiles' fuel mix.

On the bridge of the disintegrating ship, Titus von Blucher issued his last order as master of the *Graf Orlok*. 'Boost all remaining power to communications arrays. The other ships must be warned!'

Seconds later, several direct hits on the command tower brought the roof of the command deck crashing in. Trapped beneath a gargoyle-carved support column, bleeding out onto the cracked marble floor, his legs and spine crushed, von Blucher could only watch in disbelief as a flickering, fading surveyor screen showed the enemy ships turning and moving away, disdainfully passing up the chance to deliver the final killing blow to the helpless Imperial ship.

Battlefleet Gothic records and the proud family history of the Ravensburg-von Blucher clan would later attest that Captain Titus von Blucher died as he should have, giving his life valiantly in battle against the enemies of the Emperor and dying at the helm of his vessel. What such histories could not know was the true terrible truth of the situation. Von Blucher would die, but not at the helm of his ship, and not for many long, agonising months after the destruction of the *Graf Orlok*, and in a place and manner which could not be easily imagined by those who compiled such noble and glory-strewn histories.

Out in space, and as arranged, the dark eldar cruiser emerged from its hidden lurking place and bore silently and swiftly down on the dying Imperial cruiser. Even after the pillage of *Medhbh's Shield*, there was still plenty of room in its slave holds for the remnants of the crew of the *Graf Orlok*, and it was all too happy to claim the prize left to it by the Chaos ships. Mon-keigh flesh was a less precious and valuable commodity than the craftworld eldar captured earlier, but there was always plenty of demand for such slave stock and torture fodder back in Commorragh.

'SIGNAL FROM THE *Graf Orlok*, captain. They report they're under attack from enemy vessels. A Carnage class cruiser and two escorts.'

'And?'

The question hung in the air of the *Macharius's* command deck for a moment. The communications officer who was reporting to Semper shifted nervously, before hesitantly answering his captain. 'And that's all, sir. It's just a partial signal – all communications were then cut off, and we haven't been able to establish contact with the *Graf Orlok* since.'

Semper cursed, a vicious, voluble oath which caused several nearby officers to blanch at the sound of language more fitting to deep below-decks than the bridge of an Imperial warship. He turned, looking towards the two figures standing nearby.

'A two-pronged attack, the eldar in alliance with the Despoiler? Admiral Pardain, could such a thing be possible?'

Pardain opened his mouth to answer, but it was the other figure standing beside him, that of Horst's man, who replied first.

'In my opinion, no, commodore,' said Monomachus, with clinical Adeptus Mechanicus efficiency. 'While the eldar are known to be a piratical race, and while many of the human pirate fleets have gone over to the enemy's side, or at least sworn oaths of fealty to the Despoiler since the outset of the war, there are no reported incidences of eldar pirates directly aiding the enemy at any point. Indeed, Inquisition records show many confirmed incidents throughout Imperium history where eldar forces have, for whatever reasons, actually aided Imperium forces against the servants of the Powers of the Warp. There are also many recorded accounts to suggest that the eldar are also not above taking direct action themselves against the servants of Chaos, independent of any Imperium involvement.'

'Yes,' burst out Pardain, 'and for every one of these "reported instances", I can give you a dozen more proven examples of eldar treachery. You know well enough what they're capable of, Semper. Colonies wiped out, convoys attacked, garrisons assaulted and warships ambushed. The aliens may not be in league with the Despoiler, but they've proven here yet again that they can never be trusted. I had my doubts about this endeavour, and so did Ravensburg, and now we've seen who was right all along. Horst's notion of an alliance with such a race was a brave one, but also a foolish one, as we now plainly see.'

'There is no one single eldar race,' countered Monomachus, smoothly and calmly. 'Rather, our studies have revealed there are many different factions or clan-like groupings, each one with its own distinct perspective and methods. It is a mistake to assume that the proven hostile actions of one group of eldar reflect on the likely behaviour of another. Indeed, internecine warfare between different groups of eldar is not unknown, and there is evidence, much of it Inquisition-sealed, to suggest that the worst atrocities ascribed to the race in general may in fact be the work of some kind of renegade faction or pariah offshoot which is itself extremely hostile to the rest of the eldar race.'

'Could we be dealing with just such a group here? Could Inquisitor Horst have inadvertently made contact with these pariahs? Would that explain why they have attacked our vessels?'

The tech-priest paused before answering Semper's questions. 'I think not, commodore. The inquisitor's methods in making initial contact with the aliens were, by necessity, circumspect and confidential, but he has a thorough working knowledge of xenos matters, and I do not believe he would be so easily duped. The eldar we have seen here are the ones he set out to make contact with in the first place.'

Yes, Horst, Semper thought. He got us into this mess, but where was he now? He looked towards his communications section.

'Still no word from Ulanti or anyone else on the planet's surface? Or from the *Drachenfels*?'

Unhappy shakes of head from several communications officers gave him the answers he feared. They were on their own in orbit around this blighted world, facing an enemy in front of them and now more in the system beyond. They had launched several ineffectual broadsides at the eldar cruiser, watching in helpless anger as it effortlessly eluded each of them, its speed and manoeuvrability taking it out of reach of the *Macharius's* weapons batteries, where it hovered now, proud and mocking. The initial bomber attack on the ship had been successfully repelled, and now a dense screen of fighters surrounded it, protecting it from any further ordnance attacks. The *Macharius's* full complement of Starhawk bomber squadrons sat stacked in their launch bays, patiently waiting for the word to launch in a mass assault on the eldar ship.

So what where they waiting for, wondered Semper? Did his eldar counterpart, like he himself, have doubts about what was truly going on here? It was undeniably true that the eldar ship had fired upon them first, but hadn't he been preparing to do the same and had merely been beaten to the draw by a faster opponent? What had happened to the *Mosca* and the *Volpone*? Where were the eldar cruiser's own escort vessels? Why were they not coming to offer it support against the *Macharius*? Did the eldar ship know of the presence of

Chaos ships in the system? Were they truly, as Pardain suggested, in league with the Despoiler?

There is still so much we don't understand about them, Semper thought to himself, unknowingly echoing the earlier thoughts of Horst. *That's where the danger lies: in our own ignorance.*

'Communications – we still have those open comm-net frequencies to the eldar ship?'

Hard-bitten, veteran navy officers, Admiral Pardain amongst them, gawped at him in surprise. 'Yes, sir,' an astonished communications officer managed to reply.

Despite the seriousness of the situation, Semper almost smiled. If Commissar Kyogen was here, he would surely already be lining up his aim to put a swift bolter round through the skull of the *Macharius's* captain.

'Open up hailing frequencies,' he ordered. 'Tell them I want to speak captain to captain to their vessel commander.'

'A brave idea, but a foolish one.' That was how Pardain had characterised Horst's gambit in initiating this whole rendezvous. In light of what happened next, barely before the words were even out of his mouth, it might equally have described the desperate and highly unorthodox strategy Semper had just tried to set in motion.

'Energy surge from the enemy ship's launch bays,' shouted a surveyor officer. 'It's launching bombers, waves of them.'

FIFTEEN

THE WORLD KNOWN to the Imperium as Stabia had known violence before. The ancient races which had come long before the humans had fought their wars amongst themselves, and between each other, and those wars had on occasion touched this world. After those ancient ones, following purposefully in their footsteps, had come the eldar. The eldar did not wage war amongst themselves, it was widely believed, although their earliest legends and most dimly-recalled and secretly-held histories contained much evidence to suggest otherwise. Such ancient, fratricidal conflicts had not reached Stabia, and the world had remained at peace until the cataclysm of the Fall, when the eldar race turned on itself in one terrible, orgiastic moment of self-destruction.

Stabia had remained undisturbed since then, but the dust that covered its surface knew the taste of blood, and the remnants of those long-vanquished civilisations, dotted across the face of the planet, knew well enough the sounds of screams and conflict echoing amongst their ruined palaces and thoroughfares.

Now, after long millennia of silence, death had come once more to Stabia.

Ulanti ran forward at a crouch, aware of the sounds of death from all around him: screams and shouts, mostly human, mixed with the dry crack of las-fire, the solid, angry roar of shotcannons and the unfamiliar sound of the eldar weapons fire – a strange, high-pitched sibilant hiss. Even over the dull, smothering growl of the dust storm, Ulanti could still hear the loud insect whine of deadly projectile objects passing close by at supersonic speed. It wasn't until a senior armsman close beside him screamed and crumpled to the ground, clutching at his face, that Ulanti, who even with his goggles on could only see a few metres in front of him through the swirling dust, realised that these were no random shots; the enemy was close, and actively firing at him.

He rolled to the ground, landing beside the twitching corpse of the armsman. The man's face was gone, torn away by the impact of whatever had struck him. In amongst the oozing ruin of where his face had been, Ulanti could see jagged shards of some kind of crystalline substance buried into the pulped flesh and bone of the man's skull. Smoke, or possibly poisonous vapour, arose from the terrible wound, and Ulanti could actually see the acidic substance of the shards dissolving as they ate a deeper path into their victim's body. The acid or venom, seeping into the corpse's bloodstream and nervous system, caused it to spasm and twitch violently, giving it the horrid illusion of life.

In spite of himself, Ulanti shuddered. Weapons were designed to kill, yes, but whatever manner of arms the aliens were using was also designed to inflict the worst kind of suffering on anyone merely wounded or maimed by a hit from such a weapon. Cold and aloof, that was his initial impression of the eldar. To that list he had now happily added deceitful, but what kind of cruel and malignant being would purposefully use a weapon like that?

Almost in answer, from out of the dust storm there came a banshee shriek of malevolent pleasure, and a shape came hurtling towards him. He saw a dark silhouette, moving fast and with inhuman agility, its body seemingly and confusingly made up of a series of whirling jagged blade-shapes.

There were blade-shapes in its hands too, although one of them might have been a pistol of some sort, although Ulanti was unsure if they were actually weapons or merely extensions of its blade-constructed body.

All this he saw and tried to take in during one confused and terrified second, and then a heavy booted foot painfully trampled him into the dust.

'Watch yourself, sir. I'll see to this pointy-eared bastard!' called Borusa, stamping over his commanding officer's body as he rushed towards Ulanti's attacker. Inhuman speed and agility met all-too-human brutality and pragmatism.

Borusa put a studded boot into the eldar's stomach, bringing its charge to a bone-crunching halt. He ducked the first, lightning-fast blade that came at him, but the weapon in the alien's other hand cut through the meat of his forearm to the bone. Even before Borusa had registered the pain from the strange, cold metal of the alien blade, he had already dealt the creature a crushing blow with the stock of his heavy bolter, smashing the weapon down upon the creature's skull.

The eldar crumpled to the ground. Roaring in anger, blood spurting from his wounded arm, Borusa planted a foot on the eldar's chest, pinning it to the ground, and blew its head apart with a single heavy bolter round.

Getting up, Ulanti saw the source of his earlier, momentary confusion. The eldar's armour and weapons were studded with long, scythe-like blade attachments. Even the long, crescent shape of its helmet was fashioned into a cruel-edged blade. The alien's armour was mixed, muted shades of black and red. Everything about the alien and its appearance signified a dark and twisted malignity. It was also quite unlike any of the eldar Ulanti had seen so far here, sharing none of the bright peacock colours and delicately flamboyant design that he had seen in their weapons and armour, but he would be the first to admit that he was no damned Inquisition expert on xenos-related matters. However it might be different from the others the thing lying in the dust in front of him was unmistakably still an eldar.

They had come here to cautiously rendezvous and parley with the eldar, a race with a long and bloody history of attacks on Imperium forces, now they had come under attack from eldar. You didn't have to be some damned Adeptus Mechanicus construct to work out what was happening here, Ulanti thought to himself.

It was left to Borusa, cursing and grinning savagely as he applied a hasty battlefield dressing to his wounded arm, to unsubtly set the situation in context.

'Alien or no alien,' he grinned, gesturing to the corpse at his feet, 'the bastards still bleed good enough, sir. As long as I know they can bleed, then I know I ain't going to have too much problem killing them.'

He took up the heavy bolter again, sending a long, chattering stream of bolter shells into the dust storm in the direction the eldar had come from, dissuading any others that might still be lurking out there from trying the same thing. Then, grabbing Ulanti, he ran off into the storm, probing out a path ahead of them with short, menacing bursts of bolter fire.

STUMBLING THROUGH THE confusion of the dust storm, with the muffled sounds of battle coming from all around them, they soon came across other corpses, mostly crewmen from the *Macharius*, but with the lifeless forms of Horst's Inquisition retinue and also several eldar warriors mixed amongst them. Passing the corpse of one of the eldar, Ulanti could not help but notice that it was twitching and jerking in a way identical to the body of the armsman just moments ago, and that there were several identical smoking puncture wounds in its torso.

A victim of alien friendly fire, Ulanti wondered, cut down in the crossfire from one of his brother eldar? In the confusion of battle, in the urgency of the moment, there was no way of stopping to wonder what might have happened.

And there were other survivors too. Looming out of the murk, appearing so quickly that Ulanti almost sent a brace of las-shots into them, came Horst's man Stavka, accompanied by several of his group. Following them came Commissar Kyogen with half a squad of naval armsmen. There were casualties amongst both groups of Imperial servants, one of Stavka's men nursing the hastily-cauterised stump of an arm severed just below the elbow. There was the tell-tale glazed look of heavy doses of kalma in the man's eyes, inuring him from the immediate pain and shock of his wound.

'They took us by surprise, coming at us from all sides,' said Stavka. There was blood smeared across the Inquisition man's face – not his own, apparently, since he showed no sign of injury – and a look of fierce determination in his eyes. He gripped his weapon, an expensive and rare forge world-manufactured plasma pistol/bolt pistol combi-weapon, tightly. The plasma pistol element of the weapon emitted a faint whining noise as it recharged, and the barrel gave off an acrid-smelling vapour as its internal cooling element fought to combat the potentially disastrous effects of the weapon overheating. The gun had been fired recently and repeatedly.

'Are there any more of you?' asked Stavka, looking at the two naval men.

'Perhaps, but I can't raise any of them on the comm. I sent a squad to check on the shuttles, but my chief petty officer here is the only one who made it back.'

Stavka swore in the Low Gothic dialect of his homeworld. 'Alright, then we assume they're all dead and what you see here is all we've got left. They've hit us hard and fast, but there's still enough of us left to do them some damage. First thing we've got to do now is find the inquisitor and get him out of here.'

Ulanti nodded his assent. Stavka clapped him on the shoulder, grinned a humourless grin and then led them at a sprint towards the building where Horst had been meeting with the eldar leader. The sound of weapons fire was heaviest from that direction, although all that could be heard was the strange, mixed sounds of the aliens' guns. Briefly, Ulanti wondered if, in the confusion of battle and the dust storm, the eldar had mistakenly opened fire on each other. If that were truly the case, he mused, then all the better for their own chances of survival, perhaps showing that the Emperor's favour was with them.

One of Stavka's retinue, a female with a powerful physique and primitive warrior tattoos carved into her disfigured face, gave a shout of alarm. She was equipped with augmetic eyes,

which could apparently see further into the murk of the
storm than normal human vision, and she had clearly spotted some imminent threat. Raising her bulky grenade
launcher, she sent a brace of frag grenades flying out into the
dust.

The action was answered seconds later by a series of explosions and the sound of alien screams as lethal hails of
razor-edged shrapnel sprayed out amongst the eldar. The
warrior woman grinned in triumph and raised the weapon
to fire again, but was abruptly cut down by a volley of spinning razor disc projectiles which cut through flesh and bone
seemingly just as easily as they cut through the dust-filled air
of the storm. Struck by several of the missiles, the woman
tumbled to the ground in pieces.

Stavka gave a yell of anger and charged off into the dust
clouds. Ulanti followed suite, snapping off shots with his
laspistol. From out of the dusty gloom, the distinctive
shapes of the eldar began to emerge.

The attack from their rear had apparently caught them by
surprise, but they were reacting with bewildering speed,
turning from behind the low walls and tumbled ruins they
had sought cover amongst to confront their human attackers. Ulanti saw an alien warrior in brightly-patterned armour
turn the long, slender barrel of his unfamiliar-looking
weapon towards them. The weapon spewed out a thin, arcing stream of fire, revealing itself to be some kind of alien
flamer device. The weapon's reach was longer and more
deadly than its bulkier human equivalent; the alien's aim
even deadlier still.

The fireball consumed two of the men from the *Macharius*,
and one of Stavka's lieutenants, a dark-skinned mutant wearing the glowing snake crest skin-markings of one of the
infamous bounty hunter clans of the feral world of Wagner's
Landing. Two of the victims, immolated almost completely
by the potent chemical mix of the alien weapon, were ashes
almost before they hit the ground. The third, one of the
Macharius men, ran onwards blind and screaming as the fire
ate hungrily away at him. One of the eldar disc projectiles,
whether mercifully intended or not, struck him and brought
his agony to an abrupt end.

The wave of fire rolled towards Ulanti, the heat of it igniting the dust in the air, as the alien continued to direct the weapon's deadly reach towards more of his intended targets. Panicking, Ulanti snapped off several las-shots at the alien, seeing the eldar stagger slightly as at least one of them impacted against its armour. Before it could recover and readjust its aim, there was a distinctive screaming-roaring noise from somewhere close to Ulanti's right, and the eldar was struck square on by an angry ball of white-hot stellar energy, killing it instantly and igniting the fuel of its flamer weapon. The eldar and the area around it disappeared in a fiery roar, the flames from the explosion and its scattered debris casting an incandescent glow over the battlefield.

Panicked by the explosion, the other eldar pulled back to another line of ruins. Stavka crouched on the ground and fired his combi-weapon at them in an expert two-handed stance, picking off at least one more of them with short, carefully controlled bursts of bolter shells. Even amongst the loud bark of the bolter fire, the complaining whine of the plasma pistol element of the weapon could clearly be heard as it recharged once more, getting ready to unleash more catastrophe into the ranks of the aliens.

'We've got them on the run now,' shouted the ex-Arbites officer, the gruff authority in his voice evident even over the sound of gunfire and the ever-rising howl of the storm. 'Don't let them regroup or try to slip around us under cover of the storm!'

He was moving again, Ulanti and the others quickly following him. Ulanti had his laspistol in one hand and his master-crafted naval officer's sabre in the other. The shapes of two eldar reared up at him. A solid blast of heavy bolter fire scattered one of them in pieces back into the gloom where it had come from; clear evidence that Borusa was still with him and watching his back. The other, too close for Ulanti's hiveworld cutthroat guardian angel to risk a shot at, was upon the navy officer in an instant.

Ulanti and the eldar traded blows fast and furiously, the metal-working skills of the long dead craftsmen who had fabricated the sabre Ulanti wielded sorely tested by the impacts from the strange bone-like material of the alien's own sword. Remorselessly, he found himself losing ground to his opponent, forced to take the defensive by the alien's relentless and unorthodox fighting style. He looked into his opponent's eyes, the eldar's face at times only a hand's breadth away from his own. In previous duels, he had been used to seeing various emotions in his enemy's visage: hate, fear, desperation, determination. Even the faces of the most inhuman or warp-mutated servants of the Dark Powers showed some kind of emotion, even if it was often some kind of twisted glee at the thought of death, even their own. The face of the eldar betrayed nothing. Its graceful, alien features were set in an expression unreadable to Ulanti's merely human experience. Its eyes, dark and wide, reflected back only Ulanti's own face, and in it Ulanti saw the same expression he had seen in so many of his own opponents in the past: fear and desperation, and a growing realisation of death at the hands of a superior opponent.

He felt rather than saw Borusa's closing presence nearby, but shouted out an angry command forbidding the big hive-worlder bodyguard to interfere. Parrying a sudden thrust of the eldar's blade and barely managing to sidestep the alien's lightning-quick follow-through attack, Ulanti stepped unexpectedly into the alien's guard. Too close to use his own blade, and moving before the alien could dance out of reach again and bring its own blade to bear, he used a move which owed considerably more to the vicious tenets of combat during brutal, no-holds-barred boarding actions than it did to the stylised if lethal etiquette of the art of Necromundan duelling, bringing his knee hard up into his opponent's groin.

Ulanti had no idea about any peculiarities of eldar physiology, or even what gender – if any – the alien might be, but the move seemed to have the desired effect. The alien grunted in pain and surprise, and staggered back for a moment. Swiftly, before the creature had a chance to recover, he swung his sabre at its exposed face, cleaving its skull.

For all the eldar's inhuman grace and speed, it died just like any other opponent Ulanti had slain in the past, falling heavily to the ground with a surprised gurgle.

'Caught it a shot there right in the bilge decks, sir,' grinned Maxim, giving Ulanti a congratulatory clap on the shoulder. 'Maybe we'll make a decent bit of hivetrash out of you yet.'

He had to duck, grabbing Ulanti and dragging him down with him, as the air around them was again rent with the strange, frightening sound of the aliens' weapons fire. There were several screams from nearby – Ulanti saw one of the Inquisition bodyguards, a middle-aged Imperial Guard veteran, sprawling in the dust, disembowelled by one of the deadly razor-edged disc projectiles – and then the answering bark of the Imperial guns.

The outlines of the alien warriors started to manifest themselves out of the murk of the storm. Ulanti checked the charge on his laspistol, as Maxim ratcheted back the loading lever on his heavy bolter, locking a full magazine of the lethally explosive rocket shells into place. He looked at Ulanti as he took aim at silhouette targets moving towards them.

Maxim grinned again, shooting a glance over at the officer. 'Not to worry, sir. Like I said, we've seen the colour of their blood now, and, xenos bastards or not, we know that they bleed and die just like the rest of us.'

He was just about to fire, just about to, by his own expert estimation, shred apart the nearest two eldar, when the shout came to them from somewhere close and to their right.

'Hold your fire. Stop, in the name of the Holy Emperor!'

The voice was shocking in its immediacy, and there was something in the command which demanded complete and instant obedience. Almost involuntarily, and to his own very great surprise, Maxim found that his finger had frozen on the trigger, just short of sending out a long, lethal burst of bolter fire. He looked at Ulanti, seeing the doubt and confusion that must have been evident on his own scarred, brutal face reflected in Ulanti's own expression.

They both became suddenly aware that all the other sounds of gunfire had ceased, human and alien. Whatever power that voice held had apparently held sway with the eldar too. Human and eldar faced each other uncertainly and in silence amidst the swirling screens of dust. The moment, probably only a few scant seconds in reality, seemed to stretch on forever in the minds of the participants, and then the spell was broken as Horst and the others appeared.

Ulanti and several of the others instinctively made to raise their weapons to fire at the sight of the armed eldar accompanying the inquisitor, especially when he saw that same tall, menacing eldar warrior lord amongst them. An unmistakably forbidding gesture from Horst, backed up by a command in that same compellingly dictatorial tone, brought a swift end to such intentions.

'I said cease fire. You'd do well to consider those words as immutable as if they were handed down to you from the Golden Throne itself.'

Ulanti's weapon dropped down to his side, and he rose to his feet. The others did likewise, as did the eldar. The old eldar – some kind of seer or lord, Ulanti surmised – walked beside Horst, his presence commanding instant respect and obedience from the other eldar. He heard no words from the eldar lord, and saw little in the way of commanding gestures, but, somehow, the same command which had frozen the human combatants in place also communicated itself through the ranks of the aliens. The eldar also lowered their weapons and pulled back a short distance, standing warily and suspiciously eyeing their opponents while Horst, the eldar lord and the eldar's peacock-attired bodyguards held the ground between the two hostile groups.

Suddenly, the eldar ranks opened, and the tall, menacing eldar warrior-lord strode forward, gesturing angrily at the seer. The seer's bodyguards clustered nervously around their lord, uneasy at the presence of the armed humans, and the anger of the knight. Ulanti strained to hear over the smothering sound of the dust storm, catching only snatches of the aliens' strange lilting, musical speech, shrewdly noticing that as much seemed to be communicated in silent gesture or body stance as it was in actual speech; noticing too the strange moments of silence and stillness in the conversation which would then resume without apparent interruption, almost as if the aliens had some secret means of communicating between themselves.

The knight's voice became more strident, notes of unhappy discord evident in the aliens' lyrical-sounding language. The bodyguards' unease increased. Finally, at a gesture from the seer, one of the bodyguards threw something down on the ground before the knight. The effect was instantaneous: the knight stepped back almost in fear. His own group of warriors, catching sight of it, also drew back in revulsion from the object lying in the dust at the knight's feet. The seer bent down and picked it up, holding it up for all to see. Ulanti saw it was an armoured helm, black, barbed and sinister, unmistakably similar to the one worn by the strange dark-armoured eldar warrior that Borusa had killed earlier in the battle.

The eldar saw what their lord was holding, and, even over the sound of the storm, Ulanti and the other humans witnessing all this heard the word – half whispered in fear, half shouted in revulsion – which rippled through the aliens' ranks like a palpable wave of shock.

'Druchii,' they said amongst themselves, making the strange word sound like a curse.

'WE HAVE BEEN betrayed, Darodayos, both we and the humans. The Dark Ones – the druchii – are here amongst us, spreading their deceit and setting us and the humans against each other.'

Darodayos stared at the hateful mask in Kariadryl's hand. Like many of his race, especially those of the aspect warrior castes, he was suspicious and hostile to all human-kind, and all too ready to believe that they had been betrayed by the humans. It would not be the first time that the followers of the human corpse-god had turned on the eldar, and Darodayos doubted that it would be the last.

Nevertheless, the eldar warrior was unable to deny the evidence in the farseer's hand. He had fought the Dark Ones before, and knew well enough the kind of trickery and deceit they were capable of, and seemed all but second nature to them. Still, with his own eyes, had he not just seen the humans turning their guns on his own people?

The two things, an innate and deep-seated suspicion of the humans and the equally deep-buried dread of his race's own darker, one-time kinsfolk, fought for supremacy in the mind of the neophyte exarch.

Sensing the confusion in her commander's mind, Freyra, one of the Striking Scorpion warriors and kinsman to the farseer lord, stepped forward, making the third aspect of the fourth gesture of respect – respect due to a war leader from a notable lieutenant – as she did so.

'What the lord farseer says is true, Darodayos. The druchii are upon us. They must have come through another webway portal elsewhere on the planet's surface, and closed in on us under the cover of the storm.' She pointed off into the storm-hidden distance behind her. 'The ones I encountered came from the south. At first, we thought like you did, that the mon-keigh had betrayed us. Then I found the first druchii corpse lying amongst three of my brethren.'

She broke off, pointing grimly to the object still held by Kariadryl. 'I took that off it and brought it to the lord farseer.'

Freyra and the other eldar relaxed somewhat, seeing the subtle but unmistakable signs of understanding and belief in the shifting stance of Darodayos's body language. Nevertheless, the same tone of hostile suspicion remained in his spoken words.

'And the mon-keigh?' he asked.

'My people have been attacked too,' answered Horst in inelegantly-phrased but adequately spoken eldar, in one of the older trading dialects used amongst those eldar who travelled widely amongst the many different craftworlds and Exodite colonies. 'Look upon them, Lord Darodayos. Can you not see the marks of battle upon many of them? We have not betrayed you, and your enemies are our enemies also.'

The eldar knight blinked once in a show of startled reaction. He had never before encountered a human who could speak, however inelegantly, the language of his people, nor had he even heard of such a thing. There were those amongst his kind who sneered that the language of the mon-keigh was little better than the crude grunting and snarling of orks and other lower classes of animals, and it was widely believed that the subtleties of the eldar language, with its many hidden meanings and additional mind-speech and body gesture inflections, was far beyond human comprehension.

A mon-keigh with the gift of speaking the eldar language, and possibly other hidden gifts as well? This mon-keigh, this 'inquisitor', as the humans seemed to term their sage-warlords, was either some kind of racial aberration or disturbing evidence that he and many of his brethren might have dangerously underestimated the humans and their abilities, Darodayos realised.

Now was not the time to debate such matters, though. In the distance, over the noise of the storm, his keen eldar senses were already picking out the sound of the thin, rising whine of approaching danger. The humans had not yet detected it, but already Darodayos and the several of the other eldar were exchanging warning gestures and urgent mind-speech alerts.

'*Dakiilithyli!*' shouted Darodayos aloud in warning to the others who may not yet have sensed the danger.

THE ELDAR KNIGHT shouted something unintelligible and the surrounding eldar reached for their weapons in sudden response to their leader's command. Ulanti was just reaching for his own holstered laspistol when, suddenly and without warning, the new threat came out of the dust storm at them.

Dakiilithyli.

Jetbikes.

Stavka ran forward, roaring in anger, to protect Horst, just as something came speeding out of the dust screen. Ulanti glimpsed gleaming dark metal and barbed blade edges honed to a cruel perfection, and then there came a sound like something you would hear from a butcher's shop or execution block, and a thin wetness sprayed across his face. The object was past before Ulanti had even quite registered what it really was, and Stavka fell to the ground in two sections, the top half of his body landing a metre away from the lower part, his mouth incredibly trying to form words as his twitching hand reached out pathetically towards the fallen pistol lying nearby.

A few moments later, mercifully, he died with a final shudder. The object which had killed him – some kind of small alien jet vehicle, Ulanti realised – flew on into the dust storm again, its rider brandishing a sword in triumph, the Inquisition man's blood still wet on the vicious wing-blades jutting out from the sides of the vehicle.

'More of them are coming. Defend yourselves!' shouted Horst, as more of the alien engine noises came to them over the sound of the storm.

The words were barely out of the inquisitor's mouth before the alien jetbike assault was upon them. Ulanti saw one eldar lose his head to a passing sword sweep from one of the jetbike riders, while one of the *Macharius's* armsmen was swept off his feet by another of the attackers. One moment, the man was standing several metres away, trying to draw a bead on the fast-moving alien vehicles with his unwieldy shotcannon, and the next he was gone, carried screaming off into the storm, impaled on the prow blades of one of the vehicles which had struck him full on.

Ulanti fired off several las-rounds at the speeding targets, but at best only succeeded in managing a glancing hit or two off the black, chitin-like armour of one of them. Any attempt to make any improvements to his marksmanship was rudely interrupted by the screaming engine sound of another one of the vehicles coming straight at him.

He ducked just in time, avoiding the wing-scythes, and then had to keep on moving, rolling across the ground, as the vehicle's angry rider swung out at him with a short-hafted polearm weapon. Ulanti rolled, the weapon blade slicing a line in the ground just beside his head, and then the vehicle was gone, speeding off into the cover of the storm, its rider no doubt intending to make a tight, sweeping turn and come back to finish off his elusive target.

Ulanti came out of the roll, sending a flurry of las-rounds into the storm in the same direction the vehicle was going. His aim was guided more by sound than sight, following the noise of the vehicle's strange alien power source. The glowing las-shots were instantly swallowed up by the dust storm, and Ulanti was none the wiser if they had had any effect or not, when, through the howl of the storm, he thought he heard a more urgent note creep into the sound of the alien vehicle's engine. Ulanti had no idea how these alien craft operated or what kind of power source they used, but the sound made by a damaged and stricken engine was unmistakable.

The over-stressed pitch of the thing's power source grew in volume, becoming a loud, complaining whine, before abruptly fading away to almost nothing, then completely disappearing. Ulanti could have sworn he heard the sound of an impact over the noise of the storm and the surrounding gunfight, but could not be certain. Reasonably assured that the vehicle and its rider would not be returning for a second attack, he turned his attention back to the rest of the battle.

The second wave – or perhaps merely the first wave returning to attack again – of jetbike riders was coming in at them now. Two more of the eldar went down, cut apart by streams of projectile fire from the oncoming vehicles. The eldar on the jetbikes – for that was what they were, Ulanti realised, even if they were members of some rival faction within the same race – were mostly ignoring the men from the *Macharius* and were instead concentrating their fire on their erstwhile brethren.

Whatever the cause of this seeming hatred for the eldar led by the knight and the sage, the Imperium men were more than happy to take full advantage of the fact.

Maxim knelt and took aim with the heavy bolter, patiently tracking one of the speeding enemy vehicles and then pressing and holding down the trigger and sending out a long, stuttering stream of fire. Maxim was not exactly a marksman with the heavy bolter, but the point of a weapon like a heavy bolter, with its high firing rate and lethal stopping power, was that you didn't have to be; with a weapon like this, all you had to do was fire off enough explosive-tipped rocket shell rounds, and you would eventually achieve the desired purpose.

The air around the jetbike and its rider was suddenly filled with screaming, glowing tracer rounds. The rider tried to swerve a path through them, and for a brief moment it looked like he might actually succeed. Then a round struck the vehicle's nose, shattering its armour, while at the same time several ripped through the engine innards at its rear.

The vehicle dipped towards the ground. The rider opened his mouth to scream or curse, but then several more heavy bolter shells struck home and blew him out of his saddle.

The burning, riderless vehicle crashed into the ground, exploding apart and transforming itself into a hail of razor-edged fragments lethal to humans and eldar alike.

Meanwhile, if the eldar were the targets of some special enmity from their darker-souled kin, then it was a hatred which they returned with equal fervour.

Eldar warriors knelt or stood, holding their ground, returning fire at the oncoming wave of jetbikes. The air was filled with deadly, whistling razor discs and crystal splinters from the differing alien weapons, and several eldar screamed and fell, struck down by enemy fire, while more than one jet-bike suddenly swerved away, the vehicle or its rider hit by fire from the eldar disc weapons.

One of the sage's peacock-attired bodyguards – a fearsome-looking eldar female warrior in delicate bone-white armour and flaming red face-mask – ran forward to meet a jetbike which had peeled off towards where the eldar sage-lord stood. Pirouetting through a hail of fire from the vehicle and its rider, she leapt into the air, emitting a loud and inhuman, mask-amplified piercing shriek as she did so. Passing over the top of her target, she struck out with the crackling power sword in her hand, neatly decapitating the jetbike rider as he passed beneath her. She landed nimbly on her feet, but was unable to evade the first vehicle's partner, which brutally rode her down, ripping her apart with a burst from its nose-mounted weapon.

Another of the eldar bodyguards – a warrior in glittering, flame-decorated heavy armour – gave a cry of anger and swung round the barrel of his heavy weapon, immolating both jetbike and rider in a blast of searing heat-energy.

Two of the other riders bore down on Darodayos, perhaps drawn in by the eldar aspect lord's commanding presence and ancient and ornate armour. Darodayos unsaddled one of them with a single, lethal shot from his laspistol, and then stood his ground in challenge to the remaining one, lower-ing his pistol and brandishing his power sword in a show of unmistakable invitation to the other attacker.

It was a challenge which was enthusiastically taken up. The second rider discarded her own pistol and took up a scythe-like lance weapon, snarling in anticipation as she increased her vehicle's acceleration and bore down on her intended victim.

Darodayos continued to stand his ground, unblinking, as he stared down the approaching bike and its rider, apparently heedless of the weapon in the rider's hand, or the blades mounted in vicious, sweeping patterns along the length of the bike's flanks.

Then the bike and its rider were upon him. Darodayos leapt, jumping clear of the lethal blades that passed centimetres beneath his body, swinging his sword out in mid-air to meet the blow from the rider's lance-scythe, the buzzing energy sheath which surrounded the ancient blade shearing through both the haft of the dark eldar weapon and the hand which held it.

The hand and the broken weapon fell away, and the bike and its crippled, cursing rider passed by, apparently escaping. Darodayos knew otherwise. The laspistol, holstered against his leg, seemed to actually leap unbidden into the eldar's hand, even though he had never even tried to reach for it, and then, still in mid-air, he shot the eldar rider three times through the back. She slumped forward dead across the vehicle's controls, and the bike spun out of control, crashing into the rubble ten metres away.

Darodayos's feet touched the ground again, just as the bike exploded. The entire duel had happened in the blink of an eye. Watching, almost mesmerised by the incident, and only able to mentally reconstruct the sequence of events after they had happened, Ulanti was stunned by the eldar warrior's devastating show of speed and masterful precision.

Remembering his own recent and hard-won duel with an eldar who had appeared to be nothing more than an ordinary rank-and-file warrior, Ulanti was forced into an unhappy consideration of how he would have fared in combat against a warrior like this knight. It did not make for pleasant thinking. Ulanti saw the eldar look towards him for a second, almost as if it sensed something of his thoughts, but then abruptly the alien turned away again, raising his weapons and calling out urgent warnings to his kinsmen.

'BEWARE! MORE OF the Accursed Ones. They have raider vehicles!'

The words were barely out of the neophyte exarch's mouth before the first dark shape glided ominously out of the dusty murk. The eldar instantly directed their weapons fire at it, but the cannon weapon mounted on the armoured skimmer vehicle's prow swivelled round and unleashed a blast of dark-hazed energy at them.

'Disintegrator!' The same horrified mind-speech thought flashed through the minds of all the eldar, just as two of Freyra's Striking Scorpion brethren were struck by the weapon strike, and were instantly wreathed in a dark halo of crackling, black energy. When the dazzling black energy glow faded away, all that remained of the two aspect warriors was two fused, smoking masses of twisted bone and armour fragments.

Chiron of the Dark Reapers stepped forward, picking off the disintegrator lance and its gunner with an expert shot from his missile launcher, but the dark eldar skimmer continued to advance, its narrow deck crowded with more battle-eager dark eldar warriors while, behind it, the shapes of several more fast assault vehicles appeared out of the gloom, accompanied by scattered lines of infantry on foot.

The druchii – the Dark Ones – had arrived on this world in force, and Darodayos and his brethren, as well as their human allies, were clearly outnumbered.

'We must retreat,' warned one of Freyra's remaining Scorpions, in mind-speech thought. 'They are too many, and we are too few.'

'That cannot be done,' mind-spoke Kariadryl, the farseer's voice commanding instant respect from all the other eldar. 'The webway gate link to this place is weak and damaged by age and neglect. It is closed now, and will require too much time to re-open, time which the druchii will not allow us.'

'Then what are we to do?' asked one of the mid-ranking Guardian warriors.

'We flee,' commanded Darodayos, tingeing his mind-speech words with the power of his aspect rank, in a clear indication that, as the most senior warrior here, this was a military command decision, not to be questioned, even by Kariadryl. 'You must protect the lord farseer, he is all that is important here. You will hide from the druchii, and you will await rescue from the *Vual'en Sho* and the other craft of ours who are here to watch over us.'

'And what of you, Lord Darodayos?'

The question came from Kariadryl, even though the aspect lord suspected that the wise old farseer already knew the answer.

'I will remain here, lord farseer,' the aspect warrior commander replied, 'to face the druchii and allow you more time to escape. I pass the favour of Asuryan to your blood kinsman Freyra. To her now falls the duty of protecting you.'

There was a chorus of mind-speech voices from the other warriors, many of them beseeching the aspect lord to rethink his decision to stay and fight alone, some of them requesting permission to join him in his stand. He silenced them all with a single, irrevocable mind-speech command.

'And the humans?' asked Kariadryl. 'What will become of them?'

'With your permission, lord farseer, we will go with you.' It was the voice of Horst, spoken in slightly awkward but still comprehensible mind-speech. Shock and consternation – quickly masked – flashed through the minds of the eldar. How much of their mind-speech conversation had the human been able to listen in on and understand, they asked themselves in fearful doubt?

Horst continued, making no show of noticing the alarm he had caused amongst the aliens. 'As I said, your enemies are our enemies too, lord farseer. We wish no harm to come to you and your companions, and our ships are also in orbit above us. Perhaps they will come with your people to rescue us from our mutual enemies.'

'So shall it be,' Kariadryl commanded, ending any further complaints or doubts from any of the assembled eldar.

With the issue settled, the eldar immediately began to follow their designated tasks for the chosen course of action. To the watching humans, it must have seemed as if the eldar were able to act together in eerie and silent synchronisation, for, in real time, the mind-speech conversation amongst them had only lasted a few moments.

'Lieutenant Ulanti,' ordered Horst, drawing the remnants of his own people around him and running over towards the contingent of navy men. 'We're pulling back. Get your people together, anyone that can walk and still hold a weapon is coming with us.'

Quickly, moving together, the two groups moved off away from the advancing dark eldar and into the safety of the cover of the dust storm. Behind them, Darodayos and the small group of aspect warriors who had elected to stay with him prepared to sell their lives dearly in combat against those who were once their kin.

THEY RAN THROUGH the storm, Maxim staying close behind Ulanti, barely slowed down by the extra weight of the heavy bolter he carried. The eldar, naturally faster-moving and less encumbered by the clumsier equipment, weapons and armour of the humans, were ahead, forging a path through the storm, although several of them ran behind, forming a small vanguard to guard the two groups' retreat.

Which left only the flanks to worry about, thought Maxim, holding the heavy weapon alertly and peering through his goggles into the depths of the storm around them, trying to detect any sign of danger.

It was not his eyes, but his ears, finely tuned for survival by the brutal necessities of existence on the hiveworld of Stranivar and its orbiting prison-moon Lubiyanka, which warned him of the first signs of approaching danger.

'Jetbikes!' he shouted, swinging the barrel of the heavy bolter round in the direction that the now familiar thin, whining sound was coming from. 'They must fancy having another shot at us.'

Forewarned, the others in the party swung their weapons round in the same direction. Maxim opened fire with the bolter weapon, spraying a non-stop stream of shots out in a generously wide arc, not even able to see what he was shooting at, but desperate to lay down a heavy field of fire in the path of the oncoming vehicles. A second later, the crash of shotcannons and crack of las-weapons signalled that the rest of the human group were following his lead.

Two dark eldar jetbikes roared out of the murk, spraying weapons fire into the midst of the Imperial troops. Maxim heard screams and the fearful whisper of the deadly alien projectiles passing close by, but the sounds were immediately drowned out by the chattering boom of the heavy bolter as he fired off a second long burst at the oncoming targets.

One of the vehicles targeted him directly, drawn in by the threat of the heavy bolter. Maxim's second or third burst of fire blew apart its nose, bringing an end to the splinter rifle shots now hissing dangerously close to him. The bike, although damaged, still kept on coming. Its rider drew a pistol weapon and sprayed shots at two nearby armsmen who were drawing a bead on him with their shotcannons. The razor-edged alien projectiles took one of them off at the knees, effortlessly slicing through flesh and bone.

Cursing, Maxim readjusted his aim, zeroing in on the rider's central body mass, and pressed the trigger again, but the bolter only fired off a handful of shells before its cyclic firing mechanism suddenly juddered to a halt.

Ammo jam.

The jetbike rider grinned, sensing its target's predicament, and lowered its pistol, manoeuvring the bike to bring its blade points to bear on Maxim. Maxim judged the closing distance between him and his would-be slayer and compared that to how quickly he could draw, aim and fire any one of the several pistols he was carrying.

The likely answer to that equation was not encouraging, so he did the only thing he could, hefting the now useless bolter weapon and hurling it with all his considerable strength into the face of the oncoming alien vehicle.

It struck the rider with bone-crushing force, knocking him clear out of the saddle. The riderless craft spun past, its momentum carrying it forward, and Maxim still had to duck and twist gymnastically to avoid the fate the vehicle's rider had intended for him. Nevertheless, the edge of one of the sweeping tail blades still clipped him, and he hissed in pain as he felt the chill alien metal slice through the meat of his shoulder.

Clutching at the wound with one hand while drawing an autopistol with the other, he instinctively scanned the area for any other threats, and was relieved to see that, for the moment at least, the danger was over. The other bike had been brought down by massed volleys of shotcannon and las-fire, but the cost to the Imperium force had been heavy: of Horst's retinue, only the inquisitor himself and three of his bodyguards remained, while, of the party from the *Macharius*, only Maxim, Ulanti, a chief armsman and four of his troopers were left standing.

And Kyogen, although, from the looks of things, Maxim was delighted to note, the issue of the Ship's Commissar would seemingly not be a problem for very much longer.

The big naval commissar officer had been struck low in the back by a shot from one of the alien weapons. There was a lot of blood soaking through the thick material of his commissar's coat – probably a punctured kidney, and, under the current situation, almost certainly fatal, was Maxim's expert judgement – and the skin of the man's face was pale and waxy-looking from shock and blood loss, and tight with pain.

He was a goner, Maxim knew, so perhaps the situation wasn't such a complete cluster-frag after all. Perhaps those prayer-droning bores in the Ecclesiarchy were right after all, the big hiveworlder thought, and that amongst even the darkest catastrophe there was a hidden blessing from the Emperor.

'We've got to keep on moving,' ordered Ulanti. 'Gather up any spare weapons and especially ammo supplies from the corpses. Emperor knows, I imagine we'll be needing every round we can lay our hands on, soon enough.'

He broke off, looking at the injured commissar. 'Maxim, see to Commissar Kyogen. We're taking him with us, and you're the strongest back we've got.'

Maxim grinned as he bent down towards Kyogen, his grin spreading a little wider as he heard the sniffled grunt of pain from the man as he laid hands on him and roughly raised him to his feet.

'Come on then, commissar, sir, you heard what the lieu-tenant said. Time to be moving on. No need to worry though, old Maxim's here to look after you.'

They moved off again, looking for refuge deeper within the heart of the storm, seeking another place of shelter somewhere amongst the planet's inhospitable surface.

Behind them, back at the ruins, the sounds of distant com-bat could still be heard.

BLACK SMOKE FROM the burning dark eldar raider craft drifted in thick banks across the battlefield, mixing with the effects of the dust storm and further adding to the confusion. Dar-odayos, dropping his spent laspistol and taking up an almost fully-loaded shuriken catapult from the hand of a dead Dire Avenger warrior, gave up a silent mind-speech prayer of thanks for the favour of Asuryan, knowing that this confusion benefited him far more than his enemy.

It was Chiron who had sown the seeds of that confusion, moving swiftly and nimbly through the shifting dust storm eddies, firing off shots with his missile launcher, almost every shot striking its target without fail. After each shot, the cunning Dark Reaper warrior had vanished back into the cover of the storm again, leaving behind him only the sounds of blazing destruction and the angry, frustrated cries of his dark eldar hunters. Darodayos and the others had cov-ered for him, drawing the hated druchii away from Chiron, even at the cost of their own lives, and allowing the veteran aspect warrior to accomplish his set task.

It had been minutes since Darodayos had heard the trade-mark roar of Chiron's missile launcher speaking in anger, and he knew that the Dark Reaper warrior was dead now, since he had heard Chiron's mind-speech death-cry as, finally hunted down and hacked apart by the talons and finger-blades of some of the druchii's most twisted and mindless servant-things, Chiron had commended his soul to the safe keeping of his brethren and detonated his remain-ing stack of missiles, despatching his killers into the ever-hungry maw of the Great Enemy. Nevertheless, the burning wrecks of the three destroyed druchii raider craft were testimony to the effectiveness of Chiron's tactics; if the druchii planned to pursue Kariadryl and the others, then they would surely now have to do so without the advantage of their deadly and lightning-fast skimmer craft.

Another sound tore through the noise of the storm: a terrible, wailing, screaming sound. The death-scream of a Howling Banshee; that of Alarriele, he knew. He had not known her well, for she was young and had only recently begun her journey on the path of the warrior aspect, but she had fought and died well, and her Aspect brethren amongst the warrior path shrines back on An-Iolsus would honour her spirit.

She was the last of those who had elected to stay behind with Darodayos, and now only the Aspect Lord remained. He knew now that his task was even more vital than ever. Every second he further delayed the druchii, every drop of extra blood he shed here increased the survival chances of Lord Farseer Kariadryl and the others.

The shapes of several dark eldar warriors loomed up before him, calling to each other in their own debased version of true eldar speech. To Darodayos, even the crude word-shapes made by the mouth of the mon-keigh inquisitor when he had endeavoured to speak the eldar tongue were more honest and acceptable than the sound of the maliciously twisted but still recognisable parody of eldar speech spoken by these druchii.

Forewarned by a prescience sense which he had become more and more aware of, the closer he drew to the level of true exarch, Darodayos raised and fired the shuriken catapult before his eyes had even properly picked out the silhouettes of the two approaching targets. Both of them crumpled silently, near decapitated by the expertly-directed hail of razor discs, neither of them even able to get out any kind of final mind-speech death-cry that Darodayos could detect, if in fact fallen abominations such as the druchii still retained such abilities.

Nevertheless, no matter how swiftly and silently they had been executed, the deaths had still been detected, and others of their kind were already converging on him from all around.

Pain and death, that is what the druchii thrive upon, thought Darodayos as he despatched another over-eager dark eldar pursuer with a shot from his shuriken weapon. Perhaps that was what their vestigial psychic senses were attuned to now, and that was what drew them in.

More of them came at him. The shuriken catapult in his hand whispered once, twice, three times, and then he discarded it and drew his power sword in one smooth, quick reflex gesture as the next wave of them attacked.

Something screeching, with venom-dripping barbs where its hands had once been, threw itself at him. He cut it in half with one sweep of his power sword, leaping clear to avoid becoming entangled in the thing's potentially lethal death flails. Another twisted abomination, another product of the pain-artistry of the druchii torture-masters, followed in close behind its sibling. It too died swiftly beneath the Aspect Lord's blade.

Still more of them charged, and Darodayos slew them all in turn. These things were nothing more than pets, he realised, grotesques created in the laboratories and torture gardens of the druchii's hidden fastness for the Dark Ones' own amusement and hunger for cruelty and pain. They were using them now to wear him down, he knew, to test his strength and speed without risk to themselves. They were out there somewhere in the gloom, watching and studying him, circling round as they waited for the right moment to attack and take him unaware.

Well, let them come, he thought to himself. No matter how many of their pets they sent against him, they would find him ready.

His power sword rose and fell, the energy current running in a glowing sheen across the surface of its rune-decorated blade, almost singing as it cleaved through druchii-altered flesh and bone, bringing a merciful end to the existences of things which may once have been living, sentient beings before they fell into the hands of the Dark Ones.

As he fought, Darodayos felt his psychic senses and martial skills merge together and become heightened to a degree he had never before experienced or suspected could be possible. Every blow he struck unerringly found its target, every move his opponents made, even their death spasms, had been anticipated by him seconds earlier. He felt parts of his life – whole centuries of experience, memories of valued friends and precious-remembered lovers – slewing away. All that mattered was the here and now, and the joy of combat and killing. In his mind's eye, he saw the lonely, final pinnacle at the end of the path of the warrior, and he knew that he was now ascending to that place, now on the cusp of becoming a true exarch, of abandoning all he once had been and could still be, instead giving himself over wholly and completely to the warrior aspect. Some rational part within him mourned the loss of self, but the greater part of all that remained now rejoiced in the freedom of combat and slaughter, so different from the paths followed by many of his kinsmen.

He fought and killed with wanton abandon. His enemies died around him, and, as they died, so too did the mind and spirit of the being once known as Darodayos. He was an empty shell now, hollow and spiritless, living only for combat and killing the enemies of his race.

And then, suddenly, there were no more druchii things to kill, and the druchii lord and his retinue were making their assault. Despite his anticipation of the attack, though, Darodayos was still almost fatally caught by surprise.

There were five of them, the druchii lord and four of his squires. They moved swiftly and with lethal intent, but little of the ill-cautioned eagerness which seemed to be a mark of many of their kind. The lord led the attack, but Darodayos's exarch-elevated senses saw him as little more than a dark, shifting blur. Darodayos could see the squires and their intent with perfect clarity, could see ahead to what they would be doing vital moments in the future, but to Darodayos's prescience sense, the druchii lord was a blind spot, his actions taking place in so many different, unknowable futures.

It was the *fhaisorr'ko*, the shadow point, Darodayos realised with a shock. Part of it was centred around this druchii lord, concealing him and his actions from the perceptions of those blessed with the gift of future-sight. Suddenly, the druchii commander was transformed into a far more dangerous and ominous opponent than he had seemed just seconds ago.

The druchii lord came on. Darodayos stood ready to meet him. Then suddenly, at the last moment, the dark eldar drew back, allowing the henchman to his left and right to launch their own simultaneous attacks on the Aspect Lord. Darodayos had not seen the move coming – the forces of the *fhaisorr'ko* that surrounded the druchii lord had left him blind to the ploy – and was almost skewered on the blade of the henchman to his left, while only the quickest parrying thrust with the point of his power sword saved him from a similar attack from the enemy on his right.

Darodayos leapt up and back, avoiding his two opponents' lightning-quick follow-up attacks, all the time aware that the third druchii was circling round towards his unprotected back.

His leap brought him down on top of this third enemy, his power sword cleaving through the druchii's body from shoulder to sternum before the druchii had even registered the manoeuvre. Still in mid-air, before his feet had touched the ground, Darodayos brought the sword round in a tight sweep, sending a fine mist of dark eldar blood flying from its crackling blade, and struck down one of the other squires with a single, disembowelling thrust.

His feet touched the ground and he brought the sword up to meet the already pre-determined attack from the last remaining squire and, then, shockingly, the druchii lord was upon him.

The druchii commander fought with two short, hand-held, multi-bladed weapons which were part dagger, part scythe and part glaive. His manner of combat with these dangerously unfamiliar weapons was furious and lethally uncompromising. Darodayos, with the longer and more powerful weapon, was forced back on the defensive, his sword weaving a barrier before him to fend off the barrage of stabbing thrusts and sudden lunging sweeps from his opponent's blades. Crystallised matter was smeared across the blade edges of both those weapons, and Darodayos had no doubt that death, slow and agonising, lurked there.

Forewarned by his prescience-sense, the Aspect Lord saw the last remaining squire unfurl some kind of long whip-like weapon. The tails of the weapon were woven together from black, glistening cord, which twitched, sinew-like, with grotesque life.

The druchii warrior lashed out with the weapon. Again warned by his prescience, Darodayos twisted away on instinct, out of reach of those twitching cord tails, just as his prescience vision screamed at him in warning, showing him the mistake he had just made.

The druchii lord was on him instantly, one of the poison-frosted blades in its hand flashing past the Aspect Lord's parry to slash mercilessly through Darodayos's fatally exposed throat.

Feeling the blade's chill bite through his flesh, feeling the hot rush of blood from his severed jugular, feeling the first burning sting of the poison seeping through his flesh and veins, Darodayos followed the guidance shown to him by his dimming prescience vision, hurling his power sword out with the last of his failing strength.

The corpse of the last of the druchii squires, his body transfixed by the hurled blade, hit the ground even before that of Darodayos.

KAILASA OF THE Kabal of the Poison Heart stood over the corpse of his victim, dispassionately watching the tremors and convulsions run through the dead Aspect Lord's body. The corpse would retain this grotesque semblance of life for hours, he knew, as the venom ate its way through its nervous system, firing off random pain signals amongst dead nerve endings and lifeless brain matter.

He lifted the blade with which he had dealt the final, masterful killing blow, licking its edge with his tongue and relishing the taste of the crystallised venom mixed with fresh blood. After a lifetime of patronage of the many poison bars and venomfeast-houses of Commorragh, Kailasa was a connoisseur of all toxins and poisons, and was completely immune to many of the more mundane ones such as this.

Still, mixed with his victim's blood, the effects of the venom gave him a pleasingly exhilarating sensation which helped offset his anger and impatience at the unexpectedly costly losses the craftworld weaklings had inflicted upon his force.

He reached down to the corpse of the defeated craft-world warrior, casually removing its helm and plucking out the small jewel set into its forehead. He ran it between the delicately talon-tipped fingers of his gauntlets, peering into its misty, opaque depths. He sniffed at it, and then licked it.

'Exarch,' he breathed to himself in pleasure, pleased that there should be such a fine soul-prize to show for his victory. He threw it over his shoulder, into the midst of the pack of warp beasts behind him. Immediately, the creatures began tearing and clawing at each other, fighting over the rare morsel. One of the haemonculi snickered in morbid plea-sure as the creatures rabidly tore into each other.

Kailasa smiled. Afterwards, when this mission was over, he would lead a hunt for the victor of the battle, for the largest and most ferocious of the pack, and reclaim his soul-prize, ripping it out of the creature's belly with his own hands.

He turned, sensing the lurking, expectant presence of the Mandrakes behind them. He looked at them for a long moment, holding them in his gaze. Four pairs of eyes, full of hungry malice, four dead, gaunt faces, stared back at him.

'Find the farseer,' he told them simply.

THE STORM WAS lifting now. Kariadryl sat at the entrance to the shallow gully where they had chosen to seek shelter and, most likely, he knew, make their last stand. The landscape of Stabia, revealed now under the lifting storm, was even bleaker than he had imagined.

From where he sat, though, everything seemed bleak at present.

Only moments ago, he had heard the psychic death-scream of Darodayos, and was still mourning the Aspect Lord's loss. He had already foreseen the warrior's death – had caught glimpses of it in amongst the shifting deceptions of the shadow point – but the inevitability of the moment made it no less sorrowful.

The shadow point. The *fhaisorr'ko*.

It was here at last, all around them. They were caught in the midst of it, and his far-sight was useless now, leaving him just another weak old man, depending on the strength of others, sacrificing the lives of the young to prolong his own already over-extended existence.

'Honoured kinsman. Lord farseer, you should not be here. It is too dangerous to be here alone.'

He turned, seeing Freyra, the Striking Scorpion warrior who was kin to him. Her tone was politely respectful, but also scolding. Her stance, and that of the two aspect warriors who stood with her, was firm and unyielding; he was under her protection, a duty which she took with deadly earnestness.

He allowed himself to be taken back to the others. His discussions with the human called Horst had not been concluded, and further conversation with him would be a pleasing and enlightening experience, and would help pass the time before the druchii inevitably tracked them down to this lonely and desolate place.

Suddenly, he paused, turning as he sensed something else out there. Freyra sensed his disquiet, as did the other two warriors. Kariadryl sensed the hot psychic rush as their combat senses bristled in agitation, and hands tensed on weapons.

'You sense something, honoured kinsman?'

Kariadryl remained motionless, staring out into the depths of the storm, staring out with his far-sight into whatever hint of the future had briefly been revealed to him by the mocking blank face of the shadow point.

He saw nothing. Not even the phantoms of false ghost-futures.

'It is nothing, kinsman,' he answered, finally. 'Just the dying breath of the storm,'

He allowed them to lead him off again, mentally mulling over the lie he had just told them.

He did not yet know what it was, but something was out there. Something was coming.

THE BURNING GOD strode through the dying storm, and the storm retreated and parted before it in fear.

It had exited the webway through a long-disused portal amongst ruins far to the south. Nothing lived on this barren world, but the wind whispered its forbidden name in awe, and the sand and rocks beneath its feet trembled at its passing. Its pace was steady and measured, its progress constant and immutable.

It continued on, knowing that the end was close, but not knowing whether it would be destined to arrive in time to intervene in the fates which converged at that end point.

SIXTEEN

'Alien attack craft are inbound on a direct assault approach. Still no response to our hails from the alien carrier vessel.'

All eyes on the command deck of the *Macharius* were fixed upon Semper. He felt the nervous, expectant gaze of his crew upon him, and could almost sense the anxious babble of thoughts going on beneath the tense, silent atmosphere which filled his vessel's bridge.

What's the old man playing at, they were no doubt thinking. *We're under attack, several of our sister ships have been attacked and destroyed, and he wants to parley with these xenos scum? We should be opening up at them with torpedoes and broadsides, not hailing frequencies.*

Semper understood his crew's frustration and anger. Nevertheless, something compelled him to try this most unorthodox of strategies.

'Enemy attack craft squadrons still approaching, commodore,' warned Remus Nyder, never lifting his gaze from the vital information relayed to him from lectern point's surveyor screen. 'They're fast, these xenos crates, damned fast.'

The unspoken warning in his report was obvious: whatever it is you're hoping for, you'd better hope it happens soon.

Semper paused, his mouth suddenly dry. Again, some ineffable sense told him there was much more at stake here than just the safety of his ship and the lives of his crew. Somehow, he knew that what happened here would have important ramifications far beyond this moment and far beyond the borders of the Stabia system. Something told him that the fate of the entire Gothic sector could be at stake, depending on what he did next and how his alien opponent reacted.

'Hailing frequencies?' he asked, struggling to keep any hint of inner turmoil out of his tone.

'Open, sir, but still no response to our signals,' answered a communications officer.

'Then open them all, damn it. Use every frequency we've got. They may not want to talk to us, but, by hell, I'll make sure they can't pretend not to hear us.'

Semper waited until a communications ensign gave him the signal that all comms channels were now open. Drawing himself up to his full height and automatically and unconsciously assuming his most imposing and authoritative voice, he cleared his throat and began to speak.

'Attention, commander of the alien vessel. This is Commodore Leoten Semper, captain of His Divine Majesty's Ship the *Lord Solar Macharius*. You have attacked my vessel and we have been forced to defend ourselves. I know that there has been conflict between our two forces already, and I know we have both suffered the loss of sister vessels and the deaths of valued comrades...'

'...IT WAS NEVER our intention for any of this to happen. We came here as you did, in good faith. We came to talk, not to do battle. There is suspicion and hostility between our two races, perhaps with good cause, but I am a warrior, just as you are. As warriors, we must follow orders, and my orders were to watch and guard, not to attack. It was never my intention to engage in battle with you and your forces, and it is not my wish to do so now. Your vessel's strike craft are even now approaching my ship on a direct attack course. My own ship's squadrons stand ready to meet them, just as my vessel's gunners stand ready to open fire on you, to defend my ship against any further attacks. If you continue in this current course of action, we will defend ourselves with all the force at our command, and then there will be no turning back for any of us, for either of our two races. As one captain to another, as one warrior to a fellow warrior, I beg you to reconsider your actions. There… there are things here hidden from us both, I think. Do not ask me to explain, for I cannot, but I believe there is some other force at work here, a force which neither of us is responsible for.'

The mon-keigh's words, barbaric, alien and incomprehensible to most of those listening, echoed through the bridge of the *Vual'en Sho*. Lileathon, listening along with the rest of her crew, had to wait several more seconds for one of her vessel's Mind Talker crew to finish translating the alien commander's words.

As soon as the mind-speech translation was finished, Lileathon and Ailill exchanged looks. In contrast to the captain of the *Vual'en Sho*, there was hope and surprise in the face of the vessel's second-in-command.

'You heard what the alien commander said, craftmistress. He has doubts, just as we have. We must call off this attack before it is too late.'

'More mon-keigh lies! More mon-keigh tricks and deceit! They are filled with lies, filled with deception. That is all they are capable of, that is all their animal souls can conceive!'

Lileathon's voice was a shriek, the unshielded emotion that filled her emphasized by the blast of unmasked contempt which she mind-speech sent out to accompany her spoken words.

Ailill staggered as if physically struck, so powerful were the raw emotions of hatred and contempt psychically broadcast by his commander. There was a hushed, shocked silence all across the bridge. Several crew members made brief, frightened gestures while casting nervous glances at their ship's commander.

Ailill recognized it. The fourth aspect of the second invocation of protection, seeking protection from any eldar whose animus was possessed by powerful emotions. It was a powerful signal, rarely seen in eldar society, and used only in extreme circumstances as a show of severe disapproval at any eldar whose emotional behaviour had gone beyond acceptable bounds. It harked back to the dark time of the Fall, and carried with it the eldar's fear of events of that time, and of the cause of those events.

Raw, unchecked emotion was what the eldar feared most of all. Unbridled, their race's darkest and most sensual emotions had once almost destroyed them. Now, every eldar kept this side of themselves in careful check, and maintained a secret but equally close watch over the passions of their comrades.

Lileathon recognised the gesture too, and knew all too well what it meant. She stepped back, struggling to rein in the fierce emotions raging inside her. All eyes were on her, all eldar minds thinking the same carefully masked thoughts, and Ailill could only imagine how aware she must have been of the secret words those minds were now whispering to themselves.

Outcast. Renegade. *Eshairr.*

'Ailill, my old friend, my craft-comrade... I apologise...' Her voice was harsh and broken, her gesture of contrition clumsy and confused. Tears welled in her eyes, bringing more signs of fear and disapproval from her crew.

Compassion welled up within Ailill. 'You feel the loss of Kornous deeply, honoured craftmistress, as we all feel the loss of any of our brethren. There will be a time for mourning, and then we shall remember our brother Kornous in a way which is fitting and honourable, but this is not that time, Lileathon, and this hatred you are filled with, this vendetta you pursue against the humans, these are not fitting ways to mourn those we have loved.'

He was looking directly at her now, his body language emphasising the nature of the relationship between them. 'You are the craftmaster, but I am the *Lann Caihe*. It is my duty, when required, to bring water to quench your fire.'

All was still on the bridge of the *Vual'en Sho*. Although it had been unspoken, Ailill had made clear his intention to have Lileathon replaced as craftmaster, as was his right as the ship's *Lann Caihe*, if he believed that his superior was no longer fit for command. Never before that anyone could remember in the history of craftworld An-Iolsus, had a vessel's second-in-command ever had to invoke this ancient law. If it were to happen now, Lileathon's shame and disgrace would be great indeed, and she would have no other choice than to leave the safety of An-Iolsus and become a true *eshairr*: a renegade without ties or allegiance to any craftworld, a homeless exile.

Lileathon realised the enormity of what she had done, of how close she had just come to crossing that forbidden line which her race drew around themselves long ago. She looked at her second-in-command.

'Ailill, wise Ailill, tell me what to do, and I will make it so…'

THE FLIGHT DECKS aboard the *Macharius* were a hive of activity, as yet more Fury fighters and Starhawk bomber craft were brought up from the hangar decks and prepped for take-off. The *Macharius* and its attack craft squadrons were going to war.

Strapped into the seat of his Fury, Kaether cursed loud at his ground crew, angrily urging them on to hurry up and get his fighter prepared for launch, even though he himself knew it would take several more minutes to familiarise himself with the status of the craft. Behind him, Manetho intoned techprayers under his breath as he communed with the fighter's machine-mind, running diagnostic checks on its systems. Their own fighter was a write-off, crippled beyond salvage after the earlier battle, and Manetho himself had conducted the rite of expiration over the remains of their former craft.

This new one was a training craft. No two craft were identical, and even though Kaether knew the dangers of entering combat in an unfamiliar craft, he was still impatient to be underway. The rest of his squadron was already launched and facing the incoming wave of alien attack craft, and Kaether was keen to rejoin them before the battle began.

'How long to launch?' he asked impatiently.

'Eight minutes,' answered Manetho, in between snatches of the fourth passage of the rite of blessed synchronisation, 'it being exactly one minute and fifteen seconds since you last asked the same question.'

Kaether's reply, good-natured but typically foul-mouthed, was cut off by the booming voice broadcast over the flight deck vox-callers.

'Flight deck commander to all flight crews and ground crews. Stand down, that is an order. All launch missions have been put on hold. Complete pre-flight preparations and then stand to and await further instructions.'

Kaether could not believe what he had just heard, and this time his comment to Manetho was less good-natured but equally foul-mouthed.

'Vandire's arse! The enemy attack wave is almost on top of us! Just what do those stupid scavving bastards up on the command deck think they're playing at?'

'CONFIRMED, SIR. THE alien attack craft formations are turning back. It looks like they're intending to maintain a wide holding pattern in orbit around the alien carrier cruiser.'

Semper looked to Remus Nyder for confirmation of his own reading of the situation. The grizzled Ordnance Officer nodded in agreement. 'A climb down, but not a complete back-off. So where do we go from here?'

Semper looked at the enigmatic image of the eldar ship on the bridge's main auspex screen.

'A good question, Mister Nyder,' he breathed to himself. 'A very good question indeed.'

THE ANSWER WAS not long in coming.

The ship was cruising on three-quarters speed, carefully managing its tell-tale power emissions, gliding in amongst the invisible and unpredictable radio wave currents thrown out by the pulsar star. It blanketed itself in their static interference, using them to further mask its presence from its prey.

Finally, though, it had to emerge from its concealment. When it did, it would be quickly detected by its prey's surveyor senses. It didn't matter, judged the ship's commander. He and his vessel still had a second means of concealment at hand. By the time the prey detected the subterfuge, it would be too late.

'CONTACT!' SHOUTED A surveyor ensign aboard the *Macharius*. 'A capital class vessel, coming in at speed off our portside.'

'Identify!' barked Semper, aware that it would take only the slightest thing to destroy the fragile ceasefire they had seemingly only just managed to achieve with the eldar.

Or perhaps you are the one who has been betrayed, said a worrying voice inside him. *Perhaps it is another eldar vessel, and this 'ceasefire' was only a ploy to allow them time to gather their forces against you.*

'Its shields are raised and it's powering weapons... wait, I'm picking up a registry code. It's an Imperium ship... it's the *Drachenfels*, sir!'

'Open hailing frequencies. Get me through to Ramas immediately.'

Communications officers and adepts hurriedly carried out their captain's orders, but to little avail. A senior communications officer nervously informed Semper of their failure.

'No response, sir. *Drachenfels* appears to be running deaf. Either her comm-net is down, or she's refusing to talk.'

Semper's angry oath sent the officer scurrying back to his station. Raising his head, Semper stared at the surveyor screen, seeing the target icon of the *Drachenfels* bearing down on his position and that of the eldar ship. Erwin Ramas was a fine captain, he knew; one of the best he had ever had the privilege of serving alongside, but he was also a hard and uncompromising man. And he was an eldar-hater of long and bitter standing.

'Ramas, you cantankerous old bastard, what are you playing at?' Semper murmured to himself, fearing the worst.

'A SECOND HUMAN vessel,' intoned one of the *Vual'en Sho's* bridge crew. 'It is the same one which we believe destroyed the *Lament of Elshor*. It is coming in on an attack approach, with weapons armed. The first human vessel is hailing it.'

'What response to their hails?' asked Ailill, anxiously.

'None so far, that we can detect.'

Lileathon and Ailill looked at each other, communing quickly in silent mind-speech. Both soon came to the same mutual decision.

'Signal the attack craft squadrons. Tell them to prepare for battle again.'

Eldar crewmen glanced towards Ailill, who countenanced Lileathon's order with an impatient gesture of command to them. With two powerful human warships apparently ranged against them, now was no longer the time to counsel caution.

ABOARD THE *DRACHENFELS*, cocooned in his armoured strategium shell, Erwin Ramas pored over the information fed through to him by his ship's surveyor senses. They were closing in rapidly on the target. All he needed was a few more precious moments to catch his prey unawares.

ABOARD THE *MACHARIUS*, Semper could feel the situation slipping out of control again as more and more information came through to him.

'*Drachenfels* still inbound on our position. Still no answer to our hails.'

'Alien cruiser is manoeuvring away. Could be swinging round to begin its own attack.'

'Alien attack craft are changing course, speed and formation. They're reforming for an attack.'

'Commodore, we must do something.'

This last came from Nyder, who was staring hard at his captain. Swiftly, Semper came to a decision.

'Bring us around. Put us between the *Drachenfels* and the eldar ship. If Ramas wants to fire upon the alien ship, he'll have to go through us first.'

The order brought blank looks of surprise and consternation from the bridge crew. If they were caught by surprise by their captain's first order, then what came next was to truly shock them.

'Arm two torpedoes and get ready to fire on my orders. Our target is the *Drachenfels*. Perhaps a shot across Ramas's bows will encourage him to start talking.'

Reluctantly but efficiently, the bridge crew prepared to carry out their captain's orders. Powerful manoeuvring thrusters swung the *Macharius* round in space, bringing it onto a direct target bearing with the oncoming *Drachenfels*. Semper was awaiting final confirmation that torpedoes were loaded, aimed and ready to fire, when the urgent call came in from the command deck's surveyors section.

'Contact! Another capital class vessel incoming on the same approach vector as the *Drachenfels*. It's following on right behind it.'

'Identify immediately!'

The seconds seemed to stretch out forever before Semper got his answer.

'Another Imperium registry code, wait, it's the same one… energy signatures match too! Golden Throne, according to the readings, the second ship is also the *Drachenfels*!'

ABOARD THE DARK eldar cruiser, all was silent as they awaited the order to fire. Suddenly, there was a commotion amongst the crew manning the ship's sensor systems. Their captain's threatening hiss of displeasure was abruptly cut off by a warning shout from one of his crew.

'Mon-keigh vessel detected, directly astern. It's powering up weapons and locking onto us with targeting scanners!'

The dark eldar captain hissed in fury. His plan had been a good one, but he had been out-thought and out-captained by a mere mon-keigh animal. His humiliation would be great indeed, if he ever survived to return in disgrace to Commorragh.

ERWIN RAMAS SMILED as his mind-link to his ship's systems confirmed that targeting systems had locked onto the alien craft. It had been a difficult chase, and only luck and skilful navigation had allowed him and his vessel to follow the alien ship and remain undetected on its tail for so long. The enemy vessel was a hunter, all its senses focussed on the prey ahead of it, little suspecting that it itself was also being hunted.

Yes, it had been a difficult chase, but now the chase was over.

'Fire,' Ramas commanded.

A full quartet of torpedoes rumbled out of their prow silos and roared away towards their target. Caught by surprise, with its attacker appearing at such close quarters, the dark eldar vessel did what it could to evade the attack, turning rapidly to port and putting on a sudden burst of speed to escape the reach of the torpedoes. Had it been shadow-cloaked in the usual manner of a dark eldar vessel, its manoeuvre might have succeeded, but there had been no time to disengage its mimic engines, and it was still broadcasting the energy signature of a larger and more powerful human cruiser vessel, giving the crude machine-minds of the torpedo warheads a clear target to lock onto.

One of the torpedoes went astray, while another struck the target astern, inflicting serious damage on the dark eldar cruiser's engine systems. The remaining two torpedoes missed their target, but, armed with proximity fuses, the warheads detonated close enough to the target to cause widespread minor damage to the ship's thinly-armoured hull, and to violently buffet the cruiser vessel from prow to stern.

The damage was not crippling, but it was more than enough to achieve the intended purpose. The cruiser's mimic engines imploded, unmasking its true shape to those watching on the viewing screens on the bridges of both the *Macharius* and the *Vual'en Sho*.

Human and eldar eyes alike saw the same thing, as the image of the first detected vessel claiming to be the *Drachenfels* suddenly wavered and flickered weirdly in and out of existence in the direct aftermath of the torpedo hits. For a brief second, those watching thought they saw the images of ships of many different classes and races appear in rapid, bewildering succession, but then the cascade of false images was abruptly gone, and all that remained was the image of another different kind of vessel entirely.

To human eyes, it looked like something more akin to an engine-powered blade than a space vessel. Its lines were sharp and cruel, its silhouette vicious and dagger-like. It had little exterior hull detail, and the black, non-reflective material of its hull seemed to suck in the available light from the starfield around it, so that its shape blended into the blackness of space.

An assassin's blade, that was what it looked like: sinister and concealed, fast and lethal.

Aboard the *Vual'en Sho*, Lileathon and her crew looked at the newly-revealed vessel in dread, instantly knowing it for what it truly was.

'Druchii cruiser!' spat Ailill, his tone full of utter loathing. Lileathon looked at the image on the screen, suddenly realising the full implications of the discovery of the dark eldar presence in the Stabia system, suddenly realising the game their enemies had been playing against her and the humans, and realising the terrible mistake she had come so close to making. Anger welled up within her, but was quickly subdued again. Instead of any personal anger, all that remained in her was the cold, calm fury and hatred and loathing all those of her race bore towards their once-kin.

'Signal the attack squadrons. They have a new target. *Mael dannan:* No mercy to the druchii abomination.'

'GOOD TO HAVE you with us again, *Drachenfels*. You had us worried there for a moment.'

Erwin Ramas's rasping, electronically-created laugh sounded over the comm-net of the *Macharius's* bridge.

'The Emperor's favour was with us, Leoten. We caught a glimpse of that damned thing on our surveyors, after it goaded us and one of the alien ships into attacking each other. We pursued it, and since then we've been chasing ghosts and shadows all over this damned hole of a star system. After we finally found it again and got on its tail, we couldn't break comm-net silence and risk letting them know we were there.'

'Understood, *Drachenfels*,' smiled Semper. 'Do your gunnery crews require any help finishing the target, or do you think you can handle this one without our help?'

'Let the damn xenos-kind kill each other, Leoten,' snarled Ramas in reply. 'I've found better targets for our gunners to practise on.'

In his stratagium, Ramas directed his bridge crew to send their gathered surveyor findings through to the other Imperial Navy ship. Moments later, its contents sifted through by the living machine-mind that inhabited the *Macharius's* logic engines, the data was fed through to the bridge crew and, instantly, three new target icons appeared on the surveyor screens.

Ramas chuckled to himself, and the sound carried over the comm-net, even as the startled cries of 'Contact!' rang out through the *Macharius's* command deck.

'Yes, Leoten, there are still more surprises. Three of the Despoiler's fleet, one Carnage and two escorts. The cruiser and one of the escorts have been clipped once or twice already, so it would appear that von Blucher gave a good account for himself. They were sneaking round your flanks, hiding amongst all this damned pulsar interference, when we crossed their path and picked up traces of their energy wake.'

'They're working with the other alien vessel?' asked Semper.

'You have another explanation for their presence here?' answered Ramas.

Semper did not. He turned to the communications section. 'Relay the information we've just received to the eldar vessel. Tell them that their enemies and our enemies are the same. Our enemies have united against us, so let us do the same.'

He turned to Nyder, but the *Macharius's* Master of Ordnance had already anticipated his captain's next question. 'All attack craft squadrons are mobilised and ready. The eldar squadrons are already closing in on the other alien target vessel. We follow them in?'

Semper smiled. 'We do indeed, Mister Nyder. We'll let the alien bomber pilots have their fun, and then we'll have our pilots show them how a precision bombing run should really be done.'

LIKE AVENGING HARPIES, the formations of eldar Eagle bombers fell upon the dark eldar cruiser. All their race's hatred and loathing of their fallen kin came to the fore as the bomber pilots and their crews attacked the fleeing cruiser with unsurpassed fury. Heedless of the fire from the cruiser's own defences, they flew in recklessly close, not releasing their payload until they were sure of striking the target at some vulnerable point, not peeling away from the curtain of fire thrown out by the dark eldar vessel's defence turrets until they were satisfied that their missiles had caused sufficient damage to the enemy ship. Of the Eagles that had left the *Vual'en Sho*, only three quarters would return to their wraithbone cradles within the cruiser's launch bays.

The dark eldar ship staggered under the fusillade of missiles. It threw out a protective shadow-field to conceal itself from the enemy craft, confusing pilot's senses and targeting scanners, but these were not human eyes and human targeting scanners they faced now, and the eldar pilots and the infinity circuit systems of their craft easily saw through such evasions. Sonic warhead missiles, designed to impact against the far denser armour and hull structure of ork and human ships, pierced the body of the dark eldar craft with ease, exploding deep within it and wreaking bloody havoc amongst the ship's shadow-haunted decks and galleries.

The crews of the eldar attack craft were well aware that this vessel was probably responsible for the loss of *Medhbh's Shield* and possibly also at least one of the missing human vessels too. The slave pens in its dismal holds were most likely crammed with captured prisoners – fodder for the druchii's abominable appetite for cruelty and pain – and it was also likely that there were eldar amongst those prisoners. Such awful knowledge did not deter any of the bomber crews as they brought their craft in close-range attack against the dark eldar ship, and more than one pilot or bombardier mind-spoke the words of prayers of solace to themselves as they launched their deadly payload at the target, knowing that the death they were now condemning the captured slave-fodder to was a far cleaner and quicker one than whatever fate otherwise awaited them in the druchii's secret citadel base.

By the time the last of the eldar bombers peeled away from the target, they left behind them a vessel transformed in minutes into a shattered, broken ruin. The ship's hull was pierced in dozens of places. Fires raged out of control on many of its decks, while others had been blasted completely open and exposed to the hard vacuum of space, sweeping them instantly clean of all life. Panicked by the explosions which had wracked the ship from end to end, and hunger-maddened by the pain-filled psychic screams broadcast from the minds of the dead and injured, the warp beasts and haemonculi-created monstrosities imprisoned in their lightless kennels in the hold decks broke free of their restraints and went on the rampage, killing dark eldar and terrified prisoners alike. For those slaves who had survived the initial bomber attack, the interior of the crippled ship must have seemed like hell itself. Some decks were an inferno of flame, others were gripped by the stellar chill of open space, while the mindless abominations from the ship's darkest depths wandered freely through its chambers and passages, killing everything which crossed their path in the most brutal and terrible ways imaginable.

Fortunately for any innocents still alive within the dying craft, this particular vision of hell would prove to be mercifully brief.

As the eldar attack wave peeled away, the slower-moving Starhawks from the *Macharius* followed in their wake. What the eldar had begun, the pilots of the Imperial Navy craft would complete. Waves of plasma warhead missiles smashed into the dark eldar cruiser's fatally-weakened body. Entire sections of the ship were vaporised: the prow section blew apart, struck by ten or more missiles. The vessel's dark matter reactor was breached, releasing the pent-up fury of the ship's nameless power source in an all-consuming blast of destructive energy. The rear portion of the ship was disintegrated, disappearing in a lightless explosive flash which seared itself into the surveyor screens of the Imperial craft, appearing as a brief and miniature black hole which hungrily sucked in every available piece of matter in the vicinity, including three luckless Starhawk craft trailing in the rearguard of Firedrake squadron's formation.

The dark eldar ship's commander need have no fear now of the prospect of the cruel wrath of his kabal lord when he returned in failure and humiliation to Commorragh, for there was literally nothing left to show that he and his vessel had ever even existed.

THE CARNAGE CLASS cruiser *Despicable* and its two escorts had expected to take their targets by surprise, coming in with their energy patterns subdued and following the surveyor-confounding pulsar lines already mapped out by their temporary allies. They had expected to find an enemy force divided and possibly even warring amongst themselves, an enemy thrown into doubt and confusion by the subterfuge tactics of the dark eldar.

What they found instead were three cruiser class vessels, including two powerful Imperial ships of the line, already alerted to their presence and bearing down upon them fast and hard.

The *Vual'en Sho* darted ahead of the slower Imperial ships, drawing the enemy fire upon itself. Lance shots from the *Despicable* and torpedo shots from its escorts reached out into space in search of the eldar ship, but its speed, manoeuvrability and baffling cloaks of holofields eluded the enemy's best efforts. Then, suddenly turning and effortlessly slipping past a brace of torpedoes from the escorts, it quickly closed to within firing range and opened fire with its pulsar lance. One of the escorts, already damaged from the early battle against the *Graf Orlok*, took the full brunt of the stream of tightly-focussed laser energy, and exploded apart. The *Vual'en Sho* attempted to slip away again, but the manoeuvre brought it within reach of the *Despicable's* rows of powerful flank batteries.

Even with its holofields fully deployed, the eldar ship could not evade the full effects of the punishing curtain of fire projected from the Chaos cruiser's weapons batteries. The delicate crystalline membranes of its topsails were partially shredded by the impacts of half a dozen macro-cannon rounds and a bleeding, ragged gash opened up along the length of its portside hull by the slashing beams of batteries of laser cannons, the *Vual'en Sho* retreated out of range of the Chaos guns again, its holofields projecting a rearward display of confusing multiple false images to cloak the escape manoeuvre. Lileathon knew that many long and painful months awaited her ship in its berth on An-Iolsus, as the Bonesingers and Fabricators repaired the damage done to the living psycho-plastic material of the *Vual'en Sho's* structure.

The gambit had paid off, however. By seizing the Chaos gunners' attentions, the *Vual'en Sho's* risky manoeuvre had permitted the two Imperial ships to close to within firing range of the Chaos force.

Dual torpedo salvoes from the *Macharius* and the *Drachenfels* hammered into the *Despicable*, registering several successful hits upon it. One struck the base of its command tower, bursting through the thick armour there and sending columns of fire roaring up through the interior of the tower. Another detonated amongst the galleries of gun batteries on the cruiser's forward portside, knocking out of action the weapon emplacements located there.

Moving in closer, and coming under fire from the *Despicable's* prow batteries, the *Macharius* opened up with its own portside batteries, goring the Chaos cruiser's void shield defences. The *Despicable's* remaining Infidel class escort darted in towards the Imperial cruiser, launching torpedoes at its vulnerable underbelly and engine sections. A patrolling swarm of Fury interceptors, launched for just such a task, moved in quickly to intercept the ordnance weapons, subjecting them to a bombarding hail of lascannon and missile fire and detonating them harmlessly in space before they could reach their target. Any further annoyance value the Chaos escort ship might have had was brought to a swift end when the *Drachenfels* turned its starboard side lance turrets upon it. Eviscerated by the sweeping lance beams, the craft was quickly reduced to a blazing and lifeless wreck.

Outgunned, outnumbered, stripped of his escorts and with the fighting capability of his ship dangerously reduced, the master of the *Despicable* chose to withdraw, trusting to his vessel's superior speed to carry him away from the Imperial vessels, judging also that the faster but lightly armoured eldar vessel would be unlikely to give pursuit on its own. Disengaging, he turned away, presenting his undamaged starboard side toward the Imperial ships and allowing the gun batteries there to bring their sights to bear on the enemy cruisers. The *Drachenfels* took the full brunt of the fire from the Chaos cruiser's formidable array of weapons batteries. Its void shields vanished in moments, and Erwin Ramas barked in pain and anger as he felt the enemy gunfire punch through his vessel's armoured skin, several particularly wounding hits penetrating deep into his vessel's body to damage its most vital systems. Every surveyor screen on the bridge and gunnery bay command posts went temporarily blank as one salvo of plasma missiles smashed into the ship's surveyor system, knocking them out of action, while a stream of laser fire also crippled the ship's void shield generators. Blinded, and robbed of its shield protection, the *Drachenfels* would be of little use for the time being in any further engagements.

Staying close by to protect its damaged sister ship, the *Macharius* had little choice but to allow the *Despicable* the prize of its fortunate escape, although Semper ensured that a brace of launched torpedoes would further speed the Chaos vessel on its way, and give the enemy's defence turret crews something to occupy themselves with.

Standing on the bridge of his ship, still flushed with the unnerving euphoria of battle, Semper at first did not hear the report from his communications officer.

'Incoming ship-to-ship communications signal, sir,' the man repeated again, finally catching his captain's attention.

'From the *Drachenfels*?' asked Semper.

The officer paused before answering. 'No, sir. From the alien ship. They're hailing you by name.'

At Semper's signal, the communication from the *Vual'en Sho* was put onto an open comm-net channel.

'Craftmaster Semper, I/we are Lileathon, second-born of the union of Faryiarda and Morgyell, who is also now known to you as craftmistress of this vessel which we term *Vual'en Sho*.'

The eldar's voice was strange and eerie, her phrasing of the Gothic tongue of the Imperium stilted and awkward. Semper and those listening could not know it, but Lileathon did not speak one word of the language, and was speaking the words as they were psychically communicated to her by the Thought Talkers who had some fluency in Gothic.

'This is Semper, *Vual'en Sho*. Go ahead.'

Again, the strange alien voice sounded over the command deck comm-net. 'You fight well, human. I/we thank you for the aid you have given, and I/we regret what nearly came to pass between our two ships. But we still have comrades trapped on the world below, Semper-human, both your people and those craft-brethren precious also to us.'

'What do you propose, *Vual'en Sho*?' asked Semper.

The answer he received made perfect sense, and flew in the face of everything he had been taught in his entire life regarding the well-known dangers of having any dealings with cunning xenos-creatures such as these eldar.

SEVENTEEN

IT BEGAN WITH screaming. It would end with screaming too.

Sheltering in what little cover there was on offer in the ravine, Ulanti tried to snatch a few hours' much-needed rest after the battle in the ruins and the desperate flight through the storm and across the barren surface of the planet. Minutes or hours later – he couldn't tell, and the deadly, muscle-numbing weariness which had gripped him earlier seemed no less diminished – he was awakened by the sound of screaming.

With a shock, he realised that it was one of the eldar sentries screaming: Banshee warriors, Horst had called them. The sound seemed to start off as a scream of warning, or defiance, but at some swift point became transformed into a scream of pain, a long, ululating howl which could only have been caused by some awful abomination being inflicted upon living, vulnerable flesh. The scream ended, perhaps mercifully, in a dying, choking gurgle, horribly amplified by the vox-caster systems build into the eldar warrior's helm.

Seconds later, the gunfire began. The harsh, dry hiss of dark eldar weaponry, answered seconds later by the quieter, different-toned sound of the eldar's own armaments.

Ulanti was on his feet in moments, almost colliding with Maxim, who had armed himself with a shotcannon following the loss of his heavy bolter. The big hiveworlder's eyes were red-rimmed, his pupils fixed and dilated. He had been chewing tajii root for hours, and was pumped up on aggression and pain from his wounds. Ulanti knew that if Maxim Borusa was going to die today, he wouldn't die easily.

As Ulanti hurried off towards the sounds of battle, Maxim paused to recheck the load on his shotcannon; he wasn't yet too narcoticised that he would forget to do what, for him, was so basic and elementary a survival precaution as to be second nature to him. He felt eyes on him, and looked up to see Commissar Kyogen nearby, propped up against the rock wall of the ravine. By all rights, Kyogen should be dead by now; one of Horst's retinue was a qualified medic and had done what he could for the Ship's Commissar, but the dark eldar round which had struck him down had been imbued with some kind of anti-coagulant poison, and the medic had been unable to staunch the flow of blood that seeped out from the deep wound in the man's flesh.

Kyogen was big, as big as Borusa himself perhaps, but the hiveworlder had been amazed that even a body as large as that could contain so much blood. Kyogen's uniform and thick felt coat were heavy with the stuff, and the dust of the ground around him stained dark by the creeping tide of blood still oozing out of him. He was still conscious – perhaps the medic had given him something to prevent him passing out, or perhaps, Maxim mused with a smile, a stickler for the rules such as Ship's Commissar Koba Kyogen wasn't allowed to pass out and die until he received the properly authenticated orders to do so. He gripped his bolt pistol tight in one hand, and a small book – probably something about naval regulations and discipline, Maxim supposed – in the other, holding it tightly to his chest, and glared at Maxim.

Maxim looked back, and laughed. 'Don't forget to save the last round for yourself, commissar. We can't afford the likes of you falling into the hands of the xenos and spilling your guts about the precious secrets contained in all them regulation manuals and loyalty codices you're so fond of.'

The only reply he got was a mute, hostile glare. Still laughing, Maxim turned his back on the dying man and ran off after Ulanti.

KAILASA MOVED FORWARD with the first line of dark eldar warriors, keen to ensure that his orders were carried out. The Mandrakes who had gone on ahead of the rest of the dark eldar force and who had successfully tracked down and located the prey's hiding place had been allowed to keep and do whatever they wanted with the enemy sentries, but Kailasa had ordered on pain of death that no one else would be allowed to kill any of the prey. It was vital that the farseer was taken alive, and the kabal commander did not want to risk any chance that his prize might be killed by mistake.

The dark eldar advanced into the face of sporadic, scattered fire from the craftworld eldar and their mon-keigh allies sheltering in the scant cover of the rockfall at the mouth of the ravine. They had no heavy weapons, and not enough ranged ones to count.

Given time, Kailasa knew it would be a simple matter to surround them and pick them off at leisure with massed volleys of splinter rifle fire, backed up by covering fire from the several heavy weapons still possessed by what remained of his force, but time was something the dark eldar lord no longer had. He had received word that the ships belonging to the craftworld eldar and the mon-keigh had not only failed to destroy each other, but had united together and were in the process of driving off his own vessels. Soon, they would send shuttles to rescue their kin trapped here, but it was Kailasa's intent that all these would-be rescuers would find would be dust and a pile of corpses, with the dark eldar long ago escaped through a webway portal, taking their captive prizes with them.

And besides, he still wanted to take as many captives alive as possible. His losses so far had been higher than expected. Added to this, the loss of an entire Torture class cruiser, as now seemed highly likely, would not carry much favour back in Commorragh, and so, in order to help assuage his Archon's potentially lethal displeasure and save face, it was now in his interests to bring back as many prize captives as possible.

One of the warriors in front of him cried out and fell, struck down by a well-aimed shot from a shuriken catapult. His companion instinctively raised his splinter rifle and returned fire, sending out a hail of deadly, poison-coated splinter shots towards the rocks. Just as instinctively, Kailasa raised his own splinter pistol and shot the warrior in the back.

'Agoniser rounds only,' he commanded. 'I want live flesh, not corpses.'

Mindful of the brutal lesson just displayed, the rest of his troops took greater care in firing upon their enemies. Although agoniser shots could still kill, they were intended to subdue their targets and render them incapable of escaping, inflicting mainly minor superficial wounds, but introducing a nerve toxin into the target's bloodstream which would subject them to the most horrific agonies for a short time, but leave them still alive afterwards. Living targets struck by agoniser rounds would frequently break their bones and wrench apart joints and muscle, so severe were the spasms and contortions caused by the toxin. Kailasa had seen victims chew through their own tongues on occasion, paralysed by pain and choking to death on their own blood, but it was still his most favoured and amusing method of taking captives.

Laughing in anticipation of the glory that would soon be his, he ran on into the battle.

THE DARK ELDAR were in amongst them now, overrunning the defenders at the entrance to the ravine and falling upon those behind. An armsman in front of Ulanti cried out and fell to the ground, screaming shrilly and writhing in agony, although the only wound Ulanti could see on him was a tearing flesh wound to his shoulder from a passing shot from one of the dark eldar weapons. This was the third time Ulanti had seen one of his men or the eldar so struck down, and he swiftly realised that they had just discovered yet another form of the maliciously perverse warfare favoured by these dark eldar creatures.

The dark eldar warrior who had just picked off the armsman sighted Ulanti and swung its pistol weapon round to fire at him. Ulanti ducked, hearing the sinister hiss of the crystalline shot as it skimmed past him.

He came up firing, sending two las-shots into the target's central body mass. It went down hissing in pain, its armour partially protecting it from the worst of the damage. Ulanti kept on firing, sending more las-shots into the thrashing body of the dark eldar, only stopping when he had completely depleted what remained of his weapon's power charge. When he had finished, all that was left of the dark eldar was scattered pieces of charred flesh and fused armour.

He was still reloading when another dark eldar warrior charged down the side of the ravine towards him, brandishing a sword and a crackling whip-like weapon. The roar of a shotcannon lifted the warrior off its feet, smashing its body ragdoll-like against the rocky wall of the ravine.

Ulanti looked round to see Maxim nearby, the shotcannon in his hands firing off more volleys of explosive scatter shells into the ranks of dark eldar following on behind the first.

'Best fall back, sir,' the big hiveworlder shouted. 'I'll cover you. The inquisitor and that alien magician are back there. If we're going to die then we should at least make sure we die in the best company. Arriving before the Golden Throne alongside a senior inquisitor might help when the Emperor makes his judgement on our immortal souls. Mind you, I'm not too sure what he'll have to say about all these aliens we'll have brought with us.'

Ulanti did as commanded, the distinctions between first lieutenant and chief petty officer blurring in the heat of battle. Maxim swung his shotcannon round, searching for more targets amongst the shadows of the ravine, when one of those shadows suddenly detached itself from amongst a cluster of nearby rocks and leapt upon him, knocking him off his perch and sending both him and his attacker hurtling down the slope of a steep side gully.

MAXIM HAD FOUGHT many tenacious opponents hand to hand before, but nothing like this creature. It was one of the dark eldar things, but unlike any that Maxim had seen so far. Its naked flesh was pierced by hooks and barbs, many of which seemed to be holding parts of it together, with the glistening red of raw viscera clearly visible through the splits in its flesh.

As they rolled down the slope, Maxim's hands scrabbled for purchase on the creature's slime-coated flesh, one hand finally finding purchase round its throat, piercing himself on the blades set in its flesh as he tried to throttle the life out of the thing. The creature giggled as Maxim's powerful grip crushed its windpipe, grinding together the bones of its throat. It cackled as the sharp rocks of the gully tore and bruised both their bodies as they rolled over them.

The two of them were momentarily thrown apart by the bone-jarring impact of their landing at the foot of the gully. Maxim felt some of his ribs break under the impact, and coughed up blood as he tried to shout in pain.

The creature was on him again in an instant, tearing at the skin of his chest and face with the metal blades hammered into the tips of its malformed fingers. Maxim's grasping hand found a fist-sized rock, and, roaring in pain and anger, he swung it up into the creature's face, repeatedly smashing it into its nose and teeth. The creature sniggered to itself through the ragged hole of its mouth. Its fingers were round Maxim's throat now, not so much strangling him as working their way into the flesh of his neck, leisurely searching for the arteries and veins.

Maxim felt himself starting to black out, part of him grateful that he probably wouldn't feel anything when the creature's questing fingers finally found his jugular. Dimly, from far away, he heard a familiar voice calling distantly out to him.

'Up! Get its head up, Borusa, damn you, so I can get a clear shot at it!'

There was something in the voice which compelled obedience. With the last of his strength, Maxim's fingers found the creature's throat and jaw. Pushing upwards, he forced it to raise its head.

The bolter round caught the creature in the centre of the face, blowing away most of its skull and throwing it several metres back. Groggily, Maxim watched as, incredibly, the thing began to rise to its feet again. Another bolter round blew it backwards again, followed by another and another.

The detonations rang out in quick succession, until the shredded remains of the dark eldar Grotesque fell to the ground in a ragged, bloody heap.

Maxim heard the sound of another body falling to the ground nearby, behind him. Before he passed out, he just had time to glimpse the prone figure of Commissar Kyogen, the man somehow having dragged or staggered his way down here from further along the ravine. The now empty bolt pistol was still clasped in his bloodless hand.

KAILASA KNEW THE prize was close now. The craftworld weaklings and what remained of their mon-keigh allies had fallen back as far as they could and attacked what remained of his own forces with desperate fury.

A female Striking Scorpion – one of Arhra's cowardly brood, who had refused to follow their Fallen Phoenix lord father into the dark embrace of Chaos – leapt forward, cleaving in the skull of the retinue bodyguard beside him, spitting another warrior on the point of her blade with her return blow. Kailasa stepped over the tumbling bodies of his two dead followers, and casually swept aside the Scorpion warrior's attack upon him. His own blow severed her weapon arm at the shoulder. Numbly, in shock, she fell to her knees as the dark eldar lord swept past her.

A mon-keigh in the uniform of the second-in-command of one of their warships – Kailasa had seized enough slave-fodder in successful raids along the mon-keigh shipping lanes to know something of the hierarchy of their rankings – brandished a laspistol weapon at him. Kailasa stepped aside, dodging the mon-keigh's shot, and felled him with a single agoniser round from his splinter pistol.

Another mon-keigh in elaborate robes of rank barred his way towards the prize. Kailasa brought his pistol up to bear again, but was made to stagger back by the invisible impact of a psychic blow emanating from the upstart mon-keigh. The blow was weak – the rune-wards carved into the dark lord's armour were enough to protect him from the full force of it – but it was enough to knock him off-balance for a moment.

In that moment, Horst raised and fired the plasma pistol in his hand, but the shot missed, striking the ravine wall behind where Kailasa had been standing, turning the rock into molten slag. The dark eldar moved with preternatural speed, closing the distance between him and the human inquisitor and felling him with a stunning strike with the pommel of his sword.

At last Kailasa stood before his prize. The figure of the aged farseer cowered before him, frail and helpless. Kailasa doubted that this one would be able to withstand the ordeal which would soon be his for long, but there were haemonculi surgeons and skilled flesh-sculptors and pain-artists who knew ways of trapping life and sensation within the ravaged forms of their victims for longer than could ever be thought imaginable.

'Grandfather farseer,' the dark eldar lord sneered, affecting a mocking bow. 'If only you knew what pleasures await you when I bring you back in triumph to Commorragh.'

KARIADRYL STARED IN awe and dread at the figure before him. The dark eldar lord was everything he had ever imagined, a piece of black legend from his race's darkest and most secret myths come to terrible life. More terrible still, with his mystic far-sight, he was able to see the swirling black halo which surrounded the dark eldar like a living cloak of shadow.

This creature, this abomination standing before him, was the focal point of the shadow point, even if the dark eldar itself did not perceive it. All the elusive glimpses of possible futures, all the false prophecy images, all the tantalising hints of what might still come to pass, coalesced into this place and moment of time.

And then, like shadows retreating and shrinking before the rise of the dawn sun, the black light aura around the druchii warrior lord dwindled and shrivelled away, scorched by the light and heat of something far greater and more powerful.

Kariadryl looked, with his eyes, with his inner far-sight. And then he laughed in genuine pleasure, for now he knew what was coming along the ravine towards them.

The burning god was here at last.

EIGHTEEN

THE AVATAR ADVANCED down the neck of the ravine, the stone of the walls glowing cherry-red in places as they were touched by the heat of his passing. Where he walked, dark eldar died before him.

Some ran, trying to flee his terrible wrath. Others stood and tried to fight, spitting blasphemous curses against his holy name. Flee or fight, it did not matter. They died, no matter what they tried to do.

Three Mandrakes hurled themselves onto the avatar, clinging to its burning skin and hacking at it with their blades. They clung on to it relentlessly, screaming their hatred as the meat of their flesh was cooked from their bones.

Dark eldar warriors retreated before the avatar, shots from their splinter rifles vapourising against its glowing iron skin. Some it cut down with its black blade, or incinerated with fiery blasts of the blade's arcane power, others it crushed into the dust beneath its iron feet, others it struck down with its terrible molten gaze.

It did not matter. Flee or fight, they all died, no matter what they tried to do.

A pack of warp beasts leapt snarling at the burning god. One creature it smashed aside with a blow from its glowing fist; another it spitted on the end of its wailing blade. The third managed to land and raked at it with its talons. Magma blood boiled up out of the rents torn in the burning god's iron flesh.

The burning god seized the creature and ripped it away from its body, smashing it against the unyielding rock face of the ravine wall.

Kailasa charged at the burning god, screaming his hatred. His first blow cut deep into it, splattering the dust and rocks with burning blood.

One blow, however, was all the burning god would permit him.

As he swung again, aiming at the iron skin of its neck, the avatar reached up and simply caught the blow in its hand. Its great fist closed around the blade of the sword, melting through it. Magma blood welled up and fell in steaming drips to the ground from where the unnatural metal of the blade cut into its divine flesh.

In seconds, the dark eldar lord's sword glowed red hot. Kailasa screamed as the heat seared the palm of his hand, and he released his grip on its pommel, just as the molten blade broke apart and fell uselessly to the ground.

He raised his splinter pistol and aimed it up into face of the avatar, but was stopped in his tracks as he saw the god staring down at him, the cold fury in its burning eyes holding him in a paralysing stasis more compelling than any poison or nerve toxin.

Slowly, helplessly, he watched as the giant warrior laid down its sword and reached up with two massive hands to unfasten the bindings of its helm.

Slowly, helplessly, he watched as the giant warrior removed its helm and turned its naked face towards him.

The burning god looked upon the dark eldar. Kailasa looked up into the god's terrible, beautiful face. He tried to scream, but the flesh of his face was already melting away as the unbearable light and heat radiating from the visage of the burning god's unmasked face fell upon him.

All that was left of Kailasa of the Kabal of the Poison Heart
fell to the ground in a smouldering ashen heap, which the
avatar trod unnoticed into the dust as it strode over to Kariadryl.

The farseer bowed in awed abeyance before the burning
god, not daring to look up into its forbidden face.

'My lord Kaela Mensha Khaine, what would you have me
do?' he asked, trembling.

He felt the burning god lay one fiery hand upon him. Its
touch did not harm him, even though the air around its skin
shimmered with the searing heat radiating from its iron
skin.

Kariadryl understood what was required of him. Slowly,
helplessly, he raised his head and looked into the god's face.
Light, bright and unbearable, washed over him, obliterating
everything.

He gazed into the true face of the burning god. And at last
he understood.

Everything.

STILL SICK WITH pain, Freyra of the Striking Scorpions
climbed groggily to her feet, slowly taking in the details of
the carnage around her. The stump of her severed arm still
burned with pain, but, as one who walked the warrior path,
she knew mental incantations and secret body disciplines to
numb the pain and staunch the life-threatening flow of
blood from the wound.

She remembered being struck down by the druchii warrior, and, dimly, as she lay semi-conscious, she remembered
a burning giant looming up over her and looking down
upon her with a face that blazed like the heart of a star. She
was still trying to remember what had happened, when she
saw the the body of the farseer. She ran towards it.

The bodies of two mon-keigh lay nearby. Both were alive,
although the one in the uniform of those who manned the
warships of the humans' corpse-god emperor had been
struck by a druchii agoniser round. He had mercifully passed
out from the effects of the venom, but the toxin was still in
his blood, and it would require a rare anti-toxin to fully flush
the poison out of his body. From the marks in the dusty

ground and from the attitudes of the two unconscious humans, Freyra could tell that both had been struck down while trying to defend her honoured kinsman. She would see that the human received a plentiful supply of the anti-toxin.

She knelt by the body of her farseer kinsman, knowing already that he was dead. The ground around him was black-ened, seared as if touched by a great heat, but, strangely, Kariadryl's body had been left completely untouched by whatever force had been unleashed here.

Stranger still was the look of utter calm and even the hint of a contented smile on the face of the aged farseer.

Freyra knew there were things that needed to be done. Kneeling over the corpse of her kinsman, she began to recite the necessary incantations of honour and mourning to mark the passing of her craftworld's most venerable seer, stopping only briefly when she heard sounds in the sky overhead.

It had begun with screaming, and now it ended with screaming: the screaming of thruster engines as a trio of human shuttle craft came into land nearby. Given all that had happened since she arrived on this forsaken world, she did not find it strange at all when the landing ramps of the craft opened to disgorge mixed groups of human troops and eldar Guardian crewmen from the *Vual'en Sho*.

THE SEARCH PARTY from the *Macharius* found Maxim's uncon-scious form at the bottom of the gully. He was covered in so much dried blood from the slashes across his neck and chest, as well as the numerous other minor wounds, that at first they had assumed him to be dead, but he had stirred groaning to life when they began to roughly haul his body back up the rocky slope.

Stretcher litters were brought down, to carry Maxim and the corpse of Kyogen up from the bottom of the gully. Maxim watched as the commissar's body was lifted onto the other stretcher. The bolt pistol was still gripped in the corpse's hand, but, as the stretcher bearers hauled the body into place, Maxim saw the small, gilt-edged book slip out of the dead man's other hand and fall to the ground.

'It's funny,' Maxim grunted, gratefully accepting the tajii stick offered by one of his own stretcher bearers, who he knew to be a long and valued customer of his, and a useful source of pharmaceutical supplies from the ship's medical stores. 'Me and that silver skull bastard, we hated each other. There was probably nothing he'd have liked more than to send me to the Emperor with an execution round to the back of the head, but in the end he still saved my life.'

Pain and the effects of the drugs he had been administered – and those others he had earlier self-administered – might have dulled his senses, but he still caught the look shared amongst the apothecary crewmen.

'You must be mistaken, chief petty officer,' one of the surgeon's assistants said in a tone reserved for politely humouring those whose brains had been scrambled by serious head wounds. 'The commissar's been dead for hours. He must have died before the battle even began.'

Maxim painfully hauled himself out of the stretcher litter, angrily shrugging off the attempts by the stretcher bearers to restrain him, and staggered over to Kyogen's corpse. He bent down and picked up the small book the dead man had been clutching.

It was no book of naval regulations or Imperium political doctrine, which was what he had assumed it to be. It was an Ecclesiarchy prayer book, of the standard type issued in their billions to the officers and men of the Imperium's armed forces. The fake gold-embossed aquila emblem of the Holy God-Emperor winked up knowingly at him from the book's scratched and battered cover.

SOMEWHERE OUT ON the edge of the Stabia system, the last remaining dark eldar cruiser made its escape, unscathed and undetected. Its crew knew that their mission's failure would not win them a warm welcome from their kabal lord back on Commorragh, but the vessel's captain was quietly confident that the greater part of the blame would settle on the dead shoulders of Lord Kailasa and on the unworthy nature of their Chaos allies.

And, besides, her holds were filled with slave-fodder taken from the attacks on two of the vessels belonging to the mon-keigh and their weakling craftworld allies, so she would not be returning home to face her lord's displeasure empty-handed.

Down in the suite of rooms assigned to him by his dark eldar hosts, Siaphas of Eidolon was plotting the details of his continued survival in the face of the recent disastrous events.

By now, with the escape of the *Despicable* back into the warp, the Despoiler would know what had happened here, so Siaphas knew the folly of even thinking about returning to the Warmaster's court to attempt to give his version of events. He was irrevocably tainted with failure now in the unforgiving eyes of the Despoiler, and not even the patronage of his protector Zaraphiston would shelter him from Abaddon's wrath.

No, the Chaos sorcerer decided, he would remain here amongst these dark eldar creatures. As he had realised before, they could easily be fashioned into a powerful and effective force by one with the imagination to see the unique possibilities they represented. Of course, their ridiculous and self-destructive kabals and their love of intrigue and in-fighting would have to be done away with, but, given time, Siaphas was certain that a being of sufficient guile, intellect and mystic power could easily manipulate events so as to ensure their rapid rise to a position of command over such a force, and was he not just such a being?

Siaphas was still considering the pleasant details of his future empire-building over his unwitting hosts, when his reverie was interrupted by the sound of the door to his chambers sliding open.

One of the creatures known as a haemonculus stood there. Several more lesser members of the same kind stood in the shadows behind him. It was only when the lead one started to speak that Siaphas noticed the cutting tools and restraining devices in their hands.

'A pity that your master's plan has come to nothing, Chaos-thing,' it snickered, 'but do not fear, for if you cannot serve us in one way then you can still do so in another. The voyage home is a long one, and our commander requires we provide her with some form of diversion to pass away the time. It should be an interesting experience for us too, for never before have we been gifted with such exalted, Chaos-altered flesh to work with. When we are finished with you, Chaos-thing, there should be enough of you left to fashion some new and novel kind of pet to present to the Archon himself. He keeps a large menagerie of such things, and you will enjoy your new home amongst them in the kennels of his citadel.'

Siaphas was still trying to frame the words of a spell as the gaunt figures of the dark eldar flesh-sculptors glided silently forward towards him.

AFTER THE HORRORS of Stabia, the interior of the dome of the crystal seers of craftworld An-Iolsus was a reminder of all that they had fought for and died to protect. The delicately perfume-scented mists clung like wisps of vaporous silk around the bodies of the trees, while the tiny jewel-cara-paced insect-drones drifted from tree to tree in lazy pursuit of their endless, slow maintenance tasks. Peaceable musical-sounding chimes sounded from somewhere deeper in the crystalline forest, while the air gently pulsed with the sound-less psychic whisperings of the minds which inhabited this place.

Freyra finished her task, planting the spirit-stone two hand reaches deep within the rich loam of the forest floor. She stepped away, still aware of the pain from her wounded arm, still aware of her awkward control over the new limb there. The healers had done their work well, but it would take much effort for her to learn how to master the movements of her new wraithbone-crafted prosthetic arm with anything like the dexterity she had previously taken for granted. She was unsure, and the healers were unable to make any promises, if she would ever be able to wield a weapon again effectively in combat. She had thought of abandoning the warrior path and finding other ways to serve her race and craftworld, but she knew what would soon be required of all of them on An-Iolsus and the other craftworlds, and she realised that soon enough the eldar would need every war-rior they could find.

In honour of her fallen kinsman, and in recognition of the coming sacrifices that would still be required of them, she would persevere and regain the skills her injury had robbed her of.

She bowed silently to the trees around her and exited the dome.

The dome's occupants waited until she had gone before linking minds with the new arrival. An invisible psychic breeze stirred to life amid the mists and bowers as the spirits of those who had gone before gathered to commune with the new mind amongst them.

It is good to be amongst you all again, my old friends, sounded the mind-speech voice of Kariadryl the farseer. *I have much to tell you…*

EPILOGUE

Ships of the line, they called them. Now, for the first time, Leoten Semper understood just what exactly that phrase meant.

In carefully manoeuvred formation, in wide, serried rows, the Imperial ships advanced into battle. Seventeen capital class ships, including two battle cruisers and also two battleships, the fleet flagship, the mighty *Divine Right*, amongst them. Twenty smaller vessels, frigates and destroyers mostly, swept out across either flank of the formation or formed a rearguard, following in the wake of the lumbering but majestic cruiser squadrons.

It was a line of giant leviathans, the greatest ever force assembled in Gothic sector history, the cream of Battlefleet Gothic, under the direct command of Lord Admiral Ravensburg himself. It was an awesome sight, possibly the largest single naval force gathered together for battle since the long ago and almost forgotten days of the titanic struggles of Warmaster Horus's treacherous rebellion against the Emperor. Looking out from the bridge of the *Macharius* at the lines of ships as they gathered prior to battle, Semper had turned to his second-in-command and smiled in grim humour at the vista before them.

'Vandire's teeth, Hito, I don't know what it'll do to the enemy, but just the sight of all this is enough to scare the life out of me.'

And now the *Macharius* was there amongst them, moving forward with the rest of the fleet formation, taking its place alongside its sister ships. They were surrounded by illustrious names well known from Battlefleet Gothic history: the battleships *Divine Right* and *Cardinal Boras*, venerable old warhorses which formed the solid backbone of the Imperial line; the Mars class battlecruiser *Imperious*, under the command of the near-legendary Compel Bast, whom even Erwin Ramas was said to be in awe of; the cruisers *Iron Duke*, *Minotaur*, *Zealous*, *Hammer of Justice*, *Sword of Orion*, *Mjollnir*, *Legend of Romulus* and *Sirius*.

Amongst them too were other, less familiar names. Newly-built ships which had come into service only in the last few years, to help replace some of the catastrophic losses suffered by Battlefleet Gothic in the earliest stages of the war. These ships may not have carried the same illustrious pedigree as some of their more venerable sister vessels, but already several of them – the Lunar class cruisers *Lord Daros* and *Jotunheim*, the Gothic class cruiser *Invincible*, the Overlord class cruiser *Cypra Probatii* – had distinguished themselves sufficiently to have already assured their place in the annals of Battlefleet Gothic history.

Yes, we'll all see our names mentioned in the history books, thought Semper, taking his customary place on the command deck. *Assuming any of us actually live through this day.*

They had been hounding the Chaos fleet through the Gethsemane system for days, trying to bring it to battle. Now at last, spotted and flushed out of its hiding place in the surveyor shadow of the system's second world, the enemy had been forced out into the open and made to stand and fight.

No man within the Imperial fleet had any illusions about just how critical this battle was. So far, Battlefleet Gothic had been slowly but inexorably losing the war. Barely-won holding actions were falsely hailed as major triumphs, scattered retreats were disguised by Imperium propaganda as defiant withdrawals, worlds retaken from the enemy were trumpeted as significant milestones on the path to final victory, with no mention made of the dozens of Imperial worlds still under the yoke of the Despoiler, nor the stream of worlds which continued to fall to his endless attacks.

'We need this victory, gentlemen,' Semper had told Ulanti and the other senior officers of the *Macharius* in the private briefing in his quarters before the commencement of the battle. 'This is the first time an enemy force of this size has been detected and identified, and the first time we of Battle-fleet Gothic have been able to assemble a force of sufficient size and strength to bear on it and bring it to open battle. Have no illusions, gentlemen. If we win today, the war will continue, but we will have dealt the enemy a grievous blow, and we will have shown the Despoiler and our own people that we are indeed capable of defeating him.' His voice had lowered then, and he had looked his assembled officers in the face, repeating the same words which he had heard from Ravensburg himself just a few hours ago aboard the *Divine Right*, during the Lord Admiral's final briefing to his fleet captains.

'But, if we lose, gentlemen, then we will have lost the greater part of our battlefleet's strength, and the Despoiler's final victory is all but assured. What we do here today determines the fate of the entire Gothic sector, and we can depend on none but ourselves to determine what that fate might be.'

Semper himself had looked up sharply at this last comment when he had first heard it, catching the eye of Ravensburg, and, more significantly, also that of Inquisitor Horst, standing anonymously and unnoticed amongst the scrum of scribes and Administratum and Munitorium officials that formed part of the Lord Admiral's vast personal entourage. Horst held Semper's gaze for a moment, and then glanced away, eyes downcast. To Semper, the meaning seemed unmistakable.

Everything that happened in the Stabia system, was it all for nothing, he wondered? *Did we completely fail in our mission there?*

Now, standing upon the bridge of his ship, Semper stood to attention, his officers and crew immediately following likewise, as the ship's comm-net system crackled into activity, patching into a fleet-wide broadcast from the *Divine Right*. The distinctive voice of Lord Admiral Cornelius von Ravensburg, clipped and supremely confident, commanding and autocratic, echoed round the command deck of the *Macharius*, and round every deck level of every ship in the Imperial formation.

'Hah, here we go, gentlemen. Into the jaws of death, into the mouth of hell. Damn his eyes, may the Emperor bless and bugger us all!'

At those semi-blasphemous words, which Imperium historians would subsequently alter to make sound a little more eloquent and noble, waves of torpedoes were launched at the Chaos armada, the combined energy signatures from their massed launching momentarily blotting out surveyor screens on many ships throughout the fleet.

The Chaos fleet, still manoeuvring for position, scattered wildly to avoid the menacing waves of torpedoes, in the process tearing apart their own lines of battle. Bright starbursts of plasma detonations blossomed amongst the Chaos ranks, signalling at least a dozen or more successful torpedo impacts. Those Chaos ships which had avoided the first torpedo wave now brought their own superior-ranged weaponry to bear on the advancing Imperial fleet. Lance and battery fire, sporadic but deadly, reached out across the gap of still tens of thousands of kilometres between the two fleets, seeking targets amongst the Imperial line. Several vessels, the *Drachenfels* and *Lord Daros* amongst them, shook under the impacts of direct hits, but, able to present their heavily-armoured prows to the enemy, the Imperial line continued its advance into battle with only minimal damage.

Inside the torpedo rooms of more than two dozen Imperial vessels, crews sweated and strained to load more volleys of the huge, thirty-metre long missiles into their firing chambers. On the gun decks of every Imperium ship, and on every command deck, anxious gunnery officers checked their firing solutions over and over again and maintained a careful watch on the green-glowing lines of gun deck status runes.

The *Imperious*, leading the charge from the vanguard of the Imperial line, was the first to draw serious blood. Even before the other ships could launch off a second torpedo wave, the Mars class battlecruiser's nova cannon was firing with its deadly trademark accuracy. Its chosen target was the Murder class cruiser *Deathblade*, an old and bitterly-hated adversary from several actions the *Imperious* and its crew had waged against the enemy in the Orar sub-sector. The front section of the *Deathblade* was consumed in a sudden and fearsome explosion. Broken and ablaze, the cruiser fell out of the Chaos formation, its sister vessels hurriedly manoeuvring to get away from it as its surveyor signature showed all the wild and tell-tale energy fluctuations from damaged and out of control plasma reactors heading towards imminent and explosive overload.

Cheers rang over the Imperial comm-channels at the fate of the stricken enemy ship. Then, in the roaring blast of launching torpedoes, the deck-shaking earthquake rumble of gun batteries unleashed and the incandescent scream of lance fire, the two fleets clashed together.

Ravensburg's plan was simple. A mass front assault with waves of torpedoes would, and now did, split the enemy formation into two. The Imperial fleet, formed into carefully staggered lines, would then advance through this newly-formed breach, taking fire from enemy ships on both sides, but simultaneously bringing their own port and starboard batteries to bear on different enemy targets.

As a strategy, it was brutally direct. In execution, it was simply brutal. Ravensburg was well known for his jocular references to battle casualties as 'paying the butcher's bill'. The price of the butcher's bill for the Battle of Gethsemane would be steep indeed.

The Imperial formation, passing through two lines of intersecting fire, was buffeted and blasted on both sides by the enemy gunners. The Tyrant class vessel *Zigmund*, singled out by the gunners of four different enemy vessels, two on each side of it, was the first to fall. Its shields stripped away in seconds, it staggered under the impact of multiple simultaneous hits on both its flanks. Its engines destroyed, its gun decks reduced to burning wreckage, it lay stricken and helpless as its sister vessels mercilessly passed it by, abandoning it to its fate. Enemy torpedo destroyers and attack craft bomber squadrons, hiding nearby in the cover of the larger cruiser vessels, quickly closed in for the kill like schools of hungry barracuda.

The Lunar class cruiser *Excellent*, famous for its defiant no-retreat stance in the face of an ork space hulk monstrosity two centuries earlier at the Defence of Platea, was set ablaze prow to stern by a series of devastating torpedo and lance hits from the grand cruiser *Foe-Reaper* and its phalanx of escorts. The last act of the *Excellent's* captain, Leonardus Mathieu, was to bring his dying vessel up to ramming speed, sending it crashing catastrophically into the hull of the *Foe-Reaper* and bringing to an end the Chaos ship's litany of atrocities against the Imperium, which stretched back for millennia. Captain Lagardo Mathieu, who had commanded the *Excellent* during its most famous action at Platea, would surely have approved of his descendant's own final and very effective act of defiance.

The entire Omega squadron of Sword class frigates was destroyed in a vicious duel with the Carnage class cruiser *Wanton Desecration* and its squadron of Infidel escorts, finally succumbing when bomber waves from the nearby Styx class cruiser *Violator* entered the fray.

The Firestorm class frigate *Europa* fell prey to the guns of the Desolator class battleship *Nergal*. For Lord Admiral Ravensburg, this particular item on the butcher's bill would come at an especially heavy price. His son Mannfred, the youngest of his eleven children and one of his favourites, had been first lieutenant on the *Europa*.

On every ship involved in the engagement, surveyor screens swarmed with target icons. On both sides, members of gunnery crews simply dropped to the decks in exhaustion, overwhelmed by the heat, noise and toxic off-spill from weapons overheated to the point of catastrophe. On flight decks, ground crews worked numbly and robotically on a seemingly endless number of attack craft, prepping them for launch just as previously-launched craft, battered and missing many of their wingmen, returned to their carrier vessels for refuelling, re-arming and urgently-required repairs. The void around the giant cruisers was filled with a bewildering, swirling maelstrom of attack craft, fighters and bombers, Chaos and Imperial craft alike, all caught up together in one vast, straggling dogfight, spread out over tens of thousands of kilometres of space. Unable to distinguish friend from foe under such conditions, turret gunners on both sides often simply opened fire at any attack craft which came within striking distance, and more than one bomber or fighter pilot, having managed to survive the lethal gauntlet of the battle, found himself coming under fire from the defences of his own mothership.

In a final, deadly series of salvoes, the dual Imperial formations broke through the Chaos lines, the *Divine Right* brutally ramming and smashing apart a damaged and powerless enemy frigate which drifted into the battleship's path. As Ravensburg's flagship pulled away from the enemy fleet, ships on both sides still exchanging lethal bouts of weapons fire, the punishing damage taken by both sides quickly became apparent. If the Lord Admiral cut his losses now and fled back into the warp, then he would do so without three of his capital ships and five of his escort vessels. Some badly damaged vessels would be unlikely to survive the dangers of the immaterium, while several more, including the *Lord Daros* and the Dauntless class light cruiser *Guardian*, would surely face many long months or even years of repair work in orbital dry dock.

Still, despite the damage his fleet had suffered, Ravensburg's plan had succeeded. As his ships continued to put distance between themselves and the enemy, gaps in the Chaos battle line quickly became visible.

The *Foe-Reaper* was gone, reduced to a tangled mass of burning wreckage from its collision with the dying *Excellent*. The *Malignus Maximus* and the Murder class cruiser *Steel Fang* had been similarly reduced by concentrated salvoes from the Imperial formation, while *Steel Fang's* sister ship *Krotos* had been the victim of wave after wave of combined attacks from the bomber squadrons of the *Macharius* and the *Imperious*, and was now little more than a gutted hulk. Similar massed bombing waves from the *Divine Right* had relentlessly harried the Styx class cruiser *Corpsemaker* and its escorts, crippling its launch bays and effectively knocking it out of the fight. Elsewhere, a wide ring of expanding super-heated gases and wreckage fragments was all that remained of a nameless Slaughter class cruiser which had explosively succumbed to combined fire from three different Imperial cruisers, while the *Nergal*, flagship of the Chaos Warmaster admiral, Baal-Hierophant Lokkis Vanama, bled out a telltale plume of burning plasma from its rear section, indicating the probable loss of one of its reactors from the numerous torpedo, lance and weapon battery attacks which had been directed at it during the battle.

Aboard the *Divine Right*, Ravensburg watched the progress of the injured enemy battleship with his trademark cold, remorseless gaze. He would not learn until after the battle about the destruction of his son's ship by the guns of the enemy flagship, but it would add little to his already firm determination to see the notorious battleship mercilessly hunted down and destroyed today. Once he learned of the vessel's presence in the Gethsemane system, then its destruction and the death of one of Abaddon's chief lieutenants immediately became one of his main aims in this conflict.

'Our fleet?' he asked without looking away from the enemy positions.

'Still battle worthy,' answered one of his adjutants, thinking of the number of crippled and seriously damaged ships in the Imperial line, and tempted – but only briefly – to add the word *barely* to his report.

'Good enough,' nodded Ravensburg, turning to his waiting command staff. 'Signal the ships and tell them to come about and re-engage the enemy. Tell them we're going back through the gates of hell to finish the job properly this time.'

AT RAVENSBURG'S COMMAND, the lines of Imperial ships swung ponderously round, presenting their prows once more to the enemy. As they turned, flank-mounted batteries were able to open fire at the distant enemy, which dutifully returned the favour. The void between the two battered fleets was filled with sporadic weapons fire, as both sides steeled themselves for the second round of battle.

The Imperial force advanced in a rag-tag formation, its original line of battle broken by the rigours of the first encounter and the losses sustained then. The Chaos fleet, split apart by the first Imperial charge, was in even greater disarray.

Torpedo launches streaked from the prows of various Imperial craft, seeking individual targets of opportunity within the confusion of the enemy ranks. Other ships, damaged or with their torpedo payload already fully expended, were unable to launch anything. Aboard the Tyrant class cruiser *Incendrius*, its captain screamed vicious, bloody obscenities into his internal comm-net, threatening death, damnation and the worst punishments allowed under naval regulations if his loading crew didn't get their fingers out and fire off some damned torpedoes, all the time unaware that his entire torpedo room had been transformed into a derelict morgue. A lucky melta missile hit had struck that section in its weaker flank side, opening up a catastrophic breach in the cruiser's hull. Those torpedo room crew not fortunate enough to be immolated in the initial blast had instead been sucked screaming out into space through the giant molten hole in the chamber's wall.

Aboard the *Macharius*, Leoten Semper faced the prospect of his probable and imminent extinction with all the aplomb expected of a product of Cypra Mundi's thousands of years of breeding officers for the Imperial Navy.

'What's our status, Mister Ulanti?'

'Two starboard gundecks ablaze, captain. We have a minor conflagration raging in the secondary rear arsenal, and a larger one in the upper portside launch decks, but that perhaps doesn't matter so much, since we've accounted for and recovered rather less than half of our attack craft squadrons, and we really have no more need for those decks any more. External communications are shot half to hell, but that doesn't perhaps matter so much either, since there's so much battle interference and comms babble going on out there that no one can hear anything anyway. Crew casualties are currently running at almost twenty per cent and expected to rise even without any further battle damage. Our void shield generators are dangerously overloading, and I believe Magos

Castaboras is down in the enginarium now, in the process of performing the last rites on our number three plasma reactor.'

Semper almost smiled. Ulanti could make the second coming of the Traitor Warmaster Horus sound like nothing more than a petty inconvenience. 'What's your opinion of our current battle status then, Mister Ulanti?'

Ulanti's answer was immediate and unblinking. 'I think there's a damn good chance we'll all be getting reacquainted with a few long-dead old comrades before the day's out.'

Semper looked shrewdly at his second-in-command. 'Did you think you would end your days back home on Necromunda, Hito, telling bored grandchildren tales of your glorious exploits amongst the stars in the service of the Emperor's navy?'

'The thought had occurred to me, sir, but only in a pleasing if somewhat abstract sense.'

This time Semper did smile. Laugh, in fact, as he clapped his second-in-command on the shoulders. 'A fine daydream, Hito, but you're Battlefleet Gothic now. For us, and all those like us, this is always how it's supposed to end.'

The *Macharius*, along with the other ships in what remained of the Imperial line, drew closer on their targets. The bridge rocked as the first enemy weapons hits impacted against the ship's beleaguered, failing void shields.

'Torpedoes, Mister Nyder?' asked Semper.

'Six in the pipe, six more on the shelf, captain,' reported the *Macharius's* ordnance officer, the strain of the engagement showing on his face. Semper knew that the loss of so many of his attack craft crews had affected the man deeply, even if he would never openly admit it. 'That's all I can give you for the time being, sir. The loading track from the forward arsenal is smashed, and I can't release anything from the rear arsenals until those fires back there are under control.'

'Very well. Twelve it is,' nodded Semper. 'No sense letting them go to waste. Find a target and fire when ready, Mister Nyder.'

The *Macharius* shook, and shook again as it fired off two salvoes, sending three missiles apiece streaking off towards two different targets. Semper studied the surveyor screen closely. At first he thought the ships within the Chaos fleet were simply manoeuvring to evade the many individual torpedo salvoes from the Imperial line, but then, even before the shout from one of his helm officers, came understanding about what was really happening.

'Their fleet's breaking up! They're attempting to disengage!'

On surveyor screens and augur displays all through the Imperial formation, the truth quickly became evident. The enemy fleet was breaking off from battle, those vessels which could running for the warp jump point at the system's edge and abandoning their damaged brethren to the mercy of the Imperial guns. Ravensburg's attention was still almost solely fixed on the escaping fleet and the prize of its fleeing flagship, but he was not about to pass up the free opportunity now being presented to him.

'Open fire,' he commanded to his fleet, as they swept past the drifting clutter of damaged Chaos vessels, firing broadsides into them at something close to point-blank range. 'We'll gladly accept these scraps, but only as an appetiser for the rest of the feast.'

Many of the ships within the Imperial line channelled extra power to their engines, pushing ahead to catch up with the faster enemy ships. Speculative shots from lance turrets and torpedo tubes ranged out in pursuit of the escaping enemy, seeking to hit and hopefully cripple engines and power systems.

Suddenly, a Sword class frigate, speedier than the larger capital ships and racing ahead of the main Imperial formation, exploded apart, its prow bursting open. At once, the alarm was passed through the Imperial fleet.

'Mines!' captains and surveyor officers shouted to helm crews, as emergency surveyor sweeps were made, and new courses urgently laid in to avoid this latest threat.

Aboard the *Divine Right*, Ravensburg cursed violently and volubly. The enemy had dropped mines in their wake, to cover their retreat. Scattered widely amongst the other debris of battle, they would be a real hazard to the pursuing Imperial fleet. By the time his ships had picked a safe passage through the drifting minefields, or had sent out attack craft squadrons to clear a path through them, the Chaos fleet would be long gone.

How many casualties could he afford, he wondered, if he simply ordered his already-weakened force to simply push on ahead and run the gauntlet of the minefield?

He was still pondering on the variables in that cold, harsh calculation when he heard the astonished shout from one of the bridge officers.

'Vandire's teeth! Ships, a whole new fleet of them! Where did they come from?'

ABOARD THE *MACHARIUS*, aboard every ship in the Imperial formation, the reaction was the same. Looking at the images on the augur screen, seeing the distinctive energy signatures of the new arrivals on the surveyor screen, Semper could only imagine the mood of consternation amongst his counterparts on the command decks of the enemy ships.

Ulanti confirmed what Semper already knew. 'Eldar vessels, more than twenty of them, including a dozen or more capital class warships. Emperor only knows where they came from, or how long they've been here watching everything.'

And Emperor only knows what they're going to do next, Semper thought to himself, almost afraid to watch, but unable to tear his gaze away from the lines of newly-emergent icons on the surveyor screen, their strange energy patterns shifting and fluctuating as they drew closer towards the Imperial and Chaos fleets.

The eldar ships were coming in fast on a tangent course intercepting the escaping Chaos fleet, but which, with a minor change of heading and brief burst of speed, could just as easily bring them into attack range of the Imperial ships. Everyone aboard the command deck of the *Macharius* knew all too well just how fast and manoeuvrable the alien vessels were, and how such a sudden but significant course change could be made effortlessly and without warning.

'ALIEN BASTARDS, I'VE known their treachery before,' cursed Augustus Ortelius, captain of the *Divine Right*. 'They're going to attack us, admiral. We must open fire upon them now!'

'No!' It was the voice of Horst, standing on the command deck beside Ravensburg, the full weight of authority of his rank of senior inquisitor and envoy of the Council of Terra evident in that single word. 'We wait. Let them act first. Then we will know what their true intentions are.'

ABOARD THE *MACHARIUS*, the mood was equally tense.

'Damn it, we still can't positively identify any of the eldar ships?'

The surveyor officer wilted before his captain's impatience. 'It's notoriously difficult to identify an individual eldar vessel's energy signature, even if you already have previous sightings of that vessel on record, captain. The fact that there are so many of them together only makes it–'

A shout from the communications section put the man out of his misery. 'We're being hailed, captain. By one of the alien ships!'

Semper and Ulanti exchanged quick, alert glances. 'Open comm-net channels,' ordered Semper.

'Good hunting, *Macharius*?' The voice on the bridge comm-net speakers was proud and confident, with a slight mocking edge to it. The familiar words of Battlefleet Gothic's customary greeting between vessels sounded strange too, framed in the inhuman voice of an eldar. Both Semper and Ulanti were grudgingly impressed; Craftmaster Lileathon's spoken Gothic was nearly flawless, and the haughty eldar commander had clearly learned much about the Imperial Navy and its customs since they had last encountered her and her ship.

'Good enough, *Vual'en Sho*,' answered Semper. 'When we first met, we were mostly enemies, when we parted, we were mostly allies.'

'What are we now, you wonder?' Again, that slight mocking tone to the eldar's voice. 'This time we bring a gift with us, *Macharius*. The gift of *mael dannan* for the servants of the one you call the Despoiler.'

Ulanti looked at his captain, puzzled. 'Mael dannan?'

'Total and merciless extermination,' smiled Semper, as the eldar ships opened fire.

A cruiser at the head of the retreating Chaos fleet was blown to pieces, struck multiple times by the withering, relentless fire from the eldar vessels' pulsar lance armaments. Seconds later, more hits registered all along the front length of the Chaos formation. Some returned fire, their gunners desperately seeking targets amongst the elusive, fast-moving eldar ships. Others manoeuvred in panic, seeking another escape route, their course taking them back towards the guns of the waiting Imperial fleet.

Both fleets, human and eldar, with the Chaos fleet trapped between them, opened fire. The Battle of Gethsemane would rage for days yet, with elements from both fleets hunting the remnants of the Chaos formation through the system, and there would be fierce losses on all sides, but the final outcome of the battle was no longer in doubt.

Mael dannan. Total and merciless extermination of Warmaster Baal-Hierophant Lokkis Vanama and his entire fleet.

A new chapter in the Gothic War had begun.

More Warhammer 40,000 from the Black Library

EXECUTION HOUR
A Warhammer 40,000 novel
by Gordon Rennie

AN INHABITED WORLD. An Imperial world, far from the nearest warzone. Once again, the guidance of the Powers of the Warp has served him well. Already the name and location of this new target are being relayed to the rest of the fleet. The Planet Killer is making ready to strike another blow for the Dark Gods. The doomed inhabitants could not possibly realise or understand it yet, but the hour of their appointed execution has just been set.

THE VILE AND unholy shadow of Chaos falls across the Gothic Sector at the onslaught of Warmaster Abaddon's infernal Black Crusade. Fighting a desperate rearguard action, the Imperial Battlefleet has no choice but to sacrifice dozens of worlds and millions of lives to buy precious time for their scattered fleets to regroup. But what possible chance do they have when Abaddon's unholy forces have the power not just to kill men, but also to murder worlds?